Mike Berry

Thanks to Annie, without whom I would never have reached this point. I love you loads.

Thanks also to Kia and Lana. One day, I'll write something that you're allowed to read.

Thanks to everybody who has followed me, humoured me, retweeted me, amused me and encouraged me on twitter.

Thanks to the other authors who have supported me, specifically but not exclusively: Steven Montano; Scott Whitmore; Tyr Kieran; D.H.Nevins. When I am Lord, you will be spared.

And thanks most of all to you, for reading. Without you, I'd be talking to myself here.

Mike.

INTRODUCTION

Of course the corporations won, in the end. What other entity could have endured the formative generations of Old Earth, could have grown larger and stronger even as the individuals who had founded them perished and were forgotten?

In the early days there was some protest as the strongest nation-economies of Earth gradually fell under the spell of the Super Corps. But such dissent was badly organised and under-funded, being bankrolled almost always by the poor. Before long, nobody really tried to stop the corps at all. They had grown so all-encompassing that virtually everybody, at least everybody who mattered, depended upon them in some way. They owned the raw materials, funded the schools, provided the jobs, paid for security, ran the hospitals, distributed the food. When the overcrowded Earth began to provide scarcer and scarcer opportunity, these emergent mega-companies began to turn their eyes skywards.

Gone were the days when space exploration had been the province of governments. Gone were the days when leaders had been chosen at the ballot. Those times were soon relegated to the creaking databases that slumbered in the bowels of information corporations, those organisations that grew to trade in the once-ubiquitous right to knowledge, history, fact itself.

Economic power became the linchpin that held the whole sociological and societal model together, the bedrock on which the system was built – became, in short, politics itself: Corpocracy. Leaders were chosen at the checkout, the net-node, the stock exchange. Shareholders' profits, not national interests, would drive the explosion into space.

The strongest corporations struggled to climb over the carcasses of their unworthy fellows, scrambling upwards as if time were not only finite, but distinctly limited. They planted flags in rocks, planets, stars. They claimed any celestial body their grasping

1

tentacles could reach.

Naturally, there were armed disputes. The richest usually won. Those who died in the Corp Wars were considered to be economic frontiersmen, traders in danger whose stock had simply fallen. Or more often, they were not considered at all, outside of the theoretical columns of numerals in the blurring minds of the company director-machines. Such was life. Such was the march of progress.

This expansion, planned by computers, executed by the brave, the radical, the dispossessed – any and every extreme of the human spectrum – continued apace despite the increasing remoteness of the frontier from humanity's poisoned cradle. The corps became adept at terraforming, using this technology to warp every possible planet and moon the cosmos provided to their own ends.

The new worlds were fortified, fought-over, sometimes obliterated. Armies were grown in vats, raised in the corporate security forces, wiped out in wars with other clones. These soldiers were men and women who never knew what it meant to even *be* human; humans-as-tools, whose war was a pointless and inexplicable necessity to their fleeting lives.

And as the battlefield expanded in this tumultuous, bloody manner, so the distances that must be traversed in order to make war became more and more vast. Some corporations, driven to the brink of extinction, were spared the final coup-de-grace simply because the logistical costs of bringing the war to their doorsteps became more expensive than any potential victory was worth. Once again, balance sheets dictated a change in strategy.

As the distances grew, empires were consolidated, cemented in their vastness. Their sprawling borders became their armour, the vast distances of interstellar space their castle walls. And as the deep-space corporations became increasingly isolated from each other they began to tolerate each other's distant existences.

Gradually it became apparent that there was not only enough for everyone but there was in fact *too much* – an effective infinity of space and materiel – so much that the abundance obscured any notion of *claim*, any necessity for *rights*, any will to fight expensive wars over bites of an infinite pie. The corps eventually pared back their support structures, securing only a handful of liveable offworlds each. They let their armies dwindle, keeping careful check on their fellows' relative forces in an uneasy lockstep disarmament.

And as relative peace became the normal way of life for the pioneers of the space-faring corps, so a sense of disappointment spread with it. What had all the hurry, all the violence and destruction been for?

The corps had grown to rule their home world, had eventually *out*grown it, had battled across a thousand worlds and lost nine billion soldiers. . . and all for what? The cycle of expansion, consumption and exhaustion had become its own goal and its own propulsion. Some prominent thinkers suggested that this was the nature not just of humanity, but of the universe itself: it simply *was*; it simply continued; there was no point as such, and that it would be best to come to terms with that as soon as possible. Then, perhaps, the human race could settle down and work out what came next. Whatever divergent course could be contrived, humans themselves would have to choose it and engineer it into being. But for now they mined, they built, they gradually settled into a sort of stasis.

The great warp engines of the empire-building pioneer ships fell victim to disrepair or decommission. The director-machines had plotted the value of further growth against the projected upkeep costs and reached the inevitable answer. Soon the only interstellar ships in service were those sub-light vessels essential to the maintenance of the status quo – freighters, troop ships, civilian shuttles.

Clearly, another race had gone before. Deepseeker Mining probes first found evidence of their existence on the frozen world of DSH-3, moon of the gas giant Maxima Omega. Once, DSH-3 had borne an Earth-analogous atmosphere, but the relics seemed to pre-date even the long-ago existence of any such hospitable environment. They came from an age of much greater temperatures and thinner air, and who could have built such towering spires of diamond-hard carbon and then deserted them without trace remained a mystery.

People named these others the *Predecessors*. But the knowledge that they had been and gone, leaving nothing but empty shells, served only to heighten humanity's feelings of loneliness and increase the numbers of people who questioned the point in any sort of advancement.

Other Predecessor settlements were found near to ancient gas giants. All were as empty and deserted as those of DSH-3. A rumour circulated that the new psychoactive drug *fader*, which swept through human space leaving a trail of social devastation behind it, had been found on one such world. This, however, was generally discounted as a simple public relations exercise by the drug's real manufacturers.

The corps declared a non-exploitation pact, unthinkable a few hundred years earlier, to cover all Predecessor worlds. After all, the Predecessors had only left their habitat-shells of carbon, an element more easily extracted elsewhere. Doubtless, the director-machines had measured any value in the exploitation of these ruins against the chance, however slight, that one day the vanishing Predecessors would reappear and want them back, and decided not to risk it. Humanity was alone again. Still.

Soros: an unremarkable star, with a mass about one-point-three times that of Sol; older by a billion years or so, but still expected to last long enough that humanity would go the way of the Predecessors long before its fires could burn out. It marked one of the furthest extremities of the great expansion into space.

The Soros system was also a mostly unremarkable one, except that nobody had ever bothered to terraform any of its planets. Farsight Exploration, one of the original deep-space corps, owned the only habitable outpost there, which is to say that they effectively owned the system itself, for what it was worth.

Far from exploration, Farsight had long-since turned its hand to mineral extraction. Many believed that they maintained the station there, with all the expensive supply-chain issues this

4

implied, merely as a launchpad for a second great rush for resources, should one ever occur. The mineral wealth sent back to the more occupied regions of Farsight space just about paid for the outpost's existence.

Macao Station: a standard Farsight mining base, made from prefab pieces shipped from the neighbouring Platini system in the great echoing bellies of the original pioneer-ships, then bolted together more as cost than liveability dictated. An island at the extremity of human space. A singular, distant monument to the fallen drive for expansion. A sentinel at the trailing edge of infinity.

Alone. . .

CHAPTER ONE

Darkness, cold, an echoing icy tomb without air. The man moved slowly, suited and clumsy, floating down the tunnel. He didn't know why he was there. But he had been drawn. . . compelled. It made no sense.

Onwards into an impenetrable world of shadow. His suit-light flowed over shiny rock, a hostile microcosm of frozen stone. The suit respired clouds of rolling vapour that streamed around him like ghosts. He dragged himself across the rock, drawn onwards into that midnight abscess. His mind was calm and empty. He knew no fear.

He emerged into a larger space where his light didn't even touch the far wall. The darkness was so deep as to be almost deliberate − a velvety, living medium in which anything might grow. His own breathing filled the universe.

He floated there, suspended, a drifting angel alone in the whole of creation. Immense mass hung poised around him, waiting to crash down, a held breath of darkness. He looked around, seeing nothing. He floated in a tank of purest void − weightless, singular, at peace in isolation.

He was alone. Yet something else was in there with him.

He felt a living wave that oozed from the frozen matter around him, a radiation, a thing that lived inside the folds, woven into the fabric of space itself. It was there. He could feel it. His skin was tingling. His heart began to race. He knew now why he had come. He cast his light around, but the space in which he floated was like a sensory deprivation chamber. There was nothing.

But within that nothing, within that blackness, there was *something*. . . A pattern. . .

And then it spoke to him.

'My emissary. You have come to me. . . Listen. . .'

CHAPTER TWO

Macao Station hung above the rotational plane of the Soros system like an overlooking god. Below, if such a direction could be said to have meaning in space, the asteroid belt sprawled vastly across an expanse of some four hundred million miles – an apparently endless sea of glittering shards. From their scarred surfaces, pockets of concentrated metallic ores caught the light of Soros and flung it back, tinted with the shades of iron, copper, nickel, even gold. These colourful lights winked on and off as the rocks rotated gently in their timeless ballet, the station keeping perfect step. Icebergs moved amongst the swarm like pale shades.

Occasionally, a rogue element would come crashing through this ordered procession – usually an incoming meteor from Platini-direction – and smash into one of the belt objects, either causing obliteration in a cloud of dust or setting off a chain of collisions. These legacies of disorder could continue for long, long periods, complicating navigation through the belt, but eventually the mostly-uniform motion of the great mass would correct any errant rocks, and the timeless discipline would be restored.

Lina McLough looked out over this vista from the window of the canteen, whose floor was on the middle level of the rotating wheel of Macao Station. She was swirling the unimpressively lumpy dregs of her coffee in its plastic mug.

Most of the denizens of the station found the real-view mode of the windows somewhat nauseating. After all, the whole thirteen-hundred-metre wheel of Macao spun one full revolution every fifty-one seconds, causing the field of asteroids to whirl past at a somewhat dizzying rate. The windows were usually set to display the feed from cameras mounted on tracks that encircled the station, whose steady movement in a counter-spin direction offset the rotation and created a merciful, much less sickening, impression of relative stillness. But Lina preferred the real-view.

7

The canteen was quiet at this time: a few other miners using up their last minutes of freedom before joining Lina's shift on duty; a small group of admin staff; two off-duty members of the security team; and Lina, waiting for Eli to return from the toilet.

Si Davis, Niya Onh and Petra Kalistov, the other miners, were laughing and shoving each other over some mutually-insulting exchange of words, obviously completely at ease together. After all, most of the inhabitants of Macao had been here for many years. They were an odd and disparate bunch. Some of them had fled from Platini system due to personal or professional tragedy. Others had actively sought the quiet of the frontier life. Many had been drawn here by the salary, which easily outstripped what they might receive for similar work at Platini. Some of them had even been born on-board. These three, like Lina herself, were immigrants, but they'd all been here as long as she could remember. She knew these people like family. It was a strange family, admittedly, but one that was bound by undeniably strong ties despite its numerous sub-sects and inner cliques. After all, they daily depended on each other's diligence to stay alive.

She absently cycled through the view-modes of the window, tapping it to change them. Three of the seven didn't work at all, and one showed only an inward-looking close-up of the station's own hull. She settled again on the real-view of the belt – a seemingly endless swathe of mineral wealth, an infinite job of work.

It was said that Macao could justify its expensive existence for many billions of years based on the volume of metals out there. She would have thought that the company would pay a little more attention to upkeep, bearing that in mind. It was believed, though, that Macao was kept alive mostly as an outpost, a launchpad, against the contingency that a second great interstellar land-grab should one day ensue. Its outlying position would give Farsight a natural advantage over most of its competitors in the unlikely event that this should happen.

Macao, as the expression went aboard, was just spinning itself – just about paying to keep itself turning. The investment required to increase production, and supply this produce first to Platini, and from there further into more densely-occupied space, would be so great as to be simply uneconomical. And for all their faults, Farsight could never be accused of poor economy.

So Macao just spun itself, ad infinitum, its failing systems replaced or repaired only as necessity dictated, sometimes not even then. The K6s, the in-system mining ships that supplied Macao with its lifeblood of raw materials, only ever flew due to the ingenuity of the maintenance team and ground crew, aided by Eli, a truly inventive scavenger and maker-do. It was not uncommon for a K6 to take off in a condition that would be considered un-flightworthy elsewhere.

Macao ran at a barely sustainable level of production at the best of times, and Halman, the Farsight company bigwig and station controller, feared that any loss of production could easily result in the closure and mothballing of the facility. So the usual policy on unsound or even unsafe K6s was to run them anyway. Eli did his best to stick up for his miners, but it was a constant balancing act between profit and safety. Even he knew that some concessions to operational danger must be tolerated.

And here he came, crumpled in his aged flight suit, heavyset and scarred, a friendly-looking veteran of the frontier, fifty-five standard years old but still crunching rocks with the best of them. He paused to share a brief laugh with the other miners, slapping the huge Si Davis on the back before moving to the coffee machine. His grizzled face studied the arcane panel of the device as if he hadn't used it thousands of times before, wearing its usual expression of barely-restrained amusement. He shot a questioning look at Lina, who grimaced, held up her cup and shook her head. He chuckled, ordered just one drink from the machine and came to the table. He kicked his chair out and sat, placing his cup on the discoloured surface.

'I wish you wouldn't have the windows like that, Li,' he said. 'Makes me sick.' He sipped his scalding coffee and winced.

'No,' replied Lina, 'I'm pretty sure that's the effect of the so-called coffee. What's that, your third?'

9

He sipped again, pointedly. 'Lifeblood of human civilisation, Li.' He checked his watch and grimaced comically.

Lina cycled the window and the asteroid belt stopped moving. 'Better?'

'Thanks.'

'Any more news from the lifers' wing, then?'

'What – the last news wasn't enough for you?'

'Just looking forward to the next exciting instalment, is all. I wonder what it'll be? Maybe a full-on prison break, take the station by storm and establish Macao as the leading frontier pirate base.'

'Don't even joke about it. Did you know that Murkhoff is being sent back to Platini on the next shuttle for reconstructive surgery? They say he'll be blind in his right eye until they can grow a transplant organ. You know what that animal did to him?'

'No. I didn't realise it was that bad. Wow.' They were silent for a moment in homage to the injured man. 'At least the shuttle is due soon, right?'

'Any day, by my reckoning. Assuming Farsight haven't forgotten us. So until then I guess Murkhoff isn't going to be winning any games of pool.'

'Pool?'

'Yeah, depth perception, right? Your three-dee vision requires two working eyes.'

'And you told *me* not to joke about it. Damn, Eli, that wasn't even funny.' She arched an eyebrow at him, a slight smile on her lips, an expression that, added to the effect of her well-defined cheekbones, shock of tangled blonde hair and wide green eyes, had been known to melt some men, at least in her younger days.

'Maybe not, but I can get away with it, because Murkhoff said that himself. Anyway, poor guy. Our sec-teams aren't made for this. What's the worst they had to deal with before this whole prison thing started? A bit of graffiti and maybe kids breaking into the vending machines. And now this. . .'

'Well, I guess it keeps us spinning. Although I would say that it takes a special kind of idiot to look at an under-supplied mining outpost full of civilians and think maximum-security prison.'

'Yeah, well keep those thoughts to yourself is my advice. I get the impression that the company is a little touchy about the whole affair. Halman too. Doesn't matter what you or I think. We just get paid to crunch rocks.'

'Speaking of which, hadn't we better saddle up in a minute?'

'I make it five,' Eli responded, gulping his coffee. He motioned to the window with his cup. 'Rocks aren't going anywhere.'

'Pardon my enthusiasm. It wasn't genuine, I assure you.'

'I should hope not. Such a startling break from character would demand a referral to Hobbes.' He gave her a serious look, but his face was too sculpted by laugh lines to really pull it off.

'Does such a referral come with any sort of a rest?'

He chuckled, shaking his head. 'Dream on.'

For a minute or two they both watched the belt. The exhaust plumes of the finishing shift's K6s were converging into a rough group and heading back to base.

The canteen door suddenly whined open and Halman came in whistling brightly. He greeted the three miners at the other table, then wandered over to Eli and Lina.

'Mind if I take a seat?' asked Halman.

'You're the boss,' said Eli. 'Sit wherever you like, I reckon.'

Halman coughed laughter, his brown eyes sparking, and sat. He was a bear of a man, as broad as Eli but taller, possessed of a surprising grace of movement, balding and borderline-ugly, at least on the outside. Much of his once considerable muscle mass had lost its definition in his early fifties, leaving him a slightly slouching, hulking individual. He'd been a soldier in the corporate militia at Platini in his earlier life, where he'd fought guerilla warfare against the union insurgents. But apart from his habitual swearing, his gentle demeanour belied his violent past. He wasn't exactly intelligent in the traditional sense, but he made up for this by being practical and resourceful. 'You have to work with this asshole?' he asked Lina, indicating Eli with one thumb.

'Yeah, I do. About that pay rise. . .'

'I don't think so,' replied Halman seriously. 'I need that money

11

for duct tape and nails. You know this place is only held together by duct tape.'

Lina sighed theatrically. 'Yeah,' she agreed grudgingly. 'I know, I know.'

Eli leant towards Halman, giving him a sidelong, conspiratorial look. 'About that. . .' he said.

'What?' asked Halman suspiciously. He was all-too used to being harassed about the latest thing that had broken down. He did, in fact, consider it to be one of his main duties.

'Well, the cooker in my quarters has been broken for two months now. I don't have time to fix it myself – you know how hard you people work me – and more importantly, I don't have the authority to sign for the parts myself.'

'And?' asked Halman warily.

'Well. . . have you spoken to Nik Sudowski recently?'

Nik Sudowski was the head of Macao's put-upon maintenance division, and as such was a man in great demand.

'Of course I have,' said Halman, uncertain as to where this was leading.

'Well, I asked him about it again this morning. He wasn't exactly helpful. In fact, he wasn't exactly conversational. The guy kinda looked like crap, to be honest.'

'I saw him yesterday,' said Halman. 'And he seemed okay. Maybe you've pissed him off, Eli.'

Lina laughed. 'Yeah, Eli,' she agreed. 'You do have that magic touch with people.'

Eli nodded towards Lina. 'And she asks for a pay rise!' he exclaimed. He turned serious again and added, 'It just seemed unlike him, is all. Nik, I mean. He didn't really seem himself.'

Halman shook his head. 'Nik's fine,' he said. 'I'll remind him about the cooker. Right now, it's you lot I'm concerned about. Hadn't you better get out there and make me rich?'

Eli grimaced and necked the last of his drink. 'Rich,' he muttered incredulously. He stood up, shoving Lina on the shoulder. Reluctantly, she also rose. 'See you later, Dan,' he said to Halman. 'If, that is, we don't die from exhaustion first.'

12

'Hardly in the risk-group for that are you, Eli?' replied Halman, grinning. 'Everyone knows you guys do jack shit in those ships. They do everything for you, right?'

Eli rolled his eyes and groaned, but he didn't allow Halman to bait him. 'Come on, Lina,' he said. They filed out of the canteen, gathering the other members of their shift along the way. Lina glanced back at Halman. He was staring out of the window, watching the belt, lost in his own thoughts, his large fingers drumming on the grimy table-top.

CHAPTER THREE

Lina snapped her four-point harness into place, yanking the straps tight from where the much-larger Bickes had been using it. She didn't really like how her vessel had become the unofficial stop-gap in the fleet lately – she liked to keep it set up to her own specifications. Still, complaining wouldn't change anything. Having tried it at length, she knew this for a fact.

She woke the computer, which reconfigured the readouts to her preferred settings and began to pre-flight all the systems. The reactor-cells were starting to show several developing hotspots – problems in the making, effectively. The more use K6-12 got, the sooner it would end up in maintenance itself – a fact which the ground crew seemed oddly oblivious to.

Never mind. She began to leech gas into the nozzles – not enough to move the craft yet, just enough to diagnose the injection and thrust characteristics. Everything looked fine.

'Okay then,' said Eli's voice through the speaker. 'Everyone green?' There was a chorus of affirmatives, some a little uncertain. 'Then let's roll. By the numbers, now.' The channel clicked off, making the slightly-blown speaker in Lina's cockpit pop quietly.

The Kay-pilots dialled up the gas and the machines converged on the central runway in perfect synchronisation. Lina trundled past the much larger in-system loader, the heavy grey vessel used for loading and unloading supply shuttles. HUD-markers on the cockpit canopy illuminated and tracked her companion vessels, tagging them with pilot names and bearings.

The huge hatch in the floor began to open, making a ramp, disgorging a condensing rush of air into space. Supposedly, the air in the hangar was vacuumed out before the space-door opened, but like everything else on the station, the pumps were gradually failing.

Eli was first out, his Kay weaving slightly as its little wheels left the deck, adding thin new strata of rubber to the many layers already plastered there. The craft veered, exposing the imbalance of its gas-jets. Eli corrected quickly, though, used to the vagaries of the ship, and headed off towards the belt. One by one, the others followed him, making a total of seven vessels.

The spinning station spread the emerging Kays into a regular fan, and they maintained this formation as they headed towards the belt, which lay below and before them like a rocky shoreline. Lina noticed that K6-8's navigational lights were out. She told the pilot – Sal Newman – as much. Sal just tutted, unsurprised.

Eli's voice crackled over the comm, somehow intrusive and over-loud in the eerie silence: 'One, two and four – head to sector Blue-Nine. Eight, nine and twelve – sector Blue-Eight.'

The various pilots responded in the affirmative. Lina, though, was the only one to voice the common thought: 'And how about you, Eli? Are you going to be shirking the work again?'

There was a slight pause during which Lina wondered if she had been a little too disrespectful. She forgot sometimes that Eli was actually her superior. He generally bore the teasing well enough, but that pause suggested to Lina that this might be one barb too many.

'I'm going to prospect the unnamed sector counter-spinwards from Blue-Ten, maybe map it for mining next. That okay with you?'

'Sure,' she responded, turning smoothly towards Blue-Eight, flanked by her companions. 'Make us rich, Eli,' she added, trying to inject a lighter note into her voice.

He laughed in response, making it all right again. 'I'll certainly try, Lina, but no promises.' His own Kay headed off alone towards the distant haze of the uncharted sector. The comm went dead again. Lina watched his gas-trail dissipate into space.

They reached their assigned sector and the Kays settled into their positions, matching the average rotational velocity of the belt objects. Rock and ice loomed coldly all around them – a jagged, three-dimensional stew of tiny shards and vast, house-sized boulders. Lina nudged K6-12 close enough to one of the larger chunks. An arm extended from the vessel, thin and angular like an insect-limb, with a drill-headed probe at its tip, and began to feel blindly for the rock. The probe pushed forwards, boring quickly, extracting a tiny sample of matter. The analysis came back good – double-M, like so many of the rocks here – and the vessel unfolded its tool arms and got to work. Shiny disc-cutters flashed in the pallid light of Soros. A plasma beam flared whitely, making the canopy darken protectively. The cutting sent a steady vibration through the hull – a quiet, soporific hum. Rock was flayed away, gripped by claws, shaved and diced and trimmed, passed back to the mass driver.

'So how's the kid, Lina?' asked Rocko.

Kay 6-12 jolted violently as its mass-driver launched the first bolt of rock towards the distant station's hopper and the jets rapidly compensated to prevent the craft from crashing. The first bolt hit a rock, spun away and was lost. Sometimes it could take a lot of bolts to forge a path through the belt to the station's receiver. Lina had often wondered if it was really the most efficient method, but she supposed that brighter minds than hers had come up with it. Already, the tool arms had made the next cut.

'Kid has a name, Rocko. I'd have thought you'd know that after the twelve years he's been around.' She craned to see his ship – above and to her left, picturing Rocko's face – his dark skin, handsome features, clean-shaven head and the star tattoo on his cheek that showed him to be an ex-member of Platini's Democratic Workers Union, essentially a now-dissolved insurgent group. Halman, in Platini Alpha's Farsight militia, had fought urban battles against the DWU in his younger days. Here, though, all things were forgiven. Rocko was family now. His Kay launched a bolt towards the station. This one got quite a bit further than Lina's had done. Below them and to the right, far off, a shuttle-sized iceberg was ploughing through the field like a juggernaut, silent and inexorable, bulldozing smaller objects out of its path.

'Sorry. How's Marco then?'

'Not too bad, thanks. Doing pretty well at school. I guess he couldn't help but pick up a little touch of genius from his mother, right?'

Sal laughed, a bright and tinkling sound. 'Genius, is it? Is that why you're out here in the middle of nowhere crunching rocks for some faceless corporation?'

'Hey, remember who has rank right now, Sal. And consider how easy it would be to have an *accident* out here.'

Sal laughed again. 'I don't think you'd have to engineer one, Lina. Have you seen the reactor diags on this piece of crap?'

'Can't be much worse than mine,' she answered.

'Or mine,' Rocko chipped in.

They were silent for a minute or so as the Kays continued their work, vacuuming up any errant dust from the cutting, which otherwise would only add to the communication barrier already presented by the belt. A hydraulic-pressure warning lit up on Lina's dashboard. She set the computer to run a deeper diagnostic on it, but the system seemed to be working for the moment.

'He's a good kid, anyway – say hello from me, would you?' said Rocko after a while.

'Sure, I will do. Though you can come say it yourself any time, you know.'

'He's too busy for the likes of us these days,' commented Sal in a voice that barely contained her amusement.

'Piss off, Sal,' Rocko replied automatically.

Lina laughed – she couldn't help it when she heard the wounded innocence in Rocko's voice. 'Oh yeah, I forgot,' she said. 'How is the *lady friend*, Rock?'

'She's fine. And she *is* just a friend, whatever you dickheads think.'

'I'm sure that's true,' answered Lina. 'Well say hi from us, next time she lets you get your breath back.'

There was a click as Rocko pointedly switched his comm into ignore mode. But he soon switched it back on again and Lina knew he wasn't really pissed.

The cut chunks of rock formed three tightly-converging dotted lines now, pointing back towards Macao Station. With a bit of zoom Lina could also see the bolts from the other wing, over in

Blue-Nine, forming their own ordered procession, if a little less advanced than her own wing's. The others must have had a delay in starting.

The diags came back from the hydraulic system. It was losing pressure at an increasing rate from a rupture in one of the reservoirs, probably caused by a minor accident station-side. The ground crew should have spotted it really. That was supposedly what they were for. The cutting arms would likely become inoperable within the hour. Lina ran through all the camera angles, and eventually she spotted a microscopically-thin trail of leaking fluid that formed an inky ribbon, stretching off into space. She cursed under her breath, but not quietly enough to prevent the others hearing.

'What's up?' asked Sal with forced casualness. Sometimes, when things went wrong in the belt, somebody ended up dead or hurt. Not often, but it had happened before. Everybody feared the inevitable next disaster.

'Nothing serious,' Lina said. 'I'm just losing some hydraulic fluid.'

'Wanna head back? We'll be okay.' Sal, despite being ranked below Lina, suffered from a persistent desire to look after her. Lina knew this stemmed from the time when Sal had been involved in a brief affair with Lina's then-husband, and Marco's father, Jaydenne. Marco, born on board, had still been a baby at the time. Sal, a pretty redhead several years younger than Lina, had offered him the attention that Lina herself had been unable or unwilling to supply. But Sal, who had still been a newcomer to Macao, had given Jaydenne up because of her conscience. Lina suspected Sal had loved him. She couldn't imagine how hard Sal's decision had been. Sal had worked hard across the intervening years to ingratiate herself to Lina, and to be fair, it had worked. Jaydenne had gone to Platini Alpha, leaving his wife and infant son behind like unwanted baggage. Their relationship had, by that point, been dead for some time anyway. Sal had remained, and had become a friend.

'I'll see if I can last it out. If the tool arms stop working I guess

I'll have to drop it back. Maybe there's another ship that I can grab.'

'I don't think there's a spare at all,' replied Rocko. 'Unless you want to take one that hasn't been pre-flighted.'

'I guess I might have to,' said Lina, her voice slow and unenthusiastic. 'Maybe some of them will be done by then. Anyway, this one *was* checked.'

'Maybe it just sprung,' suggested Sal. 'Could be from a micro-impact. Otherwise, the power-on diags should have caught it.'

'Could be,' Lina said. 'I didn't notice an impact, though. Maybe they can just bodge it – quick weld, bleed and refill.'

'Maybe,' said Sal without conviction.

For a moment then, Lina felt how tenuous, how fragile their existence was out here. She could actually *sense* the delicate, straining bonds that held everything – the Kays, the station, the people, their whole overburdened frontier world – together. The vastness of space loomed around her, endless in every direction, a vista without horizon. She felt tiny and vulnerable, a single byte lost in the cacophonous datastream of creation. She looked up at Macao. The station loomed through the rock-haze, turning darkly about its hub, its two huge spokes like muscular arms that gripped its outer rim. It didn't look like a place that could sustain life. For all its bulk, it looked too fallible, too delicate. This was a feeling she had suffered from more and more of late. She shook herself, shivering, and turned up the heater.

'When's that damn shuttle getting here again?' asked Sal after a while.

'Soon,' answered Rocko. 'It should be soon, right?'

'It better had be,' said Sal. 'I heard Gregor's out of real beer.'

'Oh that's just bloody great! Thanks for that!' enthused Rocko falsely. 'I'll sleep easy now I know that, Sal. We'll expect a riot, then.'

'You two, cut the crap!' demanded Lina. It was unusual of her to curse, and it surprised the others into obedient silence. 'The supply shuttle is due next week. Maybe everyone can restrain the urge to riot until then.'

'At least we'll get our new batch of psychos for the lifers' wing,' added Rocko quietly, possibly expecting further reprimand.

Lina's Kay had diced up the last of its asteroid and she pointed it towards the next likely-looking candidate. The face of the new rock loomed huge and cliff-like, glinting in the ship's spotlight. She wondered briefly what epic journey had brought this chunk of stone to Soros, what cosmic furnace had originally smelted it, long before humanity existed. The belt was an archive – a stone recording of ancient stellar history. It would still be here when Macao fell into final, terminal disrepair and was forgotten.

Lina mentally shrugged and relaxed back into her chair. The asteroid was rotating gently in the vertical plane and the ship struggled briefly, feathering its thrusters, to match the rock's motion, little blasts of gas hissing into space. It aligned itself and anchored on. A few marble-sized stones pinged gently off the hull and ricocheted away.

'Yeah, well, I don't think any of us are too thrilled by *that*,' agreed Lina, remembering her own similar comment to Eli. 'But I guess it keeps the station spinning. And I think there's only gonna be one this time.'

Rocko's Kay moved gracefully above Lina's, its waving tool arms like jellyfish tentacles, coming about and lining itself up with a new rock. There was another cushioned jolt as Lina's mass driver launched its next bolt towards the station.

'Yeah, but he sounds like a pretty rough customer,' said Sal. Her Kay was off to Lina's left, industriously sawing and processing, tool arms moving in a surgical ballet.

'So I hear,' agreed Rocko. 'Guy called Carver. Another nutcase, originally from Aitama. Shipped from there to the high-security prison at Platini Alpha. I guess even they got sick of him, though, so we get him next. Multiple murder, of course.'

'Of course,' agreed Lina, having nothing else to say. She shivered again, even though the heater was on high now. Why send psychopaths and murderers to a remote mining outpost? Surely there was a better, more central place to incarcerate them? Maybe somewhere a bit better prepared than Macao.

Her Kay's arms were weakening now, struggling to apply the cutters forcefully enough to the rock. She willed them to persist but could do little else. In theory, one of the other craft could have attempted to patch the external skin of the reservoir in space. In practice, it would be a pretty dangerous manoeuvre – a job best left to the ground crew.

'So,' said Sal in a brighter tone. 'You guys reckon Eli's gonna find gold in the uncharted sector?' Her Kay was coming about now, too, having exhausted its first rock. Sal moved it deftly through the shifting maze and approached a new one.

'Maybe,' said Lina. 'Who knows what's really out here? Must be something worthwhile somewhere.'

Sal laughed lightly. 'Here there be dragons, right?' she said. 'That's what they used to write on the uncharted parts of the map in times of old.'

Lina laughed, too. 'And a big X where the gold's buried!'

'Right,' agreed Rocko. 'Let's hope.'

CHAPTER FOUR

'Come in,' called Halman's voice from behind the door. Hearing this, Nik Sudowski hit the pad to open it. It stuck, motors singing treble, near the top of its track. Ducking slightly, he entered the austere grey room, feeling sheepish.

'How's it going, Nik?' asked Halman, pushing aside a datasheet that he had been studying. His stubbled face peered up at Sudowski warily. Halman indicated the chair opposite his own and Sudowski sat in it.

For a moment, his hands twisted nervously in his lap before he managed to still them. 'Not great, Boss.'

Halman sighed resignedly. Sudowski guessed that whatever he had been looking at on the datasheet had already put him in a bad mood. 'Spill it,' he said.

Nik took a deep breath into his skinny chest. He caught sight of his reflection in Halman's window. His face was deeply lined and drawn, his growing army of wrinkles more pronounced than ever. It wasn't a great face, he knew, but he had grown to tolerate it, and he supposed everyone else had, too. 'When is the shuttle due?' he asked.

'Should be in the next few days. We had the standard message through from Way Station One a few weeks ago, claiming that the shuttle passed by them on schedule. It shouldn't be far behind the laser-message, although of course it must be slowing down by now. Why?'

'It's that PCB in the air scrubbers – a little thing, really, but one that's going to be a problem any time soon. We've made a liquid-nitro jacket for the chip but it's on the verge of burning out. Can't do much else, I'm afraid.' He suddenly caught a whiff of the distinctive workshop smell that emanated from his own dirty overalls – a bitter mixture of metal and machine-oil.

'How soon is "any time soon"?'

'Like any time *now*, really. As in, for all I know, it'll die while I'm sat here talking to you.'

Halman looked out of the window, which showed the usual, stable image that most people preferred. Nik's gaze followed his. The tiny planet Vagar was a cold speck in the distance, Platini an impossibly great distance beyond even that. Such a fragile lifeline. Something groaned vastly, deep in the bowels of the station – a shuddering, metallic sound that startled the two men from their reverie. They looked at each other, fearing the worst, but no alarms went off.

'Probably just the baler jamming,' said Sudowski after a pause.

'I expect the refinery guys are on it. Isn't there anything we can cannibalise to get the PCB part?'

'It's possible. Or maybe my guys can reverse engineer it, bodge together some sort of functional stopgap. Crude would be the best we could do, but it might work for a few days.'

'Well let's get everyone we can spare onto it and hope that it doesn't become a matter of life or death before the shuttle gets here. Keep it quiet, though, okay?'

'Sure.'

'And apart from that?'

Sudowski wiped a hand across his face and exhaled deeply. 'About the same as usual. Trouble with the Kays. The dead-lifter needs replacing, too. The whole control console is gone, as are two of the motors. We've had to patch in an auxiliary terminal just to move it out the way.'

'Well, I'll certainly add it to the list, but the chances of us getting a new one this side of eternity are pretty slim, I'd say. You'll have to figure out how to drive it through the auxiliary.'

'If we can't, then the ground crew are gonna have a nightmare time. Lina's old crate sprung a hydraulic leak today.'

Halman laughed, but it wasn't a particularly humorous sound. 'Don't you ever have any good news, Nik?' he asked, rocking back in his chair and spreading his hands questioningly.

'No,' Sudowski admitted. 'Not often.'

23

'Anyways, I have every confidence in you and your team. If anyone can keep the scrubbers going and the Kays flying, it's you. If you need personnel to move them around by hand, let me know and I'll find people somehow. But personally I'm expecting that you'll patch up and make do, as always.'

Nik Sudowski sighed, flattered by the compliment, but subdued by tiredness and the burden of expectation. 'I can't promise anything, Boss.'

'Sure. Well, I'd better let you get on, then, Nik,' said Halman. Behind him, the asteroid field rotated gently, like a vast cog. The gas trail of a solitary Kay was threading its way through the minefield of rock and ice. Neither man noticed it go.

'Guess so. See you later. Let me know as soon as the shuttle radios in, would you? Then I can stop panicking.'

'Of course,' said Halman.

Sudowski let himself out into the dimly-lit corridor and headed off back towards his office, which was one floor hubwards, or up. Turning a corner, he came across one of his maintenance teams, comprising Alphe Ridenhour and Fionne Sinclair, both of whom were on their backs on the corridor floor and immersed from their waists up in an open wall space. He stopped and coughed politely. Alphe jerked, banging his head on some unseen hazard, and swore. There was an agitated clanging sound and then Alphe twisted his body and his oil-smeared face appeared, complete with look of irritated inquiry, which faded when he saw Sudowski. He combed a hand through his dark, untidy hair.

'Hi, Boss,' he said, shuffling out and sitting up. Fionne also wriggled free of her confines, holding a well-worn spanner in one small hand. The knuckles of the hand were skinned and raw, caked with machine oil and blood.

'What's up?' asked Sudowski.

'Damn water pipes. Failed one-way in the main branch of the hot. There's boiling water pouring from the ceiling in corridor 146.'

Fionne laughed, lighting up her grubby face. Underneath the dirt she was an unusually pretty young woman – blonde and clear-skinned, handsome bone-structure and slightly upturned nose –

24

though she wore her good looks with complete indifference. 'The only way we can come at it is from the floor above, of course. But we have to pinch the supply off here or we'll be boiled alive. We taped the area off, so if you're heading up you'll have to detour.'

Sudowski sighed heavily. 'It's almost as if Farsight weren't thinking of us at all when they paperclipped this pile of junk together, eh?' He found that he was massaging the side of his head with one hand. It was beginning to ache, he realised – subtle, pulsing waves of pain that showed promise of intensifying later.

'Yeah,' agreed Alphe. 'Almost seems that way.'

Fionne began rifling through a heavily patched canvas tool bag. She produced a gunmetal-coloured power clamp as long as her forearm and began to dial settings into it with the ease of long practise. She hefted it meaningfully. 'We'll get the bastard,' she said, and slid back into the dark recess of the wall. Sudowski heard the growl of the power clamp from inside.

'How long?' he asked.

Alphe's face – the face of a country bumpkin, despite the intelligence it concealed – wrinkled in distaste. 'Ohhh. . . The dreaded question. . .'

'Ballpark.'

'By the end of the shift, I guess. But it is a guess.'

'Thanks, Alphe, that'll do for me.' He gave Alphe a nod and turned to continue down the corridor. The voices of the two engineers faded into the distance. He reached his office without passing anybody else, and let himself in.

The room was generously furnished compared to most of the station – two-seat sofa, small meeting table, desk in one corner, pictures on the walls – but somehow the starkness of the underlying structure still showed through, like bones poking through skin. An ugly rust stain that stretched from ceiling to floor in one corner had repeatedly thwarted any attempts to paint over it, showing through again and again with impressive determination. Nobody had been able to find what was causing it, but it was presumably some splitting, slowly failing pipe in one of the hubwards floors, that would eventually show itself by creating

25

some entertaining disaster, much like the one Alphe and Fionne were dealing with at that very moment.

Sudowski went to his desk and sat. He fired up the computer – they were all off by default to prolong the lifespan of their heat-generating components – and opened the parts files. He found the chip, and the related board, that was currently dying in the air scrubbers, and enlarged the schematic, turning it this way and that.

He was rubbing the side of his head again, where the interface chips had been removed. In his previous life, he'd driven plant equipment by neural link on Aitama, in the Platini system. The chips had been taken out when he'd left for Macao, but he still felt their legacy sometimes. More and more, lately, it seemed. It was really beginning to ache now, and the harsh light of the computer screen was making it worse. Maybe he was coming down with something, although transmissible illnesses were rare on board, brought in yearly batches by the supply shuttles.

He pulled up the attached specifications file and ran through it, biting his lip. He began to enter details into the search utility. Nothing. No match. Of course not. He got up, went to the coffee machine, and let it make him its own version of the classic drink, which was basically brown-coloured chemical sludge plus caffeine, then returned to the computer. He set the cup down and began to adjust the parameters of the search, shifting margins and tolerances to find a part – *any* part – that would do in a pinch. Gradually, the figures he entered grew further and further from the ideals. And then, just as he was about to give up, there it was. It wasn't a perfect match, of course, but it would – *should* – do the job.

He pulled the part up and inspected it. He felt reasonably confident that it would do to replace the chip in the scrubbers, if it came to it – if, for example, the shuttle was late, as they sometimes were, and the scrubbers failed. Only problem was that it was a key component of the communications array, and they only had one – the one that was in use.

'Okay,' Sudowski said under his breath. 'I guess that's good to

26

know.' He felt like either laughing or crying, maybe both. Instead, he shut the computer off, poured the remaining coffee away, and headed back towards his own quarters and his bed, massaging his head as he went.

CHAPTER FIVE

Halman began his tour of the station – *his* station – by checking into the machine rooms where the air scrubbers were situated. He found, surprisingly, nobody there, although the huge cabinet that housed the scrubbers was surrounded by patched-in terminals and pincushioned with probes. The whole contraption was humming softly, and the air felt tense and electrified. Fearing that even his presence there might somehow upset the delicate equilibrium of the machine, he stole from the room and away into the maze-like corridors of Macao. Strange that there was nobody there, he thought, but he supposed somebody was monitoring the data from the probes remotely.

He headed downwards – rimwards – from the machine rooms, walked past rows of living quarters, and took the next stairs, down again. He went through the warehouse, wondering where Charlie Stenning was, to the hangar. Alphe was there with his head under the open cowling of the dead-lifter, surrounded by members of the ground crew. Liu Xiao, head of the ground crew, looked up as Halman crossed the tyre-marked flight deck. He came towards Halman, smiling his usual polite smile.

'Hey Liu,' Halman greeted him. 'What's up?'

'Hello Dan,' Liu replied. He was smartly uniformed, unmarked by oil or other grime despite having recently had his head inside the dead-lifter. The ground crew hadn't had new uniforms for five years now and Halman wondered exactly how he had maintained the condition of his clothing for so long. Halman himself wore sturdy but scruffy work trousers and a long-sleeved shirt with worn-out elbows, and all *he* did was sit behind a desk most of the time.

'You managed to get hold of young Alphe, then.' Halman indicated the tech, who was now on his tiptoes with the whole upper half of his body inside the machine. Alphe was almost always half-buried in some machine or other when Halman saw him. 'I understand he's much in demand right now.' He laughed, adding, 'As usual.'

'Indeed,' said Liu, still smiling. 'I managed to lure him down to my lair.' He looked around himself at the hangar: high ceiling, festooned with drapes of cable and oily hydraulics; ranks of roosting Kays; patchwork textures of rusty metal and stained surfaces – a veritable machine crypt. His smile widened a notch. 'Technically, I think he's due for a break.'

Halman thought again of the air scrubbers and the humour went out of him. 'Aren't we all, old man. Can he get it going?'

'Alphe?' asked Liu, as if Halman could possibly have been talking about anyone else. 'Yes, I should think so.'

Halman put a hand on Liu's shoulder, turning him away and leading him off towards the glasspex-fronted control room. Liu came along willingly, his small, trim form dwarfed by Halman's massive bulk.

'How's production, Liu?' Halman asked when they were out of earshot of the crowd round the dead-lifter. 'And things generally?'

'Come into control and I'll give you exact figures, if you like,' offered Liu. 'We've managed to set-up the system to auto-collate the logs from the Kays.'

'No, it's okay – rough'll do.'

'Well, the miners have hit targets consistently across the last twenty-plus shifts. Despite their obvious obstacles. We're okay, generally. The usual concerns – things breaking, Kays falling apart. General struggle for survival. K6-13 is still out of action, as you know. We're hoping to get the parts on the shuttle. It's just the injector control from the standard servicing kit that we need. I ordered it from Way Station One last year but they told us to wait until Platini sent it.'

'Good. You're doing well, Liu. I know it isn't always easy, but I appreciate your efforts down here. I consider this the business end of our whole operation.'

Liu shrugged. 'No problem.'

29

'How're fuel supplies?'

'Gas, we're okay. Some of the Kays need fission material, as always. Most of them, to be honest.' He shrugged. 'They keep flying.'

'No two-three-five from refinery recently?'

Liu's attention was briefly distracted by a loud bang from the direction of the dead-lifter and Alphe's voice, cursing tiredly but vehemently. He craned to see, then shook his head, dismissing the incident. 'Sorry?' he asked.

'No two-three-five from refinery?' Halman repeated.

'They haven't sent any down for a while, no,' admitted Liu. 'I've been meaning to have someone run up and check.'

'Don't worry about it,' said Halman. 'I'm heading that way myself in a bit.'

Liu nodded amicably. 'Good, thanks.'

'Who's out there at the moment?'

'Ilse Reno's shift. She's going to radio in any minute, though, so we'll have to clear the decks to let them land.'

'Well, I'll let you get on, then,' said Halman. He turned to regard the little group around the dead-lifter. They were replacing the heavy cowling, three men struggling to fold it back into place. 'Looks like progress,' he suggested.

'Let's hope so,' said Liu. And with that, he turned away and walked back towards the stricken machine.

Halman left the hangar and ambled back through the warehouse, feeling tiny beneath the high, vaulted ceiling and skyscraping shelves of spare parts and other equipment. Charlie Stenning, in charge of warehouse, was now on the mezzanine, conversing with one of his staff, waving a datasheet in one hand.

Halman called in at the aeroponics department, where white-coated technicians tended plants that hung with their roots suspended in a nutrient-rich vapour. The heat and humidity were stifling, almost suffocating. It was a strange place, where the plants themselves, with all their organic randomness, looked like alien visitors in the bright, sterile environment. Shiny steel shelves stretched away into the distance, pinched by perspective.

Tomatoes and peppers, almost artificially red, dotted the greenery like bright baubles. Cabbages hung like beach balls that had frozen in mid-air.

Aeroponics was one of the few departments on the station that typically took care of itself. Or at least, its staff took care of its running without too much cause to bother Halman, which amounted to the same thing from his point of view. Even so, he liked to walk the floors, talk to the people, be seen to show an interest.

Halman was an honest creature at heart, and he found himself wanting to tell everyone about Nik's concerns for the air system. When he spoke to Ola, the woman in charge of the department, the truth almost spilled out and he had to bite his lip to restrain it. He reminded himself that there was no need to scare people, least of all the slightly-nervous head of aero. She was efficient, but she was a known worrier at the best of times. Anyway, he was confident that Nik would fix it. Satisfied that he had done his duty by the aeroponics team, he continued onwards.

He took the stairs up to Macao's plaza, one of the more spacious areas of the station. Except for Gregor's bar, *The Miner's Retreat*, the retail units of the plaza were dead-eyed and shutter-mouthed. There weren't many entrepreneurs willing to set up private businesses on a far-flung mining outpost, it seemed. Gregor, thank goodness, was the exception to the rule. Even at this hour, *The Miner's* was open. Tobacco smoke and the smell of stale synthihol wafted from its shadowed doorway.

From there, he wandered through the rec-area, between the massive tubes through which materials were shuttled from the refinery to the dispatch area of the hangar. The tubes were ten metres wide each, grey and heavily-armoured, and they always looked like the exposed bones of the station to Halman. Off-duty workers promenaded between them, looking out of the windows, chatting, drinking coffee, laughing together.

He passed the kitchens, checking in to chat briefly with the head chef – a slightly pretentious title for a man with little more culinary skill than Halman himself. Stocks were getting low, but

31

that was normal this close to resupply. There had been a temporary glitch in the water purification system a week before and the kitchens were still full of jury-rigged sterilisation equipment that nobody had yet dismantled. Halman requested that they take care of it sooner rather than later. The head chef shrugged and went back to his work. Halman didn't have the heart to pursue it.

He walked past the admin offices, pleased that nobody collared him on the way. His own door stood invitingly open and he could see his half-eaten apple browning on its plate amongst the detritus of his desk. Amy Stone, his second-in-command, bustled past, distracted, offering a token greeting.

He continued into long rows of living quarters, occasionally stopping to exchange small-talk with someone or other, taking his time. If it hadn't been for his perpetual concern about the air system, he believed he would even have been enjoying himself.

He headed up the stairs, hubwards, to the refinery. He entered the department through thick sound-deadening doors hung with plastic curtains, emerging into a huge, shadowy cavern of deafening noise and massive crane-arms. Staff members crawled between the metal megaliths like ants. Sealed vats large enough to play football in stretched away into the distance. Control panels flashed; robotic arms tipped giant crucibles of searing molten metal into chutes and hoppers; steel walkways criss-crossed the ceiling, connecting mezzanines and observation platforms.

The heat was far worse than inside aeroponics and Halman began to sweat at once. The concavity of Macao's floor could be clearly seen here, this being the inside, hub-most layer of the ring and the view being unbroken by walls or bulkheads. Above Halman's head, beyond the high ceiling of the refinery itself, was the spindle of the station – the hub of the great wheel – crammed with kinetic defence systems and communications equipment.

He walked across the steel mesh platform and descended a short flight of steps to the main floor of the refinery, his boots crunching through rock dust and metal particles. His entrance was heralded by shuddering metallic groans and ear-splitting screeches as the robot arms went ponderously about their work. As he approached the nearest of the grinders – a huge, squarish lump of a thing that took raw material straight from the main hopper and crunched it into gravel – the refinery's second-in-command, a serious woman named Sarissa, rounded the corner of the machine and almost bumped into him.

She looked up, startled. She had an intelligent, if unsmiling face, haggard and pockmarked by tiny burns. She was holding a datasheet in one hand and a lump of glossy stone in the other.

'Halman!' she exclaimed in surprise.

'Hi, Sarissa!' he shouted back. A head-splitting, repetitive clanging noise began in the distance of the refinery as some heavy piece of equipment began its work.

Sarissa lifted her ear defenders and slid them back on her head, pushing back her strawlike grey hair. 'What?' she yelled.

'Hi, I said. How're things?'

'Fine, fine,' Sarissa shouted, nodding emphatically.

'I spoke to Liu,' Halman continued as slowly and clearly as he could. 'They're short on two-three-five down there.'

Sarissa frowned heavily, shaking her head. 'We've hardly had any in lately. We still don't have a batch for them.'

'Why not?'

A refinery worker in full hazmat gear squeezed past Halman and scampered away between rusty metal towers.

'No reason,' Sarissa explained. 'Just random. Some'll come in sooner or later. Maybe today. Who knows? Is it urgent?'

'Not yet, I don't think. But if you have any at all, just take it down, will you?'

'Sure, I'll send it today.' She hefted the lump of stone – presumably some item intended for analysis – and Halman got the impression that she would like to be away about her business. 'Anything else?' she asked, seeming to confirm this.

'How are we for the rest of it? Oxides, copper, iron, nickel, heavy metals?'

'Good,' she said. 'Good. Lots of silver – a surprising amount. Once again, it's just a random spike. The hoppers, overall, are as full as they ever get at this point in the cycle. We'll be glad to get it all onto that shuttle.'

'That's great, Sarissa. Keeps us spinning, right?'

'Right,' she agreed, still not smiling.

'What about water ice?'

'Oh, loads. They ran a couple of shifts' worth of just ice last week.'

Halman nodded. 'Good,' he said. 'Everything else okay?'

'Well. . .' she said uncertainly, looking away. Her fingers clenched and unclenched nervously on the lump of rock, massaging it.

'What?' Halman asked, sensing something wrong, something she didn't really want to tell him.

'We've, er, we've. . .' she trailed off, still not looking at him. Her face worked with conflicting emotion but no sound came out.

'Yes?'

'People have been reporting some slightly weird occurrences these last few days.'

'Weird?' parroted Halman, his brow furrowing. 'Weird like what?'

The noise was increasing in volume now and Sarissa had to raise her voice to a bellow in order to be heard. 'Things have been going missing. You know – safety equipment, mainly.'

'That is a bit weird,' agreed Halman. Why would anyone take safety equipment? 'Maybe people are misplacing stuff.'

Sarissa shook her head. 'I don't think so,' she yelled. 'Stewart was burned yesterday because he didn't have the gloves he should have had – couldn't find them.'

'Pull someone off duty and get them to go through the whole place,' Halman shouted. 'Actually, two people. We can't be having accidents because of shit missing. That's just insane. Farsight'll scrag me if someone dies.'

'And. . .' she started uncertainly. She looked up at Halman, seemed to steel herself and began again. 'And. . . some people are saying the place is haunted. I know it's ludicrous, but there you are. One of the guys was almost hit by a falling block yesterday, down at the far end near the crucibles. When we got up there, there was a shackle-pin missing.' She puffed her cheeks out and shrugged, visibly lost for an explanation. 'Those things don't just come out on their own – they can't. At least in theory. Nobody wants to go down there now. I pretty much have to force them, and even then they'll only go in pairs.'

'That is *very* odd,' agreed Halman, genuinely puzzled. 'But I expect it's nothing. Even so, check the whole place out. Even if you have to stop production entirely for a day.'

'I don't know about that. . .' she replied, looking away into the clanking, living depths of the refinery. 'I'm sure it *is* just nothing. I mean, I wasn't going to even mention it. I filled in an incident report, of course, but. . . The shackle pin is weird – it shouldn't be possible – but I'm sure there's a good explanation for it. And I'm also sure that it *is* just a one-off. Pretty sure,' she finished unconvincingly.

'Even so, I want this place checked over. That's an order. Full safety survey. This talk of haunting is just the sort of bullshit we don't need. I can't have people scared to work, and I can't have somebody killed if we could have prevented it.' He stooped low, catching her eye. 'Okay?'

'Sure,' she said. 'Okay.' And then she scurried away between billowing shadows and swinging cranes, quickly lost from sight.

Halman stood for a moment, sweating, his ears ringing. 'Haunted!' he said aloud. 'Bullshit!' And then he turned and wandered back the way that he had come.

CHAPTER SIX

Lina found Marco lying asleep on the sofa in the living room with a piece of half-eaten toast balanced on a plate on his chest. He had been watching the holo, which was still showing the final scenes of a Farsight film about the Corp Wars called The Bitter Frontier. It was a favourite of his, and one that she disapproved of. The holo was the only light source in the room, and shadows lurched across the walls in time to its hectic strobing. The fridge-freezer, which was slowly dying, could be heard even over the crashing sounds of interstellar warfare.

Lina sighed and cautiously approached the prone form of her son. Her suspicions were confirmed – he was sleeping.

She smiled to herself, wanting to reach out and touch him, maybe brush his tangled blond hair away from his eyes. That hair – an unruly shock that resisted all attempts at styling – was the perfect image of her own. She contented herself by simply standing and regarding his expressionless, slumbering face for a moment. He was a good boy, and a wave of simple love – an ache, almost – washed over her. How he could have turned out so well with a mother who was always at work and a father in Platini system, she couldn't imagine. But there it was – somehow it had happened anyway.

Suddenly, he started, some deep part of his brain alerting him to her presence, and sat up. The plate slid slowly off his chest and clattered onto the floor. The toast, of course, fell butter-side-down. Lina vaguely remembered hearing some scientific explanation as to why that usually happened – something to do with aerodynamics, she thought. Never mind.

'Mum,' he said, sleep-slurred, blinking up at her.

'Hi, kiddo,' she answered, gently forcing herself onto the sofa beside him. His face was endearingly confused. He craned to see the fallen toast, then relaxed against her.

'I was watching the holo,' he said unnecessarily.

'You know I don't like you watching that Farsight propaganda film,' she said, putting an arm round his shoulders.

'No, Mum, I know.' He sounded like he was coming more fully to his senses now. 'I just like it. I know nobody really won the Corp Wars. Farsight was no better than anyone else, right?'

Lina nodded, looking into his face. That face was still a little cute around the edges, but soon it would be a handsome face, she reckoned. The flickering red and green that pulsed from the holo in alternating waves cast him in a surreal light, making him look like some sort of alien visitor from a more perfect universe. 'That's right,' she said. 'But now, they're better than they were, and the Corp Wars were a long time ago. The company provide us a living, right? But I still don't like you watching that film, on principle.'

'Okay,' he agreed. He paused for a moment, then changed the subject: 'I'm hungry, Mum. I didn't eat my toast.'

'No,' she answered. 'I reckon the floor ate your toast. Holo — change, random.' The holo obediently flicked to a scientific documentary about Predecessor ruins. There wasn't really that much to say on the subject, in Lina's opinion. Everyone knew they hadn't actually left anything behind. Except, of course, for the hard core of idiots who insisted that the drug fader had come from DSH-3. 'I'll fix you some proper dinner.'

'Thanks, Mum.' He snuggled against her appreciatively.

'No worries. I'll see what we've got.' Reluctantly (in truth, she was tired enough to fall asleep next to him) Lina forced herself to stand up and go into the kitchen.

'Maybe we could have those burgers?' Marco called from the other room.

Lina rearranged the jumble of brooms, pipe-offcuts and shoes around herself so that she could actually access the fridge-freezer. She managed to get into such a position that she could open the door and extract the burgers — real meat burgers saved from the last shuttle — and some salad grown in the aeroponics room. 'Yeah,' she called back. 'Burgers it is.'

She managed to wriggle her way free from the clutches of a broken vacuum cleaner that she had never quite managed to fix, snagging a half-loaf of bread as she went. She picked her way to the stove and began to cook dinner.

'Mum?' said Marco from the kitchen doorway, making her jump a little.

'Yes?' she answered, turning to face him, spatula in one hand, flight suit speckled with cooking-oil spots.

'I heard at school that the air scrubbers were wearing out, and that if they fail then we'll all die.' Although the tone was nonchalant, Lina couldn't fail to detect the note of worry hidden underneath.

She smiled reassuringly, uncertain of who she was really trying to reassure. 'You know Sudowski's guys won't let that happen, honey. The station's always been like this, since long before you were here. Before Nik Sudowski, it was his uncle. And the maintenance teams have always kept this place together. *Always*. Okay?'

'Okay,' he replied, nodding. He sounded a little unsure, although he looked happier.

Lina turned to the cooker again and flipped one of the burgers to check its readiness. Satisfied, she dumped both of them onto the hunks of bread that she had laid out ready on two plates, salad piled alongside.

'The shuttle is due any day now, anyway, and it should be carrying the part for the scrubbers. The maintenance team have known it was going for ages. Even if the old one fails before that – which it won't – then they'll find some way of keeping the system running. Dinner's up.'

'Yeah!' Marco enthused, his stomach overriding any concerns his mind may have had. He hungrily accepted the proffered plate and they headed to the metal table in the living room. Metals were about the only things that were in genuine plenty at Macao, and one kind of got used to seeing them everywhere, usually in their bare, untreated forms. Pretty much the whole of the station was furnished with whatever functional metal happened to be in abundance at the time.

Lina killed the holo and turned on the overhead light, which was set to so-called 'environmental mode' and accordingly emitted a ruddy evening-hue. They both tucked in, equally famished.

'How was school, Son?' asked Lina around a mouthful of burger. She wiped a smear of tomato ketchup from her chin.

'Mmm, okay,' he answered. 'We're learning chemistry, but Miss Greene says all chemistry is just stamp collecting, and we should remember that all science is physics really.' He shrugged and took another bite.

Lina laughed. 'She did, did she? She should tell that to the chemists at the refinery – they'd like that!'

Marco took a swig from his water glass. 'Ella told me one of her guards was attacked by a prisoner,' he said conversationally.

Ella was Ella Kown, security chief and mother of Marco's best friend, Clay. Lina didn't really appreciate her telling Marco about the prison attack, but she had never knowingly lied to him and she wasn't going to start now. 'Yeah, 'fraid so. He's gonna be okay, though, the guy who was attacked. Murkhoff, it was. I think Ella's team just need a little more experience in handling the prisoners. It's still a bit new to them.'

'Oh, right,' he said, seemingly dismissing the matter. 'Is Eli still gonna take me to the game?'

'The soccer? Yeah, I should think so – he hasn't said otherwise.'

He nodded. 'Good. I like Eli.'

Lina nodded, too. 'So do I. He's one of the good guys. Even though he works us half to death sometimes.'

'Keeps us spinning, right, Mum?'

'Yeah,' she agreed, picking up a piece of salad with her fingers, grinning to hear him say those words. 'That's the line.'

CHAPTER SEVEN

Darkness, cold, an echoing icy tomb without air. The man moved slowly, suited and clumsy, floating down the tunnel.

'Are you there?'

Nothing. . .

'Hello?'

Nothing. . .

He moved further down the tunnel, gloved hands trailing over slick, unseen surfaces, assuring himself of his bearings. He gave a little kick of thrust from the jet in the suit's arm, being careful not to hit the wall. This *was* the right place, wasn't it? Suddenly he was afraid. Maybe he was lost – a man could lose the way, run out of air or power, suffocate, freeze and die in here.

'Hello?' More fearfully this time, hearing the note of tension in his own voice, struggling to subdue it. 'Are you there?'

'I am here.'

Relief, then. He heard his own breathing, heavy in the stillness, emphasised by the hissing of the suit's respiration system. Sensing the possible beginnings of hyperventilation, the suit restricted his oxygen intake slightly.

'I thought perhaps you had left me.' He laughed to hear himself say this – a short cough of laughter, an exorcism of worry more than anything. Now that it had spoken, he could *feel* its presence – it was like a crackling in the air, a latent electrical charge that prickled the skin even through his suit. But there was something else, too – a sort of *hunger* – the sort of feral tang that a person might experience when they felt the breath of a wild animal close upon their skin. 'Or perhaps that you were never here.'

'I am here. And I will never leave you.'

'Good.'

'You have done the small tasks I asked of you?'

'Yes.' He waited for a reply, but there was only silence. Silence and his own breathing. 'You said that you would answer some questions for me.' He waited again. 'Will you do that?'

'What would you know?' The voice sounded a little cagey, thought the man. Suspicious.

'What are you?' he asked. Suddenly, he was afraid. Had it been foolish of him to return here?

'I am a living thing,' said the voice. 'I am a hungry, trapped, living thing. You might think of me as a sort of. . . *dragon*. And I am your friend.'

'My friend?' repeated the man. *Friend*. . . That word carried with it a soothing, calming association. It was good. Everybody needed friends. The fear dissipated like water boiling off into steam. 'A dragon?'

'Do not misunderstand me,' added the voice – the dragon. 'For I can be a dangerous friend.'

'Yes,' whispered the man, awed. His head felt fuzzy, stuffed with cotton wool. He shook it, trying to clear it, but the fuzziness persisted. Never mind. . . It was a pleasant fuzziness really.

'Fear not, though,' said the dragon. 'It was you who sought me out. You who came to me, showed your fealty with the tasks I set for you. You have returned. You are my emissary. The chosen one. And we will be *good* friends, you and I. I have no cause to hurt you.'

'I am your emissary,' repeated the man, entranced. He floated like a wisp of smoke, a shade of himself, the merest mote in that maw of darkness. His suit-light was a single interior star.

'So,' said the dragon in a lighter tone, 'how are you today? You sound a little. . . *tense*.' The man failed to detect the slight hint of amusement that floated just below the surface of these words.

'I'm okay. I just. . . I thought you might have gone for a moment, or that I might be lost. I'm okay. A little tired. . . we work hard. . . but otherwise. . .' And he did feel okay, now that he was here.

'Did you not enjoy the tasks I set for you?'

'Oh no, no,' stammered the man, concerned that he had been misunderstood. 'It isn't that. I did enjoy them. . . It's good to have a purpose.'

'You do not have a purpose without me?' It sounded like a question, but the man thought it might be a statement.

'I suppose not,' he admitted. His suit-light played across ice-slicked rock, trickling through the darkness, the smallest living spark.

'Was it not easy to do these things? To evade detection? Did it not excite you?'

'It was kind of fun,' said the man thoughtfully, struggling to extract the right words from his uncooperative brain. 'But you said, that if I did these things, then you would tell me more about yourself.'

'I have told you already. What more would you know?'

'I don't know. . .' said the man stupidly. Somehow, his proximity to the dragon seemed to reduce his own intelligence. It made him feel childish and slightly confused. It was a shame, because when he had been away from it he had thought of many questions to ask, but floating here in its very court, its temple, its home, he could not remember what they were.

'Well?' asked the dragon.

The man thought deeply, his brow wrinkling. 'You have told me you are a dragon,' he began cautiously. 'But what *are* you? I mean, really? How did you come to be here?'

'I tire of this. Enough. Do not ask me these questions any more. They have begun to bore me.' The voice was calm, but the man sensed that this was dangerous ground now. The dragon had said that it wouldn't hurt him. But it had also said it was a dangerous friend. These two concepts seemed to contradict each other. Which was the truth?

'Yes, of course,' the man agreed, eager to please. 'That is enough.' He had gone too far. Perhaps the dragon would bite. He waited, breathing deeply, for judgement to be passed.

'Do not be afraid,' said the dragon. 'And do not make me repeat myself again. I intend no harm to you. Nor to anybody else.'

42

'Good,' said the man.

'Now *I* have a question for *you*.'

'P-please,' stammered the man reverently. 'Ask me anything.'

'Do you think, having completed some simple quests already, that you could do something else for me?'

'I don't know. . .'

For a moment the dragon said nothing. The man began to fear that he had offended it with his uncertainty and he cursed his own stupidity. There was a pause, pregnant with possibilities. He waited nervously.

But then, just when he could bear it no longer and was about to break into grovelling apology, the dragon spoke again: 'It is a simple question. Will you help me or not?'

'Yes,' said the man hurriedly, grasping at this lifeline. 'I will.'

'Good.'

He felt the dragon smile behind the curtains of depthless shadow, a sensation that faintly stung his flesh, both chilling and exhilarating. 'What,' he asked breathlessly, 'do you need?'

'Simple things,' said the dragon. 'Little things, really.'

'Anything,' whispered the man, awed. 'Anything.'

CHAPTER EIGHT

'Prisoner Welby,' said Ella Kown. Welby was sat on his metal-framed bed, head bowed and hands together, back towards Ella. He slowly raised his head and looked round over his shoulder. His expression was a serene blank, but his dark eyes were glazed and slightly narrowed. It was not a face that Ella could ever come to trust.

Welby slowly stood – he was only averagely-built, but he seemed larger than he really was in the tiny cell. He crossed softly, catlike, to the plastic screen, a thin smile on his lips.

'Officer Kown,' he said, standing before her. He was only about her size – she was stocky and tall for a woman, and in truth she'd back herself if it ever came to a fight – but she found herself wanting to step away from him all the same. She managed to resist the urge, though. 'What can I do for you today?' he asked.

Ella ran one hand over her wiry blonde hair, shaved number-three short, feeling a little uncomfortable beneath that steady gaze, not as if he was looking *into* her, but as if he couldn't really see her at all, as if she was merely a disembodied voice. His skin looked like plastic in the neon light, smooth and fake.

'I wanted to talk to you about Murkhoff.'

Welby shook his head slowly, eyes cast down, but Ella could see from the line of his jaw that the smile never left his lips. 'That was an. . . *unfortunate* incident,' he admitted. He looked up again, right through Ella's face. 'It will not happen again.' His breath misted gently on the plastic screen between them, evidence that he was real, human like her. 'How, may I ask, is Officer Murkhoff?'

Ella regarded him silently for a second, letting the silence speak for itself, emphasise their relationship. 'Not happy, Welby,' she said at last.

'Hmm,' said Welby, his brows pinching into the tiniest frown. 'I

44

have spoken to the man responsible.'

Ella saw his frown and was unimpressed by it. *Is that supposed to be an expression of concern, Welby?* she thought. *I don't buy it.* 'What exactly is the nature of the influence you have over the others?' she asked.

Welby's smile broadened in a grin that would have been innocently disarming if not for the eyes that floated above it like dark gemstones, sparkling and distant. 'I speak the truth. For those who wish to hear it.'

'I'm told that you have requested the facility to begin some sort of church here.'

'No, no, Officer Kown. Ella.' She squirmed a little to hear her own forename slip from that smiling mouth, but managed, she thought, to hide it from him. 'A place of meeting, of discussion. I need only a small room for us to gather in from time to time.'

'I can tell you, Welby, that isn't likely to happen.' In one of the cells further down the corridor somebody began to yell mindlessly, interspersing their cries with loud bangs on their glasspex screen. One of the sec-team, unidentifiable in their black combat armour, strode into the corridor from the direction of the control room and began to converse with the occupant of the cell. Their body language was a little aggressive for Ella's tastes, especially after what had happened to Murkhoff.

Welby listened to the sounds of disturbance for a moment, unable to actually see what was happening from his side of the screen, then turned his head back to Ella. 'And why not, may I ask?'

'Look, if you want to start some sort of cult here – here, of all places, in the asshole of the universe – then frankly I couldn't care less. But first, you need to do something for me. You need to demonstrate that you can be trusted. And I'm not sure if you can do that.'

'It is hard to gain trust without the means to demonstrate trustworthiness, Officer Kown.' He was still smiling, but she thought he was getting annoyed with her now. A tiny tick was beginning to work steadily in his jaw. A part of her was sadistically glad to see it. 'I ask only for that opportunity. Those who will listen will be reformed. Those who will not. . .' He shrugged benevolently. 'I care not. I have no intention of forcing my beliefs on anyone else.'

'And what, pray tell, are those beliefs? Specifically.'

'That those who came before have left a puzzle for us, a test. That they are to be revered.' He spoke as if to an ignorant but well-meaning child, full of tolerant patience.

'Predecessor cults are generally harmless enough, Welby, in my opinion. Even in a Predecessor system, such as this one. Personally, I don't think there's a scrap of truth in it. They were just some loser race who quit the game altogether millions of years ago, and I can't see any actual harm in people wanting to worship them. People have worshipped dumber stuff than that. I'm not saying that this meeting place of yours is an absolute impossibility. But it does look unlikely. What happened to Murkhoff – or anything remotely similar – must *never* happen again. Do you understand me?' And she gave him her own thousand-yard-stare, one practised over many years, right hand resting emphatically on the stun-baton that depended from her belt.

Welby recoiled a little, his face a caricature of innocent injury, his palms spread. 'Of course, Officer Kown. I regret the incident as much as you. It is not outside of my abilities to. . . *discipline*. . . the man responsible if you should require.'

'Absolutely not,' she said forcefully. 'This is what I mean about earning my trust. My people tell me you have influence with the other inmates here – *some* of the other inmates – and I ask you to use that influence to promote good and peaceful behaviour. And then. . .' She held up a finger to forestall the interruption that she could see he wanted to make. '*Then* you might get what you ask. *Might*.'

He beamed at that, but it struck Ella as a crocodile smile. She wondered if she would ever be able to grant his wish, or if it was madness to give this man *anything* he wanted. But if he could somehow make the others behave, surely it would be worth it.

Another Murkhoff must not happen. Too many Murkhoffs could shut Macao down for good.

'Thank you, Officer Kown. I will do my best. Though I ask you to remember what materials I have to work with.'

'I will be keeping a close eye on you, Prisoner Welby.' She nodded curtly to him, not bothering to wait for any response, turned on one heel, and strode away down the corridor towards control.

In one of the cells she passed, a skeletally-thin prisoner whose standard red prison-suit hung from his frame like loose skin, was singing softly in a language she didn't recognise. He didn't acknowledge her passing. Another murderer – she forgot his name – and one of Welby's cult friends.

On the other side of the corridor was the cell whose occupant had been shouting while Ella had been talking to Welby. She stopped outside it and peered through the screen. The occupant, a man by the name of Mercer, was lying naked on the floor with pieces of his latest meal strewn around his body, smeared on walls and furniture. His eyes were closed and he looked to be either asleep or dead. Closer inspection revealed his chest to be moving slowly up and down, confirming that it was the former. Unimpressed, Ella strode the rest of the way into control, ignoring the other cells – some empty and some inhabited – as she went.

Control was a low-ceilinged cylindrical room with a large central desk. A couple of surveillance monitors hung from a metal beam just above the desk, which was littered with datasheets and pieces of paper. The armoured guard who had conversed with the naked prisoner was talking to Theo, the duty admin.

'Guard – who are you?' demanded Ella sharply, stopping before the desk.

The suited guard started guiltily and turned to face her. 'Er, it's Jayce,' answered a voice from inside the suit. Safe behind the desk, Theo, a slightly chubby, friendly young man in his mid-twenties, set his face impassively, aware that somebody was about to get in trouble, hoping to shield himself from any fallout by virtue of neutrality.

'Why is that prisoner lying there naked, Jayce?'

'Er, Ma'am, I don't really know,' mumbled Jayce. Despite being larger than Ella as well as fully-suited, he managed to wilt somewhat, seemingly shrinking into himself.

'Well what are you going to *do* about it?' she demanded angrily.

'Er, I, I don't know, Ma'am.'

'I thought he was fucking *dead* for a minute there, Jayce! Get the doctor and get him examined, will you? Macao makes more than your yearly wage from each one of those poor bloody human battery-hens in there, as long as we keep them alive.' Jayce wouldn't – or couldn't – look at her any more. 'Do you know how much they're worth dead?' Silence from the defeated Jayce. 'Hmm?' she prompted. He shook his head. 'Take a guess.'

'Nothing, Ma'am,' he admitted guiltily.

'Damn right! Now get Doctor Hobbes and get in there. This isn't a concentration camp, Officer. These people may be closer to vermin than human beings, but you'll damn well treat them like human beings anyway. That man is ill.'

'Yes, Ma'am,' whispered Jayce.

'Go, then!' yelled Ella into his black-visored face. He scarpered.

'Sorry, Ella,' said Theo, shuffling from foot to foot behind the only partially-safe barrier afforded by the control desk.

'I saw Jayce yelling into that man's cell while I was talking to Welby,' she explained more calmly. 'We have to take a more professional line with them. Strict, distant, but not unnecessarily harsh. Okay?'

'Sure.' Theo shuffled a stack of papers together a little nervously. 'We'd have got him out, Boss, if we had a couple more guys here to help. But everyone's scared to go in there after Murkhoff. I didn't want to force Jayce, and I'm supposed to stay at the desk, right? I didn't think one guy could do it alone, and Rachelle's off sick today.'

'Even so, Theo, it isn't right to just leave him like that. I'll stay and lend a hand. Also, at a time like this I'd rather you left the desk than just stood there helplessly. Use a little common sense.'

'Sure, okay.' Ella felt a little calmer now and Theo seemed to sense this. 'Get you a drink?' he suggested cautiously.

'No, thanks, Theo, I'm fine. I'll take a look through the records for a minute.'

Ella wandered round to the other side of the desk, making Theo move aside so that she could see the monitor, and began to call up the prison-wing's records. Here was Welby's name, one of the more recent prisoners to arrive at Macao. Multiple murder, like most of them. He had killed three men – co-workers – at Platini Dockyard. Tortured them to death in horrifically brutal fashion. Apparently they'd been bullying him about being a homosexual. For the record, he'd denied the accusation about his sexuality. He had, however, admitted the murders. He had never shown any remorse or regret. Now, of course, he had religion. Double bonus. Ella had read Welby's record before, but she was still nauseated afresh this time. She turned to Theo, puzzled.

'What makes Welby so influential with the other prisoners, Theo? I don't get it. Physically he's unremarkable, if a little creepy. His record is nothing special for the sorts of scum Platini Jail send us. He doesn't seem unusually intelligent or persuasive to talk to.'

Theo looked over her shoulder at the monitor, studying it as if the answer might simply be written there. It clearly wasn't. 'I don't know, to be honest,' he admitted. 'He seems to talk a lot at mealtimes and exercise breaks. To the others, I mean. When we try to overhear he tends to go quiet. I assume he's talking that cult rubbish to them. But he's always polite to us, never showed any signs of wanting to make a problem. This about that church he wants to start?'

Ella Kown rubbed her chin thoughtfully. 'Kind of,' she said.

Just then, Doctor Hobbes came dashing in, Jayce trailing after his small but purposeful form like a black leaf sucked along in his wake. Hobbes looked a little flustered.

'What have you been doing to them?' he demanded simply, coming to a stop, a little out of breath.

'Us?' replied Ella innocently, putting a hand to her chest.

'Nobody with anything sticking out of their eye this time, I

49

trust?' Hobbes continued. It was hard to tell if he was joking or not.

'Not yet, good Doctor, but the night is young,' said Ella levelly. 'Number twelve is lying naked on the floor of his cell.'

'Naked,' repeated Hobbes tonelessly. His white jacket was torn on one elbow, Ella noticed. This was a little at odds with his usual clean and dapper appearance, which was a good trait in a doctor, she thought.

'Correct.'

'Great. Does he look alive?'

'You're the doctor. You tell me.'

CHAPTER NINE

A voice was calling from the darkness, silken and sibilant, its words twining together like snakes, hypnotic, compelling, beckoning him onwards. He swam through a field of asteroids, following that voice like a shark homing in on the merest trace of blood in water. The blackness smothered him, enfolded him, threatened to ink him out of existence. And yet he knew no fear – that blackness was also blanketing, womb-like. He sensed the proximity of invisible rocks that tumbled and rolled around him, poising to crush him like unpredictable living things, masses of malcontent.

But the voice was calming, drug-like, a loaded needle leeching its soothing medicine into space. He tasted it, smelled it, felt it infuse his being and fill him, dissipating him smoothly into the matrix of the universe, melting and moulding him into a bodiless shade. He rode his own quantum probability wave, neither here nor there, yet everywhere.

Above him, the station hung like a festive decoration in hell – dark and sharp-pointed, turning disinterestedly about its axis. He could hear the people aboard it talking. Their words drifted to him on the solar wind – little scraps and breaths of poison vapour. They were planning. They didn't – *couldn't* – understand. He knew, with an ache of sadness, that they never would.

And then he was in a tunnel – *the* tunnel – and he knew that he was almost home. He braced himself against jagged walls of rock, feeling the now-familiar twists and outcrops as he threaded his way down that throat of stone. He was dimly aware that he should be wearing a suit, that he wasn't really here. The dragon had reached out to him this time. It was getting stronger.

He continued, swallowed by shadows, breath steaming in the frozen vacuum. Somewhere nearby, something else was breathing, too. The voice called him onwards, but it didn't call him by name. It called him *Emissary*, and he smiled with satisfaction at that.

And then he emerged into a vast cavern, inexplicably bright, whose walls crawled with scaled skin that pulsed and glistened and lived. He floated in that organic cave, at peace – happy. No harm could befall him here.

'My emissary,' said the voice from everywhere at once. 'You have come to me. . . Listen. . .'

'Yes. What do you need from me?'

'Look. . .'

And the walls of the cave melted and dripped, scales bleeding away into space like oil dispersing across water. He saw a ship – a shuttle – sliding through the void on a plume of blood that seeped and blossomed behind it, globules breaking away and drifting through the vacuum like raining confetti, spattering grotesquely on asteroids. The shuttle was bad, he knew.

'I see it,' he breathed, repulsed, his stomach clenching. Who would build such a thing? Who could allow such a thing to exist? Its ugliness made him want to turn away, but the voice bade him look.

'You must stop it,' said the voice. 'This is what I ask of you.'

'I must stop it,' he repeated. He thought for some time, trying to understand. 'It's bad, isn't it?' he said at length. 'I never saw anything so foul.' The shuttle continued onwards, a mindless dead thing, a relentless pill of poison. It stank – even from here, it stank.

'This is a little thing, a simple enough task,' said the voice. 'But. . . *important*,' it added, enunciating the word carefully, its voice elongating into a protracted hiss, bleeding away into nothing.

'Yes.'

'Can you do this for me?' The voice was fading now. Fading. . .

'Yes,' he whispered, awakening in front of his bedroom window. His face was pressed up tight against the pane, the palms of his hands also flat against it. The belt hung silently before him. He was wearing pyjamas, his feet bare on the cold metal floor. 'Yes,' he whispered again, his heart racing in his chest. 'Yes. . .'

CHAPTER TEN

Deep in the hubward-most layer of Macao, in the station's machine rooms, a frenzy of activity was taking place. The deep, shuddering crashes and bangs that came through the bulkhead from the refinery next door only served to increase the tension inside.

Sudowski's team, everyone who could possibly be pulled from another job, were all in attendance. Some of them were wiring diagnostic terminals and datasheets into the main console of the air scrubbers. The unit that housed the scrubbers was a dense tangle of wires, pipework and humming electrical components. It stretched fully from floor to ceiling and wall to wall. Cooling ducts and armoured cables stitched the whole assembly into a sort of technological cat's cradle, taking away heat, bringing in coolant, shuttling data back and forth. A deep, bassy hum emanated from the machinery and the smell of frazzled ozone mingled sickeningly with synthetic oil and overcooked plastic. Unusually for a room on this floor, there was a single window in one wall, but it showed only the dark, convex hub of Macao itself.

Sudowski was talking to Alphe, who was holding a datasheet in one hand. They were discretely separated from the core of the activity, conversing in hushed voices. It was usually fairly dark in the room, but the team had flooded the space with harsh, blueish LED strings to compensate. Sudowski was squinting and shielding his eyes as he talked with Alphe, as if his head was hurting. He looked tired and somewhat slow.

Technicians were swapping data, taking readouts, rushing to get further equipment. Occasionally, one of them shot Sudowski and Alphe a suspicious glance. There was a definite atmosphere of worry, barely held in check. The nitro-jacketed circuit board was impaled with temperature probes, blindingly illuminated, its protective casing flayed away, and it was this around which most of the attention was focused.

This was the scene that Halman arrived to, and what he saw immediately confirmed his fears. So the chip was finally burning out. He felt a lump rise in his throat. It had been some time since Macao had faced an equipment failure this serious. Where in hell was his shuttle?

Sudowski spotted him and dashed over, tripping on a bunch of loose cables that snaked from the cabinet and away into an open floor hatch. He recovered, a little shakily, but dropped the datasheet he had been holding. A technician dashed past, almost stepping on it.

Halman stooped to retrieve the small, translucent device and offered it back to Sudowski, who took it with a slightly wan expression and pocketed it.

'What's going on, Nik?'

'I wish the damn intercom worked,' said Sudowski by way of answer. 'I've been trying to get you for half an hour.'

'Well you have me now.' Halman bent to look into the smaller man's face, his rugged features arranged into a picture of concern. 'No offence, but you look like death, Nik.'

'Er, yeah, thanks,' muttered Sudowski, wilting. He looked to Halman as if he was wincing from the light – certainly his eyes were half shut. 'I think I'm coming down with a bug. Typical, really, at a time when I need my shit firmly together.'

'Take a moment, Nik, it's okay.'

'As you see, this is the death-knell for the FS-AS1.'

'The control chip?'

'Sorry, yeah.' One of Sudowski's hands, as if of its own volition, began to rub his forehead, pinching and kneading the skin there. 'Any news from the shuttle?'

Halman led Sudowski by the elbow to a quieter corner of the room. Alphe, he noticed, watched them anxiously for a moment before continuing with his work. A small tuft of Alphe's dark hair was sticking up at an untidy angle, greased into place with machine oil.

When he was sure that nobody was actively eavesdropping, Halman continued. 'No, I'm afraid not. Why it has yet to arrive is anybody's guess, but if it isn't today or tomorrow then we can assume something has gone wrong.'

'Right, then I need the go-ahead to try the cannibal part I've found. If you enjoy breathing air, that is.'

Halman's broad, slightly ugly face broke into a transforming grin. 'Bloody hell, Nik, why didn't you say so? I didn't know you'd found a part! What are you waiting for? Do it!' But when Sudowski didn't return his grin, Halman's face gradually fell again, his exultant expression crumbling away like an unstable cliff. 'What?' he asked suspiciously.

'The closest match I can find for the FS-AS1 is a critical part of the communications array: the processor from a board whose purpose is to translate tracking data for the laser relay satellites and adjust the lensing of our lasers.' Halman's face took on a distant look as he considered the implications of this. Sudowski left him to it for a moment.

'How critical?' Halman asked at last.

Sudowski looked around clandestinely, and leant in closer to Halman so that he could speak in a stage whisper. 'It's a *critical* component,' he repeated. 'With the communications array working, we could scatter laser messages into space and hope to hit the shuttle, maybe find out if something has gone wrong with it. But without the comms. . . well. . .'

'Shit. . .' whispered Halman. His mind began to churn, incapacitating him. He stood that way, with his mouth slightly open, for some time before recovering. 'No wonder you don't feel so good,' he said at last.

'Do I do it? Because my team are waiting for the word.'

'How long will the air stay breathable without it?'

'Usually, we'd have a few days leeway. But we've been running the scrubbers at minimum power for days now to reduce data-flow through the chip.'

'How long?'

'Well, if the shuttle arrives tomorrow. . .' Sudowski shook his head. Halman saw that his lower lip was a little raw, as if he had been biting on it. 'Not long enough, I'm afraid. It could take us all day to patch in the replacement chip, maybe longer. We're on the fine line between just in time and just too late right now. We can't rush the job, because if somebody fries the chip accidentally then you can kiss Macao Station goodbye. When that shuttle finally gets here it could well find a tin can full of corpses.'

Halman exhaled heavily. He felt as if he had been gut-punched. 'And if one of your guys frazzles the chip from the array, then we have no air *and* no communications, is that right?'

Sudowski nodded seriously. 'Right,' he said.

Halman had to clench his teeth to avoid a loud and obscene exclamation that could only serve to increase panic and distress amongst the scurrying techs. He breathed deeply for a moment, then finally said, 'Let me send a last message to Way Station One, explaining what we've had to do. Hopefully the parts for the scrubbers and the comms are already en-route. But if not, I'll ask them to flag the next shuttle down and load them. But with the extra acceleration time, the next shuttle will be delayed by almost a year if they have to do that. It isn't much help, if that's the case. But I'll send the message.'

Sudowski was silent for a few seconds. His fingers massaged the flesh between his eyes. Halman could see the scars beneath Nik's hair, standing out purple against his pale skin. 'Do you think the way station might send a special transport just for the bits we need?' Nik asked in a doubtful voice. 'Like right away? I mean, if the part for the comm, or – even worse – the part for the scrubbers isn't already en route for some reason?'

'I don't know,' admitted Halman. 'Remember last time we asked for a special transport? They told me we'd have to pay for it ourselves. But then, this time it's really fucking urgent. They might. . . I don't know. . .' He trailed off. It seemed unlikely that the company would commit to such extra expense, even if lives were at stake. Perhaps this additional cost would be the final push they needed to just write the station off altogether. He felt a cold sweat on his brow. Could some company desk-jockey light years away really concede to kill him with the push of a pen? He'd worked for Farsight all his adult life, even fought for them. Could he really be of that little worth? He hoped he'd never have to find out for certain. He could pay for the shuttle, if he had to – and he *would*, if he had to. But the expense would virtually eradicate his savings, accrued over his years of service on Macao. *My retirement fund*, he remembered bitterly, aware that he was still, as always, getting older every minute.

'Okay,' Nik said softly, looking up into the Halman's face. 'I'll have a team head up with you, then as soon as the message is sent they can begin removing the chip.' He turned to go, but then stopped and looked back over his shoulder. 'Good luck,' he added.

'Yeah,' Halman said. 'And you.'

CHAPTER ELEVEN

The pilot came to his senses gradually, the silken layers of sleep slipping away like a series of shrouds, one by one. His mouth was dry and his eyes stung, even in the relative darkness of the shuttle's bridge. He groaned aloud and tried to lie still, inwardly cursing the suspended-animation cask he had slumbered in. All his joints ached, his head ached, even his damn *teeth* ached.

There was a muted hiss as the cask injected him with a reinvigorating drug. The effect was almost immediate, though faint at first. He tensed his limbs against the close confines of the cask, yanked away the straps that crossed his chest and wincingly sat up.

He looked down at his own body. He was in the navigator's seat, which was in sus-an mode with its plastic cocoon still half-formed around it. He always slept in the navigator's seat because its life support system was newer and presumably more reliable than those of either the pilot's or co-pilot's places. He was reassured by the familiarity of his surroundings. He looked across towards the main screen and the flight console, unconsciously intending to check the HUD.

There was somebody sitting beside the cask, magnetted onto a metal floor-chest, watching him. At least, it was the *shadow* of a person, framed against the weak multicoloured light from the control console.

The pilot jumped, his heart kick-started into a hammering drumbeat in his throat. 'What the fuck?' he cried, but it came out in a hoarse and unintelligible croak: *Whurrthafack?* He tried to recoil, but his muscles were still unresponsive. The shadow-person was within arm's reach, much too close and too unexpected for the pilot's liking.

'It's okay,' said the shadow. The voice was clearly male. 'It's okay. Take a minute.'

The structure of the shuttle groaned and creaked – a faint, whining chorus of metallic voices. They were the sounds of a hull recently subjected to sharp braking forces, but the pilot's mind was currently unable to snag on this detail.

The pilot nodded dumbly, trying to control his own panic response, struggling to get a grip. There was surely a good reason for this unexpected awakening, and the stranger seemed benign so far. It couldn't be the prisoner, could it? Who would have woken *him*? No, it wasn't possible. But that greasy little ball of fear kept trying to block his gorge. He reached down and fumbled the IV-lines from his thigh. Their loose ends floated away like coiling snakes.

'I have taken the liberty,' said the shadow conversationally, 'of waking you early. I do hope you can excuse my impertinence.'

'I. . . need. . . water,' croaked the pilot.

The shadow nodded slowly but made no attempt to fulfil this request. 'All in good time,' it said.

The pilot wanted desperately to rise from the cask now, put a little distance between himself and this unexpected stranger, but he knew that if he tried to get up he might tumble out of the cask and go cartwheeling away across the bridge, possibly hurting himself on some protruding piece of equipment. Also, he wanted very much to turn a light on. The shadow watched him impassively. It disturbed him to think that this man had sat here beside him, in silence, all the time he had been waking up. 'What do you want?' he managed to ask.

'It's not me,' said the man. 'It's the dragon.'

The pilot felt his face take on a puzzled expression. Had the shadow said *dragon*? 'What?' he whispered. His head felt stuffed with stupefying cotton wool. This would probably all make sense in a minute. Wouldn't it? He tried to push his fears away – the world always seemed a little random on waking from sus-an. But man, he needed a drink.

'It's not me who's the problem,' said the man slowly, clearly labouring to be patient. 'It's the dragon.'

'Dragon?' parroted the pilot. He knew, suddenly, that this man was not right in the head. There was something implacable in the tone of that voice, something robotic and unreasoning. The thought landed like a bomb in his mind. He could well be in trouble here after all. He'd have to play this carefully – not an easy task when he still felt badly befuddled by his years in the cask.

The shadow's head nodded seriously. Behind the man, the pilot could just make out the shuttle's large viewscreen, now that his eyes were beginning to work better. It showed the expected asteroid field, in its familiar oblique spread, but it looked somewhat thinner than it should have been. Macao Station was not visible. And the shuttle was at a standstill. This man, whoever he was, had intercepted the vessel en-route, somewhere very close to its destination. The pilot's heart began to race anew, his breath coming in odd lumps that were hard to swallow and hurt his chest. He felt like crying.

'You have a man on board. One Prisoner Carver, if I'm not mistaken.' The pilot, transfixed, could only nod. 'I have to get the code for his restraining device.'

Was that all? Was that really all this man wanted? He wanted to free the prisoner who right now lay strapped and trapped in his own cask down in the hold. Maybe that was all that would be required of him. He knew it was a mistake to capitulate, but in his current condition what else could he do? And in truth, he didn't even pause to consider the consequences. He just wanted this situation to end.

'It's on the datasheet over there,' the pilot said in a small and trembling voice. He raised one shaky hand to point towards the control console. The datasheet lay magnetted onto the main dashboard. He couldn't see it from here, but he knew it was there.

'Good,' said the man brightly. He rose and swam to the console, weaving around hunks of equipment and items of baggage. To his amazement, the pilot heard that he was singing softly and cheerfully under his breath.

The man began to root around on the dashboard, discarding rejected items that floated this way and that dreamily, silhouetted against the main screen. The pilot began to realise sluggishly that this might be his chance. He made to rise, but was confounded to find that he couldn't get up. Panic began to boil inside him. The shadow-man was still facing away from him, searching the dash, but surely he would return any second now.

And then he remembered that his legs were still strapped into the cask! With desperate, fumbling fingers he began to undo the straps. Why were there so damn *many*? And then there was a hand on his chest, pushing him back down onto the bed of the cask. He heard a frightened whimper escape his own lips, but he was too weak to resist. The man floated above him now like a dark angel, his face a shadowy blank, the datasheet clipped to his belt.

'One more thing,' said the man, pressing down on the pilot's chest, pinning him in place even more tightly than he already was.

'What?' whispered the pilot. He felt his bladder let go and was dimly surprised that he had that much liquid left in him.

'This,' said the man. And he drew a lumpy shape from his belt. 'It's not me,' reminded the shadow-man. 'It's the dragon.' And then the pilot saw that the shape was in fact a large – a *very* large – spanner. Coloured telltales reflected off its silvery surface as it fell towards his unprotected face.

CHAPTER TWELVE

Lina took her coffee from the machine and weaved through the randomly scattered chairs of the canteen. She nodded and smiled knowingly at Rocko, who sat discretely in a corner with Fionne Sinclair, their heads bowed together and conversation quiet. Rocko scowled at her in response, but his face immediately resumed its expression of boyish happiness, his white teeth gleaming in contrast to his dark skin. Fionne laughed prettily at some remark of his, her face dimpling. Lina resisted the urge to wink and went to Eli's table at the far side of the room, ducking under a loop of armoured cable that hung from a hole in the ceiling.

'And what, may I ask, are you smiling about?' asked Eli, eyebrows arched.

'Young love,' replied Lina, feeling her smile grow. She liked Rocko, and Fionne.

'And much good may it do us,' said Eli. Outside the window, the trails of the last shift's Kays could be seen returning to base on schedule. One of them was out of formation, though, lagging somewhat behind the others. This was almost certainly K6-3, a problem vessel that seemed to suffer from an unfixable irregularity with its gas injectors.

'Bit cynical, Eli,' she said, lifting the cup to her lips. The liquid smelled faintly of some plasticky chemical. Lina, who was not good at eating breakfast however much she insisted her son did so, felt her stomach clench in response. She lowered the cup of noxious fluid, crestfallen.

Eli chuckled at her disgust. 'Just realistic, Li,' he corrected.

'So what is it now?' she asked resignedly. 'Besides the fact that we're about to go on shift.'

The lights in the canteen flashed off briefly, then on again. This was not an uncommon occurrence on the station and nobody really paid the phenomenon any heed.

'Didn't you hear?' asked Eli. 'Sudowksi's boys are having to junk the comms array to fix the scrubbers.'

Lina couldn't believe she'd heard this right for a moment. '*What*?' she demanded.

'They're junking the comms array,' he repeated more slowly, 'to fix the scrubbers.' He sat back, satisfied with the stunning effect that this had on his friend, and took a swig from his own revolting coffee with apparent impunity. The grimy window behind him showed the impassive vista of deep, cold space, speckled with glinting asteroids. The Kays were out of sight now, on their final approach to the hangar.

'No way,' Lina breathed. Eli nodded his grizzled head. That look of near-amusement was still on his face, she noticed with mild irritation. Didn't anything bother him? 'Where's the shuttle?' she demanded, looking around as if she might locate it within the confines of the canteen itself.

Eli leant in close, secretive. 'That,' he confided, 'is very much the phrase of the week.'

'Oh hell,' she said in a small, hollow voice. 'But what if. . .'

'I saw Sudowski running about like a headless chicken near the admin offices. He looked half dead, to be honest. Poor guy. He hasn't been looking too good all week. However much our jobs may suck at times, it does inspire some joy in me to know that at least I'm not him. He told me about the array.'

'But Eli, this could be really serious,' Lina hissed. She leant on the table, which wobbled, spilling her coffee. She didn't notice. 'So we can't talk to Platini? And if the shuttle buzzes us with a problem, we can't even hear it?'

Eli sighed, and she could see that he was worried, too, underneath his implacable exterior. She was kind of glad, to be honest. 'Well, I think the radio'll still work. But no laser, so no Platini, no.'

'Where's the fucking shuttle?' she cried in an unintentionally loud voice. Fionne glanced up briefly from her hushed conversation with Rocko, her pretty face inquiring, and shot Lina a puzzled look.

'Beats me,' admitted Eli, waving her to keep her voice down. 'I don't think they really want this getting to the drones, okay, Li? Privileged information, etcetera. And mind the potty-mouth – it's unbecoming in a lady.'

'Well. . . what if. . .' Lina trailed off, her brow furrowed. Had he just made a joke? 'I mean. . .'

'Come on, we'd better get a wiggle on.' Eli drained his cup and stood. He zipped his flight suit all the way to the top – it was unusually cold in the canteen – and indicated the door. 'We're on shift, remember?'

Lina stayed in her seat, struggling to get her mind around what he had told her. Was this really such a serious development? Surely the shuttle would arrive any time now, with its usual hold full of spares. The scrubbers were due for a service, so Platini Dockyard would have sent the parts. A shuttle had never failed to arrive before – surely that wouldn't happen now. But why, then, did she feel as if something was wrong? Maybe badly wrong?

'We're just carrying on as if nothing's happened, then?' she asked. Her fingers were drumming nervously on the dirty surface of the table and she had to actually concentrate to stop them.

'Yeah, of course. If anything, we need to go up a gear now. If something has happened to the shuttle then Farsight are gonna throw a fit about the loss.' He stared deeply into her face, a look of concern on his features. Lina guessed she looked as pale as she felt. 'You okay, Li?' he asked, putting one large, gnarled hand on her shoulder. It was a comforting hand – a worker's hand – something real and reassuring.

'I guess. I just don't like it, Eli, that's all.'

'Don't sweat it – it's going to be all right. You need a nice back-rub or something?'

Lina shoved him away. Eli staggered, laughing. 'Dream on,' she said seriously, getting to her feet. 'Actually, don't even dream about it.' She felt herself smiling again. Somehow Eli always made it okay. She guessed that was why he was so popular on board.

They filed out of the canteen and into the corridor, which was dimly lit by small LED-strips, its walls studded with rivets that had bled rust. The ceiling was low and patched. Little jags and corners had been built into the passages of Macao to limit line of sight and prevent people from noticing the curve of the floor, which apparently unnerved some folks. They headed through this deliberate snarl of passageways, past the kitchens and admin offices. Halman's door was closed and raised voices could be heard from behind it. They exchanged warning looks and hastily continued towards the crew quarters and the stairs to the rimwards floor.

They rounded a corner and bumped into Sal Newman, who was coming out of the shower block looking tousled and clean, towelling her long red hair. She was dressed, however, in the typical threadbare miner's flight suit, and looked essentially ready to go. Her face was bright and cheery, although deeply scarred across one cheek from an accident years ago, and the sight of her made Lina's mood go back up another notch. Sal, who had nearly stolen her husband, whom Lina hadn't even wanted any more. Forgiven, but never to be forgotten. Sal, who was now a friend.

'Hey Sal,' Lina said.

'Hey, fancy bumping into you here,' Sal replied.

They headed down the stairs and emerged into the warehouse, which led to the hangar itself. The yawning space was piled with pallet racks loaded with what the techs generously referred to as 'spares,' but were in fact mostly used and broken K6 parts under plastic sheets. A wire-floored mezzanine was suspended from the ceiling on long rusty poles, and one of the ground crew was standing up there examining some huge and oily item on one of the rack's upper shelves. Lina couldn't tell who it was, and the figure didn't look at them as they passed below.

Eli didn't mention anything about the scrubbers to Sal and Lina followed his lead. She felt a little bad keeping the information from Sal, but she didn't want to get Sudowski, Eli, or – even worse – herself, into trouble.

When they reached the hangar door, the light was on above it, indicating that the hangar was pressurising. As they waited, making good-natured small talk, Rocko Hoppler sidled up to them, looking as casual as he could.

'Hey Rocko,' crooned Lina. 'How's Fionne?'

Rocko nodded non-committally. 'Well, thank you,' he said, and then wandered off to lean against a wall. He looked lost in his own thoughts, but happy. Eli arched his eyebrows. Sal grinned.

From inside the hangar they heard a series of loud crashes and thumps. Something impacted against the massive bulk of the door itself, causing a shockwave of reverberation that they felt through the floor.

'Bloody hell!' cried Sal, wide-eyed.

Eli laughed. 'I guess Waine is driving again,' he chuckled. Waine was one of the ground-crew, a man famed, and teased, for his continual crashing of the dead-lifter. Many of the Kays bore the scars of his well-intended ministrations.

As they waited (it seemed to be taking a particularly long time to flood the hangar, in Lina's opinion) the other members of the shift joined them one by one: Si Davis, Niya Onh and Petra Kalistov. Niya looked as if she might be a little hung-over. She kept rubbing her temples, and her delicately-slanted eyes were squeezed almost shut against the bright light.

They waited in increasing boredom until eventually Si boomed 'Right! That's it!' He strode up to the huge hangar door, his head almost level with the top of it, and hammered on it with one massive fist. 'Open up, you lazy bastards!' he bellowed.

Several of the miners chuckled, including Eli, who had always been the laissez-faire kind of leader, and Si repeated the procedure for emphasis. He pressed his ear to the door.

'Well, I don't know how they could miss your deafening voice,' Petra said coldly.

The light above the door went off suddenly. Si stood back, palms spread and grinning. 'See?' he asked. 'They didn't.'

The massive door groaned, shuddered and reluctantly began to rise with a protracted shriek of grinding metal. The hangar had a tendency to over-pressurise slightly, and there was a muted whistle as air rushed out from under the door.

'Good job, that man,' said Eli. 'Top of the class.'

The rising door revealed the booted feet of the finishing shift, then their legs. Without further waiting, they ducked under and squeezed past Eli's shift into the warehouse. Ilse Reno, the leader of the opposite shift and second only to Eli himself amongst the miners, paused. She was a shortish, petite woman, but was nonetheless imposing for it. This was possibly because her straggly grey hair and glowing red eye-implant lent her something of the appearance of a pirate. 'We left a couple of rocks for you, Eli,' she said in her gravelly voice, deadpan, then followed the rest of her retreating team.

'You didn't have to do that!' he called after her, but she was gone into the maze of towering racks, swallowed by shadow. 'Strange woman,' he muttered to himself. Then, to his team: 'Shall we?' He turned and led the way into the hangar.

The hangar was vast, its ceiling a jungle of cabling, the mining ships squatting in the gloom like gargoyles in their alcoves. A couple of ground crew were struggling with the infamous K6-3, trying to free a seized nut on one of the jets using a gas-driver. The dead-lifter was limping across the floor, one of the Kays dangling from its mandibles, followed by the bald-headed Waine, his wrinkled face contorted in concentration as he struggled with the controls of an auxiliary terminal. The lifter's huge solid-rubber tyres crunched slowly and deliberately through the mush of oil and dust. There was a gaping hole like a tooth socket where its main console should have been. It narrowly squeezed between a stack of oil drums and a thick metal pillar, then disappeared round a corner.

'All set!' yelled Liu Xiao, the leader of the ground crew, popping his head up from behind the computer screen that stood on a lone desk incongruously placed right in the middle of the space. 'Two minutes!'

'No sweat,' responded Eli, giving him a wave. 'To your chariots, soldiers!' he cried enthusiastically, ushering his team towards their vessels. They moved with the traditional reluctance of the overworked.

The miners found their respective Kays and climbed into the cockpits. Some of the ships bore fresh scars, presumably from Waine's efforts with the troublesome dead-lifter, but most of them were already so battered that it was hard to tell.

Lina seated herself in the familiar pilot's seat and booted up the computer. Clearly, the other shift hadn't used her ship today, although that was probably set to change again if K6-3 continued to malfunction. Still, it was good to find everything set up the way she had left it for once. She dutifully checked the diags. As usual, they showed reactor patterns that would have made the vessel unusable in most places, but that were well within the tolerated limits on Macao. The ground crew had repaired the hydraulic leak, as promised, though, and the gas was full. She wriggled in her seat, trying to embed herself in some manner that would prove at least bearably comfortable, gave up, and closed the hatch. It snicked smoothly into place, tinting the shadows of the hangar orange and overlaying the scene with a HUD readout that tagged the other Kays with their ID-codes and pilot names.

The ground crew were leaving the flight deck now, heading towards the control room. A klaxon, accompanied by a brief strobe of red light signalled that the deck was clear. As the last Kay sealed itself around its pilot there was another klaxon, and this time an orange light. There was a pregnant pause, during which the Kays sat poised and humming gently in their alcoves, steaming with exhaust gas, waiting for the air to flush. There was a subdued rushing noise as the air was cycled out of the hangar and then a pulse of green before the door in the hangar's deck began to open, forming a ramp that dropped away into space – a yawning mouth of darkness with glittering rock and ice caught in its throat.

The Kays trundled across the concave flight deck and assumed launch formation. One by one, they accelerated down the short ramp and out into space, fanned by the station's spin into a broad front. They converged, rotating, into their two usual wings, with Eli in the centre, and headed towards the belt.

'I'm with you today, Lina,' said Eli's voice over the comm,

peppered with static.

She glanced to the left, where his ship coasted along beside her, thirty metres away, keeping lockstep.

'Oh really?' she asked. Usually, it was Eli's job as flight leader to prospect for high concentrations of double-Ms in the unexploited sectors. She realised that he was probably hoping to increase production, fearing that Farsight might demand reparations for their lost shuttle. This hardly seemed fair to Lina, but it certainly seemed feasible.

'Yeah, eight, nine and twelve – Blue Eight. One, two and four – Red One.'

The pilots confirmed their instructions and the shift split into its two wings, Eli taking point in Lina's wing and Petra leading hers. They diverged gracefully, dialling up the gas as they went.

Lina remained unable to shake her concerns about the air scrubbers, despite the job at hand. She found herself flying by instinct, her mind repeatedly wandering from the task. Luckily, the ship's computer had the matter safely in hand.

She checked the rear-view, half expecting to see the prodigal shuttle coasting up to the station. But she didn't. Rocko and Sal kept up a stream of chatter over the comm, but it was distant and muted to Lina, far-off static.

She realised that she was starting to get the fear that she had felt last time in the belt, and hopelessly tried to tell herself to stay calm. They were so cut off out here. She could almost *see* that fragile silver thread – the intangible, essential lifeline that stretched away through space, joining them to the way stations, then Platini, and beyond that the inhabited universe Sol-wards. That thread was nothing, really. They were alone. But then, they always had been. So why did it suddenly bother her so much? This thing with the laser array – did that really make any difference? It took years to talk to Platini, anyway. So did it really matter? They had always depended on the shuttles to survive, and the loss of communications didn't change that. But that thought only led her to the real problem: Where was the shuttle? *Phrase of the week*, she thought and smiled humourlessly to herself.

Lina realised that they were in the outskirts of the belt when the vessel's manoeuvring jets began to give their customary little nudges here and there, trying to adhere the Kay to its planned trajectory while at the same time avoiding the sometimes-erratic asteroids as they rolled and drifted through space, occasionally bumping into each other.

'Are you listening to me, Li?' asked Eli's voice, making her jump.

'Huh? Sorry?'

'Oh, you are alive in there, then. I called you three times.'

'Sorry, I guess I was gathering space-dust for a minute.'

'I don't wanna go too far in, okay? This is almost dense enough, now.'

'Yeah, sure, just say when.'

They flew onwards for another thirty seconds or so before Eli gave the word to decelerate and set up shop.

'The only problem with having you along, Eli,' said Rocko as the Kays slowed to a near standstill and began to choose their rocks, 'is that we'll have to actually do some work today.'

'Not that you aren't welcome, or anything,' added Sal with a hint of mischief in her voice.

Eli's Kay coasted smoothly in between Lina's and Rocko's, its tool arms flexing like the fingers of a metal hand, reaching for a large asteroid that shimmered in its spotlight.

'Too right,' said Eli. 'Have to keep an eye on you slackers, don't I?'

'*We* have to keep an eye on *you* more like,' suggested Sal as her Kay coasted away from the others towards the far left of the group. It anchored onto a rock and began its work.

As they mined, Lina and Rocko drifted gradually away from the others, leapfrogging from one likely-looking asteroid to another. Typically, their samples showed almost entirely good double-M-types. The pilots were all well-experienced, adept at identifying the best targets by sight. That was one of the few things the Kays actually needed a human pilot for. The confusingly-similar albedo ratings of silicate-heavy non-double-M asteroids in the belt made radar scanning worthless. The ships rapidly analysed samples to confirm or deny the humans' judgement. They usually confirmed it.

Sal and Eli were soon left some distance behind and to their left. Lina tried hassling Rocko about Fionne for a while, but in truth her heart wasn't in it. He responded with steadfast patience: no, she wasn't sick of him yet; yes, she had been keeping him up at night, thank-you-very-much; no, Rocko wasn't suspicious of the amount of time she spent with Alphe when Rocko was on shift. Lina soon gave up this line of enquiry, defeated by his relentless good spirits. They worked in silence for a while.

Macao sat far above them, locked into its infinitely-repeating spin-cycle, a monolithic wheel in space. Even from this close, she could hardly see it at all. It looked to her like it could easily just slip below those waves of stone and sink forever, unnoticed.

The vibration from the Kay's cutting equipment became soporific, and Lina had to literally pinch herself to stay awake. She tried to engage herself by running a full batch of system scans, but they didn't tell her anything new and the process was an inherently tedious one. She glanced up at the HUD-marker showing Rocko's K6-9, which was partially hidden by a huge, gnarled asteroid that looked strangely like a clenched human fist.

'Hey, Rocko,' she said, bored of silence now.

'What?' he asked, clearly suspicious of another Fionne-related enquiry.

'Talk to me,' she said.

'About what?' he asked. His Kay looked spectral in the milk-light of Lina's ship, only half-real, an alien avatar of the man.

And then Sal spoke, her voice small and tinny, distorted even over this short distance by the belt debris. She said one word: 'Eli!'

Lina was alert at once. There was something in the tone of that voice, a note of shrillness, even fear. That one word echoed again in her mind, portentous. She tried to quell the sudden racing of her own heart. It was probably nothing, just her own unfounded fears.

'What is it, Sal?' she asked, trying to inject her voice with calm,

71

but her words were suddenly drowned by a harsh rush of noise from the cockpit speaker. Sal screamed, once, high and wavering, the top-notes clipping over the comm, then the rush erupted into a roar, devouring her voice. And then, before Lina could react in any way, there was silence.

Silence. . .

'What the hell was that?' asked Rocko's voice, trembling and breathy. His Kay was still at work, its tool arms efficiently cutting and vacuuming, its thrusters giving little kicks of gas here and there, machine and mineral caught in a mindless dance.

Nobody answered. Rocko's Kay detached from its asteroid and came about slowly. Lina also commanded her own ship to raise anchor and turn around, but her hands were shaking and it took several tries to hit the *Manual Resume* control and initiate the manoeuvring jets. She was struggling to breathe, her mind completely blank and paralysed, her hands reacting of their own accord, her eyes frozen so wide open that they hurt. Her heart was a wild, jittering thing that shook her whole body. A cold sweat was on her brow. She didn't feel real. It couldn't really be happening. . .

'Sal. . .' said Eli's voice over the comm, but it didn't really sound like Eli at all. That voice sounded thin and scared and childlike.

'What the hell happened!?' demanded Rocko again, almost screaming now. 'Eli! What *happened*!?'

His Kay was close behind Lina's own – too close, really – but for all she knew she could have been in the belt completely alone. Time spun out; empty space became a viscous fluid that her ship struggled to force its way through, desperately slow, and the blackness around her gathered in like drawing curtains, threatening to close on her. *Not real it's not real it's not real it's–*

Spat!

Spat!

Spat-spat-spat!

Blood was raining across the cockpit window of Lina's Kay. She recoiled in horror, releasing the ship's controls, and the autopilot smoothly took over, correcting her flightpath to avoid a large and

72

twisted hunk of metal that came whickering towards her from between two rocks. As it flew past, narrowly missing Rocko, too, Lina managed to read the legend *K6-8* stamped onto its twisted surface. More debris flowed around her ship, twisted bolts and splinters of metal that bounced off the cockpit window and away into her wake. And the blood. . .

But it wasn't just blood, now. There were specks and flecks of gristly, fibrous matter in there, too. Then when something that looked horribly like a human tooth ricocheted off the front of Lina's ship with an audible *ping*, she put her head between her knees and vomited onto her boots.

CHAPTER THIRTEEN

Danyal Halman sat at his desk, watching the slow but continuous activity out in the belt, shown magnified in his office window. The Kays were doing their best to clean up after the accident, which mainly, sickeningly, meant vacuuming up the all-but vapourised and homogenised remains of Sal and her ship, now stirred into a diffuse cloud by the roving asteroids. At least nobody else had been caught in the blast. Thank whatever god you may subscribe to for small mercies.

Explosive decompression – the words wandered darkly through his mind, for about the thousandth time that night. He tried to imagine – tried *not* to imagine – the sucking, ripping, terrifying sensation that Sal Newman must have felt in that brief moment before her grisly death, when she had been blended through a tiny hole in the skin of her Kay, just before the ship's structure disintegrated into flak.

He sat, watching, feeling physically weighted down, his stomach burning with acid indigestion, as if someone had lit a fire in there. He wondered absently if he was developing a stomach ulcer. Wasn't that a fairly normal reaction of the human body to prolonged stress? Didn't matter, he decided. He could use some time off in sick-bay, maybe let somebody else have a turn at being Station Controller for a bit. His large hands idly toyed with a small square of ceramicised germanium, turning it this way and that, twirling it between their fingers. It was the burned out chip from the scrubbers, its label blackened into unreadability. It was as light as a shard of bone.

The belt lay spread out like a solid swathe of desolate, rugged landscape – a hostile vista across which a man might stumble, dying, beneath the cold light of Soros forever. The little glimmers of the Kays were as insignificant as fireflies, the merest seeds of life.

Sal. Sal Newman. Sal was dead. She was not the first to die in a belt accident, but she was the first in many years now. Halman felt cheated. It shouldn't have happened. *How*, damn it, *how* had it happened?

Eli said that her Kay had bumped into a pointed rock, piercing the hull. Simple. But that wasn't the whole story, was it? Because the Kays weren't supposed to be that damn stupid, or it would happen every time someone flew one through the belt. The Kays – the bloody unreliable, treacherous Kays that any humane and sensible company would have condemned – were supposed to know better. Something else had failed, and this time a person had died. Make that one more fuck-up for those greedy Farsight tight-asses. It was almost good that the array was down or Halman might have been unable to help sending them some sort of damning, ranting, career-ending message. He'd worked his whole life for the company – hell, he'd even *fought* for them – but he'd never been as angry with them as he was now.

On the upside, if there was one, Eli was seemingly okay. He had seen Hobbes, who had given him the once-over, offered him a sedative, which he had refused, then released him. He was shaken, but he would live. Lucky Eli. Lina had refused even to see the doctor, and had just gone home to her son. Halman thought that Marco's company would be more beneficial to her than Hobbes's at any rate, so that suited him just fine. Rocko had gone to see Fionne. Ditto there.

He wondered if Ella Kown should be involved, maybe interview the survivors. But what, really, was the point? Statements would have to be taken, he supposed, but there was no real rush. After all, they couldn't be sent back by laser, and until – *unless* – the shuttle arrived, they couldn't be sent via that, either. So fuck it.

The little lights moved, swarming, in the belt. They looked like carnivorous fish excited by blood in water, and the analogy made his stomach turn. He supposed that he should eat something. What time was it? Late, he thought, but the wall-clock in his office had been broken for months. It was on Sudowski's list of things to fix, but it was way down near the bottom of Sudowski's list of things to fix, and as such, remained broken.

And also, worryingly, the air was beginning to taste bad. At first, he'd thought he was imagining it. But as the hours ground on, he became more and more convinced that he was right. The air was beginning to taste bad. There was a chemical tang to it, like burnt ozone, that caught in the back of the throat. The scrubbers were scrubbing, but at a reduced, cautious rate designed to prolong the life of the barely-suitable replacement chip. How long did they have before it, too, burned out?

He held up the scorched square of the original chip, superimposing it over the dark rectangle of the office window where endless rocks processed away into infinity, letting the light catch on its dull edges. He turned it over, running his calloused thumb across its surface, inwardly cursing it. He felt like crying. And then, with no knowledge that he had intended to do so, he dashed it against the wall of the office with sudden ferocity. Brittle with heat-induced fatigue and age, it shattered into dust with a dry and understated little noise, its remnants raining down like ash.

Halman put his head in his hands, elbows propped on his desk, massaging his temples. His stomach ached and burned inside. He looked at the fragments of the chip, shocked that he had destroyed it, appalled at himself. What if Nik thought of some way to repair it? That, he decided, would barely surprise him at all. He tried to imagine how he'd explain his actions if that happened: *Er, sorry, Nik, I smashed it in a fit of childish rage. Yeah, I guess we are all going to die, then. Did I mention I was sorry?* But really, logically, he couldn't imagine that the possibility of fixing it would ever come up anyway. Was that a good or a bad thing, bearing in mind that he had just destroyed it? He couldn't work it out.

Sal.

Dead.

Shit. . .

He sat like that, head cradled in his big hands, smoothing the hair around his ever-enlarging bald spot, for some time. His mind

76

became mercifully blank. He didn't know how long he stayed that way.

And then, decisively, he got up, tapped the window several times with one knuckle until it went blank, and strode from the office without bothering to lock the door behind him.

He walked down bare and rusting corridors, large boots clanging and banging loudly, passing nobody. The heavy equipment of the refinery, usually audible through the ceiling here, was conspicuously silent.

He walked through the rec area, between the pillars that housed the supply-chutes to the dispatch department. The place was deserted, the benches below the long windows unusually empty. He exited into the plaza and soon stood in front of *The Miner's Retreat*. As he approached its understated exterior, Halman heard the bubbling sound of conversation from inside. So this was where everybody had got to. He briefly considered turning away, maybe heading off to bed. But he knew that he wouldn't be able to sleep if he did.

He pushed open the scarred and slightly-buckled door, making a bell above it ring, and surveyed the interior of the bar. It was a low-ceilinged and dimly-lit room: stark metal furniture crammed closely; small corner bar made from hideous plastic wood; a few windows, boarded over. Usually the air inside lay in blueish strata of tobacco smoke, but smoking was now banned on board in the hope that this would reduce the load on the scrubbers.

People were pressed into every available nook and cranny, talking in muted, secretive tones. There was none of the usual pleasant atmosphere, no music playing, nobody at the games machines, nobody laughing.

He pushed his way to the little bar, turning sideways and using his powerful shoulders to force through the crowd like a human wedge. He noticed, with a pang of loneliness, that his mere presence was enough to kill several conversations as he passed. Off to his right, in a shadowy corner, he saw two women from the refinery leant together, crying together, over two apparently-untouched glasses of beer. The rest of the crowd, despite the

77

cramped confines, had left a small, respectful circle of space around them. In fact, there seemed to be a few other people crying, too. Halman knew how they felt.

He leant against the drink-slicked surface of the bar and tried to catch the eye of Gregor, the proprietor. Gregor was deep in conversation with Petra Kalistov, serving drinks mechanically to other patrons almost without looking. His hands logged sales on the computer and gave out glasses with deft autonomy.

Halman turned, looking about himself, huffing impatiently, hands stuffed into his pockets.

'Hey,' said a voice at his right elbow.

He started slightly and turned towards the source of the sound. It was Lina, sitting on a bar stool and cradling a tall glass of beer. She looked wan and tired, but somehow her sadness had turned her faded prettiness into a kind of ghostly beauty. Her face was paler and more drawn, but her delicate bone structure stood out more clearly than usual. Her bright green eyes and tangle of blonde hair accentuated the pallor of her skin even further, giving it the appearance of fine porcelain. Halman wondered how that idiot Jaydenne – now somewhere in Platini system – could ever have left her. He supposed that should have been a good thing for the remaining men of Macao, but Lina had never shown an interest in any of them. She was all about Marco these days. Marco first, friends second, mining firmly third. That seemed like a fair order of importance to Halman.

'Hey,' he said. 'How long does it take to get a fucking drink in this place?'

She seemed to consider this question more deeply than it really warranted, biting her lower lip as she did so. 'Kinda busy, isn't it?' she said at last.

The person to Halman's left abruptly rose and weaved away through the throng, and Halman grabbed the vacated seat immediately, pulling it closer to Lina's.

'Yeah, it is,' he agreed.

'What d'you want?' she asked. For a moment, he thought she meant *What are you bothering me for?* but then he realised she was offering to buy him a drink.

'Oh, er, just a beer, please. Real beer. Thanks, Lina.'

She signalled with one slim hand and, to Halman's amazement, Gregor responded immediately, as if by telepathy, flicking her a little wave in return.

'There isn't any real beer, remember?' she said.

'Oh yeah,' he agreed, a little perturbed. He hated synthi. 'No shuttle,' he added quietly. Lina just nodded.

Gregor plonked the two glasses down in front of them and hit the relevant key on his bar-side computer terminal, automatically charging Lina's station account, then whirling away to serve the next customer. Nobody bothered to insist on verification at The Miner's – they all trusted Gregor implicitly. After all, he wasn't going anywhere.

'Eli's looking after him,' Lina said, as if Halman had asked her a question. 'Marco. Eli's looking after him.'

'Good,' replied Halman, sipping his beer. It tasted artificially-yeasty, slightly disgusting, really. 'How is he? Eli, that is.'

Lina shrugged and drained her glass. Halman noticed the unsteady way she replaced the vessel on the bar, and that she was actually quite drunk. 'He's okay,' she said, brushing an errant lock of hair back behind her ear. She seemed to be studying some tiny detail on the surface of the bar itself, tracing with one finger in a pool of spilled liquid.

'I'm sorry,' said Halman, and immediately wished he hadn't. 'About Sal,' he added stupidly, unable to stop himself.

Lina breathed deeply for a moment, not looking at him. 'Yeah,' she said at last. 'Me, too.' Then she lifted her head and offered him a smile so sad and empty that something melted inside him.

They sat in silence for several minutes, but it was a comfortable silence, and Halman found something oddly reassuring in it. He didn't really want to talk, to be honest.

After a while, Lina said, 'Jaydenne had an affair with her, you know. Back in the day.'

Halman, shocked, managed only to say, 'What?'

'Sal,' explained Lina, looking up. Her bright eyes were a little

79

watery around the edges. 'Jaydenne had an affair with her, back in the day,' she repeated.

'Shit, Lina, really? I didn't know that.'

She nodded. 'I never really told anybody,' she admitted glumly. She sighed, tracing patterns in the spilled beer. 'I think she loved him, Dan,' she said at last, reflectively. 'More than I did, by then.'

'Lina, you don't have to tell me this. . .' Halman started, embarrassed by her sincerity. He took a large gulp from his beer – the situation seemed to warrant it. Some things were best left unsaid. Halman was a great believer in that theory.

'And she left him. Or, more precisely, she told *him* to leave *her*. I told her she could take him – it would have been fine. We were really finished by then. I was all the time with Marco. Jaydenne was always a selfish bastard, when I look back at it. I should have seen it before then. I couldn't devote enough time and attention to him, so he found it elsewhere.' She shrugged. 'Simple.' After a while, she looked up into Halman's face, her expression intent. 'You know why she told him to go?'

Halman shook his head. The beer, amazingly, seemed to be calming the burning in his stomach, but he still felt a little queasy. He wanted Lina to shut up, in all honesty. He liked Lina a lot – hell, if he'd been younger, better-looking and more her type, he might have tried his own luck – but he didn't want her to tell him something she'd regret. 'Why?' he asked, sensing that this was required of him.

'For me, Dan. And because she wanted to do right. She thought that I might regret being okay with it later. Regardless of what I'd said. She thought that I might grow to resent her. She hardly knew me back then – she was still working in the refinery. But she gave up the man she loved because she thought she was doing something wrong. For me, it was easy to give him up. For me, it just kinda happened. But for her. . . well. . .' She shook her head, making an errant tangle of hair fall across her face. 'I don't know. . .' she finished lamely.

Halman felt tears well in his eyes, and turned away so that she wouldn't see. He was not a man who usually wore his emotions

80

openly, and he didn't want to start now. He wiped his hands over his face, clearing his blurry vision, and turned back to her. He lifted his glass in salute. 'She was a good woman, Lina. Whatever may have happened in the past. Family.'

Lina lifted her own glass in return. 'Yeah,' she said, meeting his gaze. And then, by silent consensus, they drank.

CHAPTER FOURTEEN

Eli awoke at around five in the morning, although as a long-time shift-worker, the artificial times imposed by the station clock were of little real meaning to him. His neck ached, and one of his arms had gone numb where he had lain on it. He looked around himself and saw that he was in Lina's quarters, lying on the sofa, washed in the flickering witchlight of the holo.

He knew, somehow, that Lina was back: something felt different, although he wasn't sure what. Maybe some secretly-awake part of his brain had been alerted by some small noise that he hadn't been consciously aware of. He sat up and swung his feet down onto the cold steel floor. He rolled his head in a gentle circle, trying to bring his neck back to life. There was a glass of water on the small table next to the sofa, and he took a drink from it. He had slept without a blanket, fully-clothed, and now he wanted a shower. Marco, of course, hadn't stirred or caused any sort of concern whatsoever. Eli had known the kid would be fine, but Lina wouldn't leave him alone all night. As she usually got back late from shift, this seemed a trifling distinction to Eli, but he had humoured her. She had needed to get away for a bit, and she had needed not to worry about her son.

He stood up, trying to smooth some of the wrinkles from his flight suit, and went to Lina's room. He gently pushed the door ajar and peeped in. She was asleep under a virtual mountain of duvet, snoring gently and almost-certainly drunk. He considered staying, making sure she was okay in the morning (*Hey, it already is morning*, a little voice protested in his head) but he decided she would probably rather not have to deal with him hung-over. He knew her well enough, he judged, to say that he'd be better off leaving her be.

He stood and watched her for a minute, staring at the shock of blonde hair that spilled from beneath the covers, listening to her breathing. She was beautiful. But he knew that she was also damaged. It was hard sometimes to suppress his instinct to protect her, to somehow prevent further damage. But despite her delicate appearance, he knew that she could take care of herself. They had to, out here. Far-off in the bowels of the station, something groaned vastly in an almost inaudibly-low frequency.

He went also to Marco's room and checked on the boy. He was an undefined hump in the bed, breathing quietly in the darkness. Eli watched him for a moment. Marco was like the son he had never had, another member of Eli's family-that-wasn't-actually-family, and in truth he loved the boy greatly. How would Marco take the news of Sal's accident? It would definitely be better to let Lina deal with it. Some things were a mother's prerogative.

Sal. Such a shame. Eli was not a native of Macao originally, but he had been here since before Sal had come aboard. That had made her a member of his family. Dead now. He shook his head, standing in the dark, envying the others their unconscious state. He would let himself out and come check on them later, when Lina had had a chance to talk to her son.

He went back to the living room and found a datasheet by the light of the holo. He scrawled a note on its screen with one finger:

> MARCO – LET YOUR MOTHER SLEEP IN, OKAY?
> SHE'S HAD A HARD NIGHT.
> – ELI

With that, he killed the holo, fumbled his way to the door in darkness, and let himself out.

CHAPTER FIFTEEN

Carver came to with the typical grogginess of the sus-an transportee. Wherever he was, it was entirely dark. *Maybe*, he thought, *this is the hell they always told me I was going to*, but he didn't really believe that. Hell? He wasn't a *bad* person. Okay, so he'd killed that one woman pretty good, but anyone who had heard the bitch *speaking* would have sympathised. And there had been that thing with the kids, of course. But he wasn't a *bad* person. Neither, for that matter, was he a religious person, so that kind of ruled that one out.

Where, then, was he? He tried to rise but his muscles didn't want to respond. Those fucking drones at Platini Dockyard had told him he'd feel like shit by the time he got to Macao Penitentiary, that such illness was normal in those awoken from sus-an, so he guessed it was just that.

But if he was really at Macao, the genuine asshole of the universe, then why was it so dark?

And then the darkness was suddenly lifted away like a blanket and the world was flooded by blinding light. Carver cried out, trying to shield his face, but his hands wouldn't move properly. His arms just flailed weakly, flopping uselessly like dead things.

'Put this on,' said a voice from the light.

Carver squinted into the brilliance, trying to see who had addressed him, but there was only the light. For one terrifying moment his reason failed him and he decided this was Hell after all, that the light must be either God or the Devil, come to pronounce judgement upon him. He shook his head, feeling sick, unable to think.

'Oh, right,' said the light-voice. 'You're still a little sleepy. Take a moment.'

Carver moaned aloud and lay wincing in the unbearable

brilliance for a minute or two, feeling like a piece of meat on a slab. Slowly, slowly, his surroundings began to congeal out of the pervading glow: low, metal-panelled ceiling; some rack of crates; a sign whose lettering he couldn't read. He was still in the machine rooms of the shuttle, where the passengers' casks were, so he guessed that meant he had arrived at the prison station after all. He wrenched the straps away from his body and tried to rise again. This time he made it to a sitting position.

There was a man floating next to him, holding a space suit. Just one man? Thoughts began to crowd into Carver's mind – dark and angry thoughts. One man. Just one man. Just. One.

'Put this on,' said the man again.

'Why should I?' asked Carver, his ugly pinkish face a picture of slyness, his hugely-muscled limbs shuddering as he tried to clench and unclench them, work them back to life.

'Because I have this,' said the man with the space suit, and held up an object that he carried in his other hand. It was a small rectangular device that looked a little like a datasheet, but even with his blurred vision Carver recognised it for what it was: the restraining device.

'Why the fuck do I need a space suit?' he demanded, filled with impotent rage. He began to clamber down from the cask, but he was still slippery with acceleration gel. His cramping hands couldn't hold the edge properly, and he flipped out of the cask and went flying towards the other man, wrenching the IV-lines painfully from his arms and legs, releasing droplets of blood into the air like spores.

The man shoved him back towards the cask and Carver banged his shaven head, sending bright stars shooting across his vision. 'Unhh!' he cried, flailing.

The man laughed, and that made Carver even angrier. He struggled to get back up, but he couldn't even stay still. He kept spinning uncontrollably in one direction and then the other, then back again. He guessed he probably did look pretty funny to the other man. *Laugh it up while you can, fuckface!* he thought savagely.

'Just put the suit on, unless you like gulping vacuum,' said the man. 'And if you want to play silly-buggers, I'll fry your already-squishy little brain.' He wiggled the restraining device playfully.

Carver had managed to grab onto the support frame of the cask now, and he clung to it like a man who might be sucked up into the sky by a tornado. He tried to give the other man his infamously intimidating stare, but he knew he looked too foolish for it to have the desired effect. *Whoever you are*, he vowed to himself, *I intend to fuck you up badly as soon as I get a chance.*

'Why,' snarled Carver, his throat full of either phlegm or acceleration gel, 'do I need a space suit? What the fuck sort of a prison is this?' He could feel the shuttle flexing and groaning around him, a living leviathan of cratered metal.

'This is my own special prison, Carver. We're not at Macao, but nearby, in the asteroid belt. We are quite alone out here, hidden from prying eyes. And here, we do what I say. And I,' explained the man cheerfully, 'do what the dragon says.'

'What fucking dragon?' demanded Carver, still hanging onto the frame, quaking with anger. Whoever this guy was, he was a proper fruitcake. Carver tried to pull himself upright, but was frustrated that his usually strong body was still almost as limp as cooked spaghetti.

'*The* dragon,' said the man, and just to make his point, he pressed a button on the restraining device and Carver's entire body went rigid, racked by agony that blazed like liquid fire through every cell at once. He screamed and spasmed, his legs floating out from under him. 'Again?' asked the man when the spasms had subsided. Carver could only shake his head mutely, eyes squeezed shut. 'Good. Now put this on,' said the man again, throwing the space suit directly at Carver's belly, making him flinch instinctively. 'We have work to do.'

'What work?' Carver snarled, wiping gel from his short-shaven hair, hair that was so blond as to be almost white and contrasted starkly with the pinkness of his scalp. He flicked the gel from his fingers, but he didn't dare flick it at the other man like he wanted to. He shook out the space suit he had been thrown, regarding it critically. Its arms and legs floated and flailed, billowing like pennants.

'Lots of work,' said the man. 'I'm a bit behind, to be honest. I keep having to return to the station. I have. . . *duties* there.' He said the word sourly, as if it tasted bad. 'But I've come back to get you. Honestly, I'd have left you if I could do the work alone.' He seemed to remember himself, and shook his head in a *listen-to-me-rabbiting-on* gesture. 'Put the suit on,' he said, a little more kindly this time.

Carver managed to work his huge, muscular form into the skin-tight suit without actually letting go of the metal frame. He also kept one eye firmly on the man with the restraining device. The man seemed to notice him staring at the little box.

'You know how this works, right?' he asked conversationally.

Carver nodded, scowling. 'I can't get too near to it, I can't get too far from it, and it can't be turned off without the code,' he parroted, recalling exactly the words of the little rat bastard at Platini who had first explained the device to him. 'It's linked to an implant in my head.'

'That's it,' agreed the man, nodding. He sounded pleased, as if Carver was a difficult student who was finally coming round.

By the time Carver had fully suited up, barring the helmet which he assumed would be in the airlock, the man was looking impatient again.

'What now?' asked Carver suspiciously.

'Follow me,' said the man, magnetting onto the floor of the ship and stretching his back as if it ached. 'There's a manoeuvring jet in the sleeve of the suit, but I don't suggest you use it. You might fly out of range of the restraining device too easily. Magnet onto the floor instead. I assume you know how. If not – learn.' Then he turned and led the way from the cargo hold.

Carver floated stupidly for a moment, wanting to make a break for it, knowing that he couldn't. He considered throwing something at the man – that seemed like a good way to hurt or even kill the bastard without getting too close to the restraining device – but of course, he still wouldn't have the code for the damn thing, and then he'd be trapped here, unable to approach the device or to leave its vicinity, possibly until he starved. It almost seemed worth it, but grudgingly he gave the idea up, clamped his boots to the floor and followed the retreating figure.

They passed between stacks of supplies in identical, coded crates and industrial-looking machines that were bolted into the deck. Their boots rang on the worn wire-mesh tiles, filling the space with echoing noise. The man in front didn't bother to check that Carver was following – what choice did he have? – he just calmly led the way through the darkness, splashed by the occasional gout of coloured light from some computer terminal or instrument panel that they passed.

The man stopped before a huge snarl of pipes and cylinders, some jumbled heap of arcane machinery that stood almost ten feet high and bore a simple set of dials and a small electronic display on its front.

'You know how to work this?' he asked, turning to Carver, who stayed the requisite distance behind him.

'Of course not,' replied Carver contemptuously. 'I don't even know what it is.'

The man sighed and tutted, as if he had expected no better. 'It's the air system,' he explained slowly. 'Tanks–' he indicated the large cylinders, '–and scrubbers,' he finished, indicating some random-looking tangle of pipework and machinery. 'I was considering removing the whole thing from here and installing it on the rock. But I was hoping you'd be some help. I don't honestly understand why the dragon has allowed you to live,' he said.

'Man, you are fucking crazy,' said Carver wonderingly. He almost felt sorry for the freak, but it was only a fleeting emotion, immediately burned away by his red and blazing hatred. He thought maybe the man would fry him again in response to this observation, but he only nodded mutely, looking at the air unit closely.

'We can still do it,' said the man thoughtfully. 'We'll just have to raise the temperature of the air-flow here. It'll get hot in this shuttle.'

88

'We can still do *what*?' demanded Carver impatiently. He was not a man who liked to be kept out of the loop or made to feel foolish, and that was what this bastard was doing to him now.

The man turned to Carver, a little smile on his lips. 'Seal and pressurise the asteroid,' he said in a voice pregnant with barely-constrained excitement. Carver could see that the freak was wired – actually *having fun*. He vowed again to make the bastard suffer just as soon as he had worked out how.

'Why the fuck,' asked Carver coldly, 'would you want to do that?'

'Because it'll make it easier,' said the man openly. He clearly wanted Carver to ask a follow up question, but Carver just shook his head and grunted. His huge hands were clenching and unclenching at his sides. When the question didn't materialise, the man continued anyway: 'Easier to dig up the dragon.' His smile broadened then, but it also became colder, as if an ice-sheet had advanced across his face. *And people call* me *insane!* thought Carver with some amazement. 'Don't worry,' said the man. 'It's all for the best, in the end. You'll see,' he said, running his hand across the worn-smooth surface of the machinery in front of them, his eyes becoming glazed and distant. 'They'll all see.'

CHAPTER SIXTEEN

Lina slept fitfully, fighting against layers of darkness that tangled around her like bodybags, smothering her, covering her. But however hard she fought, she kept finding herself back in the belt, where Sal was screaming through the comm – not the brief shriek that she had uttered in reality, but a protracted and wavering howl of agony and fear that warbled on and on into ever-higher registers as she was torn to pieces. Lina flew towards her – towards where her Kay *should* have been – through a dense cloud of blood and gore. Teeth ricocheted off the front of her ship in a virtual hailstorm. She wondered distantly how anyone could have so damn *many* of them.

And then she became aware that there was something else in the belt with her, something dark and shapeless that rode through the void like smoke; a surreal whisper of shadow; a greedy, *hungry* shade of death. She didn't know how she sensed it, but the feeling was overpowering, and the truth of it seemed bleakly inescapable.

The pitter-patter of teeth against the window of her ship grew gradually louder and louder as she neared the area where Sal's Kay had been, until it became a virtual fusillade: *Bang! Bang! Bang!* She wanted to flee, to escape before the shadow caught her, like it had caught Sal, and scatter her own insides across the rubble-strewn vacuum of the belt, but the noise was now so loud that she couldn't even think.

It was catching up to her, she knew. It was right behind her. Panic-stricken, she forgot all about Sal and turned her Kay around, maxing the gas. She thought she was screaming aloud, but the noise was distant, so distant. The ship struggled, drive system howling, wallowing in space as if caught in thick mud. . . slowing, slowing, failing. . .

The lights of the dashboard suddenly went off, dousing Lina in darkness as thick as tar. A charnel stink – a stench of rotten and putrefying meat, hideously ripe and sweet – filled her head, making her gag. And then, somehow, impossibly, the shadow reached right through the hull of the ship and *touched* her. . .

She woke, screaming, bolt upright in bed. Somebody was hammering on the door of her quarters: *Bang! Bang! Bang!* She wiped one hand across her face and it came away slicked with sweat. The covers clung to her naked body like a pallid second skin. She breathed deeply, trying to calm her rattling heart, letting the knocking continue. Her head was pounding. Her tongue felt like something had died on it. The lighting was too bright.

'Mum?' said Marco's sleep-blurry voice from the doorway.

Lina jumped, a little sound of shock escaping her throat, pulling the covers tight around herself as if they might armour her against harm.

'Marco,' she breathed.

'There's somebody at the door,' he said, rubbing his eyes with the back of one hand. 'Shall I let them in?'

Lina nodded, making her sweaty hair fall over her face. She brushed it behind her ear and saw that he was studying her intently. 'Yeah,' she managed to say. The insistent knocking continued.

Marco made no move towards the door, though. 'Are you okay?' he asked, his young face suddenly aged by concern.

She shook her head, wanting to lie but unable to do so. 'I've been better.' She could feel tears beginning to well in her eyes. She looked away from him and said 'Get the door. I'll be out in a minute.' She managed to control her treacherous face and dried her eyes on the sheet as subtly as she could. She turned back to Marco, who hadn't budged, and attempted an encouraging smile. It didn't seem to have the desired effect. He nodded obediently, but his look of concern condensed into one of outright worry. He paused for a moment longer, unsure, then turned and went to answer the door.

Lina jumped up to close the door of her room, but the blanket fell away and she stumbled, trying to gather it round her and right herself as she went. She realised that she felt like absolute crap and wondered how much she had had to drink last night. Marco was speaking to somebody in the other room now, but she couldn't discern the words. What had happened to Eli? She supposed he must have let himself out when she'd got back, whenever *that* had been.

She managed to push her own door closed and crammed herself gracelessly into yesterday's rumpled flight suit that she had apparently left lying in the middle of the floor. Her head reeled unpleasantly as she did this, making her want to throw up. The suit didn't smell too great, truth be told, which didn't help either.

Somebody knocked on the door of her room just as she was reaching for it, and when she opened it Marco was there again, in his plain grey, oversized pyjamas.

'It was Rachelle, from the security team,' said Marco, his expression a little puzzled. 'She says there's a meeting in the plaza today, outside *The Miner's*. You're supposed to be there.'

Lina struggled to process this information. For a moment, she couldn't remember what *The Miner's* was, but then she recalled that she had in fact spent most of the previous night there. She thought maybe Halman had been with her, but she wasn't certain.

'A meeting?' she repeated. Marco nodded. 'What time?'

'Half-nine,' he said. 'Can I come with you?'

'You've got school,' she replied automatically, distracted.

Marco looked offended. 'No, I haven't,' he said with a touch of irritation. 'Not today.'

Lina nodded, trying to focus. 'Er, okay then, I guess. Is Rachelle still here?'

'No. She didn't actually come in. Should I have asked her?'

'No,' Lina said, sitting back on the bed with an unintentional sigh. 'No, that's fine.' She put her head in her hands, trying to massage her brain into some sort of working order. She sat this way for a while, forgetting that Marco was there, but when she looked up he was studying her analytically.

'What's going on, Mum?' he asked. He was holding out a battered datasheet in one hand. 'Why was Eli here last night?'

'Cos I was out,' she admitted, with a touch of guilt that the more logical part of her mind assured her was undeserved. 'What is that?'

'A note,' said Marco, handing it over. 'From Eli. He says you had a hard night,' he added, and Lina thought she heard a little judgemental note in that voice, although it could have been inferred. 'At *The Miner's*, were you, Mum?'

She felt the tears creeping up on her again, and fought to suppress them. She guessed that sooner or later they would have to come. But now, with her boy here, was not the time. 'Yeah, I guess I was,' she admitted. She patted the bed next to her and Marco sat there. He looked up into her face, his eyes innocently questioning. His hair was appealingly sleep-tangled. Lina put an arm around his small shoulders and pulled him close to her, aware that she stank of stale sweat and synthihol. She put her head against his and sat there in silence for a minute. Marco allowed this familiarity, but she could sense that he still wanted an explanation.

Eventually, he broke the silence: 'Why weren't you at work? Did you go after?'

'Work finished early,' she said wearily. 'There was an accident in the belt last night, near the start of my shift.'

Marco's eyes widened. 'What?' he gasped. '*What*? I mean who? Who?'

'Sal,' said Lina, a sudden lump in her throat. She gritted her teeth, trying to control herself. 'She's dead,' she managed to add at last. 'She bumped a rock, and her Kay decompressed.'

'Mum. . .' said Marco, and this time he embraced her. His body felt frail and bony against her own. Jaydenne had been tall and athletic, and Lina supposed that his son would one day assume a similar shape. But as yet, he was still a child.

Lina sighed deeply, not even noticing that tears were beginning to seep from her eyes and down her face, to drip onto Marco's shoulder. 'It's okay,' she said, but she didn't know if she was talking to Marco or herself. 'It's okay, it was just an accident. We all know the dangers. Something just went wrong. It was just an accident.'

Marco was crying too, she realised. He released her and stood up angrily, startling her. His face was red and streaked with his own tears, now. 'It could have been *you*!' he shouted accusingly, his hands balled into fists. 'It could have been *you*!'

And there it was again – that wave of love, but tinged with guilt this time. 'Honey. . .' she said, grasping for something. 'Honey, no. . . It's never going to be me.' Marco shook his head, eyes streaming, but she stood and went to him, enfolding his reluctant body in her arms and pulling him close again. She stroked his hair and whispered, 'I'm still here, Marco, I'm still here,' until eventually he relaxed.

He stepped away from her and she saw by the new gleam of hardness in his eyes – a very *adult* look – that he was going to be all right. 'Mum,' he said with deliberate calm, drawing a deep breath. 'I've been thinking lately, and, I mean this. . . this just makes me more sure. . . I. . .' He visibly steeled himself and said, 'I want to go to Platini Alpha. Or even Aitama.' He spread his hands, as if to say *There it is*, and smiled thinly.

Lina shook her head. 'Marco, is this about your father?'

Marco's brows drew together for just the briefest instant, but when he answered his voice was steady and rational. 'No. I don't need *him*. I just want to go somewhere safer. Somewhere better. We shouldn't be here, Mum. People shouldn't live here. You could get another job. You said yourself that Farsight would take you at Platini Dockyard, and it has to be better than this.' He smiled encouragingly, cajolingly, his eyes still shiny with tears. 'Right?'

'It was just an accident, honey. A one-off.' But as she spoke, she suddenly recalled an image from her dream: alone in the belt, alone but for the hungry, greedy shadow that seemed to permeate the void with its reeking wolf-breath, its infinite tendrils of grasping darkness. 'A one-off,' she repeated, but this time it was just a whisper.

'Mum?' prompted Marco, making Lina snap back to reality.

'Yes?'

'Hadn't we better get ready?'

'What?' she asked, her brain slow and muddy. 'What for?'

'The meeting, remember?'

'Oh yeah,' said Lina, filled with fresh dread, her hangover swelling to new proportions.

Despite her pounding head, she managed to make cheese on toast for breakfast. She supplemented this with recon-juice from a can, rejecting the awful coffee she usually had in the morning as unlikely to actually improve her delicate condition. They talked about little, safe things: Marco's school-work; films; station gossip. Once he'd finished, Marco excused himself to go to the toilet, and Lina sat sipping her juice alone.

She lifted the glass and looked into the liquid suspiciously. Something tasted a little off. Okay, she was quite hungover, and it could just be that. And the Farsight-branded recon-juice never tasted *that* great, but she had an inkling that it was neither of those things. She put the glass down amongst the crumbs of toast and sniffed the air, frowning.

'What time is it?' asked Marco, reappearing in the room.

'Er, almost time to go, I reckon,' said Lina, starting guiltily and turning in her seat to face him.

'I wonder what they want,' he said. She could see that he had washed and attempted to assert some sort of control over his hair. She guessed she should probably do the same.

'I don't know,' she said. But she was sure of one thing: it wasn't likely to be good news.

95

CHAPTER SEVENTEEN

'Take your helmet off,' said the man. He was holding the restraining device in one gloved hand.

'Hey, hey. . .' Carver began to protest weakly. 'Look, I don't know about that, man. Won't it take a while to pressurise in here?'

The man's voice was tinny and inhuman in Carver's helmet speaker. 'I guess we'll see,' he said. 'And anyway, it's *been* a while. Take your helmet off.' And he waggled the restraining device meaningfully. '*Now*,' he added.

They had worked quickly, under the crazy dragon-man's direction, and Carver was almost impressed by how much progress they had made, albeit in a ridiculous madman's scheme. They had backed the shuttle carefully up to a particularly huge asteroid that the man had evidently moored it alongside while Carver still slept in sus-an. The shuttle was a big ship – the biggest Carver had ever been inside at any rate – but the asteroid dwarfed it.

Carver knew that the shuttle crossed the great distances of space, accelerating steadily for years at a time, with a shield of small particles driven ahead of it as defence against collisions. Now, the shield was dispelled, the magnetic field turned off, and to Carver this was conclusive evidence that the shuttle wasn't going anywhere soon. He didn't know if this was good or bad.

The shuttle was equipped, as all such vessels were, with an emergency boarding and rescue system. This consisted basically of an extensible tube, just wide enough to crawl through, with a rotating cutter at its business end. The cutting head had forced its way into the rock like a mosquito's proboscis, setting the whole of the shuttle's superstructure shuddering and ringing. The man had explained that this was tricky work, as they couldn't push too hard without breaking their tethering line and sending the rock flying uncontrollably away from them. But after half an hour of this they had broken through into some sort of cavity just inside the asteroid. The boarding tube had clamped itself firmly into the hole and sprayed sealing-resin around the join.

They had crawled through the narrow tube, Carver complaining fiercely the whole time and the crazy dragon-man in an annoyingly buoyant mood, with instawall cannisters raided from the shuttle's cathedralesque hold. These grapefruit-sized, bright yellow devices, when primed, would wait for a pre-set period of time and then explode in hideous, ballooning flowers of chemical foam that solidified within seconds into a rock-hard mass. The cannisters, despite their size, were incredibly dense, their contents heavily compressed, and the two men could only just manoeuvre them one-by-one in the awkward micro-gravity. Under the crazy dragon-man's instruction, they had sealed four holes in the skin of the asteroid. One of these had been large enough to drive a gravpod into, but the rest had been comparatively small. The instawall had bloomed to fill the gaps then dried rapidly to a dusky, diseased-looking yellow.

Then they had turned the scrubbers to max, raised the temperature of the air to allow for its cooling as it flowed into the asteroid, and waited for the rock to pressurise. After a while, the man had equipped Carver with an airflow sensor, taking one himself, and they had crawled back into the rock and checked for leaks around the instawall seals.

Throughout most of this procedure, the man hadn't spoken to Carver except to give him simple orders. But worryingly, he had spoken to someone *else* from time to time, in a hushed and secretive voice. Carver hadn't caught any of the words, and he hadn't wanted to, truth be told. *Here I am*, he'd thought, *pressurising an asteroid in the middle of fucking nowhere, my only companion the psycho with the dragon in his head*. He wished he'd gone to jail after all and wondered what else the bastard had in store for him.

Gradually, the rock had filled with air, as measured on the man's little device. The whole process, with Carver's reluctant assistance, had taken only two-and-a-half hours. And now here they were.

'But what if it ain't breathable yet?' objected Carver, knowing it was futile to resist.

'The meter says it is,' the man told him factually.

'Then why don't *you* try it?' suggested Carver.

The man pushed off from one of the rocky walls, his suit-light dazzlingly bright in Carver's eyes, and floated down towards him like a descending angel. 'Because,' he explained reasonably, 'I'm too valuable.'

Carver nodded sarcastically, scowling. The crazy dragon-man was almost close enough to throttle now, but he didn't dare try. *Not yet*, he promised himself, *but as soon as I find a way. . .* 'Right,' he mocked. 'You're one important guy.'

The man nodded agreeably. 'That's right,' he said. 'Now take it off before I fry your evil little brain into a paste. Okay?'

Carver took a deep breath, clenched his jaw, and without another word unfastened the clasps and lifted his helmet clear. For a terrifying moment his chest hitched, paralysed by the expected vacuum. But then he realised that he was breathing after all. The air tasted a bit shitty – worse even than it had on the shuttle – but he was breathing nonetheless. 'Fuck you, man,' he declared. 'I live to fight again.'

'Splendid,' said the man, adding, unbelievably, 'Well done.' He unclipped his own helmet and removed it, hanging before Carver in the stillness of the asteroid's cavernous interior.

'What next?' asked Carver, starting to shiver quite violently, despite the fact that the air pumped from the shuttle was heated to a temperature that was almost unbearably hot at the source. His breath steamed, rolling, in the combined beams of their suit-lights. 'What does your dragon want?'

'Well,' said the man, 'we're going to dig it out of the rock. But it wants a few other things, too. Little things.'

'And if it gets them?' asked Carver, trying to sound reasonable, like a man who could be fairly bargained with. 'Can I go then?'

The man's grin broadened, and Carver could see the vacancy behind his eyes. They were like windows of mirrored glass, revealing nothing, one-way only. And his smile, for all its breadth, lacked any warmth or humanity – it might as well have been spray-painted onto a skull. 'It hasn't told me yet,' he replied. 'And I haven't asked.'

Carver turned slowly around, letting his suit-light play across the ragged walls of glinting stone, somehow too smooth to be artificial and too rough to have been hewn at the same time, wondering if this freezing rock would be his grave. He turned back to face the crazy dragon-man. 'Do you think,' he suggested in a voice laced with cold undertones like hidden riptides, 'that you *could* ask?'

'We'll see how good you are,' said the man. 'You see, the dragon says I need to head back to Macao. I have a few more errands to run.'

'Errands,' parroted Carver. 'Right.'

'Yes,' agreed the man, failing to catch the mocking tone to Carver's voice, or maybe just ignoring it. 'It was pleased with last night's events, but it needs a few more little things before it can really help us.'

'Did I mention that you are one crazy dragon-loving bastard?' asked Carver, sure now that he was not going to get the answer he wanted and starting to get angry again. He didn't care if the man zapped him some more. He was beyond giving a shit by this point.

The man's distant stare intensified, his eyes narrowing and his gaze boring into Carver's face, such that Carver quickly regretted baiting him and wished that he could take it back. 'I know what you think of me,' said the man in a voice as slow and cold as a glacier grinding across the aural landscape. 'And I know you would kill me if you could. But this will not happen. I'm going back to the station soon, and you – *you* – will dig. And if you make good enough work of it then maybe I will ask the dragon for your life.' Carver was transfixed by the man's stare now, speared like a bug on a pin. 'But I warn you,' said the man, his smile slipping and then melting away altogether, 'that the dragon is hungry, and it is not necessarily inclined to mercy, especially for the likes of you.'

'Hey. . .' said Carver, intending to strongly defend his position, even make an impassioned plea for his life. It came out as the merest breath, and trailed away into nothing.

'Come,' said the man. 'And we'll find some digging equipment before I go. This shuttle will be rammed with mining kit.' He sounded calmer, more reasonable again, and Carver tried to convince himself that he hadn't been scared just then, that this was just some poor crazy fucker living out his schizoid fantasy on a blighted rock. But something had chilled him to his core. That frozen kernel still remained as he followed the man back through the tube and into the booming depths of the inter-system shuttle.

CHAPTER EIGHTEEN

Eli came slinking into the plaza from the direction of the rec area, but the loud whine of the un-oiled automatic door betrayed him. Everyone turned to look, confounding any hopes he'd had of creeping in unnoticed. He gave an embarrassed little wave to Halman and called, 'Sorry I'm late, Dan!'

Halman, standing facing the assembled crowd next to one of his senior admin staff, a greying and severe battleship of a woman named Amy Stone, showed him a slightly forced smile and answered over the general hubbub: 'That's okay, Eli, we're still waiting for Sudowski anyway.'

Eli nodded and pushed his way through the mass of bodies towards where Lina and Marco stood near the front of the group, which was centred more or less on *The Miner's*. The place was shut now, its grimy windows dark and shuttered. Eli gave her an enquiring look – *How're you doing?* – and she gave him a wan little smile in return – *Not too bad, thanks*. And if her head would just stop pulsating, she even thought that might be true.

'Hey, Eli,' said Marco, looking up at him.

Eli ruffled Marco's hair affectionately, a gesture that the boy wouldn't tolerate from anybody else, then he leant in close to Lina and whispered in her ear, 'Did you. . .'

'Tell him?' she asked equally quietly. 'Yeah, I did.'

'Oh good–' said Eli, but he was hushed by a chorus of cat-calls and jeers as a severely crumpled Nik Sudowski entered from the stairwell, trying ineffectually to wave the crowd into silence.

Some wag, probably Si Davis, yelled, 'You crap the bed or something, Nik?'

Sudowski shook his head tiredly and pushed his way towards the back of the crowd, where Lina supposed he hoped to fade from the collective mind as soon as possible.

101

Halman cleared his throat, a noise as loud as a gunshot, making her jump, and puffed his chest out. 'RIGHT!' he bellowed, and silence fell immediately.

Here were all of the inhabitants of Macao Station, barring a couple of the sec-team who had stayed behind at the prison and, of course, the prisoners themselves – over a hundred disparate frontiers-people, around a dozen children among them. Many of them were lifelong associates, and all of them were members of the station's extended family. Although they practically filled the grey and shadowy space of the plaza, the most open public area available on Macao, they looked a desperately small and tenuous pocket of life, a fragile bubble of humanity crammed into one little corner of this hurtling tin-can which spun mechanically on the isolated boundary of known space. *And now we are one less*, a little voice in Lina's mind reminded her darkly. That voice, so often a nagging, negative little voice, sometimes sounded like Jaydenne. But now it sounded like Sal Newman. Lina wished she'd taken painkillers before coming out.

Halman looked around the assembled group, wearing his serious-business-face, catching the eye of each in turn. 'Thanks for coming,' he said, then paused, unsure of how to really begin. 'Let's not fuck arou–,' he stumbled over the obscenity, before righting himself. 'Let's not beat around the bush here,' he corrected himself. 'We've had a few problems over the last couple of days. Most of you have probably heard what's going on already, but I just wanted to make sure that you've got the right of it.' He looked out at the earnest, enquiring faces that stared back at him. Lina felt for him a little – she knew he hated public speaking. He glanced to Amy Stone, who looked tiny next to him. She nodded seriously, and he seemed to rally again. 'I'd like everyone to be equipped with the truth rather than second-hand gossip from *The Miner's*.'

'Hey!' objected Gregor, raising a hand in protest. Lina turned to see him. He was standing at the back with an unlit cigar clenched in his teeth, the typically swarthy deep-space roughneck.

Halman grunted a brief laugh, but Lina thought it sounded

purely dutiful. 'No offence, Gregor,' he said, raising his own hand in return. And then, more serious again, and to everyone: 'There was an accident in the belt last night, on Eli's shift. I'm sure everyone has already heard, but here's how it actually happened: Sal's mining ship, K6-8, having passed a thorough pre-flight, bumped a rock, which pierced the hull and caused an explosive decompression.' He scanned the rapt faces before him. Silence reigned. 'She was killed instantly.'

Lina remembered that cry for help, that small frightened voice saying, simply *Eli!* and then the scream, and she knew that it hadn't been instant, not really. Quick, perhaps, but not instant. Sal had had long enough to be afraid, even to feel pain – to die in fear and pain. She felt her lip begin to tremble and bit down on it, hard. She had already cried in front of her boy once today and she was determined not to make it twice.

'There is nothing I can say that will have any bearing on the depth of the loss that we feel, as a family, as crewmates and as friends of hers. We do not know how the safety systems of Sal Newman's Kay came to fail, and all Kays are now grounded until the ground-crew, myself, and Nik's people are satisfied that they are safe.'

'Then how come,' somebody asked from near the back, 'they were flying again last night?'

There was a rumble of noise at this, a general hubbub of questions and contradictions. Halman held up one hand until it died away.

'Ilse Reno's shift took their Kays out last night to clear the wreckage from the crash, and to try and find out anything they could about what happened.'

'That's right,' said Ilse loudly. She was leaning against one rust-stained wall, her arms folded across her small chest. She looked around defiantly, her hard face up-tilted, her brows drawn together. Her eye-implant glowed cherry-red in the shadows. 'And if any of you has issue with that, be aware that my guys insisted, as did I. This is Sal Newman we're talking about here! Any of you shitheads think we should have just left her remains drifting in the

103

belt?' She waited, inviting response, her chin jutting defiantly. Despite her generally fearsome appearance, she was beautiful in that moment, thought Lina – proud and fierce. Unsurprisingly, nobody answered her. 'I thought not,' she said, relaxing back.

Halman took a deep breath. 'Thank you, Ilse,' he said neutrally. 'Yes, well, as of *now* all Kays are grounded until further notice.' Halman nodded at Eli, who had his hand up. 'Yes?'

Eli's face was more creased than usual. He looked like a sheet that needed shaking out. 'How, then, are we going to keep the station spinning, with no mineral income?' he asked. 'I thought we'd be stepping it up, if anything, because of. . . well. . .' he trailed off, shaking his head.

'Because they've lost the fucking shuttle!' someone shouted from the crowd. Lina glanced back over her shoulder, but couldn't tell who it was. Marco looked round nervously, too.

'Yeah, and we have to pay for it, right?' piped up the angry-sounding Jayce, one of Ella Kown's sec-team.

'As for the shuttle. . .' shouted Halman, overriding the noise. 'As for the shuttle, we simply don't know where it's got to. We still hope to receive it any day now, but we have to prepare for the possibility that we may not.' These words, from the station controller himself, fell like bombs among the assembled listeners, but bombs that spread shockwaves of stunned silence. Everybody had known that this might be the case – most people had suggested as much, at least in private – but to hear it said aloud, and by Halman, somehow made it real. 'We have to prepare for the possibility that the next shuttle we receive will be a year from now, rather than a day or two. Personally, I still think it'll turn up, but honestly that's just a gut feeling. Supplies are going to be rationed, except for what we can grow here in the aeroponics lab. That means we'll have to–'

'Develop a fondness for salad!' Si Davis interjected, somewhat inappropriately, Lina thought.

'–we'll have to collect all company-issued food supplies you have, centralise those supplies, inventorise everything, and ration it back out accordingly.' There was an uproar of noise at this, part resigned groan and part open refusal, but Halman persisted. 'Listen, if this seems a little Big Brother, I'm sorry, but we really have no choice. If the shuttle *doesn't* come, we're gonna starve if we don't pool resources and share. And by the way, this is not a suggestion, it's an order from *my* office. And it's one that the sec-team will enforce if necessary.'

Lina felt Marco's small frame tense against her. His cool, trembling hand found hers and held onto it tightly. She could feel the fear coming through his skin in icy waves. 'It's okay,' she whispered into his ear. Eli glanced at Lina. She didn't think she'd ever seen him look the least bit scared before, but that was how he looked now. Just a bit, but it was there. She didn't like it at all. Eli swallowed heavily and looked back to Halman.

'Holy shit, Boss,' said Rocko in a breathless voice. He still wore last night's flight-suit, Lina saw. His dark face was slack and incredulous. 'You saying we have to turn in all our food or, or. . . what? Ella Kown's going to *shoot* us? Really? *Ella?*' He turned from side to side, palms spread and face questioning, garnering support. 'Really?' he repeated in amazement. Ella didn't appear to contradict him. Fionne, standing next to him, pulled him close to her, quietening him, whispering into his ear.

'We'll redistribute accordingly,' said Halman calmly. 'And fairly. And we'll eat rations until either this year's shuttle or next year's shuttle arrives.' A ventilation fan in the wall above the stairwell began to cycle up with a noise that rapidly grew to be intrusive, bringing Halman to a stumbling halt. 'We. . . er, we. . .' He turned and frowned at it. 'Can somebody shut that off?' he asked Amy Stone, leaning down to her level. Amy frowned, too, and gave an answer that Lina couldn't hear, shaking her head. 'Nik?' Halman asked, looking for Sudowski and finding him at the back of the crowd. Faces turned expectantly to the chief of maintenance, who simply shook his head, too. He looked extremely pale, his eyes red-rimmed and his hair unkempt.

'Whole air system's screwed anyway!' somebody shouted. Lina thought it was Jayce again, one of the sec-team Halman would be relying on to enforce his new rules.

This comment had a disturbing effect on the assembly: a cacophony of voices rose, some berating the speaker, some agreeing, others shouting questions. Marco's hand tightened even further on Lina's, painfully, his nails digging into her palm. She squeezed back nonetheless. Eli was silent beside her.

'The air system,' said Halman in a loud but steady voice, pitched to override the racket from the fan, 'is working fine. Nik's team had to change a processor, but it's currently running at almost full capacity.'

'Almost?!' yelled a woman's voice, high-pitched with indignation.

'Yes, this is another thing I know a lot of you have been talking about,' said Halman diplomatically. Lina, from her vantage point near the front, could see a small vein pulsing in his temple, contradicting the aura of calm that he was clearly trying to project. 'We have had a problem with the scrubbers this last week. Nik's team have found an ingenious workaround for the issue. But the smoking ban will continue for the foreseeable future, to reduce the load on the system. Maintenance replaced the dead component with a processor from the comms array.' More uproar. Halman waved the crowd to silence again. 'This means that we have lost the ability, for now, to talk to Platini, or the way stations.'

'Like they were any fucking help anyway!' shouted a deep male voice from somewhere on Lina's left.

'This has been a difficult time for us,' said Halman, ignoring this comment. The fan was droning away louder than ever, now, and seemed to have settled on this new and deafening frequency. Lina thought that a bad smell was coming from it, but she couldn't be sure. If it was, then nobody else seemed to have noticed. 'It is *going* to be a difficult time for us, until we are resupplied. We are all going to behave in an adult manner, though. We will focus on the priorities. That means we're going to operate – *co*-operate – as a family, as a team.' Everybody was silent now, straining to hear him over the noise. 'Number one: another tragedy like the one that affected Sal Newman *must not happen*. That means nobody flies until further notice. Number two: we're going to centralise food resources, and ration them out, against the contingency that this year's shuttle doesn't make it. I want all food items delivered to the canteen by three this afternoon. Then the sec-team will check to make sure nothing has been *forgotten*. Number three: we're going to *remain calm*. That's the most important thing of all.' He scanned the faces before him, daring any of them to resist this last directive. Nobody spoke. 'And we *will* get through this. We're no strangers to adversity here on Macao, and this is just the way it has to be. This is why we are well paid. We are bigger than this, we can get through this. As long as we work together. That is all.' He didn't offer to field any questions, as Lina had thought he might, and this was probably wise judging by the mood of the group. Instead, with one last emphatic glare around the crowd, he turned and strode to the stairwell, where he ascended out of sight, Amy Stone dragging behind him like a ship's tender.

There was subdued murmuring all around her as Lina stood gripping Marco's hand and wondering what to do next. Eli puffed out his cheeks, catching her eye. He arched one eyebrow. What needed to be said, really?

'Let's go,' suggested Lina, looking from Marco to Eli. They made for the stairs. As she went, Lina noticed the gaunt and lanky figure of Murkhoff, the security man injured by a prisoner the week before. He was standing with Theo and Jayce, and he looked particularly glum. A white bandage covered his ruined eye and a large red welt, where his face had been glued back together, ran from under the bandage almost to his chin. Lina guessed he wasn't going to get his trip to Platini system any time soon.

Lina, Marco and Eli pushed through the remaining crowd and out of the door that led into the rec area. Lina felt shell-shocked. Eli was talking to Marco in a kindly, almost fatherly way, but she couldn't really hear him. She was lost in her own world, a world in which they sat and waited indefinitely for a shuttle that never came, as the air dried up and equipment fell into disrepair, slowly starving out here in the back of beyond.

She stopped at the large window in the rec area, falling behind the others, hypnotised by the cold monotony of the belt that filled the view like static-snow on a screen. *There it is*, she thought. *The reason we are here. Is it worth it?* She thought of what Marco had said about going to Platini, finding another line of work, another place, another life. She was biting her lip again, almost hard enough to draw blood, but she didn't notice. She reached out one hand to touch the window, as if she could make contact that way with the mineral bloodstream of the Soros system, somehow come to understand it, understand what it was that Sal had really died for. She thought of Jaydenne, wishing that Sal had gone with him to Platini, but knowing that then, maybe, *she* would have been the one in K6-8, and Marco would have been left behind with no parents at all. She thought of the shadow from her dream – out there somewhere – something dark and hungry and incomprehensible. She knew it was just a metaphor for her own fears, but she couldn't shake the image from her mind.

When she touched the window, the display suddenly flickered, changing to a zoomed-in view, and at that same moment Eli touched her on the shoulder. She jumped, uttering a little squeak of surprise. 'Eli. . .' she said, looking into his eyes. She was alarmed to see the concern there, and wondered how bad she looked. She wasn't sure if she was hung-over or losing her mind, or maybe some interesting combination of the two.

'You sure you're okay?' he asked her quietly, checking over his shoulder to make certain that Marco was still waiting for them further up the corridor.

'Yeah,' she said, her mind running in ten directions at once. And then, slowly, accusingly, she said, '*You* seem to be doing okay.'

Eli stepped back, his thick brows knitting together. 'What does that mean?' he asked, puzzled.

He looked ancient in the dim light of the corridor, she realised, like an artefact from another age, the lines of his weathered face shadowed into sharp relief. She shook her head, unsure herself of what she had meant. 'I don't–'

'You mean you don't think I'm bothered enough by Sal?' he

108

asked, his eyes widening in disbelief.

She could see his body tensing, and wished that she could unsay it. But she could only shake her head. 'Eli, I'm. . .' she began, but she trailed off, unable to finish the thought, let alone voice it. Other people were passing them in an intermittent stream now, coming from the stairwell behind them. Some of them looked enquiringly at Lina and Eli as they went by, their expressions politely concerned.

'You're what?' he demanded, and she could see the anger rising inside him in a way she had never witnessed before. 'You're *what*? Saying you don't think I care?' He cocked his head, looking right into her face. 'Really? Huh?' When she wouldn't look at him, though, he threw up his hands in exasperation. Marco was coming slowly back down the corridor towards them, his expression wary. 'Just because I've learned to smile on the outside, Lina, doesn't mean I'm not fucking human!' he spat, teeth clenched.

She knew that she'd been wrong, then, and she wished that she could take it back. She didn't even know for sure if that *was* what she'd meant. But all she could do was mouth empty words at him. Eli shook his head, the fight going out of him, then turned and stomped off back the way they'd come.

Marco appeared at her side and put his arms round her waist. People continued to pass them, trying not to stare. Her hand fell to his head and rested there amid that shock of curly hair, but her gaze was drawn again to the window. Out there, the belt processed ever-onwards, oblivious – a machine that could grind a person into single bytes of matter and never miss a beat.

CHAPTER NINETEEN

Lina spent the afternoon with Marco in their quarters. They played video games and cards, but her heart wasn't really in it. When her gaze wandered to the window for the hundredth time and lingered there, hypnotised, Marco stood up and turned it off.

Lina came back to reality slowly, seeing that she was still holding a hand of cards. She couldn't remember which game they were playing. Marco sat again in his flimsy metal chair, opposite her, and picked his own cards up.

'It's you,' he said, nodding at her.

'Hmm?'

'Your turn.'

Lina laid her cards face-down on the table. The picture cards were all holo-movie stars from Platini. Lina had no idea who most of them actually were. 'Sorry, Son,' she said. 'I was miles away. I guess I didn't sleep that well.' The off-smell had intensified now, and an accompanying bad taste had taken up permanent residence in Lina's throat. She was becoming increasingly certain that it was the air itself. She wondered when Marco would notice. Perhaps he already had.

'And you had too much to drink last night, didn't you?'

'No, honey, I. . .' She floundered for a moment, then amended this to, 'Well, yes.'

'That's okay, Mum, you're allowed sometimes.' And then he added, sounding older than his years, 'I don't see the appeal, myself. But it's okay.'

'How about you put the holo on and I make dinner, eh?'

'Mum. . .' said Marco slowly. 'We don't have any food, remember? We gave it all in.'

'Oh yeah,' she agreed. Of course they had. 'Well, they're going to distribute rations in a bit, aren't they?'

Marco checked the wall-clock, a simple silver affair that ran persistently fast. 'Five, they said. I've got an idea: *I'll* go to the canteen and pick it up, then *I'll* make dinner, and *you* watch the holo for a bit.'

Lina's heart melted a few degrees at that. 'You're going to make a fine husband for some lucky girl one day, Marco,' she said, only half-joking. She felt herself smiling – a warm and genuine smile that she couldn't have stopped if she'd wanted to – and it felt good. 'Thanks, kiddo.'

'No problem,' he said. 'I'll go now, I reckon, get to the front of the queue.'

'Okay,' she agreed. He rose from his seat, pushing the cards into a vague heap, and made to leave. 'Marco. . .' said Lina, and he looked openly at her.

'What, Mum?'

'I love you,' she said.

'Yeah,' he replied, embarrassed. 'I know.' And then he turned to go. He stood framed in the doorway for a second, small and thin and fragile-looking, and then the door closed behind him.

Lina thought his suggestion about watching some holo was a pretty good one. She thought maybe some mental chewing-gum might blot out the conflicting, disturbing thoughts that filled her head.

For a while, this was quite effective. She pulled a blanket over herself and zoned out to a programme about social trends – *memes*, which was a new word to her – and how they spread throughout the vastness of human space, raging through society like diseases. It wasn't exactly *interesting*, but at least it gave her brain something to do other than continuously replay Sal's last moments in the asteroid belt.

Marco returned with the meagre rations doled out by Ella's sec-team: a small bag of dehydrated potato mash, two suspect-looking sausages and about two handfuls worth of frozen peas. 'I guess we know what we're having for dinner, at least,' he said, holding these items up and grinning.

Lina didn't think this boded well for the future, but she

managed to grace him with a smile in return. The holo had changed to news, which was all from Platini and out of date by over five years: strikes on Aitama, presumably now resolved; murders on Platini Alpha, presumably now solved or forgotten; ships launched from Platini Dockyard, presumably now long gone on their lengthy sub-light voyages Sol-wards. She'd seen it before, anyway, so it didn't really qualify for the term *news* in the first place.

Marco asked her if she needed anything – she said no – then he went into the kitchen and began to crash around in a purposeful-sounding manner. Lina returned to the holo, trying not to think about the way the air smelled.

Presently, Marco appeared in front of her, mercifully blocking the performance of some warbling pop-idiot on the holo who seemingly could neither sing nor dance and yet was oddly in demand. He was holding out a plate of food, which though not inherently appetising, was at least steaming hot. She received it with genuine thanks, her stomach growling aloud. *Maybe this will finally cure my hangover*, she thought hopefully.

She scooched up on the sofa, swinging her legs down to make room for Marco. They usually ate at table, but neither of them suggested it on this occasion. *If the death of a friend doesn't allow you a lapse in manners, then what possible upside is there?* Lina wondered. She scolded herself for the thought: it was an idiotic one, and disrespectful, too. There was, of course, no upside at all. Feeling humbled, despite the fact that this exchange had taken place entirely in her own mind, she concentrated instead on her dinner.

Once they had eaten, they sat in contented silence under the blanket. Programme gave way to programme in a shifting, monotonous convoy of colour, bathing the room in watercolour.

After a while, an idea began to form in Lina's mind. The idea germinated, then bloomed. She sat up straight, gripped by sudden determination. Marco, who had been on the verge of sleep, uttered a little cry of surprise.

'What?' he asked, looking around.

Lina pushed the blanket off, swung her feet down and stood up. 'Come on,' she said.

Marco frowned but he stood too, bundling the blanket into a pile on the sofa. 'What is it?' he asked again.

'I want to show you something,' she said cryptically. She felt a smile teasing at the edges of her mouth and went with it. 'Come on,' she said again.

'Er, okay. . .' Marco replied suspiciously.

Lina killed the holo and went to the door, her son following curiously behind her. She turned off the light and they went out, leaving the door unlocked, as was customary on board.

'Where are we going?' Marco asked. Lina answered with a silent grin.

She led him down the corridor, following the little twists inherent to almost all the passageways of Macao. Round the next bend, two of the refinery guys were juggling plastic clubs, throwing them to each other in tight synchronisation, and they had to backtrack and take another route to avoid disrupting them.

They reached the stairs near to medical and Lina led Marco up to the hub-most floor, emerging into the machine rooms that housed most of the station's vital equipment. The artificial g-force was lesser up here – about eighty-six percent of that experienced at the rim – due to the slower rotational velocity of the smaller circle that formed the inner floor. But this was nothing yet. Lina tried not to think about the failing scrubbers, but she couldn't help glancing down the corridor towards the room where they were housed. Bright light emanated from the doorway there and she could hear voices raised in debate. She didn't think Marco noticed, though, and she led him quickly away before he could.

Deflecting his questions, she took him on a twisting route through the machine rooms, past the maintenance workshop with its massive lathes and computerised milling machines. Nik Sudowski and Alphe could be seen in there, bent over a terminal together, but neither of them looked up as the two interlopers crept past.

Lina stopped before a vast curved wall that completely blocked their way. She turned around, face scrunched, trying to remember where to go. It had been some years since she'd been up here.

'What?' asked Marco for about the millionth time.

'I'll show you,' said Lina. She turned decisively left, skirting the curved wall, and ducked through a narrow doorway behind a massive oxygen tank that reached fully to the high ceiling and was attached to the floor with bolts as thick as Lina's wrists.

Although she had security clearance to be up here, she was aware that Marco technically didn't. Even so, she couldn't imagine anybody stopping them. She'd never seen anybody else come to this forgotten corner. And, more importantly, she was having fun. She felt a little bad about that, but it was Sal who had reminded her of this place. When things had been at their worst with Jaydenne – back when Sal had been new to Macao – Lina had come here sometimes to think. Once, she'd even brought Marco with her, strapped to her chest in a baby-carrier.

Marco followed her through the door, letting it swing to behind him with a creak of long disuse. The room emerged into was almost pitch black. Most of the lights had burned out over the years and never been replaced. The room was small and empty – some old storage space. Sharp metal shavings gritted and crunched beneath their feet.

Another door led out of the room to their right. They went through it and emerged into a surprisingly large, cylindrical room that was almost as badly-lit as the one behind them. Lina was sure that Marco had realised this put them on the other side – the *in*side – of the curved wall that they had stopped at before.

The floor in here was sturdy diamond-pattern mesh, but through it they could see only blackness that dropped away below them into nothing. Ancient water leaks had left thick mineral deposits slathered onto the concave metal of the walls. Lina heard dripping, but she couldn't tell where it was coming from. Thick pillars crowded the circular space in a tight, precise configuration, leaving little room to move around them.

Marco stood, turning in place, bemused. 'Are we inside. . .' he began slowly.

'Inside the spoke,' Lina finished for him. 'Yes. The other one houses the chutes that take metals from the refinery to dispatch in the hangar, but this one is essentially empty. I don't think anyone really comes here any more. They access the comms equipment and kinetic defence systems from crawl-ways in the other spoke.'

'Wow,' he breathed, still turning in a slow circle, his eyes wide white blanks in the gloom. And then, with a touch of relish, he added, 'We shouldn't be in here.'

'It's fine,' said Lina, grinning at his amazement. 'And that's nothing. Look up.' She pointed, as if he couldn't have discerned up from down by himself.

Above them, the shaft of the spoke soared away into a singularity of perspective, an eye of utter blackness. The pillars were in fact massive cables – caramicarbide tendons, each a metre across. Marco moved towards one, entranced, and put his hand on its ancient, pitted skin, feeling the rumbling of Macao's perpetual motion that thrummed inside it like a heartbeat.

Lina stared with him, enjoying the power of the sight, relishing the thrill of fear and awe. She thought she could almost feel the immense strains and stresses that the structure was under. It practically groaned with mass, ached with physical forces. This was what they had built – this crude, majestic wheel of steel and carbon. This was the skeleton of their home amongst the stars, the innards of the great machine.

'Wow. . .' said Marco again, with real feeling.

Lina began to pace between the cables, trailing her hands across their rough surfaces, squinting into the darkness.

'What are you looking for?' Marco asked.

'This!' she exclaimed, beckoning him over. His footsteps made tiny, tinny sounds on the meshwork floor, insignificant drops of noise. 'Look: it's a lift.'

Marco came and stood beside her. He glanced from her face to the machine in front of them, uncertain. 'Is it safe?' he asked.

Lina felt a twinge of sadness at this question. Sal's death had left him uneasy, and Lina knew he was concerned for her well-being. Maybe his own, too. 'Sure,' she said softly.

The lift was basically a simple metal cage, cylindrical, just big enough for two adults to squeeze into. In the low light it looked as if it had once been painted either orange or red, but it was hard to tell for sure. It was mostly rust now. The lift was mounted on a sort of track on one of the outer-most cables of the spoke. The track threaded its way into blackness up there, thin as spider-silk, a parasitic shoot that had clung to the massive trunk of the cable itself. The teeth of the track were caked with thick black grease. There was a small door at the side nearest to them, with a simple latch to keep it closed during operation.

'Let's go,' said Lina.

She struggled to move the latch, which had probably not been used since she'd last been here herself. After a moment, though, it slipped up and Lina pulled open the door. She squeezed through into the little cage and called Marco to join her.

Once they were both inside, Marco re-latched the door and Lina took the hanging control pad in one hand. She half expected that it somehow wouldn't work, but when she pressed the *UP* button there was the click of a magnetic clamp releasing and the lift groaned, false-started, then began to rise.

'Up we go!' she cried excitedly, feeling like a little girl again. The giant cables rolled along beside them.

'So up here must be the hub,' Marco called over the noise of the machine. He was standing in front of Lina with his face pressed to the door of the cage, staring out. Weak LED lights flashed past, patching the darkness with their blueish glow.

'Yeah,' agreed Lina. 'That's right.' She suddenly wondered what they would do if the lift broke *now*. It occurred to her that nobody knew they were here. And as far as she knew, nobody ever *came* here. Would it sound some sort of alarm automatically, maybe in maintenance or the offices? She hoped so – *supposed* so – but in truth she didn't know.

They ascended through a forest of ceramicarbide trees, the gears of the lift grinding and whirring along the toothed track, accelerating smoothly as they went. The lift's pace steadied and Lina began to feel noticeably lighter as they neared the hub. Soon

116

the floor below them sank into shadow and was gone. And out of the blackness above them, a vague shape began to congeal.

'It's amazing,' said Marco frankly, turning to look up at Lina. He was stretching up on his toes, trying little hops within the cramped confines of the cage, playing with the diminishing artificial gravity. Lina wasn't sure exactly, but she supposed they were experiencing about a tenth of one gee now, maybe a bit more with the lift's own acceleration.

She smiled back at him. 'The best is still to come,' she said.

The lift began to slow down, shedding its own manufactured gees and revealing the full effect of their near-weightlessness. They grabbed onto the mesh of the cage to prevent themselves floating upwards into its ceiling. Above them, the convex floor of the hub was becoming clear. The cage rushed towards that grey surface, still slowing, and popped through a hatchway in it, emerging into total darkness. Lina felt Marco's body tense against her and she reached down to squeeze his shoulder reassuringly. Still the cage was rising, but it was clear, despite the lack of visibility, that it had almost slowed to a stop now. The whining note of the gears on the track had become a muted grumble.

'Look up,' said Lina.

She felt Marco's head move against her as he craned to see. A patch of light was visible up above and they were climbing slowly towards it. That light seemed to descend on them, godlike in the darkness, covering them and flooding them until they emerged into a bright area of shining steel walls and bare architecture. The lift sighed to a stop in the middle of the floor and they drifted gently into the ceiling of the cage, laughing and entangling. They heard the magnetic clamp crash into place.

'Let us out,' said Lina, pushing herself back towards the floor and trying to stretch her cramping shoulders.

Marco managed to jimmy the latch undone and push the door open. He practically fell out of the cage, onto a floor with a very pronounced concavity to it. He looked around, eyes wide, then attempted to stand. But he pushed off too hard and drifted up into the air, limbs flailing, crying out in surprise.

'Whoa! Mum! This is crazy!' he yelled, bumping gently into the ceiling of the room. The walls were bare, the floor was bare. Apart from the cage, and one door, the room was in fact entirely empty, which was just as well for Marco as he used almost the full space to set himself right.

Lina crammed her body through the door of the cage and stood stretching for a moment, relishing her body's lightness, feeling the aches flowing out of her muscles.

'You like it?' she asked, aware that this was his first brush with micro-gee, at least that he would remember.

Marco laughed, bouncing gingerly several feet into the air then landing with such care that he might have been doing this all his life. 'I think so. . .' he said cautiously, 'yeah.'

'Well, we're going further,' Lina said. 'Come on.'

There were no handlines here – no handholds of any kind, in fact – and they moved in slow-motion, pushing themselves from wall to floor to ceiling, swimming through the air.

She led Marco through the door into a series of cramped passages with tight crawlspaces leading off into total darkness on either side. They passed a doorless room where some huge and dirty machine lay in disuse, partially covered by a faded green tarpaulin that was tied across its body with nylon rope. Dust lay thickly on all surfaces. The LED lights were far-spaced and weak – the minimum required to actually see. The ceiling was low enough to make Lina bend her neck. Little clanks and groans could be heard, thrumming faintly in the air as if reverberated through the station's structure to be concentrated on this central space.

They came to a ladder and Lina flew up it, propelling herself easily with little touches from her hands. She called Marco after her.

The hub of Macao Station, at its core, was basically a metal cylinder about five metres across and almost fifty metres long. There were two ropes strung between sturdy hooks embedded in the curved wall, crossing each other in the centre of the space. The flat ends of the cylinder, far to Lina's left and right, were large circular windows framed by concentric steel bands – real windows, not the electronic viewscreens that the rest of the station was equipped with. The belt shimmered and shuffled on one side, dark jewels on black velvet. On the other, a host of far-away stars.

Marco emerged carefully from the hatch to float next to her, the very tip of one shoe just touching the curved floor.

'Mum. . .' he said quietly. 'It's *awesome*. . .'

'Regard!' said Lina grandly. She spread her arms to the sides like a woman about to dive into water, and jumped. She floated slowly into the centre of the cylinder, poised equidistant between those two round windows. For a moment, she hung there impossibly above Marco's head, arms and legs swimming, feeling light-headed and unreal, caught in perfect equilibrium at the centre of Macao's great wheel, effectively weightless. Marco uttered a wordless cry of surprise and amazement, then Lina grabbed onto one of the ropes and pulled. She fell, upwards and away from Marco, twisting her body and laughing aloud. She landed with a grace that surprised even her, knees bent and looking upwards at him, grinning foolishly and still gripping the rope in one hand.

Her hair was floating around her head as if caught by a strong wind and she tried to smooth it back into place, then said with a casual sniff, 'And that's how it's done.' She jumped into the air and turned a perfect slow-motion somersault.

'Whoa!' cried Marco. 'Let me try!'

He launched himself, but too hard, and flew right across the cylinder to land beside Lina, bounce, then ricochet off again to land clockwise from her, a few metres away. The surface of the floor gripped him and applied the requisite dab of rotational velocity, pinning him very gently in place. He lay there laughing and barely daring to move, clearly aware that the slightest touch would send him flying again.

'Gently!' said Lina. 'More gently than you think, even. You need to give a little push counter-spinwards and up, shedding the last bit of rotation as you fly. It's a knack. On the floor of this room you have an effective weight of less than one-hundredth what you're used to. In your case I guess that means maybe four hundred grams.'

'Wow,' he gasped again, looking down at her. Outside the windows, the view rotated slowly, asteroid belt on one side, star-speckled space on the other. 'It feels weird. How come we never came here before?'

'I guess I just forgot about it,' Lina admitted with a shrug. She pushed off again, into the centre of the drum, where she grabbed onto the rope and allowed herself to turn with it. Marco, just above her, was attempting to right himself. 'I used to come here when I was sad, I suppose. I always found it a good place to think. Most people seem to have forgotten that it's here, or they never knew. Occasionally someone goes up the other spoke to service the mass drivers or the receiver, but I don't think anyone comes this far. I always kept it to myself.'

Marco pushed off and drifted into the air, snaring the rope next to her and holding on. 'Are you sad now?' he asked her frankly, face to face with her. His T-shirt billowed around his body, too big for him, really. He'd inherited it off Ella's son Clay, who was slightly larger-built than Marco. 'Is that why you remembered about it?'

Lina looked into his eyes – *her* eyes, really, that same living green as hers, and answered honestly: 'I suppose so, honey.' She'd never told Marco about Sal's brief affair with his father, which made it probably the only thing she had ever kept from him. 'Sal was a good friend. I'd known her a long time,' she explained. And at least *that* was true.

Marco embraced her briefly with one arm, keeping hold of the rope with the other. 'Show me that somersault again,' he said, grinning at her.

'Okay,' Lina agreed. She pushed off from the rope, flew backwards away from Marco and hit the floor feet-first. Using the rebound, she bounced away and executed another somersault, this one even more graceful than the first. She realised as she landed again that she was laughing aloud.

It didn't take long for Marco to become a pro. His second somersault was as good as hers, his next one even better. Before long they were flying across the hub together, criss-crossing, hitting the floor and spinning away again, laughing and grinning and enjoying their time together. Lina had always found that the journey to the hub, through the awesome heights of the station, had given her clear perspective on events within her own life. And the weightless effect at the station's very centre had a way of freeing the mind, as it freed the body from its usual stresses and strains. And now, with Marco here as well, she was having the most fun she'd had in years.

They threw each other into the air, jumped and flipped and twirled like ballet dancers, pushed each other, bounced from wall to wall and eventually came to rest dead-centre again, clutching the rope and breathing hard despite the micro-gee.

Lina's gaze happened to settle on one of the windows. The belt hung silent outside, like something lying in wait. Her good mood drained away, like water through her fingers, into that endless space, leaving her feeling suddenly hollow and sick. Marco was saying something beside her, but she didn't hear him. There was only the belt, rotating just before her face, just beyond that circle of glasspex. . . hypnotic, almost. . . an icy, endless swathe of textured space. She stared at it for some time, and as she did so a thought came to her, revelatory in its undeniable truth: she hated it. She hated this wasteland, this soulless desert. It had killed her friend – *minced* her – and yet it carried relentlessly on as if nothing had ever happened. Humans had no place in this cosmic milling-machine. Marco was right. They should go to Platini. *Yeah*, she thought. *And maybe, if a shuttle ever comes, we will do.*

Something was out there. . . Lina craned her neck, squinting at the window. She wasn't sure, but she thought she saw the gas-plume of a lone ship, slipping out of sight and away into the belt.

'But all the ships are grounded,' she whispered, feeling her eyebrows tighten in a frown.

'Mum?' cried Marco's voice. 'Mum!' Lina realised that he was shaking her by the elbow.

She turned to face him, feeling strange and disjointed. 'Eh?' she managed to gasp.

'Mum, what is it?' asked Marco, clearly concerned. He floated in front of her, small and perfect and vital in his oversized shirt.

Lina grabbed him and embraced him and they floated away from the rope and down towards the curved metal of the floor. 'Nothing,' she said. 'It's nothing. Don't worry.'

CHAPTER TWENTY

'You've exceeded my expectations,' said the crazy dragon-man. He was floating just inside the mouth of the boarding tube that clamped the asteroid to the shuttle. The restraining device had been magnetted onto the rim of the tube, tauntingly reminding Carver as he worked that he was *Prisoner* Carver – *Prisoner* Carver, and not *Freeman* Carver any more. It didn't occur to him once that this was maybe his own fault, the ultimate outcome of the crimes he had committed back on Aitama. No – he blamed the crazy dragon-loving son-of-a-bitch who had now returned to make his life, he supposed, that little bit worse again.

Carver shot a hate-filled glare at both the device and the man floated next to it, then fired up the cutter again to exclude the possibility of the bastard talking to him any more. The cutter actually created a fair amount of heat and humidity when it was in operation, but as soon as it stopped the cold began to creep back and the cave rapidly became unbearably cold again.

Before the man had left to return to the station he had shown Carver how to bore the rock pin into the face and attach his harness to it. This prevented him from simply floating backwards away from the face as he applied the plasma cutter – a massive and ungainly piece of equipment that filled the cavern with ringing, echoing peals of sound that overlayed each other into one deafening collage. The noise didn't seem to be a product of the actual cutting, the melting of plasma through rock, but rather was generated inside the machine itself, which seemed a bit fucking unnecessary to Carver, but there you were. He was almost getting used to it.

He agreed with the crazy dragon-man on one point though: he *had* made good progress into the face, especially considering how laborious the process was. First, holding the cutter's muzzle some

123

few inches from the rock, he had to inscribe a circle for each cut, angling the beam inwards to create a cone-shape. This was not always altogether simple, though. Sometimes, the cut didn't meet up properly and he had to repeat it, sometimes more than once. Or the cut piece wouldn't release easily from the face and he had to insert another rock pin, then use this as a handle to yank the chunk out.

He had started off with big pieces, figuring this the least work, propelling them overhand into a distant corner of the cavern. However, when one of these, launched a little too hard, came bouncing back towards him as he worked and almost took his head off, he began to cut smaller pieces, of about a hand's breadth at the wide end. And as the face gradually shifted and retreated, he had to adjust his harness-point, which could take several minutes each time.

Once or twice, he had stopped, floating dazedly in the darkness. It was all just too surreal. Was he *really* doing this? *Really*? He'd considered just turning the cutter on the crazy dragon-man when – *if* – he returned, imagining the thrill he would feel as the bright plasma scythed through his body, vapourising blood and tissue as it went. He'd imagined the way the crazy dragon-man would scream, and how satisfying that would be to hear. But then he had imagined starving to death in this nightmarish tomb of cold stone, his fingers burning with frostbite, the shadows that danced in his suit-light his only companions as he slowly succumbed to madness and death, and had thought better of it. He'd wondered if he could torture the code out of the man, but somehow he knew the man would die before giving it to him. *He's insane, after all*, Carver had reminded himself glumly. And anyway, the crazy dragon-man usually held onto the restraining device when he was around, making it impossible to actually approach him.

So he'd worked. And he'd hoped that the crazy dragon-man would return, after whatever business he had to attend to on the station was completed. *And the bastard might as well be pleased with what I've done when he gets back*, he'd thought. So Carver hadn't just worked; for the first time in his life of crime he'd actually worked *hard*, worked until he'd thought he might pass out, then continued anyway, pushing through the barrier of darkness that threatened to descend across his vision.

And now the crazy dragon-man was back. Well, whoopee. *Be careful what you wish for*, he warned himself.

The man landed near to Carver, braking his flight against the surface of the rock with one hand. He waited patiently, clinging to the rock like a white bat, staring at the side of Carver's head.

With a sigh, Carver released the trigger turned towards the crazy dragon-man, his pinkish face contorted with barely-restrained anger. 'What?' he asked coldly.

'You should eat something,' said the man. 'And sleep. I can dig for a bit.'

Carver wanted to bite him, maybe headbutt him in his smug, happily insane face, but of course he didn't. 'Okay,' he said, holding out the cutter to the man.

The man shook his head. 'Bring it with you,' he said. 'I'll come with you into the shuttle, with the restraining device. We'll find you some food, then I'll leave the device by the co-pilot's seat and you can get some sleep there.'

Carver was instinctively reluctant to agree to anything this man had to say, but he had to admit that food and sleep sounded better than more interminable hours of cutting through rock in this icy hole. He nodded, not dignifying the man with a verbal response.

The man pushed off from the rock-face towards the tube that led back into the service deck of the shuttle, fishlike and surprisingly agile in the micro-gee. He unclipped the restraining device from the tube and checked its little screen as he went. Carver followed a little more clumsily, encumbered by the cutter, which he had made sure was in safe mode. He missed the tube and had to grope, one-handed, across the rock, dragging himself into it while holding the cutter in the other hand. He spilled through in a disorderly landslide of limbs.

The man was already at the other end of the tube, silhouetted

125

against the light from the shuttle, his breath pluming in the cold, waiting for Carver to catch up. They made their way into the machine rooms, where ribbed tanks of compressed gases lined the walls. The man led the way down a long ladder to the bridge, dragging himself along on handlines attached to the walls for that purpose. It was almost unbearably hot in here, especially after the the freezing cold of the asteroid.

Although the man was quiet for the moment, Carver could sense that irritating contentedness exuding from him in waves. He was humming gently under his breath, like a man happy in his work, content that he was doing his best in a tough job.

They entered the shuttle's bridge, squeezing themselves through the narrow doorway, and the man bade Carver magnet the cutter onto an equipment rack that held an assortment of battered hand-tools.

Carver looked around the bridge: it was dark and stark and oddly-angled; the surfaces and equipment well-worn; the pilot's couch stained with what looked like coffee or chocolate. A second chair sat beside the pilot's, clearly a subordinate position from the relative simplicity of the control desk in front of it – the co-pilot's chair. Carver was pretty sure these shuttles usually flew with only a single pilot, though. A third seat was positioned on the other side of the room, this one turned away from them. The large cockpit windows, actually screens arrayed across the banded expanse of the shuttle's deuterium-shielded hull, showed a grey and uninviting vista of endless, suspended rock. Soros looked impossibly distant and unreal – a dispassionate eye watching them from another dimension.

The man told Carver to sit on the co-pilot's seat, then went to a locker under the flight console and produced a handful of rustling plastic packets. He clambered back across a tangle of discarded clothing, presumably the pilot's, that was rising snakelike from the floor in response to some disruption of the air. He became caught-up, briefly, and Carver thought what an excellent moment it would be to rush the bastard. His fingers clenched, as if already seizing on the crazy dragon-man's throat. But his gaze fell unavoidably on the

126

restraining device and he inwardly sighed, forcing himself to relax. *Patience*, he told himself. *Wait for the moment. Just chill.*

'Ship's rations, I'm afraid,' said the man, floating in front of Carver, as if the poor menu choice was the worst injustice he was inflicting on his prisoner. 'There's water here somewhere, too.'

'Whatever,' Carver answered, trying to sound as disinterested as possible, even though his stomach betrayed him with a treacherously loud growl.

The man threw Carver the packets, which felt like they were filled with sand and were stamped with such uninspiring legends as *CHICKEN-STYLE DINNER* and *SWEET DESSERT*, then dragged himself off to retrieve the water he had spoken of. He stuck the restraining device onto the console opposite Carver, where he had no choice but to look at the bloody thing. The legend *ONE PRISONER – IN RANGE* glowed on its little screen. When the man came back he was grinning sheepishly and holding a metal water bottle.

'It's a bit warm,' he said apologetically, offering it to Carver.

The bottle was, indeed, almost too hot to touch when Carver unscrewed it clumsily with his gloved hand and raised it to his mouth. 'Shit!' he cried, whipping it away from his face and rubbing at his lips. 'Where've you been keeping this thing?'

'See?' said the man brightly, pushing over to the pilot's chair, where he strapped himself down and sat watching Carver eat, the asteroid belt an eerie backdrop behind him.

Carver was initially disturbed by that piercing, relentless stare, but he was so hungry that he soon forgot the man was even there. He ate *CHICKEN-STYLE DINNER*, followed it with *MEAT AND POTATOES*, then sat gulping warm water, trying to wash the lumps down his gullet and into his stomach. The contents were actually not as hot as the bottle itself, which was good because he was seriously thirsty. He drank deeply and sighed with satisfaction, leaning back against the head-rest of the co-pilot's seat, eyes closed. He ached all over now that he had stopped moving. He arched his back and stretched, as far as the chair would allow him to. When he looked up, the crazy dragon-man was still staring at him, looking particularly pleased with himself.

'Needed that, eh?' he asked Carver with a grin.

Carver thought he could actually *see* the madness, capering behind the man's eyes like a dancing jester. Despite this, though, he couldn't help but feel a little happier now that he had eaten. The endless hours of cutting in the asteroid seemed like a distant dream, something he could almost laugh about now. 'Yeah,' he agreed, trying not to smile himself. 'Guess so.'

The man nodded agreeably, then turned to look out into the belt. He sat this way in silence for a while, and then he turned back to Carver and said suddenly, 'It's beautiful, isn't it?'

Carver considered this while he opened *SWEET DESSERT*. It proved awkward, so he took his gloves off, just casting them aside to float dreamily away into a corner of the bridge. 'Yeah,' he said. 'In a way I guess it is.'

This seemed to please the man, who smiled, nodded and turned back to the window.

'So,' said Carver, pausing to bite the silver packet open, having failed to tear it along the suggested line, 'how many other inmates are there on this station of yours?'

The man turned back to him slowly, looking distant, his eyes unfocused. 'Hmm?' he asked.

'How many others are there on the station?' asked Carver again. He tried the substance from the packet. It seemed to be basically just textured sugar, but that was fine with him.

'Well,' said the man, 'there's a hundred and eleven – no, a hundred and *ten*–' he corrected himself, 'and then there are fifteen prisoners at the moment. Why?'

Carver shrugged. 'Just wondered,' he said.

'You're thinking about getting them out, aren't you?' he asked. He wagged a finger at Carver – *You're a naughty boy!* – but he didn't actually look pissed.

Carver shrugged again. Maybe this guy wasn't a *complete* fuckhead after all. *Crazy*, yes, but maybe not actually bad all the way through. Probably not actually stupid, either. Maybe just misunderstood, like Carver himself. Maybe he could be reasoned with. Carver wondered passingly what the dragon-man's eyes would taste like. He imagined biting down on one of them, maybe bursting it. 'I just wondered,' he repeated.

'It's all right,' the man said. 'The dragon told me you would.'

And there it was again. Just when Carver had thought he might be able to make some progress with the guy, there it was again. The bloody *dragon*. How could you reason with a man who listened, first and foremost, to the voices in his head? And what if – *when* – they dug as far as they could into this fucking rock, and the man found nothing there? What then? He sounded polite and almost human at times, but Carver didn't kid himself that there wasn't something badly wrong with the crazy dragon-man. Even if he *could* be reasoned with, he surely couldn't be *trusted*. Would he try to murder Carver when his little dig turned up nothing at all? Carver, despite having mercilessly butchered innocent people himself, feared his own demise as much as anybody.

'This. . . *dragon*. . .' Carver began cautiously, watching the man's face for any change in expression at the broaching of this touchy subject. '. . . You really think we're gonna find it? Like, buried in this asteroid?' He tipped more chemically-flavoured sugar onto his tongue and washed it down with the warm water.

'I know you think I'm insane,' said the man earnestly. 'But it *is* here.'

'How do you know that?' asked Carver, knowing that he was edging increasingly further out onto thin ice.

'It told me,' said the man simply, as if this constituted undeniable evidence.

Carver nodded, trying to look understanding. 'What, exactly, *is* it?' he asked, not really wanting to hear the answer but unable to stop himself.

'I'm not sure,' said the man thoughtfully. 'Maybe it's some ancient alien that was buried here; maybe some sort of sentinel to guard the belt; maybe. . .' he trailed off, turning to look out of the window again. 'It doesn't really like to be asked,' he said at last.

'Why can only you hear it, do you think?' Carver asked. When the man turned back to him his face was trembling and twitching, as if tears were threatening to overcome him. Carver realised that he had pushed it too far. That was, if anything, his major character flaw. That had been the problem with the woman on Aitama – he'd just gone a little too far. And now he'd done it again. *Never question the delusions of a madman*, he scolded himself.

'What does it matter?' the man asked emotionally. 'What does it matter when you don't even believe me?' His mood had switched again, and now he sounded like a sulky three-year-old, full of indignant anger. He stared at Carver for a moment, trembling, then looked down at his knees. He shook his head once, smartly, as if to clear it.

'Sorry,' said Carver experimentally. It was a word he had little experience with, but he'd noticed that it could be effective with people sometimes.

There was a long and uncomfortable silence while the man sat that way, head bowed and hands squeezed together in his lap. When he looked up again, though, his face wore its previous expression of indulgent good humour. 'Oh, it's okay,' he said. 'You'll see, I suppose. In time.'

'Maybe I will,' Carver agreed diplomatically. *Crisis averted*, he thought, grateful that he apparently wouldn't be getting shocked again. He looked around the cockpit, trying to think of a way to change the subject. At last, his mind snagged on something, and the question was out of his mouth before he could stop it: 'So where's the pilot, then?'

The man grinned in a slightly embarrassed way. 'Ah. . .' he said, holding up one finger as if to say *Now* that's *the question!* He released himself from the pilot's seat, pushed off, and floated across the room to the navigator's station. Carver watched him, hypnotised. The man braced himself against the far wall and spun the seat around.

In the navigator's seat sat the shattered wreckage of what had once, undeniably, been a human being. It was dressed in a one-piece flight suit, the original colour of which had probably been blue, but which was now slathered almost entirely in dried blood. The person's skull (it was impossible to tell if it had been a man or

130

a woman) was not just caved in but almost completely obliterated, and a large spanner lay across the figure's lap, matted with clumps of flesh and hair. This tool had clearly been utilised in an excessive manner: the pilot had been not just *killed*, but deliberately *destroyed*. Carver felt a lump in his throat. He imagined this gently-smiling madman beating the already-dead pilot again and again and again – as many times as the voice in his head instructed, Carver supposed. He sat, staring and stunned. Contradictory emotions bloomed within him: awe; shock; excitement; sick pleasure; fear for his own safety. Mainly the latter.

The man's sheepish grin extended slowly into something more sharklike – predatory and primal – and he turned the seat away again as if suggesting that maybe they should just forget about it. Carver sat staring, his mouth open and a thin trail of food particles drifting out of it like exhaled smoke.

'Yeah,' said the man, as if Carver had asked him a question. His eyes looked as if they were focused on something on the distant horizon. 'About that. . .'

CHAPTER TWENTY-ONE

The man worked hard, as was expected of him. The dragon had never claimed that his work as its emissary would be easy. In fact, it had warned him that sometimes he might find his tasks difficult, even *unsavoury* to carry out. And hadn't that been the case already? It would be worth it in the end, though, he knew. Good medicine always tasted bad, right? He mentally shrugged and released one of his rock pins, holding the cutter by one handle behind his back, out of the way. He moved the pin to a new position, moved the other one, then fired up the cutter again.

'You are doing well,' said the dragon suddenly. This was the first time it had spoken to him for some hours now. Oddly, despite the noise of the cutter, he didn't have any trouble hearing it. In fact, he thought its voice was a little louder than it had been before. He supposed that now that there was less material between him and it. He might have been imagining it – maybe it was just wishful thinking – but he certainly *thought* it was louder. And that must mean that he was making progress.

'Thank you,' replied the man quietly, concentrating on inscribing a cone shape with the plasma beam. It occurred to him how easy it would be to have an accident with the thing, an accident that could be as tragic as Sal's accident had been. *Yeah,* a little voice in his head told him, *but that* wasn't *exactly an accident, was it?* He ignored the voice – after all, you were crazy if you listened to voices in your head, right? – and applied himself anew to the task at hand.

'I know you are unsure about the prisoner, Emissary,' said the dragon.

The man paused, releasing the trigger of the cutter, head cocked. *How does the dragon know these things?* he wondered in amazement. He was awed by the depth of its empathy. It really seemed to be the only one who understood him these days. 'Yeah,' he admitted. 'I suppose he just seems so. . .' He trailed off, knowing the dragon understood.

'I know,' it said sagely. He could feel it breathing all around him, filling the cold, rocky womb-space with its warming life-essence. He longed to *see* it – *touch* it – marvel at its beauty in the flesh. He wondered, not for the first time, what it looked like. 'He is something of an unlikeable character,' confessed the dragon. 'But he has his uses. He is required to work here while you fulfil other duties for me on the station. I could hardly have *him* do those other tasks, could I? It is *you* who are my emissary.'

The man felt his frozen face flush with pride. He involuntarily took a deep breath, puffing out his chest. 'Well, I, I. . .' he blustered, overcome by the flattery. The shadows loomed large around him, layers of living velvet that crowded round like eavesdroppers.

'Do you trust me?' asked the dragon, a sharp edge concealed within its voice.

It was testing him again – it tested him often, probing him for any doubts. But if it knew his mind so well, why was the testing necessary? The man's brow furrowed in confusion. *It* may understand *him*, but he was starting to think *he* would never understand *it*.

'Well, of course,' said the man. 'Of course I do.'

'Good,' said the dragon. 'Because you know I want to help. My methods may seem strange at times, but you must retain your trust in me. You are my emissary, and you must believe that I have your best interests at heart, although some of your tasks may be difficult at times. The man, Carver, is a violent and savage oaf, but he has a purpose. His purpose is to dig. Your purpose is to oversee him, to be in charge of my – *our* – operations here. That means that when he has rested, he will dig again, and you will have another task.'

'Task?' asked the man, re-positioning the cutter against the rock-face. He flexed his fingers on the handle of the machine – they were beginning to seize up in the cold.

'Yes,' said the dragon. 'There is something else that needs to be addressed back at the station. You must not be missed there yet. Not yet.'

'Addressed,' parroted the man. He felt strangely detached, fuzzy-headed, as happened when the dragon spoke to him. 'Not be missed. . .'

'That's right,' said the dragon encouragingly, as if to a child who had understood a tricky maths problem. 'When he awakes, the prisoner will dig. And you will return to the station.'

'Return to the station,' repeated the man.

'Where you will do something for me.'

'Will this be another. . . *difficult* task?'

The dragon sighed sadly. The man felt the weight of its emotion, pushing down on him. He wished he could help it more, somehow. The dragon had a very great burden to shoulder. 'I fear it may be,' said the dragon. 'I fear it may be.'

CHAPTER TWENTY-TWO

Lina woke up early, her internal clock scrambled by the unexpected change from late-shifts to no-shifts. Even on non-work days, such as this was, she usually stayed as close as possible to her work-day schedule. But she had crashed out on the night of Sal's accident some three or four hours earlier than usual, and now she felt both tired and restless at the same time, completely unfulfilled by her sleep.

She tried to remain in bed, reading an ebook on one of her datasheets, but it was a particularly dreary tale about abused children in the slums of Old Earth, and it only served to depress her. She cast the datasheet aside around seven in the morning and got up, trying to make as little noise as possible.

She dressed, in a full set of clean, non-work clothes, and made a fair effort at dragging a brush through her hair. One minute she was looking at herself in the mirror, feeling dreamy with tiredness, disassociated from the reflection of her own face, and the next minute she found that she was standing in front of the window and staring instead into that.

Had she really seen a ship heading out into the belt last night? No, surely that was impossible. All the ships were grounded, right? And somebody must be keeping an eye on them, to make sure they stayed that way. Right?

She gazed out at the asteroid field: an ugly mass of matter; rocks that wore bright patches of ore like skin infections; trailing away, as always, to the very edge of sight. 'Maybe,' she said to herself in a whisper. 'Maybe not.' She thought of the shadow from her dream, chasing her implacably through the airless dark – a streamer of nightmarish, hungry intent. She thought of Sal, whose remains had had to be vacuumed up. She remembered the sound of Sal's tooth ricocheting off the front of her Kay and she shivered, shaking her head to dispel the image, and turned the window off again.

By the time Marco woke up, Lina had washed herself, brushed her teeth, and begun to feel a bit more sprightly. The bad taste of the air was more pronounced than ever, though, and somehow the added flavour of the toothpaste made it even worse. She wondered when Marco would notice it. And when everybody else would notice it, for that matter.

She was re-organising her wardrobe when Marco appeared, blinking, at her door. His opening line was a casual, 'What's that smell?'

Lina looked up from the pile of clothes that surrounded her on the floor, feeling absurdly guilty, as if it was her fault. 'Nasty, isn't it?' she said.

'Is it the air system?' he asked bluntly, drawing his dressing gown tighter around himself.

'I suppose so,' she said quietly, half expecting this to have a terrifying effect on the boy. She felt her own pulse quicken, as if on his behalf.

'Mmm,' he grunted, the matter seemingly settled, then wandered off to the small bathroom.

Lina breathed a sigh of relief and began to replace items into the metal wardrobe in almost exactly the same order they had originally been in. She knew she was just finding herself a distraction, but she didn't care – it seemed like what she needed. When she finished this task she went to find Marco in his room.

He was lying on his bed with earphones in and eyes shut. Lina didn't know what he was listening to. Marco seemed to procure a surprisingly large volume of new music from his school friends. His tastes seemed to favour no particular genre, and Lina tried hard not to influence him, although some of the sub-scream and hexno artists from Platini were, honestly, terrible.

She tapped him on the knee and he looked up, removing one of the earphones. 'Yeah?' he asked.

'I'm gonna go to the canteen and grab us some breakfast, okay?'

'Yeah, cool,' he said, replacing the earphone and shutting her out again.

It occurred to Lina how like a teenager he was already becoming, and a pang of nostalgia went through her as she gazed at his uncommunicative form. His amazement in the micro gravity of the station's hub had made him briefly childlike again last night, but now the effect seemed to have worn off. The two of them had always been good friends, and she dreaded the possibility that he might become a surly teen in the near future. *Who*, she thought, *will I have then?* She wondered about Platini, and the life they might be able to make for themselves if they could ever get there. She let herself out, and headed to the canteen in a strange mood of contented sadness.

When she got there she found that she had missed the worst of the rush, and she didn't have long to stand in line. She chatted idly to Si Davis as she waited, exchanging small talk, deliberately skirting the big issues. Si was as rude and ebullient as ever, and he fell into a general and obscenity-littered rant about *The Company* – a favourite subject of his. Lina let him run, smiling and nodding at sympathetic intervals, until he reached the front of the queue.

Amy Stone, sitting behind one of the grimy canteen tables with a datasheet in front of her, smiled a thin, efficient little smile that was virtually devoid of actual warmth, and said, 'Good morning, Simon.'

'Hey, er, Amy,' replied Si in his usual, inappropriately booming voice. 'What's for brekkie?' Lina knew as well as he did what was for breakfast, having waited while a small stream of hungry prospectors all received identical rations from the glum-looking Jayce, who stood behind Amy's left shoulder.

'Bread, de-hy eggs, coffee, powdered milk,' recited Amy robotically.

'Mmm!' enthused Si falsely, rubbing his stomach. 'Thanks, Farsight!'

Amy stared at him levelly. It was a stare that Lina thought could probably have wilted a flower, and indeed it had this effect on Si, whose grin faltered and then slid clean off his face. 'My name is Amy,' she said. 'Not Farsight. And we're all in this together, Simon.'

'Er, sure. . .' he answered, trying to avoid her eye. Lina suppressed the urge to giggle. Amy was pure battleaxe, but Lina rather liked that about her. She took no prisoners.

'Jayce,' Amy said over her shoulder, and Jayce stepped forwards, looking apologetic, holding Si's meagre breakfast rations in a single shrink-wrapped bundle. Si took the parcel without further comment then squeezed past Lina and out of the canteen, looking somewhat crestfallen.

Lina received her own parcel and took it back to her quarters, finding Marco in exactly the posture and position she had left him. She busied herself reconstituting eggs and toasting bread (*burning* bread, in the case of the first slice) then called Marco through to the table. Surprisingly, he heard her and came happily enough, presumably propelled by his stomach despite the unexciting promise of the new rationing regime. He seemed to be in fair spirits as he ate, wolfing his own food and then finishing Lina's, which she pretended not to want so that he wouldn't feel bad about it. She wondered how long the station's supplies were going to last, dished out in these conservative increments. Presumably someone had calculated that they would be okay until the next shuttle. Her mind kept trying to ask her what if *that* one didn't come, but she drowned out thought with small talk.

As soon as Marco had put his fork down and wiped his chin with his sleeve – a gesture that, as a mother, Lina found it hard to approve of – there was a knock on the door.

'I'll get it,' Lina said, already rising.

She opened the door, half expecting bad news of some sort, and was thus pleasantly surprised to find a grinning Eli standing there, hands deep in the pockets of his traditional flight suit.

'Hey,' he said simply, walking past her with the unquestioning confidence of a long-time friend. Lina shut the door and followed him back inside.

'Eli!' cried Marco with undisguised pleasure. 'How's it going?'

'Oh, you know,' said Eli, twisting one of the dining chairs

around and sitting on it backwards, elbows resting on the backrest. 'Functioning as normal, pretty much, despite the company's attempts to inflict malnutrition on me. And you guys?'

'Oh, you know, bearing up,' answered Lina for the both of them. Eli shot her a look, which although brief, said it all. They were all bearing up because they *had* to. Death in the family, missing shuttle, emergency rations. . . What could they do but just carry on?

'Is the game still on?' Marco asked, missing the significance of the moment, or else choosing to ignore it. He looked innocently up into Eli's weathered face.

'Er, no, champ, it's cancelled actually,' answered Eli apologetically.

Lina glanced back at the window behind her, where asteroids drifted like ghost ships. *There*, she thought. *That's where all the trouble has come from. That damn belt. First you kill Sal, then you take our shuttle – I don't know how I know that, but I do – and now you've taken my son's football game away. I hate you. And we're going to leave you before you hurt us any more.*

'Ohhh. . .' groaned Marco, childish disappointment creasing his face. A few years ago that expression would have been the prelude to tears, but now he simply sighed and shook his head, suppressing his disappointment.

'I thought maybe you and I could go down into Bay Seven and have a kick-around, just the two of us, instead.'

Lina's heart bloomed with warmth at that – Eli was, as she had said herself, one of the good guys.

'Yeah!' exclaimed Marco, coming alive again instantly. But his expression became suspicious quickly. 'Is that allowed, though? Nobody's supposed to go in there, I thought. Only specially authorised games, right?'

'Well that's right, buddy,' agreed Eli, helping himself to the coffee that Lina had left on the table – cold, now, as well as disgusting – and draining it in one gulp. 'But we *have* special authorisation, you and I.' He puffed his chest out importantly. 'I have friends,' he said grandly, 'in high places.'

'Cool! Nice one, Eli! Can we go now?' Marco was already up out of his seat.

Eli arched an eyebrow at Lina, who felt herself beaming back at him. 'Sure, go on,' she said. 'You kids have fun.'

'Thanks, Mum!'

'Yeah, thanks, Mum!' Eli imitated. 'Got your ball handy, Marco?'

Marco dashed out of the room to get it.

Eli turned to Lina, his battered face concerned. 'So how you really doing?' he asked, *sotto voce*.

Lina looked into his soft grey eyes and saw her own worries mirrored there. 'As I said – bearing up. Scared, sad. . . You know. . . the air, it's. . . I. . . I want to take Marco to Platini,' she stammered, unaware that she had intended to tell him this, and suddenly feeling an inexplicable pang of guilt, as if she was admitting some secret and perverse desire. Part of her wanted to scream, *The tooth! I saw Sal's tooth bounce off the screen of my ship! I saw her fucking tooth, Eli, and that was it for me, that was the end of the line! I simply cannot take it any more!* She felt tears welling in her eyes and squeezed them shut until she knew it was safe to open them again.

Eli was nodding slowly, staring back at her, and she felt that she was seeing through a mask, seeing the real man behind the laughter lines. He was becoming an *old* man – even he was not invulnerable. This thought strengthened her resolve. Time had moved on, but it was still not too late for her to make a change. She hoped.

'I think you should,' Eli said, and Lina felt a genuine gratitude swell inside her.

Just then, Marco's football flew into the room, rebounding off one of the wall-cupboards, making Lina jump. It was followed by Marco himself, who stopped it deftly with one foot. His face was grinning beneath his mass of golden curls, and he looked like any kid without a care in the world.

'Come on then!' Marco yelled, apparently surprised to see Eli still sitting at the table.

'Right!' Eli exclaimed, leaping up with a lightness that Lina knew was at least partly artificial. 'Later, Lina.' He cuffed her on the arm, kicked his chair back in, and went to the door.

Marco ran around the table and gave her a brief hug. 'See you, Mum,' he said.

'Enjoy your game,' she answered, releasing him.

And without further ado, the two of them dashed out, Marco dribbling the ball as he went. The door shut behind them, erasing them from reality and leaving her alone in the cool greyness of her quarters. She sat at the table, looking around herself and wishing she had gone with them.

Presently, she found that she was looking at the belt again, her gaze unconsciously and inevitably drawn to it. It made her feel cold inside. And uneasy.

Farsight claimed those rocks had value, but Lina knew the truth. The belt was worthless. In the grand scheme of things it mattered precisely jack shit. It wasn't worth anybody's life: not Sal's; not hers; not anybody's. She wondered if she would ever be prepared to fly through it again. *Well*, she thought, *hopefully once more. When I'm on my way to Platini with my son.*

Darkness reigned out there, cold and infinite. She wondered how many dispersed molecules of Sal Newman still drifted in that hostile void like so much dust on the solar wind.

She busied herself by cleaning the steel-tiled floor of the main living-slash-dining room, stacking the sofa, table and chairs in one corner. She didn't even care that, despite her work, the floor still remained stubbornly stained and grimy, as if it was *made* of dirt and all she could do was abrade the layers. When she was done she put everything back and sat for a minute on the sofa, at something of a loss for what to do next. Lacking any better idea for the moment, she flicked the holo on.

For a while she watched a documentary about the new and ambitious engineering works commissioned on Platini Alpha – the Grand Chasm Bridge, the new spaceport terminal, the vast network of irrigation aqueducts – but the longing this induced in her, for solid ground and civilisation, soon became unbearable and she began to flick channels.

She was surprised to find that channel ninety-nine, reserved for in-station broadcasts, was actually running. It showed the dark and cavernous space of Bay Seven, where the game was supposed to have been held today. Clearly the channel had gone live in response to some automated routine, even though the actual game had been cancelled.

And there was Marco, chasing his brightly-coloured football across the bottom left corner of the screen. Devoid of a human operator, the camera wasn't tracking the ball, and Marco quickly dashed out of shot again. This time Eli came into the picture, looking, to be honest, a little overworked trying to keep up with the boy. To his credit, though, he darted to one side swiftly enough to intercept the ball that Marco had long-bombed towards one of the goals, controlling it and moving off out of shot with it. Lina smiled to herself, ignoring the small twinge of guilt that drifted through her mind attached to the phrase *You're spying on them*. She knew they wouldn't mind.

The ball zoomed across the shot again, away into the shadowed depths of Bay Seven. The two figures – man and boy – chased after it, silent as ghosts, jostling, gone again. Back again. . . gone again. . . back again. . . gone again. . . Blades of darkness towered above them – angular flints of shadow. Two flitting figures in a holo cube. . . seeds of life caught in the dead matrix of this awful outpost at the end of the universe.

Lina reached out and killed the holo, realising as she did so that her hand was shaking. She lifted it to her face and stared at it, unable to believe that her body could betray her thus. Then she put both hands over her face and, her mind entirely blank and void of reason, began to cry.

CHAPTER TWENTY-THREE

'You can't go in there,' said Ella Kown, appearing as if by magic at Lina's elbow and making her jump guiltily.

'Ella!' she cried, whirling around. Ella's face looked serious beneath her stubbled crew-cut, neutral and stern, but Lina saw the glint of humour in her eyes. 'You startled me.'

'That,' said Ella seriously, 'is my job. You know – startling people who're sneaking around the hangars when they shouldn't be.'

Absurdly, Lina felt herself blush. Ella was one of those people who could make her feel about six years old. 'Yeah, I mean no, I was. . .' She trailed off, unable to justify herself. 'Sorry.'

'That's okay,' said Ella, smiling now. 'I was going to shoot you, but you know how much paperwork I'd have if I did.'

Lina leant against the convex slab of the hangar door, putting her head back and closing her eyes. She laughed tiredly.

'You okay, Li?' Ella asked, stepping closer.

Lina looked back at her. Although she was solidly-built, tall and strong, Ella looked almost small there, dwarfed beneath the giant rows of pallet-racking. Blueish lights far up in the ceiling cast her in a weak, ethereal glow. 'Yeah. No. . .' She faltered, genuinely unable to say for sure. She wished people would stop asking her that.

'Come with me,' said Ella decisively. She turned and led the way through a smaller side-door and into the warehouse office, from where the one-man team of Charlie Stenning usually controlled stock and storage in the warehouse. Charlie was absent now, and it took Ella a while to find the manual control for the lights, which had failed to come on when they opened the door. The room was bare and basic – much like the rest of the station – with a simple desk and computer terminal in one corner. There was a not-quite-pornographic poster of two women stuck to the wall above a small rubbish bin, but to Lina it just looked kind of sad in the almost aggressively-soulless surroundings – a desperate attempt to impose some humanity on this bare steel casket.

Ella sat on the desk and kicked the chair out towards Lina, who stopped it, spun it round, and sat.

'You wanna tell me what you're doing down here, Lina?' asked Ella without prelude. Noticing the crease that this question brought to Lina's brow, she added, 'As a friend, not a security officer, that is.'

'Ella, I don't know if I'm going insane, but. . .' She found the words reluctant to come, now, here in the cold light of day, speaking to another rational human being, but she forced them: 'I thought I saw somebody flying into the belt last night.' She spread her hands, then let them fall into her lap, as if to say, *That's it, that's all I have.*

Ella nodded, considering this possibility, and Lina inwardly thanked her for not simply blowing her off straight away. 'You thought?' she asked after a while. 'Or you did?'

'Honestly, I thought,' answered Lina carefully, screwing her eyes up as if she could intensify the memory that way, examine it more closely. 'I'm not sure, Ella. But I *thought* I did.'

'Truthfully, Lina, I doubt it. If you're not sure yourself, I'd have to say it sounds unlikely. Why would anyone do that?'

Lina exhaled heavily: Now *that* was the question. 'I don't know,' she admitted. 'Why would any of the things that have happened lately happen?' She wanted to tell Ella about her dream, about the shadow in the belt, but she knew what sort of light this would cast her in. She felt she was barely hanging onto credibility as it was.

'Crazy times, right?'

'Yeah. Crazy times.'

'How are you, really, Lina? I've hardly seen you since the Sal thing.'

'The Sal thing,' Lina repeated, amazed that it could be summarised so simply. 'I think I'm all right, Ella. But I want to take

Marco to Platini on the next available shuttle.'

Ella smiled kindly, but Lina caught a hint of sympathy in there, and felt an irrational surge of annoyance at that. 'I think you should,' said Ella.

'That's what Eli said, too.'

'We all have your best interests at heart, you know. Yours and Marco's. Clay would miss him, of course – we'd *all* miss you guys – but it might be best for you. One day, me and Clay might even come and join you there.'

Lina stared more deeply into her friend's eyes. 'This has you thinking, too, doesn't it?' she asked. One of the reasons Lina was so close to Ella was their shared history: Ella also had an ex-husband somewhere in Platini system; she too had been left with her son on Macao. Lina wasn't surprised that Ella understood.

'Yeah, I guess so,' admitted Ella. She jumped down off the desk and rummaged in the drawers, taking something from the bottom one and turning round to show Lina. It was a large bottle of whisky, about two thirds full. Ella grinned broadly.

'Hey, I don't think we should drink that,' said Lina, feeling a smile trying to surface on her own face.

'Call it a customs seizure,' said Ella, spinning the cap off. Lina laughed as Ella took a swig, her face contorting. She coughed and handed the bottle over. 'Charlie won't mind,' she said, her voice comically hoarse from the drink.

Lina swigged, feeling the liquid run like fire down her throat and explode in slow motion inside her belly. 'Man!' she coughed, turning the bottle to read the label. 'Green Goddess? I don't think that's what this actually is.'

'Nah,' confirmed Ella, taking it back. 'It's not. This is the local moonshine. The ground crew have been brewing it behind the hydraulic pumps for years now.'

'Really?' Lina wondered how many other little secrets her friend was privy to.

'Hits the spot, eh?'

'I suppose so,' agreed Lina, chuckling to herself. They sat in companionable silence for a few minutes, the bottle changing hands several more times.

'I'll have somebody check the Kays, if you're really concerned, Lina, okay?' said Ella after a while. 'But you mustn't go sneaking around by yourself. If somebody *had* been tampering with the ships – which I repeat is unlikely – then the finger would inevitably come to point at you if you were to be found creeping around down here. Make sense?'

Strangely, after a few doses of Charlie's moonshine, everything was starting to make more sense. Lina nodded. 'Yeah, it does. Has the hangar been locked down all this time, then? I mean, have you had someone watching it at night?'

'Lina, why would we do that? Everyone knows the ships are grounded. Who would try to fly one? Why?' She held the bottle at arm's length, looking at it a little ruefully, then capped it and returned it to the drawer.

'I don't know,' said Lina. And then, before she could stop herself, she added, 'I think there's something wrong here. . . in the belt, or on the station. . . something. . . *happening*.' She waited a little nervously to see what effect this would have.

Ella nodded wisely, seeming to give this paranoid suspicion genuine consideration. That was one thing Lina liked about Ella – even if she thought you were wrong, she'd still listen and consider before deciding that for sure. She never just brushed somebody else's concerns aside. 'Maybe,' she said at length. 'But then, I'm not surprised, after what happened on your last shift. It'd be odd if you felt that everything was fine.'

'Yeah, I know you're right. And the Sal thing has got me shaken up. But I feel like there's more to it than that. I know that sounds entirely baseless – and I guess it is – but I can't escape the feeling that, well, there's more to it.'

'More to it?' asked Ella. Although her tone was light, her face was serious again. 'You don't mean that Sal's death could have been deliberate in some way? Do you? 'Cause that would be a pretty serious allegation.'

Lina felt her conviction suddenly collapse. That *had* been what she meant, but in truth it sounded insane, now that she heard it said out loud. Ella was right – she was just trying to deal with Sal's death, seeking some sort of culprit for what was essentially just an accident. If anybody was to blame it was those penny-pinching corporate accountants at Platini Dockyard. 'I think I'm just tired, maybe a little shocked. I know you're right, Ella, I just. . . I guess I just want someone to blame, is all.'

'Lina,' said Ella, spreading her hands benevolently, 'it's fine. And I'll ask the ground crew to check the Kays and the ISL to make sure nothing's flown.'

'Thanks, Ella.'

'I repeat: this is a perfectly natural way for you to feel, I'm sure of it. And taking Marco to Platini sounds like an excellent idea to me.'

'Well that's another thing. . .' said Lina cautiously. 'Where is our damn shuttle, Ella?'

Ella shrugged, as if it didn't matter. 'My guess? Another bloody equipment failure. I reckon it's scattered across space somewhere between here and Way Station One. I don't expect it to come now – it's just too late – but I don't suspect any sort of sinister influence beyond that of corporate greed and laxness. Don't, of course, quote me on that.'

'I suppose. It's just funny that these things have come at once.'

'Yeah,' said Ella, standing up and pulling her uniform straight. 'Regular sitcom, this frontier life.'

'Will we be okay, though?' asked Lina. 'Until the next one, I mean.'

'The food will last, under our rationing regime. We have it all worked out. They'll be hard times, but the food will last.'

'And the air?' asked Lina in a tiny voice, catching her friend's eye. 'Will that last?'

Ella sighed, as if she'd hoped not to field this question, and looked away. Lina didn't think this was a particularly good sign. 'Honestly? Who can say. Officially? It's all under control. Nik's people are working on a standalone, jury-rigged alternative system, but you didn't hear that from me. We *should* be okay. And that's the best I can do, I'm afraid.'

'And what if there *is* some kind of saboteur on board? I know you think this is all just coincidence, but. . . what if somebody is actually trying to harm us?'

Ella bit her lip, her face thoughtful again. 'Hmm. . . I'll tell my guys to keep an eye out, Lina. We've no forensics facilities here, with which I could check the scrubbers, the Kays, or whatever. All we can do is try to remain vigilant.' She fixed Lina with a piercing eye. 'I will take your concerns on board, Lina, okay? That's about all I can do at this stage.'

'Any more of that moonshine?' asked Lina, attempting to lighten the atmosphere.

Ella laughed. 'Drink on duty? Me? Perish the thought.' She moved towards Lina, a little awkwardly, and gave her a brief hug. Ella's body felt solid and strong. Lina was glad that they were friends. 'See you around, Li. Go home, will you?'

Lina released her and smiled up into her face. 'Sure. Thanks for not shooting me, Ella. I know how tempted you must have been.'

Ella waved this away. 'Oh, no more than usual,' she said, opening the door. She let Lina out first, then followed her back into the warehouse. Lina carried on towards the stairs up, as instructed, and left Ella waiting for the hangar door to cycle.

She wandered back to her quarters, feeling foolish after her interrupted attempt at junior sleuthing round the flight deck. The little voice inside her had become a voice of reason, now, and that was good. Ella's surety, her belief that nothing was wrong apart from temporary bad luck, had genuinely affected Lina, casting a new light on her own doubts. She was glad that Ella had caught her.

She let herself into her quarters, where she played chess against herself (both losing and winning) until Marco returned from his kick-around with Eli, happy but a little wired with tiredness. Eli looked even more crumpled-round-the-edges than usual, but he seemed to have enjoyed himself, too. Lina could sense that he was worried about her from the little glances he shot her here and there, but she didn't have the chance to speak to him alone and allay his fears. Feeling a hundred times better than earlier, she invited him to pool rations and stay for dinner, which he accepted.

They ate simple pasta with dried cheese and salad from the aeroponics room, which wasn't actually bad at all. Marco ate a man-sized portion, seemingly without pause for air. Eli left them alone around seven, and Marco voluntarily turned in early, which was unusual for him. Lina had just been summoning up the courage to talk to him about Platini, but she was almost relieved when he went to bed before she could actually broach the subject. Her belly full, and her mind finally at rest, sleep took her by stealth as she lay on the sofa and carried her off into a mercifully dreamless slumber.

CHAPTER TWENTY-FOUR

Lina awoke suddenly to the unmistakeable sound of an explosion, scrabbling upright in shock. The holo was off and as she sat there, eyes darting in fear, the lights slowly dimmed away to nothing and darkness grew out of the air itself, gradually filling the room. She sat, breathing heavily, trying to still her jittering heart. Then suddenly the emergency lights came on, a weak and bloody haze of red.

She stood slowly, unsure of what she intended to do, still confused by sleep. She cocked her head, listening intently. The station was ominously quiet. The refinery had been shut down since the Kays had ceased operation, but now she heard *nothing*. The silence was almost a tangible thing, an anti-sound. The sound of a thousand machines not working. Far off, somebody began shouting in a voice that warbled close to panic.

What blew up? Something blew up. . . The powerplant? Whatever it was, it had sounded big, and therefore serious. *It must have been the powerplant*, she thought fearfully, glancing up at the emergency lights. Macao was powered primarily by a low-cost fission reactor. If something had gone wrong there then they could all be dead in minutes. *Marco!* she thought frantically, and made for his room on legs that shook and jerked at the knees, threatening to betray her and spill her onto her face. She practically fell through his door, scrabbling at the frame to retain her balance.

Marco was stirring in his sleep, on the brink of waking. Lina dashed to his side and put her arms round him, making him jump and mumble something incoherent. His eyes opened and he looked up at her.

'Mum. . .'

'Honey, something's wrong with the power,' she said,

smoothing his hair and looking into his young face, which had a spectral appearance in the red light. 'I'm gonna go and try to find out what's happening.' She hoped she didn't sound as terrified as she felt. The little voice far back in her head was chanting *What's wrong now? What's wrong now? What's wrong now?*

'Eh?' he asked, trying to sit up and failing. He looked around himself blearily, noticing the emergency lighting. 'Oh,' he said in summary.

'I want you to stay here. I'll be back as soon as I can.' She peered into his face, gauging his comprehension. 'Yes?' she prompted, shaking him smartly, once, by the shoulders.

'Yeah,' he replied uncertainly, his gaze somewhat unfocused. 'Sure.' And with that, amazing and gladdening Lina in equal measure, he actually lay back down and returned immediately to sleep.

She backed away, reluctant to let him out of her sight, as if he might simply disappear, dissolve into the red haze. Finally, she managed to force herself to turn. She ran from his room and out of the front door, banging her elbow on the table as she went.

The corridor outside was a blood-lit gullet stretching into darkness. Somebody was yelling, closer now. Another voice, answering shrilly. Lina thought she tasted an animal tang of fear in the air itself, like bitter acid, but maybe it was just the permeating foulness made by the apparently-failing scrubbers. She looked both ways down the passage, eyes wide, heart hammering, head spinning as if she could feel the turning of the station – dizzying, disorienting, sickening.

Somebody laid a hand on her shoulder and she cried aloud, a wordless shriek of shock, just about managing to hold onto her bladder as she whirled around. Petra was there, a scarecrow figure wrapped in shadows, dark hair plastered to her face, dressed in a light shift and pyjama trousers. She looked as frightened as Lina felt, which wasn't a good sign. Lina had never known Petra to worry about anything before. Petra had the figure and the face of a ballet dancer, but underneath it she was actually as hard as nails.

'Petra,' Lina whispered, her throat clamping on the word. 'You

151

scared me.'

'What happened, Lina?' Petra asked. Her fingers were combing again and again through her straight, dark hair – clawing it, really – and she was clearly shivering in her thin clothing. 'What happened?' she repeated, her voice becoming demanding, as if she could simply insist that Lina explain. 'It sounded like it came from above, from the machine rooms. Was it the generators?'

'I don't know,' said Lina, turning to go and beckoning Petra to follow. 'Let's find out.'

They dashed down the corridor, heading counter-spinwards towards the nearest stairs. Lina felt totally blank-minded, detached from her running body.

A thin stream of confused and frightened people joined them, becoming a substantial tide as they neared the stairs up to the machine rooms, where the generators and power relays were. Si Davis jogged past Lina without bothering to speak, his wide form forging a pathway through the developing crowd like an ice-breaker. He took the stairs two at a time, making them ring loudly beneath him, and disappeared from view.

Lina stumbled onto the floor of the upper deck, put one hand down to right herself, and scrambled back to her feet, hotly pursued by Petra. Voices were calling up ahead, mingling into an aural blur that conveyed only fear and surprise, no real meaning. Somebody screamed, shrill and grating, chilling Lina's blood.

The crowd thickened as they entered the machine rooms, forcing Lina to walk, pushing her way through. It seemed that everybody on the station was here, milling around, trying to see whatever was happening just outside the main generator room. The station burned with that awful red light, as if it had become a furnace.

Lina elbowed her way past Alphe, who made no effort to resist her, and stopped, stunned and open-mouthed at what she saw. An involuntary gasp escaped her throat.

Eli was leaning against the wall, hands over his face and head bowed, wrapped in the smoke that streamed from the doorway of the gennie room. A crumpled human form lay spread-eagled on the floor in front of him. A knife lay between them in a pool of glossy black liquid. But of course, it wasn't black, Lina knew. It just looked black in the emergency lighting. It was red, wasn't it? It was blood.

'Nik!' somebody screamed. 'THAT'S NIK!'

Eli raised his face, which hung slackly from his skull like an ill-fitting mask. A thin string of saliva depended from his lower lip. 'I didn't mean to. . .' he croaked, his eyes wandering to the sprawled body of Nik Sudowski. 'I didn't mean to. . .'

Ella Kown burst from the crowd like a cork from a bottle, her stun-baton crackling in her hand. She stopped in front of Eli, poised in momentary indecision.

'What the hell happened here?!' demanded Ella. Another of her team emerged to stand beside her, and Lina saw with a little dismay that it was Jayce, fully armoured-up. If you could ever count on a person to make a situation worse, Jayce was the man.

'I didn't mean to,' Eli said again, a note of pleading entering into his voice. 'He. . . Nik. . .'

'I think you'd better can it, Eli. I want you to come with me, okay? Right now,' said Ella, clearly trying to sound reasonable – a tone that was somewhat at odds with the sight of the baton that still crackled away in her hand. 'Just be cool, all right? We'll work this out. But this is not the place.' She killed the stunner, forcing her body to relax. The crowd waited in breathless silence.

'He sabotaged the power relay,' said Eli, seemingly to himself, his gaze creeping to the body that lay before him in a rapidly-spreading puddle of gore. 'I confronted him.' He looked around the assembled watchers, his eyes pleading for understanding. 'I tried to stop him.' Lina could see none of the Eli she knew in that shell-shocked face. 'He had a knife. He. . .'

Just then, the towering figure of Halman emerged from the throng, to stand between Eli and Ella, dwarfing both of them. He looked titanic and strong, and Lina instantly felt a little better.

'Eli, I want you to go with Ella,' he said in a voice that, although quiet for him, was still clearly audible from Lina's vantage point.

'Hey, Halman,' said Eli's voice flatly, while Eli's eyes looked

153

about a million miles away. 'How's it going?'

'*Now*, Eli!' snarled Halman, seizing him by the scruff of the neck and propelling him into Ella's arms. Ella, despite her strength, staggered and struggled to prevent Eli from falling. She was lucky, in Lina's opinion, not to discharge the stunner into him. Jayce came to her aid, in an uncharacteristic show of clear thinking, and between them they manhandled Eli away.

'Where's my fucking sec-team?!' bellowed Halman into the assembled crowd. They actually fell back, as one body, by a pace or two, revealing the nervous-looking Theo, still in the T-shirt and sweat-pants he had slept in, his chubby face devoid of its usual friendly glow. He stepped forwards, nodding curtly to Halman.

'Yes, Sir,' Theo said, in a voice that was little more than a croak.

'Find the rest of the team, shut this area off.' Halman turned to address the crowd as a whole: 'I want everyone except for security and maintenance to go back to their quarters!' he boomed. Nobody moved. 'NOW!' he screamed. 'GO!' The crowd faltered, losing cohesion, and began to disperse. Lina found her feet rooted to the spot. She felt as if she had woken up in another world. None of this could be happening. 'Theo – find the rest of the sec team and lock this area down. Nobody else except maintenance is to go within fifty metres of this door.' Theo nodded and sprinted off through the dispersing crowd, weaving around people with surprising agility for someone of his size.

Suddenly, the small but reassuringly-efficient figure of Doctor Hobbes appeared, as if he had simply materialised in place. He stepped past Lina with his medical holdall in one hand and a grim expression on his narrow face. He glanced at Halman without speaking, and knelt down beside Sudowski's body, opening the bag as he did so. He looked as if he had already decided it was hopeless, and Lina had to concur with that opinion judging by the amount of blood that had escaped Nik's body. Sabotage? Her mind stumbled over the word, trying to connect it with a meaning. Surely not. She had suspected *someone*. . . but never Nik Sudowksi. And he'd attacked Eli with a knife? *Nik*? No wonder he hadn't looked too good of late – he'd clearly been losing his mind!

154

This was an affliction that Lina felt she could sympathise with at that moment. Something in the superstructure of the station groaned faintly, but vastly, bringing her back to her senses.

'Maintenance!' bellowed Halman, who had always been of the school of thought that loud enough shouting could resolve any problem. His bushy moustache bristled as his jaw clenched and unclenched fiercely.

Alphe and Fionne scampered into the smoking generator room under the glowering stare of the station controller, each with a large toolbox in hand. They both made the effort not to look at the haemorrhaging body of their superior as they passed it. Fionne actually left a dainty footprint in his blood. Lina shuddered and her stomach did a single, washing-machine-like revolution at the sight, almost dumping her dinner onto the corridor floor.

'Lina?' said Halman, startling her back to reality. She looked up, eyebrows raised. 'Piss off, okay? Give us some space.'

She nodded dumbly, and turned away, finding it hard to detach her gaze from the human wreckage sprawled on the metal tiles. Hobbes had Sudowski's saturated work-shirt open to the waist and a monitoring device planted on his chest. Lina could see a long, bloody gash in the flesh there. It looked like a leering mouth. She could not believe that, even by accident, even when attacked, Eli could have done that. She caught a glimpse of bone through the wound as Halman shoved her on the back – not too roughly, just hard enough – and she finally managed to get her feet moving.

She wandered back to her quarters on autopilot, her body finding its own way there while her mind spun futilely far back in her skull, generating nothing but white noise and fragmented questions. She felt as if the station's floor was pitching beneath her like the deck of a ship at sea. The red light began to permeate her skull, eating into her sanity like acid. When she got home she found her son standing in the middle of the floor, frightened, waiting for her.

'Mum!' he yelled, as soon as the door opened, rushing into her arms. 'What's happening? I heard shouting outside. Why are the lights off?'

Lina squeezed him in her arms, held him tightly, as if the spinning of the station might snatch him from her, whirling him away into space if she let go. He was still questioning her, repeating himself over and over, but she didn't even hear him. All she knew was that he was here, he was okay. And in her imagination, pictures of Platini Alpha, culled from the documentary she had watched, scrolled like teasing glimpses of some alternate reality.

CHAPTER TWENTY-FIVE

Why hadn't the crazy dragon-man come back? *Would* he even come back? Who knew what the bastard was doing on that station? Perhaps he had been caught, jailed, even killed. What would happen to Carver then? He'd be stuck here – here in this blighted hole of ice and rock – until he died. And how long could he survive here for? He didn't have the obvious technical knowledge of the crazy dragon-man, and he had no idea how the air system of the conjoined shuttle actually worked, or how long it would continue to do so. And anyway, the restraining device was nearby, fixed to a rock pin in one jagged surface which Carver had come to think of as a wall, despite the lack of real meaning to directions such as up, down, left and right. He wouldn't be able to go far enough from it to get himself food if the crazy dragon-man didn't return from whatever demented mischief he had set off upon. The man had left him an insulated flask of water, which hung, half-full, from his belt, but no food at all.

And so he worked. What else was there to do? He clung to the fading hope that the crazy dragon-man would return, that he would be pleased with Carver's progress and would release him from the hated restraining device. He knew that this was an unlikely sequence of events, though, and as time progressed it seemed ever more so. He wondered if he might actually dig right through this damned rock and out into space. The explosion of released pressure would propel him out into the asteroid belt, where he could enjoy the twin thrills of asphyxiation and irradiation at the same time. He couldn't even go and get a helmet, because, once again, he couldn't leave the radius of that fucking restraining device. After considering this for some time, he decided he didn't really care.

He sustained himself through this difficult time by

daydreaming about murdering the crazy dragon-man, maybe bashing his crazy head in or strangling him until his crazy eyes popped out. He thought about what he'd do to the body, how he'd destroy it, humiliate it, reduce it to its component molecules. The cutter blared and screamed in his hands, sending out gouts of steam, filling the world with its enraged bellow. After a while, it even began to heat the air to an almost-bearable temperature.

He was beginning to build up a fair cache of extracted cones of rock now, which floated, jostling and knocking together in the pitch-dark volume of space behind him. Now and then, one would bump into him, and several times he came close to cutting his own leg off when this happened. He launched the chunks away again, but not too hard, having learnt that excessive force would only cause further ricochets and disorder. When he turned and aimed his suit-light into the mass, he was alarmed at how many pieces there were. He'd made his own, mini asteroid belt, but one that was trapped in this awful cavern with him. The rocky cone-shapes twisted and tumbled, looking to Carver like gnashing fangs.

Once, while he stared into this debris-filled space, he imagined that he saw shapes within the chaos, *patterns* congealing out of the surface disorder, concentrations of shape that came and went, real then unreal again, almost teasing. He screwed his eyes shut, the cutter wedged against the rock-face, willing reality to resume its course. When he opened them again, the patterns had gone, if they had ever been there at all. Shards of stone spun, glittering in the crystalline beam of his light, dangerous but entirely material.

He returned to work, moving his harness point further into the face and yanking on the line to test it before restarting the plasma cutter. His whole body ached, everything from his skin right down to his bones. He considered taking a break – after all, who would ever know? But he decided against it, knowing that he'd never be able to make himself begin again. He wondered what the crazy dragon-man would do when they failed to find anything within the asteroid. Would he fry Carver's brain until it killed him, just out of spite? Why not? How much time that gave him, he couldn't guess, but he was aware that he was probably just accelerating the eventuality by his relentless pace of work. Still, what else could he do?

And so he cut, launched the chunks into the mass behind him, moved his rock-pin, cut again. Rinse and repeat, rinse and repeat, his body aching all the time, wreathed in the steam of the cutter, possibly the single furthest human being from civilisation, alone at the frozen frontier of space, waiting for a crazy man who might never return.

CHAPTER TWENTY-SIX

'What now?!' bellowed Halman in response to the latest knock on his door. He threw his datasheet aside, grimly satisfied by the way it skipped off his desk, breaking one corner of its plastic case, and landed on the floor.

The door opened, slowly and haltingly, as the person outside turned the crank-handle in the access panel, the system that had replaced the now-defunct electrical one. Ella Kown was standing there, her posture somewhat defensive.

'Is this a bad time?' she asked, stepping cautiously inside anyway.

Halman squeezed his head in his large hands, exhaling heavily. 'Of course it fucking is, Ella!' he spat. 'When have we ever had a worse time than this?'

Ella nodded diplomatically and approached his desk. 'Can I sit down? I'm kinda beat.'

Halman indicated the chair opposite his. 'Why not,' he said.

Ella collapsed into the seat with a sigh. 'So what's the news?' she asked.

'Alphe and Fionne are working on the relay,' he told her. When he'd left them, they'd had the entire floor up in the gennie room, and had both been crawling around within the bowels of the machinery, conversing heatedly in a technical language that was, to Halman, completely unfathomable. What was clear, even to him, was that the relay wasn't the only thing to have been damaged. The turbines, which used steam from the reactor to actually generate electricity, had also been attacked. Halman wondered why Nik hadn't sabotaged the reactor itself, if devastation had been his priority, but he was relieved that this hadn't happened. Things could always – *always* – be worse. Although, when you thought about it, that wasn't a whole lot of consolation.

Alphe had burned himself quite badly on some overheated conduit, but had refused to leave his work, dignifying Halman's suggestion that he be replaced with the merest of grunted responses. Halman had decided that the most helpful thing he could do would be to leave, and this was what he'd done. He had returned to his office in a daze, walking through the newly-darkened interior of his station like a ghost, heated conversation, accusations and demands all around him, panic thrumming in the foul-tasting air itself. He had passed several rooms where helpful passers-by had stopped to release the occupants who had been trapped within by the failure of their automatic doors, and had somehow failed to understand or actually use the manual backup systems. Possibly, some of them had seized up, having never been required before. He was glad that the station's builders had, for whatever reason, never got around to automating all of the doors on board, or just opening all the rooms could have turned into a major task.

'Are they making any progress?' Ella asked, managing a surprisingly casual tone.

'I don't know, Ella. Why don't you ask them?'

'You know who we could use right now?'

'Yeah. Nik,' he replied gruffly. Ella nodded in agreement. 'The same son-of-a-bitch who apparently caused all this.'

'Unbelievable, isn't it?' They sat for a moment, considering this. 'What if they can't fix it?'

Halman looked to the window of his office. A blizzard of stone hung suspended in the night out there. He wondered briefly how the pane was still powered, but then he remembered that the windows acted also as solar panels, generating enough electricity to run themselves. He reached out and turned it off. 'They have to fix it,' he said.

'But what if they *can't*?'

'Well, then, the patched-up air system goes off when the battery dies, the Kays can't fly, aeroponics stops, the water doesn't run, or clean, the positioning jets stop, we lose gravity-effect, the heating goes off, and we die. As for how long we have. . .' He spread his hands, and offered a single, humourless bark of laughter. 'Ask Nik.'

'Oh crap. . .' Ella groaned.

'How's Eli?' asked Halman abruptly, changing the subject.

'He's in medical, with one of my guys watching him. In shock, naturally. Devastated, from what Hobbes says. He's sedated for the moment, so some small mercy there.'

'What was he doing around the machine rooms anyway?'

'He wasn't really able to explain it to me earlier, and as I say, he's out cold at the moment. He does, of course, have clearance to be down there if he wants. Going for a walk? Maybe he saw Nik and followed him up there.'

Halman huffed inconclusively, his moustache bristling. 'I suppose so,' he said at last.

'You don't suspect him of any wrongdoing, do you?' asked Ella.

Halman looked at her from beneath knitted brows. 'Don't *you*?' he replied. 'Isn't that your job? To be suspicious?'

Ella pursed her lips, considering this. At length, she said, 'Dan, this is Eli. I don't believe this went down in any way other than how he has described already. Nik's prints were smudged together with Eli's on the knife, suggesting that Eli did take the knife off him.'

'Okay, so it's inconceivable that Eli would blow up the relay then murder Nik. That's a given.' Ella nodded, attentive. 'But. . .' Halman raised a finger to emphasise his point. 'It's also inconceivable that Nik would blow the relay then try to kill Eli. I guess the whole fucking thing's inconceivable. Yet here we are.'

'Yeah, I have to agree with you there,' said Ella, nodding her head grimly. 'But in one respect, it makes a kind of sense. Nik certainly had the expertise to destroy the relay, sabotage Sal's Kay, burn out the scrubbers, making it seem like regular wear-and-tear. . . and he knew how to fly a Kay.' She sat back in her seat as if that explained everything.

Halman let this wash over him, trying to make sense of it. *Inconceivable*. That certainly did seem like the right term for it.

'Shit, Ella, you really think he did all those things?'

'I'm starting to. A lot of people have said he didn't seem himself of late. They were saying that even before. You must have noticed.'

'I thought he was just stressed. You know his head used to hurt him sometimes. Those Farsight shit-bags filled his skull with DNI rubbish at Platini. And remember, Nik *fixed* the scrubbers. Why would he do that if *he* broke them? And what do you mean, fly a Kay? What the hell has that got to do with it?'

'Well, if we've had a saboteur on board, then I'm inclined to suspect foul play in the failure of our prodigal shuttle to show up.'

Halman started, sitting up straighter. 'If somebody from here had intercepted it, then it'd be nearby somewhere, right? In the belt.'

'Right. Somewhere on the flightpath from Platini to here, within range of our ships.'

'I wish we could launch the damn Kays now, then we could look for it. That might just solve a lot of our problems in one stroke. I want to talk to the tech guys about diverting battery power to the hangar.'

'Bit of a gamble, isn't it, when we'll have to choose between launching Kays and breathing air?'

Halman suddenly slammed one huge fist onto his desk, making Ella jump in her seat. 'Shit!' he cried – a word which seemed to fit the situation well.

'One other thing. . .' Ella said reluctantly.

Halman glowered at her. 'What?' he asked through clenched teeth.

'Lina thought she saw somebody flying a ship into the belt, just after the clean-up of Sal's. . . well, you know. . .'

'And do you think she was right?'

Ella shrugged. 'I asked the ground crew to check it out, but all the Kays were cool by then, and they said that honestly there's no way they could be sure. It's not hard to fake the launch logs if you know what you're doing. The system was never designed to be secure, because nobody ever thought it necessary, I guess.'

'Nik would have known how to do it,' said Halman quietly. He felt about seventy-seven, rather than fifty-seven, all of a sudden. He passed a hand across his face, feeling the stubble where he hadn't shaved, alarmed at how sunken and hollow his cheeks felt.

'Yeah,' agreed Ella.

'For what it's worth, Ella, I'm inclined to agree with you. I can't imagine Eli being involved in all this. However, I still want him to remain in medical. And I want him properly tested under lie-detector, when you think he's up to it. Just for the records, if nothing else. And keep him secure, of course.'

'I think we need to be careful how we deal with Eli. He's a much-loved figure here, especially with the mining staff. They're already protesting his detainment, even in medical. People are pretty frightened, Dan. We're sitting on a powder keg, essentially.'

'Hmmm. . .' said Halman, lost in his own thoughts again. 'Anyway, we've bigger problems right now, haven't we? Like how to eat, breathe and stay warm. Not to mention keeping the kinetic defence system going.'

Ella laughed, startling Halman, who gave her a confused look. 'Sorry,' she said, sobering. 'It's just all so unreal.'

'Yeah, well it is bloody real, I'm afraid.'

'Is there any way I or my team can help?'

'You can try to prevent an outright mutiny, Officer – how about that?'

'We'll try, but no promises.'

'How're things in the prison?'

Ella shrugged again, as if this was the most minor of concerns. Halman supposed that, at the moment, it almost was. 'Secure. But they're pissed, of course. And frightened, like everyone else. This was never supposed to be a death sentence for any of them. But they're locked down tight, and we intend to keep it that way.'

'Good. Has the mess been cleared up properly? Nik, I mean.'

'Yeah, medical dealt with it, under my direct supervision. The body's on ice, but of course the freezer is now unpowered, so Hobbes's team will have to examine it pretty quickly. I'd imagine he intends to do just that, but don't hold out hopes of learning too much from it.'

'No,' agreed Halman darkly.

'Anything else?'

'Apart from keeping the drones away from the gennie rooms, I don't think we can do anything else. Now, we wait and hope that maintenance can fix the power. Then we get out there and see if we can find that damn shuttle. And maybe, just maybe, we'll live long enough for us both to take a day off, sometime in the distant future.'

Ella took a deep breath, sweeping a hand through her crew-cut hair. 'Sounds like a plan,' she said, rising from her seat.

'Take care, Ella,' he said as she turned to go.

She smiled. 'You, too, Dan,' she replied, and then she strode out through the still-open door and away into the crimson-hued twilight of the corridor outside.

CHAPTER TWENTY-SEVEN

'Be quiet!' called Welby into the wall that divided his cell from Prisoner Fuller's. He didn't have to shout for his words to take effect – the banging stopped immediately. 'Do you really think that's going to make any difference?'

It was almost pitch-dark in the prison, now, the scattered emergency lights casting an even dimmer glow here than elsewhere in the station. They were ranged along the roof of the corridor that ran past the cells, spaced every fifteen metres or so, glowing faintly like dying coals. Little was visible besides the lights themselves, so weak was the illumination they offered. Welby thought they looked like eyes in the darkness.

He relaxed against the wall once more, trying to make himself comfortable on the prison mattress, which was little thicker or more luxurious than a sheet. He didn't mind his new regime of hardship, really – he had earned it, he knew, by his actions. Neither did he regret those actions. Circumstance had chosen him as a weapon of vengeance. So be it.

Fuller's voice came wheedling through the wall, much smaller and weaker than the sound of his banging had been: 'We're gonna die in here, Welby. I know it.'

Welby inhaled deeply, filling his small chest with the tainted air, letting it go in a contented sigh. 'Then we die here, in the cradle of the Old Ones. Perhaps by our proximity to one of their worlds, our spirits shall know salvation in the next life. What better place than here, in one of their systems. We all have to die, my friend.' Attentive silence from next door. 'Many of us have even served as tools of death ourselves, in our lives before. Death: ha! Easy come, easy go, I say.' He laced his hands behind his head, and shut his eyes. He felt like a nap. Nearby in the station, somebody was screaming what sounded like frightened orders. The tipping

166

point was close at hand, he knew. He felt it, even from his cell – felt it in the vibrations of the air, in his bones and in his heart. Well, whatever. Let them panic, let them die – him included, if need be. Easy come, easy go.

'I suppose so. . .' said Fuller's voice faintly. There was a pause, during which Welby heard someone crying further up the corridor. 'I'm just scared, I guess.'

Welby imagined Fuller sitting in there on his own bunk, a small and nervous-looking man with a bald spot ringed by fluffy brown hair, whom Welby had always found it somewhat difficult to like. Maybe Fuller's dodgy heart was finally about to give up the ghost. Still, he was one of the faithful, and as such, was Welby's responsibility. 'It is all right to be scared, Prisoner Fuller. Those who came before are watching us, judging us. This is their system, and what happens here happens in accordance with their wishes. Don't you feel it? This is their very cradle. Trust in their wisdom, lest they return and find you wanting.'

'You really think all this – whatever's going wrong here – is their doing?' asked the voice from behind the wall.

'I trust that it is so. Perhaps they are punishing the owners of this facility for their treatment of us. Perhaps they don't *want* us to be trapped here.' Welby would have liked Fuller to shut up now. He really did feel sleepy. Funny, because he hadn't so much as walked a hundred metres all day, but it seemed that the less he did, the more tired he felt of late.

'Maybe they mean to free us,' said Fuller, a note of hungry longing creeping into his voice.

'Maybe they do,' agreed Welby, lying down and trying to get comfortable. He certainly hoped so. It would be good to have a word, up close and personal, with that snooty bitch, Officer Kown. But he was happy to wait and see. He turned over onto his side – that was better. 'Go to sleep, Prisoner Fuller, and we'll see what happens next.'

'I'll try,' said Fuller. That excited note remained in his voice, though. 'I sure would like to be out of this cell, Welby.'

'Of course,' said Welby drily. 'Now go to sleep.'

167

Mercifully, Fuller didn't speak any further. Welby drifted slowly into the peaceful, dreamless sleep of the just, safe in the knowledge that the Old Ones had a plan. They were not done with him yet. It was not his destiny to rot here in this cell. He knew it.

CHAPTER TWENTY-EIGHT

'No, he's sleeping, but that isn't the point, Lina.'

'Look, Jayce, I just want to see that he's okay.'

'He is okay, but Hobbes says he isn't to be disturbed.' Jayce managed to bristle, tensing his armoured body without actually moving.

Lina looked around herself, then leant towards him secretively. 'Hobbes isn't here,' she said.

Jayce hesitated slightly, managing to convey uncertainty even from behind his featureless facemask. 'No. . .' he said. 'But–'

'I'll be a few minutes max, all right? His friends will want to know that he's okay. *I* want to know that he's okay.'

'Ella didn't specifically tell me not to let anyone *in*. . .' said Jayce, relaxing from his guard-standing-at-attention posture. He craned his head to check the medical room's wall-clock, but of course it had stopped. He looked like some futuristic machine, made from polished ebony, but Lina knew that beneath that exterior he was at least ninety-percent idiot. She supposed Ella had been desperate, to have left him here in charge.

'Well then, that's settled,' said Lina decisively. 'Thanks, Jayce!'

He stammered something that she didn't catch, but she was already past him and into the red-lit dimness of the medical department, looking through the open doors of the treatment bays. She thought perhaps he would follow her, but he didn't.

The first room was empty. The second contained one of the medical techs, bent over some shiny piece of equipment, doing something precise-looking that took all of her attention. Lina moved on without the tech seeing her. The third room, just round the corner, contained Eli. She slipped inside as silently as she could, feeling illicit and slightly wired. The foul taste in her mouth had become ubiquitous now, an ever-present reminder of how bad things had become, like the taste of failure itself.

At first, she thought that Eli was indeed sleeping. He lay curled up on the hospital bed like a comma, with his face to the wall, dressed in light hospital pyjamas. He looked as if he had shrunk somehow, collapsed in on himself. His breathing was rapid and shallow.

'Hey,' she said softly, not really expecting any reaction.

Eli jerked as if he had been electrocuted and turned to face her, pushing himself up on one elbow before collapsing again limply. His eyes were wide and blank and his face looked vacant, paralysed in an expression of bewilderment.

'Hey, Lina,' he said in a small, weak voice.

She went to his bedside and embraced him, alarmed at how brittle he felt in her arms. It was as if something had been extracted from him, like he'd been bled by some vampiric parasite to within an inch of death. She felt a shudder go through him, and he stiffened for a moment, before becoming boneless and relaxing against her. She held him for a while, wishing there was something she could do to help him. Eventually, he pushed himself away from her and lolled against the wall, defeated-looking.

'Eli, I know this is hard to believe, but what happened is for the best,' she said, trying to look him in the eye. She wished she'd had the foresight to plan what she would actually say at this moment. Eli wouldn't look at her – he seemed to be staring deep into the wall behind her left shoulder. 'Nik was sabotaging the station, trying to kill us all, I suppose. I know that's insane, but that's what was happening. You may just have stopped him in time. Perhaps he was going to blow the reactor next. He had to be stopped, Eli.' She moved closer again, forcing him to look at her. His lower lip was trembling minutely. 'He had to be stopped,' she repeated, more emphatically.

'Yes,' agreed Eli distantly. 'I had to do it. That's right.' A wave of emotion washed briefly across his features, distorting his face for a moment into a caricature of purest misery, then was gone again just as quickly, leaving only that awful blankness behind. 'And I have to do more, yet.'

170

Lina shook her head, feeling tears well up inside her. 'Eli, you don't have to do anything now except get better. You just have to accept what happened, and somehow move on. I can't tell you how to do that, but that's what you need to do. That's all you need to do right now. Maintenance are on the power problem, and they're gonna crack it, I know they are. We're going to be okay. But you have to get better. And that means accepting that you did what was necessary.'

Eli exhaled slowly, his head wobbling slightly from side to side. He looked like one of the shell-shocked soldiers Lina had seen on the news, back in the days of the Platini Alpha Civil War.

'There's more,' he said darkly. 'There's more there's more there's more there's more there's—'

She cut him off, a little spooked: 'Eli, you're done,' she said. He turned his vacant cow's eyes on her and she couldn't even see the man behind them any more. All she saw was her own frightened face, reflected back in perfect miniature, cast in glass. She lurched upright and involuntarily fell back a step, feeling her heart beginning to race in her chest. 'You're done,' she said again, but it came out in a whisper this time. His eyes. . .

Eli's head shook ponderously, but that vacant gaze stayed fixed on her. 'No,' he said simply. That one word, filled with grim significance.

Lina suddenly felt a lump in her throat, so pronounced that it was hard to breathe. Something was wrong. *That's not Eli!* some dark and irrational part of her mind screamed. *That's not Eli in there!* In another, more stable part of her brain, a grim and undeniable thought was taking shape. She fell back another pace, her hand feeling behind her for the doorway. 'What?' she breathed. Her mind was whirling again – damn it, she felt like her whole body was whirling – as if the station had suddenly begun to spin in the opposite direction, like a waltzer in some nightmare theme park, a ride designed to induce insanity and sickness in equal measure. Eli's mouth cracked open, showing his teeth, and slowly widened in a smile. And then, without knowing she had any intention of doing so, Lina turned and simply ran from the room.

171

She pelted past Jayce without slowing, out of the medical department and along the blood-lit corridor, tears in her eyes, desperation in her heart, and a dark, swelling certainty bubbling along beneath it all. She couldn't – as yet – bring this certainty out into the forefront of her mind, where the light of reason shone brightest, and examine it. Instead, she let it simmer down there in the darkness, aware of its existence, letting it guide her body to its goal like an autopilot system, driving her towards the hangars once again.

She supposed she knew what she'd been looking for the first time now, when Ella had stopped her. She just hadn't known *then* – not really. Or rather, she'd known, perhaps, but she hadn't *known* she'd known – she hadn't *wanted* to know. But she had to have proof. She *knew*, but she still didn't *believe* – couldn't believe, not without proof. *His eyes!* Not Eli's eyes – the eyes of a grieving, damaged man – but the eyes of something mindless and hungry and reptilian.

She rounded a corner at a full sprint and skidded to a stop, almost pitching herself onto her face, hands outstretched for balance. The corridor was filled with people, clearly in two opposing groups. Somebody was on the floor in the middle, and they looked hurt. One man – Lina thought it might have been Tryka from the refinery – was shoving another man, whom she couldn't identify, and voices clamoured, competing for dominance.

Without waiting to see if whatever was going on here would turn into an all-out brawl, Lina spun around and bolted off, back the way she had come. She took a right, down a floor, past aeroponics – where she briefly saw worried, scampering figures in the darkness, desperately administering to the doomed crops that dangled in the darkness like hanged men – and right again, into the warehouse, that towering mausoleum of machine spares and oil-stains, where the stark architecture angled up into invisibility above her.

She wondered what she would do if Ella tried to stop her again. She didn't think she'd be able to explain herself verbally, the way her mind felt at the moment, so she supposed she would try her best to fight her way into the hangar, if need be. The idea sounded ridiculous, especially when you considered Ella's size, strength, and martial talents, but Lina just couldn't imagine herself reacting in any other way. The beating of her heart had become a frantic buzz, a hummingbird trapped inside her.

As it happened, though, it wasn't necessary to fight Ella Kown, because Ella Kown was nowhere to be seen this time. Neither, for that matter, was anybody else. Lina searched around the hangar door for a manual crank-handle. She found a slot, intended to receive a key that wasn't there. She ran into the side room where she had sat drinking moonshine with Ella, what seemed like years ago now. She searched through the desk, turfing objects out onto the floor behind her, and was genuinely amazed when she found exactly the item she was looking for. She held it up in the rusty light for a moment, staring at it as if it might melt into shadow and simply bleed away. It was a heavy, dog-leg spanner with a star-shaped business end and a bare metal handle. She dashed back to the hangar door, shadows lapping at her heels.

She inserted the spanner into the access panel, where it snicked smoothly into place as if it had been used a thousand times before. She tried to turn it, expecting it to move with some difficulty, but was surprised when she couldn't budge it at all. She adjusted the position of her feet, bracing herself to apply greater force, and tried again. Nothing. She swore softly to herself and stood back, chest hitching and heaving. And then she realised: she had been turning the damn thing the wrong way!

She stepped forwards again, getting a good grip on the spanner, and turned it the opposite way. This time it moved easily – almost too easily – and she stumbled and came close to falling. As she continued to turn the spanner, the massive door began to inch its way open, its motion accompanied by a hideous metallic screaming which made Lina's teeth hurt. Once the opening was a half-metre wide, she dropped to the floor and wormed her way into the hangar on her chest, pushing herself through with her feet and clawing at the sticky, oily floor with her hands.

The hangar was clotted with shadow, utterly silent and still.

173

Lina had never seen it like this before, and she was more than a little spooked, painfully aware that she was not supposed to be here. She crossed the floor in a rapid skulking crouch, half expecting somebody to grab her at any moment, eyes darting left and right as she attempted to check in every direction at once. The Kays lurked in the shadows, watching her with their dead-eye canopies.

She went to the wall beside the control room and opened the emergency cabinet. There was only one torch left in there, and she removed it from its clip to check the battery. Its charge indicator showed only fifteen percent, which was probably why it had been left. Still, that should be plenty for her purposes. She didn't expect to be long. Deep inside, where that stream of certainty bubbled darkly, she already knew what she'd find.

She moved down the ranks of Kays, the yellow beam of her torch washing over rusted machinery and muscular bunches of cable. She stopped in front of K6-10, trying to summon the willpower to continue. Her breathing was a torn, rasping sound, loud in her own ears. She stood for a moment, trying to summon the will to actually carry through with her task. Truth be told, she didn't want to. She didn't want proof, didn't want to make that certainty into fact. Really, she just wanted to go home and crawl back into bed, where she would lie in a foetal ball until either the air became finally unbreathable or the crisis had passed her by. But she had to, damn it, she *had* to. . .

She stepped towards Eli's ship, letting the torchlight wash across its blistered surface. That surface was pocked and scuffed in probably a hundred places, mostly from micro-impacts in the belt, lending it the unwell appearance of a patient in the late stages of smallpox. Here and there, it was also marked by the distinctive rectangular dents left by the dead-lifter's forks. Several of these were so deep that Lina was surprised they hadn't pierced the hull, but she supposed the Kays were actually tougher than they looked.

She crouched down, checking the underside of the ship, moving around it with her heart high in her throat. And then she saw it: a crumpled patch of metal about the size of her hand. It looked like nothing, really, the sort of thing that one could easily glance at and not even see, especially on the cratered surface of K6-10. But Lina knew it for what it was. She reached out one trembling hand, watching it as if it belonged to somebody else, and touched that damaged area of wrinkled metal, trailing her fingers across the sharp little waves and jags.

That damaged area was where Eli had bumped Sal's ship out in the belt. It was the mark of death, the black spot, the *proof* – the dreaded proof that she had needed.

'Oh no,' she sighed, her fingers caressing that crinkled patch of metal. 'Oh no. . .' She had never felt less happy to be vindicated in all her life. But that was what it had to be. It couldn't be a coincidental impact from a micro-asteroid – it was too big, and a ding of that size would have been reported and known about. It wasn't a scar from the lifter. It was what it was. Proof.

And then she was on her feet and running, the torch clattering unnoticed from her hand, rolling away under one of the Kays with its beam zigging and zagging crazily across the floor, making another shadow-Lina that briefly ran beside her. She pelted out of the hangar door, slipping in a patch of oil, almost falling, stretching out a hand to right herself, swerving round the corner and into the warehouse. She ran through a haze of red light, bunched darkness, regiments of shelving that gave way to bare corridors. She crashed into one of the techs from aeroponics as she sprinted past, knocking them flying, steel instruments spilling from their hands. She didn't even see who it was, let alone stop to apologise. She ran, on and on, her heart jumping and thumping in her chest, wishing she was fitter, wishing she would wake from this insane dream.

She rounded the door of the medical department and skidded to a halt. Where was Jayce? She looked around frantically, checking behind the door of the small canteen room that adjoined the main reception area. Nothing. She ran to Eli's treatment bay, already knowing what she'd find.

He was gone.

'No. . .' she said, but it came out in a whimper that was frighteningly small in the deserted medical department.

She checked the next treatment bay. The technician whom she had avoided earlier was lying crumpled in one corner, entwined with the equally-dead body of Jayce. Blood had formed a veritable lake around them, almost reaching to the doorway where Lina stood with her mind hitching and misfiring, unable to believe what she was looking at.

Unwilling, but unable to resist, she felt herself drawn into the room as if by some magnetic force, her feet moving slowly through the clotting blood, making little sucking and squelching noises as she went. She took hold of one of Jayce's arms and tried to turn him over. Instead, his whole body rolled and splashed onto the floor, splattering her legs with gore. His arm unfolded slowly and plopped down beside his helmeted head.

Eli had jammed something sharp up under Jayce's helmet and into his neck — maybe a surgical scalpel or something. Whatever it was, it had done the job efficiently enough, because Jayce was undeniably stone dead.

Lina looked up at the technician, whose face was a frozen picture of fear and surprise. Her mouth was locked open in a final scream, her eyes were liquid circles of terror, and she was latticed with slashes, some of them deep enough to show the bone beneath her flesh. Lina noticed that her hands were also cut to pieces — the tip of one finger was actually missing — as if she had used them in an attempt to protect herself from the onslaught. An ultimately futile attempt, then.

Lina stood back, horrified, her stomach suddenly filled with butterflies. 'He's gone,' she said to herself. 'Eli's gone. . . But where?' And then an idea began to dawn on her with slow implacability, crushing and grinding everything before it. 'Marco. . .'

When she reached the door of her quarters she found it ajar, and knew that she might already be too late. An agonising surge of fear and anger and love exploded inside her, almost stopping her in her tracks. But somehow, she made herself open the door fully and step inside.

She padded through the deserted living-slash-dining room as quietly as she could, on legs that felt stuffed full of lead. And then she heard Marco's voice, weak and frightened. Maybe hurt.

'Eli. . . *don't*. . .' that voice said.

Lina forgot all notions of stealth and burst into Marco's room with her blood keening in her ears, barging the door open with her shoulder. It smashed into something meaty the other side and she heard another voice – Eli's voice – utter a short grunt of pain and surprise.

And then she was in there, her mind filled with a savage blood-lust – the rage of the protective mother – a rage so clean and bright and pure that it shut off all conscious thought, scrubbed it into nothing.

Eli, behind the door, recovered his balance and stepped back a pace, the scalpel he had stolen from medical swishing and slicing in the air. Red light ran along its blade like blood, hypnotic and terrible. Maybe it *was* blood – Jayce's and Tamzin's.

Marco was on his bed, his back pressed up against the far wall, with the covers pulled up tight around him. *All children know that bed-covers are monster-proof*, thought Lina distantly. He looked utterly terrified, and her heart stung to see him that way.

'Eli,' she panted, stretching out one hand to keep him back, mindless of how little good it had done Tamzin, trying to circle in between him and the bed. 'Don't!'

Eli turned with her, still drawing patterns in the air with the blade, feinting left and right minutely, like a big cat about to pounce. Unbelievably, tears squeezed from his eyes and tracked down his trembling face, dropping from his chin to the cold floor. His bottom lip convulsed, then his whole face began to quiver, but he didn't relax from his fighter's stance.

'I didn't want to, Lina,' he said thickly, advancing slowly towards her. His face hung like a curtain of flesh, undulating with rage and misery.

'Then don't,' she replied, backing away from him. Her calf bumped against Marco's bed, and she almost overbalanced and

177

fell onto it, which she suspected would have spelled the end for her and her son. 'It's easy, Eli. Just don't.'

'Mum!' cried Marco in a terrified little squeak. Lina didn't look back at him, didn't dare to take her eyes off the weeping, slashing madman that had used to be her closest friend.

'But I'm the emissary!' sobbed Eli, as if that explained it all. He sounded like a toddler in a tantrum, torn by raw, intense emotion: *It's not fair!* was how it sounded to Lina.

'Eli, just be cool. Put the knife down,' she said, reaching behind her with one hand, seeking to touch Marco for what she supposed might well be the last time. 'It's *me*, Eli. Me and Marco.' As if he didn't know that.

'It's the dragon,' wailed Eli. His tears were coming faster now, and Lina wondered how much he could actually see. Maybe this was her chance, maybe her only chance. She wished she'd had the presence of mind to grab a weapon on her way in. 'It said it might be difficult. But I have to do it, Lina, I have to. I'm going,' he said in the tones of one pleading for understanding, 'to cut him up small, Lina, into little bits. And if you want to go first. . . well. . . the dragon said that was okay, too.'

'No!' screamed Marco, sending a jolt through Lina's body. Eli was itching to pounce, she knew. She could see the tension in his posture, almost hear it crackling inside him.

'Eli, no. . .' she said, feeling tears begin to well in her own eyes, knowing it was useless, that her son would watch his mother murdered, and then the madman responsible would butcher him, too.

'NO!' screamed Marco again – deafeningly loud this time– a sound that filled the room and made the walls vibrate like a struck drum.

And then Eli moved.

Several things happened at once. Lina, sensing that Eli would spring for Marco, attempting to simply bypass her, launched herself into his path. Caught against the bed-frame, she staggered and fell, right on top of her son. As went down, she saw somebody else in the room, a hulking shape behind Eli, moving in a swift and purposeful blur. Marco screamed. The sound drew out and stretched like chewing gum, hideous and tearing. Eli practically landed on her, the keystone in a veritable human pyramid. The scalpel, striking for Marco, who still cowered beneath his covers, caught Lina in the shoulder, opening it to the bone and tearing a jagged gash right down to her elbow. The breath that came from his mouth washed over her in a sickening wave. He smelled like something had died inside of him, and Lina supposed that was actually pretty close to the truth.

Whoever had entered the room behind Eli was now right on him, moving swiftly. For a terrified split-second, Lina thought it was the shadow from her dream, come to solid life and somehow inside the station itself. But the figure swung something at Eli's head, which connected with a heavy *clonk!* As the light spilled across its face, Lina saw that it was Rocko, drawn by Marco's scream.

Eli, who had until then been struggling like an enraged animal, the scalpel flitting past Lina's face like a silver wind, trailing drops of her own blood from its edge, stiffened and went rigid. He uttered a sound of bestial pain and surprise and rolled off her onto the floor, coming up in a fighting crouch.

He moved fluidly, backing into the corner, a wild beast at bay, lips drawn back in a snarl. He seemed to have forgotten Marco, and went instead for Rocko, who backed away, alarmed at the ferocity on his face. Rocko held a length of metal pipe in one hand, but it hung uselessly by his side. Rocko had fought for the Unionists on Platini Alpha, but now he looked utterly lost. He had, after all, just hit his boss on the head with a metal pipe. And by way of reprimand, said boss clearly intended to kill him.

Lina didn't waste any time. Rocko had staked his own life on saving Marco, a decision probably made in a moment – a genuine act of altruism. She couldn't allow that act to be repaid with death. And so she moved, leaping up off the bed and kicking Eli in the back of his knee. He went down as smoothly as she could have wished, and she screamed *Now! Hit him!* at Rocko, not realising that no sound actually came from her mouth at all.

179

Rocko was still stepping away, though, staring at the stream of blood that was pumping out of Eli's head where the pipe had hit him. Eli, however, recovered quickly – too quickly – and came up with the scalpel swishing. He turned to Lina, the blade held out before him, then back to Rocko, his head snapping frantically from side to side.

Lina backed away too, and Eli's attention focused on her. He moved towards her, leering. 'I am the emissary!' he shrieked, his face trembling as if he might cry again, the blade pulled back for a killing blow. 'The dragon will not take no for an answer!'

Emissary? thought Lina. *Dragon?* She saw none of the man she had known so long within that face – he had become a raving, hollowed-out shell. And then he simply stopped, momentarily frozen, head cocked as if listening for a faint sound, maybe a distant voice. A light seemed to go on inside him and his lips twitched in the simile of a smile. He turned, ducking low, then sprinted straight past Rocko and out of the door, raining spats of blood as he went.

CHAPTER TWENTY-NINE

'Halman's crazy,' said Fionne, brushing her grease-slicked hair behind her ear. Her hand left another dark smear where it touched her face. She looked round at Patrick, who was an unappealingly dirty and unkempt individual at the best of times, and now looked as if some huge carnivorous machine had chewed him for a bit and then spat him out, possibly finding him too rank-tasting to swallow. Worse still, she could only view his rear aspect from here.

Patrick didn't move from his position, on his knees with his upper body inserted into an open wall-panel, but he answered with his usual lack of humour: 'Perhaps he wants to look for the shuttle. Or maybe he wants someone to try for Way Station One. I don't think *you* are in any position to criticise his decisions. I'm nearly done here, by the way.'

Fionne sighed and rooted in her tool box, which was balanced on the square metal case of the electronic diagnostics unit. She found the item she was looking for – an insulation applicator – and crawled back into her own grimy workspace. 'I guess so,' she said. 'But it seems like something of a gamble to me. And it'd take years to reach the way station in an in-sys vessel. They only carry enough gas for a short burn.' She clamped the applicator over the cable she had spliced into the main hangar supply and dialled a setting into it, working mainly by touch in the weak light supplied by her lamp.

'It's none of our business, is it,' said Patrick rhetorically, his voice muffled inside the wall.

Fionne wished she had Alphe to work with instead of this idiot. Or Nik. Well, maybe not Nik. She was still in a state of shock to think that her boss of years – and her friend, too – had been trying to kill them all. It was insane. Unthinkable. But there you were. Life was predictable in its unpredictability, if nothing else. She was just

181

glad to have work to do.

'It kind of *is* our business, Patrick,' she answered, matching his haughty tone, aware that she should just ignore him, but unable to help herself. She needed *somebody* to talk to – it was just a shame it had to be him. Patrick could be a bully if he was allowed. Of course, Nik had usually kept him in line before. 'If a half-day of hangar costs us a whole day of air and heat, I'd say that's our business all right.'

Patrick's voice was louder behind her now, and she realised he was out of the wall-space. There came a series of metallic clunks and bumps, indicating that he was stowing his tools again. 'Halman,' he said, 'is paid to deal with those sorts of decisions. If you don't trust him, you should have really done something about it before your life depended on those decisions. Bit late now.'

Fionne paused, a wave of irritation rippling through her. *Arrogant, self-righteous bastard!* she thought. But that wasn't the worst of it. The worst of it was that he had a point. She *did* trust Halman, and always had. He was a good station controller. Okay, so he wasn't strictly the brightest spark in the fire, but he was a decent man, and possessed of a certain practical, earthy wisdom. And she had to trust him now, accept her place as just another cog in the machine, a tool that he was using to try to correct their problems in the best way he saw fit. She locked the applicator shut and felt along the cable to examine the integrity of the insulation she had applied. It was impressively smooth and unbroken. 'I think that's it,' she said when she was sure.

'Good,' replied Patrick, managing to make the word sound like some sort of curse.

Fionne backed out of the wall-space and stood achingly, her knees popping as they straightened. She had spent almost the entire time since Nik's untimely death crammed into one uncomfortable space or another. At least the perpetual physical discomfort hadn't left her with the clarity of mind to really dwell on what had happened. At least, not yet.

'Let's test,' she said, stowing the insulation tool and humping the heavy tool box off the diagnostics machine. She wanted Rocko.

Right now, she *needed* Rocko. She should be spending her time with him, not with this sweaty little rat of a man. Rocko always made everything okay. And now – just when she had finally got it together with him after years of unspoken, mutual attraction – *now* this shit storm had to blow in. Just when she was finally happy. She wondered where he was and what he was doing.

Fionne dragged the heavy machine over to Patrick, who watched with faint, detached amusement but didn't offer to actually help. Overall, the amusement annoyed Fionne more than his failure to assist her. It didn't seem like a time to be amused by a co-worker struggling with a heavy piece of equipment, or any other damn thing, for that matter. Somebody screamed nearby, but neither of them looked in that direction. They were already starting to get used to the sounds of panic and chaos that had come to their fragile, lonely little world so quickly.

They wired the tester into the circuit at as many points as they could, checking earth, current, resistance, insulation and interference until they were both satisfied beyond any doubt. Patrick stood up, a cloud of mingled oil and body smells puffing out of his clothing. Fionne backed away, trying not to wrinkle her nose. Why didn't he fucking *wash*?

'Let's go live,' said Patrick, shooting her a sidelong look that she couldn't decipher the meaning of, and moving to the twin ranks of switches that they had exposed in the floor.

'Sure,' said Fionne, trying to sound more confident than she felt.

'You're sure you didn't go into the kitchen main?' he asked her, a patronising smile forming on his face.

Fionne bit back the words that came instinctively to her lips – *Fuck off, Patrick!* – and simply nodded, turning away so as not to look at him. She heard him clambering down into the floor, his shadow stumbling drunkenly across the walls as he moved his lamp around, trying to cast some light on his work. He flicked the switch.

Click!

Fionne realised that she had been holding her breath. She let it out now, slowly, and turned around. Patrick was sitting on the lip created by the missing floor panel. He dragged the diagnostics machine over so that he could see its readout.

'Well?' prompted Fionne after a pause of only a second or so.

'Ha!' he said, his face splitting open in a broad grin. It was the first time she had ever seen a genuine smile from him. It actually transformed him into something approaching human.

'It worked?' she asked, moving closer to see for herself.

'Yeah,' he said, still grinning, turning the heavy box so she could see better. 'Look!'

Fionne squinted into the non-backlit screen of the machine, squatting down beside Patrick. 'Well, look at that!' she exclaimed – and now she felt herself smiling, too. 'It did work.'

'Well,' said Patrick, climbing up out of the pit. 'At least we can launch the ships now. Whatever Halman has planned, that must be a good thing.'

CHAPTER THIRTY

Lina didn't waste a second. She pelted after Eli without thinking, right past Rocko, who reacted slowly, dazedly, and made to follow her. Marco cried out behind her, and she yelled at Rocko to stay with him, even though she knew he would be safe now. After all, the danger was in front of her and fleeing down the corridor into the gloom, spattering blood as it went.

Eli had taken a left out of her door, and now he disappeared out of view round the corner at the end of the passage, his feet almost skidding out from under him in his haste. Lina didn't even think to cry for help. She just knew that she had to stop him before he hurt anybody else. She still hoped, in some desperately optimistic last refuge of her mind, that he could be helped, mended, made well again. But mainly she just wanted to stop him, kill him if she had to. Strangely, these two conflicting plans seemed to gel with perfect logic in her racing mind.

She rounded the corner, putting out one hand to stop herself crashing into the wall. Her life seemed to have become one long helter-skelter dash through the dying bowels of this space station, flying from one surreal disaster to the next.

This new length of passage, lined with more private quarters, was shorter than the previous one and ended in a T-junction. Lina ran to the end as quickly as she could, hoping to see Eli down one of the two branches. But he was gone.

'Shit!' she cried, spinning round in place, baffled as to what to do next. The red light seemed to pulse around her, as if she was caught in the beating heart of some immense monster. She stamped one foot in childish frustration. 'Shit!'

Where had he gone? Which way? Right was the plaza, then the rec area and canteen. Left was more quarters, then stairs up to the machine rooms or down to the warehouse and hangar. She stopped, pinned by indecision.

She looked down, trying to see more blood droplets. To her left was a thumbnail-sized splash of glistening colour on the grimy grey of the floor. The hangar! It had to be. She had no idea what he hoped to achieve by going there – the power was off and he'd be pretty disappointed if he hoped to fly out of here – but suddenly she was sure of it. She started off running again, not noticing that the blood from her own wounded arm had now completely soaked her sleeve.

As she ran past Waine's quarters, she saw Waine standing in the open doorway, fumbling with the lock. He jumped backwards, eyes wide with surprise, and yelped her name, but Lina was already gone without slowing.

'Lina!' Waine yelled again, his voice cracked and wavery, the result of his heavy smoking. 'What's up?'

'It's. . . *Eli*!. . .' she yelled back over her shoulder, quite badly out of breath now and already developing a stitch. 'Get Halman!' She didn't think he'd heard her, but she didn't care. All of her concentration was on her racing feet, her shaky legs, the madman who had tried to kill her son.

'What?' called Waine's voice from behind her, but Lina was already away, rounding the next corner.

Eli was nowhere in sight, but she saw another splotch of blood. He was not only bigger than her, with a longer stride, but he was also fitter, being a regular at the gym. Lina wished she was a little more active herself. Her pace had slowed slightly by the time she reached the steps to the next level, but her determination remained undimmed.

She paused at the head of the stairs, straining to listen over the sound of her own breathing. The descent to the next level was matted with shadows, the stairway tapering off into darkness as if the world just faded away down there. She went down, feeling as if she was descending into a pit, maybe the lair of some unseen wild animal.

She stepped down onto the floor of the warehouse. The long central gangway stretched away in front of her, a red-washed chasm between the shelves. The ceiling was a dark interior sky. Something moved at the far end – a shifting in the shadows, perhaps inferred, perhaps real. She moved along the gangway in a tense half-crouch, feeling the fear piling up on top of her like an increasing weight.

As she went, she glanced from left to right, desperately trying to look down every side-branch, scan every shady alcove of the giant racking. The place was a library of hunched, alien shapes – large pieces of engines and mining equipment under plastic sheeting, piles of substandard flight suits still in their wrapping, disorderly heaps and coils of rope and cable, boxes of bolts and electrical components with their contents spilling out. An enemy could hide anywhere down here. And even though she was pretty certain that Eli had already entered the hangar, she was unable to still the racing of her heart as she moved through that eerie vault, feeling desperately small and alone.

As she neared the hangar door, she noticed for the first time the bright light that emanated from inside. It was a white light – a *normal* light – which meant that the power was on.

She approached cautiously, her body shuddering with fear, wishing that she had just run to get Ella or Halman, or someone – *anyone* – but compelled to continue. Why was the power on? Had Eli somehow *known*? Whether he had known or not, she was sure – *sure* – that he was here.

When she was almost within touching distance of the hangar door there was a sudden creak from inside its mechanism and it began to close. She'd been right – he *was* inside.

Without further thought, she ducked under the descending door and into the hangar. As she emerged, flinching and squinting beneath the glare, the door dropped into place behind her with a deep, percussive bang. *Trapped!* her mind shrieked. *Trapped with Him!*

She could make out the slumbering hulks of the Kays, lined up like soldiers, and the dead-lifter, parked askew near the central desk, its massive forks like the mandibles of a giant insect. But Eli was nowhere to be seen.

'Where are you?' she hissed, moving off down the nearest row of mining ships, past her own K6-12. She trailed the fingers of one hand across its pitted skin as she went by – a subconscious gesture of familiarity.

Steam hissed from a vent high in one wall, with a sudden rushing noise that made her jump. She spun around, her hands flying to her face protectively, but there was nobody there. The control room was incongruously dark behind its glasspex screen, like an empty socket. Something clanged – metal on metal – the sound echoing such that she couldn't discern its origin.

She wished that she'd brought a weapon with her, and she moved towards the central desk in the hope of finding a hand tool or something. . . anything. But the desk was empty except for Liu's distinctive bright green datasheet. It was showing a cheery screensaver of a cartoon dog that was so at odds with Lina's state of mind that she stopped, unable to comprehend it. The dog bounded happily from one side of the screen to the other, its tongue waving and flapping from its mouth. Dead silence hung around her. The madman was in here with her. Somewhere.

That sound again – the sound of clanging metal. This time, she could tell where it had come from: the far end of the hangar, near the ISL and the space door.

Lina took off running, crying out Eli's name, suddenly electrified by a rage so hot that it consumed her fear in an instant, immolating it in bright fire. She pelted up the central runway, her footsteps ringing on the metal floor, and leapt across the corner of the space door to land before the in-system loader, grabbing onto one of its antennae to steady herself. Something moved, glimpsed below the loader's up-tilted nose, obscured by its heavy landing gear. Lina dropped to the deck, peering underneath the ship. Nothing. She jumped to her feet again and spun round just in time to avoid the scalpel that came whispering towards her face.

She staggered back, unbalanced, into the loader's hull, kicking out, and the scalpel's blade shattered against the ship's armoured hide. Eli recoiled, shouting with pain, his leg going out from under him. His face, an exaggerated snapshot of horror and insanity, was

188

slathered in blood from the wound that Rocko had given him. A small, vengeful thrill went through Lina at the sight of it.

She tried to turn, to dive under the loader and find some sort of weapon, but Eli was already on her, seizing her hair in one hand. She saw the deck rise towards her face as he smashed her head into it. Bright sunbursts bloomed in her vision, obscuring it, and a wave of compressive agony shot through her skull. She kicked out behind her, trying to rise, but felt only empty air. Eli drove a knee into her back, pinning her down. She felt his weight on top of her, crushing her, driving her breath from her lungs. He smashed her head into the deck again, and this time instead of light, there was a bloom of darkness.

'I have to *go*!' he hissed, right in her ear. 'And *you* aren't going to stop me!' Was that his blood she felt dripping onto the back of her neck? Or her own? She thought she smelled the insanity baking off him in hot waves – something like sour sweat and burning wires intermingled.

Again: *smash!* The darkness swelled, making Lina think of the shadow in the belt: ink in water. Darkness superimposed on darkness. Darkness filled the world. She was spinning, gasping, fading. . .

She awoke to the deafening blast of the launch klaxon, a sound like the bellow of a dinosaur. Her eyes flickered open, filling her head with pain. The rough metal of the hangar floor felt sharp and abrasive against her cheek. The hangar was awash with red, strobing light. *That's odd*, she thought. *The power was on in here. White light. It was white.*

She sat bolt upright like somebody awakening from a nightmare, her heart trip-hammering inside her, her skull throbbing. Eli had initiated the launch procedure! Somehow he'd overridden the security protocols. She glanced around and noticed that she was on the closed ramp of the space door itself. He'd dumped her body there like a piece of garbage, ready to jettison into the belt. It was about to open.

She struggled to her feet, having to push herself upright with one hand. She looked towards the ISL and saw Eli in the cockpit, working the controls, squinting into some readout. He didn't notice her – he was too enraptured in what he was doing. Why was he trying to take the ISL? Why not a Kay?

'It doesn't matter!' Lina berated herself. 'Get to a ship! I have to get to a ship.'

She clambered off the space door, feeling clumsy and injured. Her head felt as if someone had filled it with broken glass and then kicked it like a football. Her wounded arm stung and burned fiercely. But she gained the flight deck and shambled down the row of Kays as quickly as she could. She was fully cleared to operate any of the ships on Macao, but she made for K6-12 without thinking, one hand pressed to the small of her back and the other to her head. The klaxon blatted again and the light changed to orange, supposedly to signify that everyone on the flight deck was safely inside a ship.

She clawed her way up the ladder of her Kay, falling into the cockpit with tears of pain running unnoticed from her eyes. She pulled her legs in and slammed the lid shut behind her, swivelling into an upright position in the seat. Was she going to follow him out there? She supposed she was.

'I've come this far. . .' she muttered to herself as she booted the ship's computer up.

The HUD illuminated, stitching the cockpit canopy with neon stats and scales. It helpfully tagged the unseen vessel at the far end with the legend *ELI SWAINE // IN-SYS LOADER // 50.2M // 0 KPH*. She felt the cockpit pressurise and breathed a sigh of relief.

'You could have killed me!' screamed Eli's voice suddenly, clipping as its volume threatened to overload the comm. Lina jolted as if she had been goosed. He must have seen her ship appear on his own HUD and realised that she was gone from where he'd left her. She supposed he was referring to the blow he had received to his head, and she put one hand to her own battered skull. It came away bloody, as she had expected. 'I'm the emissary, Lina! The dragon wanted him dead, and now it's going to be angry!'

'Listen, Eli. . .' she began, but she faded away as she realised

190

she had nothing to follow this with.

'I have to go!' he cried. His voice, coming from the headrest speaker, was as loud in her ear as if he had been squatting behind her seat. It was a sound filled with murderous, boiling hatred, the guttural snarl of a monster. 'Don't think to follow me! It'll eat you up! It'll fucking *eat* you, Lina!'

What the hell was he talking about? And then a shudder went through her. It suddenly felt cold – icy cold, *too* cold – in the cockpit of her ship. She remembered the shadow from her dream, twining through the belt like molten obsidian – a hungry, living darkness. *It'll eat you up!* she thought, suddenly sure that this was what he meant. The reality of what she was doing came crashing in on her. Hadn't she vowed never to fly again? And yet here she was, preparing to pursue a madman into the belt where he'd already murdered Sal and dream-shadows flowed like dark blood amongst the rocks. *It'll fucking* eat *you, Lina!* she heard again in her mind. She pulled the straps tight around her chest, cinching the buckle below her breasts. She took the yoke in sweat-slicked hands and steadied herself, bracing against her backrest.

'Fuck you,' she whispered between clenched teeth, wiping blood from her eyes with one sleeve.

There was a loud rush as the hangar cycled, fading away as vacuum replaced air. Lina felt her ship trembling around her as she leeched gas into the jets. It felt like a tense little animal, itching to run. One of its tool arms twitched like a palsied limb, the result of a dying servomotor, an intermittent fault that had plagued the vessel for months.

And then the hangar was washed with emerald green as the final stage of the cycle kicked in. The space door shivered and began to drop. The belt rotated mutely out there, a carousel of broken shards. Yuwan, the neighbouring gas giant, was a creamy orange disc that soared above the plane of rubble like a rising sun.

Eli's loader was coming about, turning wide to align with the ramp, picking up speed already. Lina trundled out onto the main concourse, some fifty metres behind the ISL. She gave the dead-lifter a wide berth, her hands surprisingly steady on the controls.

'You're not getting away, you bastard!' she said through gritted teeth, not caring if he heard or not.

The loader was a ponderous and fat-bodied machine, a patchwork of black and grey, prickled with manoeuvring jets. It rode high on its suspension, only carrying empty crates, but it moved with a sort of deliberate sluggishness. Eli made a last tiny adjustment to its bearing, then dialled the gas up all the way, accelerating over the lip of the runway and out into space.

Lina had been gaining on him until his wheels left the deck of the station, but then the loader quickly accelerated off, freed from friction, flung away by Macao's rotation, banking sharply to port-side, leaving icy contrails of condensing gas behind it. Lina pushed the yoke all the way to the stop, still checking diags with one eye, feeling the vessel rattling around her as numerous loose bolts and electrical components chattered to each other. The Eli-tag on the HUD went off-screen to the left, tracked by a directional pointer. Her Kay flew from the end of the ramp and dropped away into space.

She paused for a heartbeat, letting herself fully clear the station, then banked hard to follow Eli. The greater bulk of the loader was cancelled out by its more powerful drive system and, in fact, it was slightly faster than a Kay in space. Already Eli was some hundred-plus metres in front, turning around Macao counter-spinwards, angling down towards the heart of the belt. Lina kept the yoke pinned, but he was accelerating away from her, zipping between two massive asteroids with surprising agility. She tried to turn inside his arc, wrenching the Kay over as hard as she could, but she made up only a little distance, which she immediately began to lose again. She didn't even pause to wonder what she would do if she actually caught up with him.

'Leave me alone!' screamed Eli through the speakers, making Lina's head spike with fresh agony.

No, she mouthed silently, intent on flying, her eyes checking between HUD and dashboard instruments, her knuckles white on the control stick. *It's a bit late for that*, she thought grimly, as asteroids flitted past on both sides. She jagged left, Eli's contrails washing over her screen, partially blinding her, then right, pushing on, driven by sheer determination.

'I'm warning you!' shrieked Eli in an almost comically shrill voice.

The belt thickened around her, pressing in. Macao had become invisible already. It might have been imagined – a mirage borne of wishful thinking. This endless textured space was the only reality left, and in it she might wander eternally, chasing this phantom madman who would remain always tantalisingly out of reach.

Eli swerved around a vast iceberg, maybe eighty metres across, clinging tight to its dirty surface. Lina lost sight of him, although the HUD still tracked the loader in its bright orange reticule. As she rounded the iceberg, expecting to catch a glimpse of him, the Eli-tag on her HUD blinked out. He must have killed the ISL's computer, which left him flying without safety systems. Lina thought how poetic it would be if Eli was to be killed in an accident with a belt object, as had happened to Sal. *But Sal wasn't killed in an accident with a belt object. We know better, don't we Eli?* she thought. *Because you murdered her, didn't you?*

As she rounded the large rock, she was confronted by a group of smaller asteroids which had been hidden from her sight. The loader was not visible. She dived her Kay into the mass of asteroids, gravel hissing off her canopy, the computer screaming proximity warnings and enforcing little corrective jolts of thrust, struggling to avoid the larger objects. She pressed on, though, basically guessing at which way he might have gone, blind beyond a hundred metres.

She emerged into a clearer space and spun her ship around, washing the belt with radar. Echoes came from everywhere – shifting, overlapping, useless. She could make out dispersing contrails, but couldn't tell what direction they led in. The gas trail had become a cloud already – a random organic shape.

Suddenly, she shivered, her nerves jangling. *It'll eat you up!* she thought again. That shadow. . . that living shadow. . . Whatever it was, she had voluntarily entered its lair. It would smell the blood that had soaked her flight suit and come for her. She thought she saw it – darker patches in the darkness, concentrations of nothing. . . *patterns* in the chaos. . .

'No,' she said aloud, alarmed at how her own voice trembled. 'There's *nothing* out here. He's insane. Nothing but rock and ice.'

And then she caught sight of the loader. Eli had turned sharply to starboard, almost doubling back, and she saw only the merest flash of expelled gas between the asteroids, and maybe a glint of sunlight on hull. Instantly, she was after him, half-looping and maxing the gas. She checked the HUD and saw that her Kay still had its last bolt of metal in the breech of its mass driver. The loader loomed large in her canopy as Eli slowed down to avoid a clutch of chaotically-jostling rocks the size of Kays. She targeted the wallowing ISL and hit the fire control.

The ship jolted as the bolt was released. Lina watched in slow motion as it travelled towards the banking loader, flashing once in her vessel's headlight.

'Come on!' she screamed, pushing the yoke almost through its stop, all her muscles tensed.

Eli braked hard, sending out a bloom of gas in front of his ship, rolling away below her faster than she could follow. The bolt smashed into one of the Kay-sized rocks, shattering it into dust, missing him by metres. She burst through the cloud of debris, sightless, knowing she had lost him, and tried to roll around the clutch of asteroids to resume the chase. But when she hit clear space, the loader was gone again.

Rocks hung all around her like a flock of silently-watching sheep, inviting her next move. She stopped the ship and hung there, breathing hard and inwardly cursing herself. In all directions, a total uniformity of stone and vacuum, a smokescreen of rubble.

Lina kicked the underside of the dash in frustration, immediately wishing she hadn't when a warped metal plate dropped off onto her boot with a subtle little clang. She had no idea what it was or what it might be for. She held her breath, pissed at herself, waiting to see if she had broken anything terminal. *Please no!* she wished. *Not now!* But no alarms went off and it seemed she'd got away with it.

She shoved the metal plate into a corner with one foot, casting about herself. She turned her Kay in place – once, twice – but it looked the same in all directions. Nothingness, as far as the eye could see.

Where did he go? she wondered. *Where does he possibly hope to go out here? Is he thinking he can fly right out of the system?* And then a gap opened between two asteroids, quite at random, and she saw it.

The in-system loader was heading for a massive rock – one of the largest Lina had ever seen in the belt – and the missing shuttle was somehow attached to it, *docked* with it. The rock itself was shaped a bit like a figure-eight, with a large bulb at either end and a thinner waist in the middle. The stolen supply shuttle was adhered to one of these bulbs, and Lina could see where holes in the rock had been sealed with yellow instawall foam that had formed lurid scabs on its surface. Why would he have done that? Perhaps he had been living there.

Eli closed in on the figure-eight asteroid, weaving through a cloud of smaller debris that orbited it, going much too quickly for safety. His loader hugged the asteroid's surface closely and coasted along it, closing in on the shuttle. Lina could actually see the cockpit lights in the shuttle now, could see little hisses of vapour as it vented some waste product into space.

'Go back, Lina!' shouted Eli's voice suddenly, making her ears ring. She turned the comm down to half.

'You bastard!' she yelled back, enraged, more angry than she had ever been before. She was closing in on him now as he neared the shuttle, slowing and lining himself up with it. 'You tried to kill Marco, you bastard! You were playing *football* with him the other day!' Somehow, this was the part that made her angriest of all: that he'd had the gall to take her son off and kick a ball around with him as if nothing was wrong in the world. Perhaps he had meant to kill Marco that day. Who knew? But whatever he had intended, it had been a lie, a pathetic deception. 'You stole our shuttle, Eli! All this time, it was you!' She felt tears sting her eyes, threatening to obscure her sight, and she swiped at her face angrily with one sleeve. 'You killed all those people!' she screamed. 'You *killed* those people! What is *wrong* with you?'

'I am the emissary!' he shouted back, and he sounded as angry as she was now, as if she was the one in the wrong. 'I do what I have to do!' And then, in another, calmer tone that sounded as if he was reading from a script, or maybe quoting somebody else's words: 'You are my emissary, and I have your best interests at heart. Some of your tasks may be *difficult* at times.' He paused for a moment, then added, 'You see?' as if that had proven something.

'You're a monster!' she sobbed. 'I'm going to. . . to. . .'

His loader was coming smoothly together with the shuttle now, guided with obvious skill.

'You're going to *what*, Lina?' he asked. He still sounded angry, but he also sounded tired now, as if she were an irritating child who had pestered him to breaking point. 'Hmm? *What?*'

His ship clamped firmly onto the docking platform of the shuttle, just as Lina flew overhead in her Kay. The loader, the shuttle and the asteroid scrolled past beneath her and she saw what he meant: the shuttle had only the one docking space, and the loader was in it. She swooped up and away, slowing, still jinking and jagging to avoid asteroids, not fully trusting the ship to take care of her. She turned to come around again. What *was* she going to do?

'I'll. . . I'll. . . I'm gonna go and get Ella and Halman and the others. They're gonna want that shuttle back, you *thief*! And I'm going to return with them, and Eli, there is going to be a reckoning between us.'

'That's your plan,' he replied flatly.

Lina's Kay shivered under her, strained by gees, as she looped round to head back to Macao. 'You killed all those people, Eli,' she said again.

'No, Lina, it wasn't me,' he said, but she knew it for what it was: a lie. '*You* have killed *me*, though,' he said, more quietly now. '*You* have killed *me*.'

Lina didn't have the slightest clue what he meant and she was too angry to consider it. She flicked the comm off and accelerated back towards the station, flying fast, but not as fast as she had when she'd been chasing Eli. She wondered how much of Sal Newman still drifted here. Maybe the shadow had devoured what was left like a whale vacuuming up plankton. 'It'll eat you up,' she reminded herself.

And as she flew, she felt that darkness breathing around her again – *something* within the nothing. *Patterns*. She felt as if the belt itself were a sinister, living thing, and she flew through its disseminated body like a germ.

She no longer trusted the belt at all. Her friend had clearly gone insane out here. It had eaten Sal. And she felt, as she flew alone through its jagged depths, that it would eat her too, given the chance. She concentrated on staying alert, all her senses straining, perfectly in tune with the machine. She hardly breathed until the belt began to thin again and Macao came into sight. She had never been more glad to see the place in her life.

CHAPTER THIRTY-ONE

Halman was in the rec area alone, watching the belt when Ella found him. He had been staring out at it, thinking about Sal, thinking about Nik, bathed in that hateful red light, for half an hour or more. He could feel events slipping through his fingers faster than he could react. Nik had been killed, the saboteur was dead, and yet his mood was dark and retrospective. He could have done things better. Stopped it somehow.

When Ella seized his shoulder from behind, half-spinning him around as she crashed into him, his mind just had time to scream *What now?* before she began to talk.

'Shit Halman Jayce is dead Tamzin's dead Eli's gone he tried to attack Marco and Waine says they ran off towards the hangar I don't know why but she's fucking chased him Dan I've fucked up we've fucked up come on! Come *on*!'

'What?' he asked stupidly, steadying her with a hand on each shoulder. He looked her squarely in the eyes and said, more slowly, 'What's wrong, Ella?' knowing as he said it that this was bad news, more bad news. Had she said that someone was dead? Ella's eyes were wide and jumpy, darting all over his face, and he could see that she was breathing hard, as if she had run here.

'Rachelle just came to see me,' said Ella, still rapidly, but at least understandably this time. 'I sent her to relieve Jayce at the medical department. She found Tamzin and Jayce dead – murdered.'

This last word fell into Halman's mind like a stone into a well. A slow, dark splash emanated from its impact. '*What?*' he asked again, hoping desperately that he'd heard wrongly.

'Eli killed Jayce and Tamzin. Then, while Rachelle was still in my office, Rocko appeared with Marco in tow, who was scared half to death and barely able to speak, but otherwise all right. Eli tried to attack him – Marco, that is – and Rocko heard shouting and walked in on them. Lina was there, too, and Rocko says it looked like Eli was about to cut them both to bits. He hit Eli on the head with a metal pipe – he was still holding it when he came to see me. He said Eli ran off and Lina chased him. He was yelling about dragons and emissaries or some shit. He's gone crazy, Dan! Waine saw Lina running towards the hangar.' She shook her head, forcibly detaching herself from his grip, and stood back. 'I don't know what the hell's going on, or where they've gone, but. . .' She was still shaking her head, caught in a perpetual loop of denial. 'We fucked up,' she said, staring up into Halman's face. 'We fucked up.'

Halman staggered back, almost tripping over one of the benches below the window, mouthing empty vowel-sounds. It couldn't be. . . It couldn't be. . .

'The hangar,' he said at last. Was the power back on down there by now? 'Come on!'

They ran through the rec area, dodging between the pillars that housed the huge supply chutes. They pelted through the eerily-quiet plaza where a few people moved slowly through the red haze like ghouls, looking hollow-eyed and vacant.

They ran past rows of living quarters, past medical to the stairs. Rachelle was hovering outside medical, talking to Hobbes. Her face was wet with tears. Hobbes tried to snag Halman's sleeve as he ran past, calling out.

'Not now, Kenn!' Halman bellowed, not slowing. He felt Ella's presence behind him, practically adhered to his heels, keeping easy step with him.

They virtually tumbled down the stairs onto the rimwards-most level, landing in the corridor outside aeroponics. Silence reigned here, silence and weak ruddy light that seeped from doorways as they passed, their footsteps thumping like heartbeats.

When they reached the warehouse they saw that the lights were on in the flight control room – the normal lights. They increased their pace by unspoken consensus.

Suddenly, Liu popped out of the control room in front of them.

'Come on! I've got people looking for you two!' he shouted, disappearing again from sight.

They burst into the control room, Halman breathing hard and ruing his lapsed standard of physical fitness.

The power was on in here and virtually every piece of equipment seemed to have reset itself. Numerous chimes and warning signals competed for attention like a dawn chorus of computers. The light was almost too bright. Several screens showed spooling POST-readouts that repeated desperately, vying for human input, bemoaning the fact that the system had shut down unexpectedly and now required a full diagnostic start-up.

The main terminal, however, looked like it was working. Liu jumped back into his chair, making it spin around. He corrected it quickly and bent over the terminal's screen.

'He's out there somewhere,' said Liu, not looking up. 'Eli. Lina chased him. My people are out looking for you.'

'Yeah,' said Halman between gasps, doubled over with his hands on his knees. 'Fuck, Liu.'

'Yes,' agreed Liu, spinning his seat to face outwards over the huge HUD-enabled glasspex panel that formed the control room's floor, its shiny surface marred by coffee spills. 'He took the loader for some reason. Overrode the safety system from the deck terminal. I don't know – wait! Here's Lina!' Liu leant forwards in his seat, pointing. 'Look! She's coming in!'

Halman straightened and strode into the middle of the great floor screen, casting about for Lina's tag. 'Where?' he demanded. Ella leant back against the door, head back and breathing deeply.

'She's dropping in and out of visibility,' said Liu. 'All that debris out there acts like chaff, as you know, and most of our sensors are down now. But I saw her. Watch!'

Halman watched for what seemed like a long time but was probably only seconds. An orange icon lit up on the screen between his feet, then quickly vanished again. Just before it flickered out, he had time to read *LINA MCLOUGH // K6-12 // 997 M.*

'I see her!'

'Exactly,' agreed Liu, smiling his little smile. 'She's coming in. The distance is dropping.'

'And Eli?' asked Halman, still peering down into the screen.

'Not yet,' said Liu. 'Just her.' And then he added, a little prissily, Halman thought, 'She's going a bit fast, though. Reckless.'

'But why the fuck is she out there at all, Liu? What was she thinking?'

Liu looked up into Halman's face. Halman felt the sudden and almost overwhelming urge to jump on Liu and choke him until he stopped fucking *smiling*. He balled his hands into fists and held them tight against his thighs.

'I have no idea, but in a minute or two you can ask her.' Liu's smile widened further, exposing perfect white teeth. He shrugged cheerfully, and Halman glowered at him.

'I fucking will, pal,' agreed Halman darkly.

He forced himself to relax and stalked to the slightly wonky office chair next to Liu's, where he collapsed with a groan. It looked about a hundred years old and had lost most of its upholstery, but it seemed to bear his weight. He looked up at Ella, who still leant against the door with her eyes shut tight and her head back. Never before had the station's continued existence seemed so tenuous to him. Murder. Sabotage. And now this jolly little fuckaround. Thank fuck that Lina was coming back.

As for Eli, Halman could barely believe it. His brain felt close to a dangerous overload. Had Eli really tried to kill Marco? It wasn't possible. . . And yet, somehow he knew that it was true. One of his oldest friends and most trusted section leaders had gone insane, killed a bunch of people and fled into the asteroid belt. And what the hell had Ella said about dragons? Something about dragons. . .

Halman was deeply disappointed with Ella and her team. She should never have left Jayce in charge of Eli. This was supposed to be their area of expertise. And that disappointment made him feel guilty. He didn't like to think bad of his crew. Now the guilt was turning to anger – an aimless, undirected anger. He tried to calm himself, unclenching his hands and laying them flat on his knees. 'Oh shit. . .' he sighed. In Ella's defence, it had all happened so damn *fast*, and their manpower was so stretched. . . and now two more people were dead. Hindsight, he supposed was a wonderful thing, but useless in any practical respect.

'Should I get a couple of my guys in case Eli comes in?' asked Ella, seemingly emerging from a reverie. She looked desperately eager to please.

'Yeah,' said Halman. 'Get everyone you can.' She dashed out of the door without another word.

Halman looked out at the hangar, which lay bright and empty and silent behind the transparent wall of the control room, still open to space – a stage waiting for the next act to begin. Ella was right. They should have a team waiting. Then if Eli came in, they would have him. No escape.

'Still no sign of him?' Halman asked.

'No, just her.' Liu indicated the approaching Lina-icon on the screen beneath their feet. It glowed steadily now, the distance reading dropping rapidly.

'I want to talk to her,' said Halman, staring at the orange square.

'Should be possible now,' said Liu. 'Might take a second, as we don't have main array any more, but. . .' He trailed off, his attention becoming quickly absorbed by his work. He clipped an earpiece on, dialled a couple of settings into the comm, slid the gains up on the main channel and cleared his throat as if he was about to make a speech at a wedding. 'Ahem! Lina, this is Base. Copy.' He glanced over his shoulder at Halman, who had come to stand behind him.

Lina's voice from the terminal's speaker, hissing with static and worryingly frantic: 'Copy! Get me Halman, Liu, get me Halman! I want him there when I come in!' Even with the background hiss, there was no mistaking the urgency in that voice.

'Halman's here, Lina. Take it easy, now, slow down a little. You're going too fast. I want you to back off and come round again. Over.'

'Put him on!' yelled Lina, ignoring Liu's instructions. Her Kay, visible to the naked eye now, was angling up towards the floor of the control room, approaching the station's ramp, retro thrusters firing white billows of gas.

'Lina, please back off and—' began Liu, but Halman pushed him out of the way and leant over the mic.

'Lina, this is Dan. What the fuck is going on?'

'Dan. . .' said Lina in what sounded like a relieved sigh. There was a pause during which the two men waiting in the control room had time to exchange foreboding glances, then: 'You're not gonna believe this, but. . . Eli. . .' She laughed bitterly, a sound with no real humour in it at all. 'Eli has the shuttle out there. He's been screwing with us for some time, I'm afraid.'

Halman felt the breath rush out of him as if he had been gut-punched. He had half expected the shuttle to be out there somewhere — after all, it had been his idea to route a fair portion of their precious power into the hangar. But this? *Eli* had it? Surely not. . . how long had it been out there? How long had his friend deceived him? Halman himself was a fairly simple creature, and other people's deviousness often took him by surprise.

'Hang on. . .' said Lina. 'I'm coming in. . .'

'Lina—' began Liu, but Halman shoved him on the shoulder, forestalling any further objections about her flightpath or velocity.

'Just shut up and let her land, okay?' he suggested, but not unkindly. Liu stepped back, his smile faltering for the first time that day.

Lina's Kay rose to within twenty metres of the glasspex floor, rolling gracefully to present its wheels to the hangar's ramp. The two watchers held their breath without realising it. The ship loomed large and then passed directly beneath them. Halman stood tensely as it disappeared from the floor-screen and came into view through the window that overlooked the flight deck. The ship coasted into the hangar, still firing retros at full blast, filling the space with vapour, and touched down.

Liu was at the terminal, working the controls, both hands flying over the panel with the unconscious ease of long use. The ramp shuddered, sending a tremor through the superstructure of the station, vibrating the glasspex floor of the control room, and began

203

to close. Lina's ship had decelerated almost to walking speed, bouncing gently on its suspension. It coasted past the central desk and the dead-lifter, arriving at its usual space and turning smoothly in a half-circle. Halman felt an incredible, cooling wave of relief wash over him. At least one of his endangered and diminishing crew had returned intact.

There was a rushing sound from behind the wall of the control room as the air pumps spun up and began to flood the hangar again. Lina's Kay came to a final rest and the landing lights went off almost at once. A throbbing blue strobe filled the hangar as soon as she opened the hatch, indicating to the ground crew that there were live, unsuited personnel on the deck. She swung herself out, using the Kay's tool arms as handholds, and climbed down. She looked up at Halman, who stood at the window watching her, and waved. He raised one hand in return, attempting to smile, and just about managing a grimace. Lina's blonde hair was a matted tangle, even more so than usual. Her head, face and upper body were virtually covered in what looked like blood. She came towards the hangar door at a brisk walk, one hand held to the small of her back.

'Open it up!' called Halman to Liu.

The hangar door began to rise, albeit it with its customary slowness, as soon as Lina got to it. She waited impatiently, fingers drumming on one thigh, until it was high enough to duck under. Twenty seconds later there was a knock at the control room's door. Liu hit the pad to open it and Lina walked in, slightly bent over and obviously in pain.

'Lina!' Halman cried, seizing her and hugging her briefly but tightly, forgetting that she was clearly injured. 'You dumb shit!' Her face was startled and uncomprehending as she stepped back. 'What the hell were you doing out there?'

'Glad you made it back, Li,' said Liu from his seat at the control desk. He was, of course, smiling. 'But you're hurt.'

Lina ran a hand through her hair, then looked at the blood on it as if she hadn't seen it before. 'Yeah,' she said flatly. 'I guess I am.'

'Liu – get Hobbes,' ordered Halman, but Lina waved his

suggestion away.

'No, it's – I'm fine,' she said. 'I'm fine. I'll go see him later, okay?'

'Okay,' agreed Halman reluctantly. 'Just tell me what's going on.'

'He – Eli – he tried to attack Marco,' she began shakily. 'Rocko saved his life – both our lives, I guess. Then he fled – Eli, that is – and I guess I just kinda followed. I don't know what I was thinking to be honest.' She looked as if she may be about to cry, thought Halman. He didn't blame her really, but he still hoped that it wouldn't happen.

'Hey,' he said. 'It's okay.' He struggled for something more comforting than this that he could add. After a second or two, he came up with: 'Marco's all right. I think he's still with Rocko.'

'Yeah,' Lina sighed. 'Good. That's good.' She took a deep breath in and seemed to pull herself together. 'Eli killed Jayce and Tamzin. And he killed Sal, too. That's how I knew about him. He started spouting some weird shit when I went to medical to visit him. About how he wasn't *done yet*. I knew something was up. I came down here and inspected his ship.' She looked from Halman to Liu, making sure that they were following her. 'There was an impact mark on his Kay.' Liu started to interject, but she held up a finger to stall him. 'Not from a belt object,' she explained. 'But from hitting another ship. I've been here long enough to know what a belt-impact usually looks like. You can check it for yourselves, of course. But I know I'm right. That last cry of hers – she called his name – it wasn't a cry for help. It was a cry of shock as he nudged her into the path of an asteroid. He must have sabotaged K6-8's safety systems, too.' She shook her head, crestfallen. 'When I got back to medical he was gone.'

'Surely he didn't actually expect to be able to fly away, though?' said Halman. 'As far as he was aware, the power was off here, right?'

'It was almost as if he knew. At my place, it was like a lightbulb went on above his head. Maybe he overheard someone talking about it,' Lina said uncertainly. 'And he just ran off. I followed him here. He knocked me out–' she indicated the area on her head where the blood seemed to be the most concentrated, '–then left me to die in the vacuum. I came to just in time and followed him. I almost hit the ISL with a mass-driver bolt,' she added disbelievingly. 'I almost hit it.'

'And where is our shuttle? Is he fucking living in it out there?' asked Halman.

'It's weirder than that,' said Lina. She looked a little unsteady on her feet and Halman considered forcing her to see Hobbes immediately after all. But in truth, he wanted to hear this first. He took her by the elbow and led her instead to the office chair that he himself had vacated, where she plonked herself down exhaustedly. 'It looks like he's attached it to some asteroid – one of the largest I've ever seen out there. As for why, I couldn't begin to guess.'

'Right,' said Halman, his brows descending and one hand going to his stubbled chin. He could feel the cogs beginning to turn inside his head. They felt a little rusty to be honest. 'Anything else you can tell us?'

'No,' she said after a pause. 'I don't think so.' But her face looked distant and wondering.

'You're sure?' Halman pushed.

'Yeah,' said Lina, looking down at her feet. Blood had dripped onto her boots, staining them.

'So what's all this bullshit about dragons?' asked Halman. Ella had said something about dragons, hadn't she? Dragons and emissaries and crazy mining-team bosses and metal pipes and scalpel-murders. Halman's knees felt suddenly weak. His head was buzzing, as if it was filled with flies – lots of activity but no sort of order.

'Dan. . .' said Lina, still not looking at him. 'I don't know what's going on. But Eli has gone properly insane.'

'Mmm,' grunted Halman. He looked up at Liu, who was listening politely from his seat, unsure as to whether he was still involved in this or not. 'Liu – I'm going to send two people up here – one to replace you, and one as a runner. If anything else comes out of that belt, or even so much as fucking *stirs*, I want that runner to make for my office as fast as their little legs will carry them. You're with me, okay?' Liu nodded. 'Lina – I want yourself and one other representative of the mining crew – Ilse Reno, I suppose – to report to my office. But first, I want you all-cleared by Hobbes. If he wants to keep you in, you stay. And yes, that is an order. I'm going to talk to maintenance, too. And Ella. . . Where the hell *is* Ella, actually? She'd better bloody get me my sec-team soon!'

'And then what?' asked Lina in a small and far away voice. 'What are we going to do?'

'We're going to come up with a plan – a *safe* plan – to get our shuttle back. If Eli thinks he can just take it, he's in for one big surprise.'

CHAPTER THIRTY-TWO

Carver had gone beyond exhaustion now, but still he dug. He had struggled and cursed for hours, a parasitic insect in a body of stone, working robotically, driving his aching muscles by willpower alone. At one point he had torn his glove on a piece of rock that came spinning towards him unexpectedly and crunched into his left hand, almost causing him to drop the cutter. He had screamed aloud, a fan of blood-droplets spraying from his knuckle. He'd just managed to kill the cutter without it injuring him. He had inspected the wound with a feeling of detached misery, but hadn't been able to do anything for it. For some time after that, the hand had leaked a weaving thread of blood into the air about him, that trailed from the tear in his glove like a streamer, occasionally spattering across his suit.

Once, the blood had managed to catch him in the eye, and this time he really had come close to a significant accident. He had reeled back, his feet slipping away from where they had been braced against the rock face, jerking against his harness line with a jolt that caused him to drop the cutter. For a critical second, the cutter had continued to gout incandescent plasma as it spun away, slicing a jagged lightning bolt into the rock beside him, melting one of his rock pins into bubbling slag and coming within a few centimetres of his own thigh before extinguishing.

He had dangled there from his remaining pin, the cutter hanging from his belt, weaving and snaking at the end of its line. He had reeled it in, all of his muscles a-tremble, and held it against his chest, eyes closed and teeth clenched. It had been some time before he'd been able to summon up the strength to continue. He had several spare pins in the little tool-loops of his space suit, and he'd used one of these to replace the melted one, burning the tattered end off the line with the cutter and knotting it clumsily with his damaged hands. Then he had got back to work. What else was there to do?

And so he continued like this for some measureless measure of time, a numb and senseless period of aching repetition. Was it even daytime, technically? How long had he been awake? He had no idea. His life had become a surreal blur of rocky darkness, echoing isolation and unceasing toil. After a while he didn't even want to kill the crazy dragon-man any more – at least, not wholeheartedly. He just wanted the bastard to return, feed him, and allow him to sleep again. Even the thought of the ruined body in the navigator's chair didn't concern him after a while. He didn't particularly care if his own fate was to join the shuttle's pilot in death, as long as he could have a rest and something to eat first.

Then, suddenly, he felt a vibration tremble through the asteroid. He killed the cutter and cocked his head, listening. He heard, faintly, the fading rumble that indicated that a ship had either docked with the shuttle or *un*docked. Was it possible that the crazy dragon-man had actually *been* back already, without even coming to see his slave, and had now left again? A new, and even blacker, wave of misery washed through him at that thought. It *was* possible, he knew. It certainly was. He waited in a silence broken only by the high chinking noise of colliding rock-chunks behind him. He shot a baleful look at the restraining device that was adhered to its rock pin in the wall. *Fucking little bastard*, he thought at it. Was the crazy dragon-man back? Or gone for good?

He waited. . .

Silence. . .

And then, just as he was reaching a new fever-pitch of despair, he heard a voice coming towards him from the direction of the shuttle. He almost cried with joy, putting his head back and squeezing his eyes shut to stem the tears of relief that threatened to come.

'I couldn't do it!' he heard the man exclaim from some distance up the docking tube. He was relieved to hear the voice, but a little disturbed as well. Because that voice did not sound happy, not at all. There was a note of desperate, unhinged misery in its tone, unmistakable even from here. 'I know, I know!' raved the voice, between grunts of exertion, as the man came wriggling down the tube towards Carver. 'I'm sorry, I know. . . I will do, of course, anything. . .' The voice stopped for a moment, and Carver had the sense that the man was listening for him, maybe suspicious that he couldn't hear the plasma cutter.

'Hey!' called Carver, his relief tempered by new caution. The guy really had sounded pretty distressed, and Carver couldn't imagine that that would be a positive development for himself. But fuck it – he had to eat and sleep. This lunatic was his only lifeline, desperately worrying though that thought was.

The little grunts and huffs resumed from inside the tube as the man came on again, but he didn't answer Carver's call. Carver waited nervously, his boots braced against the face and the cutter held with its muzzle safely upwards. The surface of the cave glinted exotically in his suit-light – a private night sky filled with stars.

The man emerged from the end of the tube as if born from a mother of stone and steel, tumbling out in a disorderly tangle of arms and legs. Carver noted with a mixture of satisfaction and dismay that he was dressed in what were clearly hospital pyjamas. *Proof, if proof were needed that the fucker has escaped from a mental ward*, thought Carver. The man pushed himself fully out of the tube and rotated to regard Carver, pivoting by a handle on the tube's outer edge. His face was set in a sneer, the corners of his mouth pulled down so far that the expression was almost comical until one realised that it was the manifestation of a deep and burning hatred. He was covered in blood that had apparently poured from a wound on his head.

'*You*,' said the man accusingly. 'Why aren't you digging?'

'Hey,' said Carver, hefting the cutter warningly, a little spooked. 'I heard you coming and shut it off.' The man was studying him minutely, as if suspecting some deception. 'Er, good to see you again,' Carver added uncertainly. It was even true, in a sense.

The man pushed off and drifted across the cave towards

210

Carver, swatting a pinwheeling cone of rock out of his path, and landed skilfully within arm's reach of the restraining device.

'Well, I almost didn't make it,' replied the man testily. His face had warmed slightly, but he still looked seriously pissed off, if not actually homicidal any more. 'Thanks to some interfering *fucks* I've had to deal with.'

'Didn't go well, then?' asked Carver, turning to face the crazy dragon-man, who was now removing the restraining device from the rock and inspecting its readout to ensure that it hadn't been somehow tampered with.

'What?' asked the man sharply, fixing him with a freezing stare.

Carver felt his flesh creep a little in response. 'Er, well, your problems are my problems, right?' he said hopefully.

The crazy dragon-man sighed heavily, his features lit in high contrast under Carver's suit-light, and his lip began to tremble. *Don't fucking cry, you freak*, prayed Carver internally. *I swear I'll lose it if you start fucking blubbing.* But the man didn't start to cry. He seemed to steel himself, squeezing his eyes briefly shut and clipping the unit to his belt, then shrugged.

'Maybe,' allowed the man, apparently thinking about this. 'We're gonna get some rest,' he said, turning to push off back towards the shuttle. 'Both of us. Come on – stay close or this thing'll kill you.'

And without further warning the crazy dragon-man launched himself towards the tube. Although he didn't push off too fast, Carver still had to scramble to unhook himself in time to follow within safe range of the restraining device. He couldn't for the life of him remember exactly how far that range was, but he knew he'd get a warning shot of pain if he began to go outside of it, before it actually finished him off. *Bastard!* he cursed the guy. *Don't make it easy for me, will you?*

They swam together down the grey artery of the tube and into the bleak interior of the shuttle. They wended their way back to the bridge where Carver had been allowed to rest before. Every push and pull along the handlines sent fresh aches and pains through Carver's cramping muscles, but despite this, and his new concerns about his companion, he was immeasurably glad to be out of the asteroid. It had been weirding him out a little.

Once inside the bridge the crazy dragon-man adhered the restraining device to the flight console and went to a locker in the far corner, passing the turned-away chair that had become the grave of the unfortunate pilot without so much as a glance. Carver took the liberty of seating himself in the same place where he had previously been allowed to rest, strapping himself down with the thick Velcro bands. He watched warily as the crazy dragon-man took a space suit from the locker and began to put it on over his pyjamas, expertly keeping himself in place with little touches and shoves against the walls and ceiling. Carver heard him muttering under his breath – presumably to the dragon that had somehow infiltrated its way into his head. The conversation didn't sound particularly happy, at least from the crazy dragon-man's end.

When he was done, the man swam over to the cupboards under the main console and rooted around in one of them. 'Here,' he said simply, throwing a couple of ration packs to Carver and retaining a few for himself. The packets spiralled slowly towards Carver, who caught them easily, making his wounded hand hurt afresh.

'Thanks, man,' he answered, turning his attention to the shuttle's window. He watched the tumbling, rolling play of the rocks out there, feeling utterly alone and hopeless. He was just another speck of debris lost in this horrible stellar wasteland now. His hopes of ever leaving this blighted place were at an all-time low.

The man sat himself in the next seat along, strapping in, and bit the corner off one of his own packets. 'Okay,' he answered without looking at Carver.

Carver mentally shrugged and bit the end off one of his ration packs (*CURRIED MEAT*, allegedly) as he watched the silent ballet of ice and stone outside. He chewed the spongy powder with some difficulty, wondering absently why the fucking things had to be so *dry*.

'I'm not sure what's going to happen now,' said the man suddenly, startling Carver from his reverie.

'What d'you mean?' Carver asked warily, turning his head to face the man, who was staring back at him with those empty, distant eyes.

'I mean, it might get rough here soon,' replied the man. 'They know about the shuttle – they may want it back.'

Carver considered this information carefully, crumpling his now-empty packet into a ball and casting it away over his shoulder. 'The people on the station?' he asked.

The man nodded. 'Yes,' he said. '*Them*. They do not understand the value of what we're trying to do here.'

Carver resisted the urge to point out that what *he* was trying to do, actually, was survive, escape, hopefully even kill this crazy fucker. 'I can see that they might not,' he said neutrally. Man, he was so tired. The food actually seemed to be having a soporific effect on him, and he suddenly found his arm too weary to even lift the second packet and look at it.

'You,' said the man in weary tones, 'do not understand either. You help because you must. That is all.'

Carver judged it best not to answer this accusation. It was true – he didn't understand, and he didn't *want* to, either. He did, however, fear for his future more than ever. The crazy dragon-man had the air of the defeated about him. If something had gone wrong, maybe the bastard would just decide to burn the business down and claim on the insurance, so to speak. And Carver would just be a little mark in the losses column. If that.

The man produced a small strip of plastic from down the side of his seat and held it up, regarding it critically. It looked like a strip of pills to Carver – twin lines of little blisters.

'What's that?' he asked.

'Hmm?' said the man. 'Oh, it's fader.' He shot Carver a sideways glance. 'Why?' he asked suspiciously.

'Fader?' repeated Carver, both surprised and really not surprised at all. In a way, it made perfect sense. The guy was a fucking fader junkie. Of course. 'You take that shit?'

213

'It is *not shit*,' said the man, as if explaining this to somebody who, no matter how many times they were told, was simply incapable of comprehending. 'It's. . . a lifeline,' he elaborated. 'You ever done it?' A sly little smile was spreading across his face now. He wiggled the plastic strip.

'No,' said Carver. Illegal drugs were one of the few criminal pastimes he actually had never been into.

'Do you want to?' asked the man. 'The dragon said you might want to. That I should let you if you did.'

Carver heard his own voice, unbidden, say, 'Okay.' He supposed that if the end was nigh, he might as well meet it intoxicated. Despite never taking fader himself, he'd had friends – or at least, people he knew – who had done. Right now, he saw no reason not to join them. He tiredly checked his second ration pack – *PUREED FRUIT*, it said – and discarded it unopened. It drifted off like a leaf in the wind. His raging hunger of earlier had seemingly deserted him.

'All right,' said the man neutrally. 'Why not.' He held up the strip of pills and turned it over a few times, inspecting it seriously. Carver thought he might be having second thoughts. But then he turned the strip over and pressed a single pill out of the blister. He released it into the air and let it spin in front of his face for a moment, looking from it to Carver, then back again. 'I don't know. . .' he said slowly, his brow wrinkled. 'Oh, fuck it,' he finally concluded, and he batted the pill gently towards Carver, who caught it deftly in the palm of his hand.

Carver looked at the pill for a moment, suddenly unsure. He had seen people fucked up pretty badly by this stuff back on Aitama. But then, did it really matter? That sense of finality was almost palpable, a property of the air itself. Something had gone wrong. It quite possibly spelled the end for him. So why not?

He popped the little pill onto his tongue and it dissolved instantly. It actually seemed to partially vapourise, and his sinuses filled with a sour chemical tang. A rank, bitter taste filled his mouth, unlike anything he had experienced before, making his face contort, and he almost gagged and spat the shit out without

214

swallowing what was left. It had become a thick, cloying gel at the back of his throat, seemingly ten times the volume that it should have been. But he managed, just about, to choke it down. 'Fuck!' he exclaimed vehemently, spluttering and spitting.

The man was looking at him with contemptuous amusement now, almost smiling. 'Look at you,' he said, as if he had expected no better. He studied Carver for a moment longer, then bent to his food again.

Carver felt the drug suffuse his body almost at once. It started with a fluttering in his chest, and for a minute he worried that he was having a heart attack. 'Hey. . .' he said, but he petered out, alarmed at the waver in his own voice. He held up his hands in front of his face. They were shaking. Hang on – were those *his* hands? They looked a little unfamiliar, actually. And he couldn't seem to control them. But. . . he remembered the injury that he could see on one of them, the bloody rent in the white fabric of the glove. That was pretty telling, no? Hmm. . . It really didn't matter, did it? In fact, the more he considered it, the less important it seemed.

'The dragon says I should release you,' said the man suddenly, making Carver jump.

'Whaaaat?' he asked, his voice thick and syrupy, turning to face the crazy dragon-man. Had he heard that right, or was it the fader screwing with his mind? He *had* taken some fader, hadn't he? Shit. . . how long ago had that been? Where, for that matter, *was* he?

'It says I should release you. In the morning.' The man was watching Carver quite closely now, perhaps gauging his reaction. 'You doing okay on that stuff?' he asked, sounding more irritated than concerned.

'I. . .' said Carver, his voice little more than a croak. '. . . Yeah. . .'

'The dragon says that you've done well, that you can now be trusted. *Can* you be trusted?'

His scrutiny of Carver intensified, those distant eyes seeming to bore right through Carver's skull and focus on something the other side. Carver wasn't sure if he could be trusted or not, truth be told.

215

He couldn't seem to remember. He supposed it depended to a large extent on the circumstances.

It was difficult to grasp the significance of what was happening here. His gaze was drawn again to the large window, the grim and frozen rocky shore outside. The motion of the belt objects, their distribution, seemed random at first glance, didn't it? Even as you studied it more intently, you could certainly miss the pattern. But Carver thought he saw it now. There *was* a pattern, an order, a dark, unifying thread that ran through the apparent white-noise of rubble. He could almost *see* it. . . He *could* see it. He *could*. . .

He turned his head back to face the crazy dragon-man. It wobbled heavily on his neck, which was a funny sensation, really. He laughed, and the sound filled the cockpit like pillows of down. The asteroids were moving out there beyond the window – dancing, really fucking getting down with it – and Carver studied the patterns in their motions. Order within chaos. *Patterns*. . .

'Sure,' he said, having completely forgotten what the question was now.

'I'm *not* sure, myself,' replied the man. 'But I will, of course, do as the dragon says. It always knows best.' He sniffed sadly and leant back in the flight seat. Carver sensed that he wanted to say more, perhaps spill all his secrets and confess his fears. A problem shared and all that. But he didn't.

'Yeah,' Carver heard his own voice say, somewhere off in the distance, echoing towards him through the tunnels of the ship. It was quite funny, really, this whole situation – certainly nothing to worry about. Had he been worried? He thought so. Well, it seemed laughable now.

'That stuff will help you sleep, if you let it,' said the man. He had his own eyes closed now, and he looked childish and vulnerable, a busy little tyke worn out by the day's excitement. 'I might have one myself in a bit.'

'Yeah,' said Carver's voice again. Sleep? Probably a good idea, though an alien-sounding concept.

'The dragon will tell us what to do tomorrow,' said the man with finality.

'From one killer to another,' said the distant Carver-voice, 'you work in strange ways, man.' He wondered if he should be saying this, but he didn't seem to be able to stop the words from coming. They flew into the air like slow-motion artillery shells, blossoming in explosions of sound that shook the world, completely independent of his will. 'But you get the job done, my friend.' He was okay, really, the crazy dragon-man. But was he actually going to set Carver free in the morning? He sighed deeply, feeling the tension flood out of his body, draining from his toes into the warm air of the cockpit like a bad humor exorcised. Did it matter? Not right now – he felt good. He loosened the Velcro straps then closed his eyes and rolled onto his side. The guy had said the fader would help him sleep, and that seemed to be working out pretty well. He yawned hugely, with an interesting, pleasantly weary feeling.

'I didn't,' replied the crazy dragon-man in a small, tired voice, 'get the job done.' And then he said no more.

Carver drifted on billowing sheets of darkness, borne on vacuous currents of whispering shadow, rocked by the gently wallowing shuttle, into the deepest slumber he had ever known.

He had no idea of the time when he awoke, feeling oddly disassociated from his own senses. At first, he thought that the light that flooded his eyes was part of a dream – it seemed too bright, too pure, to be real. But it dawned on him gradually, as he lay there staring at the grilled and panelled wall of the bridge, that he was genuinely awake, and still in the shuttle. The crazy dragon-man had given him some fader. He remembered now.

And then it spoke to him:

'Prisoner Carver, listen to me. . .'

A bolt of shock went through his nervous system like a flash-fire, but a fire whose flames were ice-cold, chilling him to the bone. His spine seized solid, frozen into position. He felt suddenly tiny, vulnerable, and utterly alone, curled immobile on the chair, pinned by fear. Had he really heard that?

'You're not imagining it, Carver. You really can hear me.'

'No,' he whispered, his eyes so wide that they threatened to

217

pop out of their sockets and onto his cheeks. 'No.'

'Yes,' said the voice matter-of-factly. 'Do you know who I am?'

Carver's chest was suddenly aquiver with fright, making it hard to speak at all. 'You're a fucking drug,' he managed to spit, keeping his voice low so as not to awaken the crazy dragon-man sleeping in the next seat. '*Fader*.'

'No,' said the voice. 'I am. . .'

Carver knew who it was, of course, or at least who his drug-addled mind wanted him to think it was. '. . . The dragon,' he finished in a hoarse whisper.

'Yes.'

'I don't believe it. No. That guy is fucking crazy. I'm not crazy. I don't believe it!'

'You raped and murdered a woman in front of her children,' said the dragon calmly, its voice coming from everywhere and nowhere at once, filling the world with its cold implacability.

'No. . .'

'Then you raped and murdered those children. *Children*. You cooked and ate parts of their bodies. And you wish to discuss sanity with me? Grow up, Prisoner Carver, and know yourself for what you are.'

'No. . . How do you know that?' he demanded, his voice rising in pitch. He could see the blood, the scattered and degraded body-chunks, the tiny gnawed fingers and shredded clothes. He saw himself standing there terrified, revolted and elated in equal measure, a clump of golden hair in one hand. His breathing quickened as excitement and horror warred within him. It was true. He had done those things. And it was obvious, really, how the dragon knew: it was a product of his own imagination. In fact, why was he even speaking to it? Perhaps he *had* gone crazy. When in Rome, etcetera. . .

'I know many things,' said the dragon cryptically. 'In the morning, your companion will release you.'

'He already told me that,' hissed Carver, squeezing his eyes closed and willing himself to sleep again. He didn't want this, couldn't fucking *take* this. . . He felt a pressure building inside his

218

skull, as if somebody were squeezing it as hard as they could, one hand on each side of his head. It was the pressure he had felt that day, back on Aitama, that day when he'd first seen *her* at the spaceport bar, with one of those cherub-faced brats on the end of each arm. It hadn't stopped that time until they were all dead, their perfect bodies lying in smashed and butchered pieces all around him. How would he stop it now? '*No. . .*' he wheezed again, desperate for it to end, desperate for this fucking *voice* to stop.

'I told him to wait until the morning,' said the dragon insistently. 'But I didn't tell him why.'

The dragon paused, and Carver sensed that it required a response from him. In the vain hope that he could accelerate the end of this episode, he gave one: 'Why?' *Ohhh. . . my head. . . stop talking to me. . .*

'Because I wanted to speak with you first,' said the dragon. 'About what comes next.' It paused again, as if to make sure that he was listening. 'My emissary has failed me,' it continued.

'Failed?' asked Carver weakly.

'That's right,' replied the dragon. 'My *old* emissary,' it added significantly. 'He has shown that he is not as committed to me as he claimed. He has not carried out some of the more difficult tasks I have set him. He has, however, laid a fair foundation for our next phase. You, Prisoner Carver, are to be my new emissary.'

'*Me?*' breathed Carver, wishing he could close his ears against that pervasive, persuasive voice. There was something convincing about it, something beguiling. And worse than that, there was a *hunger* in it, too.

'In the morning, as I have instructed, he will set you free. . .'

'Yes?'

'And *you* are to kill him.'

There was silence for a moment, a pregnant silence full of sinister potential. Carver's aching, swelling brain began to churn furiously, rusty gears grinding and meshing, crunching and turning. 'Yes. . .' he breathed. He opened his eyes again, turning over on the chair so that he could see the slumbering form of the crazy dragon-man next to him. The crazy dragon-man wriggled in his

219

sleep and started to snore softly. Carver began to smile – a slowly-spreading vulpine snarl of a grin. His head was fucking *pulsing* now. It felt like a fucking *battery*. It felt *good*.

'I know you have been wanting to,' explained the dragon. 'And tomorrow I would like you to do so. Go to town, if you like. Fuck him up severely, as you might say yourself.'

'Yes,' whispered Carver, putting a hand to his mouth to stifle a giggle.

'And then. . .' said the dragon, '. . . *then* we can talk about what comes next. We have great works to do, you and I.'

'Great works,' said Carver, feeling darkly empowered yet somehow confused at the same time. He saw a twining, living darkness, a room of shattered flesh, the crazy dragon-man crying out and shielding his face, a hundred images of death and hell that bled together into one indiscernible whole.

'Now sleep, my emissary,' said the dragon soothingly. Carver felt his eyes close again at once. It was hard to resist that voice. Hell, he no longer *wanted* to resist that voice. It seemed to know what it was talking about. *Dragon*, he thought vaguely as he sank back towards sleep. *My dragon. . .*

CHAPTER THIRTY-THREE

Lina looked around at the assembled group. *Halman's Council of War*, she thought without amusement. Collectively, they looked intent and tired, like scientists who'd worked through the night on some desperate weapons project. Only Hobbes had retained his usual well-groomed veneer. Si had once accused him of being an experimental robot on the run from Platini, and looking at him now, Lina could have actually believed it.

Disbelief aboard Macao had gone from height to height: the news of Eli's attempted framing of Nik, his sabotage of the station, his murder of Jayce and Tamzin. . . Surreal was really too weak a word for it. Now here they were, planning some insane deep-space commando mission in the bunker-like darkness of Halman's office.

Alphe, now technically the senior member of the maintenance division, unfurled the sheet of plastic across Halman's desk, weighting the corners down with metal coasters. Everyone craned to see as best they could.

'More light!' demanded Halman, squinting into the schematic and beckoning to Amy Stone, who passed him her own torch. Halman placed it on its base in the centre of the plastic sheet like a lantern. 'Right!' he said, turning his attention back to the diagram.

'It isn't easy,' said Alphe after a while. Lina mentally awarded him the *most-obvious-statement-of-the-day* trophy. His eyes were bleary and bloodshot in his honest farmer's face and his pale brow was smudged with machine-oil, as was so often the case with Alphe.

'No,' agreed Halman, whom Lina suspected was only managing to extract the basest level of information from the technical drawing. She didn't think she'd ever seen him concentrate so intently before. 'Why can't we just float through the personnel

221

hatch in suits?'

Alphe shook his head. 'Because it'll be locked from the inside. And if we did manage to pop it, then the airlock might not be closed properly behind it. It's too risky.'

'Hmm. . .' went Halman. 'I thought that might be too simple.' He continued to frown into the schematic, the lines in his brow deepening. 'If the only docking point is full, as Lina says, then. . . what? Can we cut our way in somewhere?'

'How?' asked Alphe, running one hand through his dark hair, sending up a small puff of dust. One of his fingers was wrapped in an unhygienic-looking bandage. He looked tired and out of his depth. He hadn't taken the news of Nik's death well at all. It had been bad enough when people had believed that Nik had been sabotaging the station. Now that Nik had been proven innocent of any wrongdoing, Alphe was clearly devastated. Usually, he was one of the calmest and most gentle people Lina had ever known, but now he was full of anger. She could see it beneath the features of his face like a subcutaneous shadow. 'What could we cut *with*?' he asked, shaking his head. His hands rested on the table at either side of the schematic – two clenched fists, knuckles white.

Ilse Reno stepped up to the table, elbowing her way in. She looked at the schematic a little disdainfully, her eye implant red in the red light. 'How about the Kays?' she asked, looking around the assembled faces: Lina, Liu, Alphe, Amy, Halman, Hobbes, Ella. 'Aren't they *made* for cutting?' She waited and let them think about this. Lina tried to envision the process of latching onto the hull of the shuttle, mentally configuring the tool arms to apply enough force. She was pretty sure she could make it work, as long as the shuttle's hull wasn't too thick.

'Hmmm. . .' mused Alphe, one finger playing thoughtfully with his lower lip. 'It's possible. I mean, we could cut a hole, probably, as long as we could anchor on, but. . . It's getting people in there that's the thing, and getting the shuttle away. We'd compromise the pressure if we cut into it, cause a blow-out. . .' His face furrowed. 'There has to be a way. . .' he said, seemingly to himself.

'So it'd kill anyone inside?' asked Amy coldly. She was famed more for her efficiency than her compassion. 'That's their problem.' She looked solid and slab-like in the near-darkness, not someone to tangle with.

'Yeah,' agreed Lina, thinking of what had happened to Sal.

'No, no, it's not just that,' said Alphe. 'We'd likely blow the whole fucking works out of that shuttle, strew the lot across space. No good.' He shook his head once, frowning, obviously displeased, and continued to study the diagram, tracing details with one finger.

'Well what about the cargo hold?' asked Lina, who was actually qualified to fly an inter-system supply shuttle, although she'd never done so for real. 'The hold is unpressurised.'

'It is?' asked Alphe, squinting into the schematic. 'It doesn't say that here.'

Lina pushed the smaller Ilse out of the way and bent over the schematic. She, too, began to trace details on its surface. She noticed that there were still flecks of blood around her fingernails. Her hair was still full of the stuff, too. She wondered absently when she'd ever get the chance for a proper wash. She'd just had time to change her clothes after seeing Hobbes, before Halman had summoned her again.

'Yeah, look here,' she said, tapping at the diagram. 'This is an airlock, into the shuttle's hold. An *internal* airlock.'

Alphe peered closely at the indicated point, and Lina moved her bloody finger away self-consciously. 'Oh yeah,' he said, sounding a little irritated as well as pleased. 'So we can cut into the hold and go through the shuttle's interior airlock.'

'Good,' said Halman. 'Are you sure the Kays will do it? Lina? Ilse?'

The two miners exchanged noncommittal looks. '*Well. . .*' they both said together.

Ilse made a *you go* gesture with one hand and Lina said, 'It does kind of depend on how thick the hull is.'

'Alphe?' asked Halman.

'Erm. . .' said Alphe, staring into the sheet of plastic. 'Of course, the deuterium shielding is all at the front of the ship. . . Here –

223

barely two-hundred-mil. Even I'm surprised at how flimsy that sounds.' He looked up, probably trying to smile. 'Economy first, right?'

'Then yes,' said Ilse, stroking back her straggly grey hair and standing to her full five-foot-two. 'If we put a bigger cutting disc on one of them.'

'Right,' said Halman. 'So we do that. We do have a bigger disc, yes?'

'Sure,' said Liu, smiling whitely. 'In the warehouse.'

Halman coughed laughter. 'And can you find it in there before the power runs out?' he asked.

Liu looked slightly offended, but his smile didn't falter. 'Charlie Stenning will know where it is,' he said.

'Good. Well, change the discs on two Kays if we have two larger ones.' He glared around the room like a searchlight. 'Backup,' he explained ominously.

'What I don't get,' began Liu, smiling that open, benevolent smile of his, as if they were just discussing what to have for lunch, 'is why he's attached the shuttle to that asteroid. Lina says he's used the boarding and rescue tube, so maybe the rock is hollow. Right?'

Lina nodded, causing an errant and bloody lock of hair to swing down into her eye. She brushed it back impatiently and said, 'Yeah, I'm sure of it. Looked like he'd plugged up holes in it with instawall.'

'Why the hell would he do that?' asked Ilse.

'Who knows?' replied Lina. 'But I'm pretty sure of it. Instawall means he's sealed the rock, probably to make it airtight. That means hollow, and that means. . . well, I've no idea what that means, really.'

'What's inside it?' asked Liu.

'Buggered if I know, old man,' said Halman.

Dragon! cried Lina's little interior voice. *No*, she told it, *that's ridiculous*. The voice retorted, sounding too much like Eli for her liking, *It'll eat you up!* She shook her head, trying to clear it.

'Will Eli know that the hull is breached?' asked Amy. 'If we cut

224

through it?'

'Well, there's supposed to be a warning system, yes,' said Lina. 'But that ship's probably two-hundred years old, and knowing who built it and supposedly maintains it, it might well just not work.'

'I don't think we can rely on that,' said Ella, who was leant against Halman's desk. Lina turned to look at her. She seemed to have aged ten years overnight, and Lina's heart went out to her despite the nightmare time she'd been having herself.

'No,' Lina agreed. 'I suppose not.'

'We have to assume he'll know what we're up to, and that he'll try to stop us,' Ella elaborated. 'That means—'

'A fight!' Halman finished for her, with a touch too much relish for Lina's liking. She looked up at him and saw that he was smiling beneath his bushy moustache, his huge arms folded across his chest.

'Well, that's great,' said Ella. 'But who are we going to send in there?'

'I'll go,' said Lina. All eyes turned to her. 'I have unfinished business with Eli,' she continued, feeling that an explanation was required.

'I should go,' said Ella, but she didn't sound too keen.

'Can you fly a Kay?' asked Lina.

'I'm sure I told you before: I flew M4s at Platini Alpha,' said Ella. 'It was a long time ago, but Kays can't be all that different.'

'Well they kind of are,' said Lina. 'Firstly, the jets are arranged in a—'

'Lina!' yelled Halman, raising one hand to stop her. 'How about if you both go?' The two women stared at him, considering this. They looked to each other, then nodded together. 'Lina, you're pretty handy with the Kays and the cutting gear. And you know something about the shuttle. How to fly it back here, for starters. Ella, you're my security controller, and you're pretty handy at kicking ass. Also, I could use a break from you.' Lina wasn't sure if he was joking or not. 'We will assume that there's going to be a. . . *hostile reaction*. . . to your arrival. You can take laser pistols from security. But make sure they fucking work first. I know some of them don't.'

'If Lina's going to cut,' piped up Alphe, 'then I'd like her with us when we modify and check over the Kays.'

'I'll pre-flight them with you,' said Liu. 'My department, my ships. You work under my supervision. No offence.'

'Fine by me,' said Alphe, nodding.

'Sure,' said Lina. She noticed that Ilse Reno was staring at her strangely, even for someone with a cybernetic eye. Was she jealous? Technically, Ilse was now the chief of the mining division. Had Lina stepped on her toes? She decided she didn't really care. She had other things to worry about.

'What if the prisoner is there too?' asked Hobbes, pushing his glasses higher up onto the bridge of his nose. Why he had never had corrective surgery Lina didn't know. Maybe the glasses were an affectation – supposed to make him look scholarly. 'And maybe the pilot, too. They could be facing three people. I really think we need to consider this carefully before anyone else gets killed.'

'This is Ella,' said Halman slowly, as if talking to an idiot. He indicated the woman in question with a sweep of one arm. 'Would you pick a fight with her? Even with two friends?'

Hobbes faltered. 'Well, *I* wouldn't, of course not,' he replied. 'But Eli would, I'm guessing.'

'I think he has a point,' said Liu. 'It does sound pretty dangerous to me.'

'What about this prisoner?' asked Alphe, looking worried. 'Do you think Eli has actually released him?'

'Some degenerate fuck from Platini Jail,' said Halman dismissively. 'Ronnie Carver. I think we can expect him to be dead, judging by Eli's record. The pilot, too. But I guess we can't depend on that.'

'I'd like to think of another way. . .' said Alphe, shaking his head.

'You are forgetting what's at stake here!' bellowed Halman with sudden, unnecessary volume. 'If we don't get that shuttle back, then we are all in very real danger. Everyone on board this station is going to die.' He enunciated the last three words slowly, beginning to pace up and down the room with his hands laced behind his back. They watched him as one, cowed by his loudness. 'Does anybody fail to understand that? Time is against us. The end is fucking *nigh*, boys and girls! We are going to get that shuttle back! Because we *have to*. If I need to do it myself, I will. I just don't think I'm the best man for the job.'

'No,' agreed Ella quietly, stilling him with a look. '*I'm* the best man for the job.'

'Maybe we can flood the shuttle with poison gas?' suggested Liu, smiling graciously. Everyone turned towards him with expressions of identical shock. 'What?' asked Liu, eyebrows arched.

'Fuck me, old man,' said Halman in amazement. 'I never knew you had it in you.'

'He has a good point,' said Ilse Reno. Her eye glowed evilly and her small face was set hard. 'Gas 'em. Fuck it.'

'Do we *have* any poison gas?' asked Halman. Lina didn't know if he was seriously considering it or not.

'Refinery could make some,' suggested Liu. 'They use all sorts of stuff.'

'Or Fionne,' added Alphe. 'She's a dual chemistry and physics grad. Something of a genius, in fact. Don't tell her I said that.'

'Right,' said Halman, nodding his grizzled head as he continued to stride about the room. 'Young Fionne will fucking love that, won't she? What d'you reckon, Liu? Cyanide? Mustard gas? Hmm?'

'Mustard gas should be fairly easy to make,' said Liu, utterly failing to catch the sarcasm. Lina almost laughed, although it really wasn't funny when you thought about it.

'Mustard gas,' agreed Halman, still nodding. 'Good. I'll get her on it.'

'They have suits anyway,' said Ilse. 'Those shuttles carry loads of them.'

'Look,' said Halman. 'I'm no humanitarian, but I'm not just flooding that ship with poison. That'd be fucking murder. You want to end up in some Farsight prison?'

'Technically,' said Liu, 'I think we live in one already. But I take your point.'

'And as Ilse says,' Halman continued, 'it's unlikely to help anyway. We'd only introduce another dangerous factor. If they go in armed, and find anyone there, then they can order them to surrender. Right, Ella?'

'Right,' she agreed uncertainly. Lina wondered if Ella hadn't actually been in favour of the poison gas approach.

'And if they don't, then shoot them. But it would be wrong of us not to offer them a chance. A choice. And the pilot, or even the prisoner, might need rescuing from Eli if they're still alive.'

'I suppose so,' conceded Liu. Although he was still smiling, he looked a little disappointed.

'How long do we have?' asked Lina. 'Power, I mean.'

Alphe straightened, shrugging his broad shoulders. 'Like this. . . maybe two days. Then we lose the lot – air, heat, kinetic defence, rotation. . . everything that matters.' He swallowed heavily and breathed silently, tensely, for a moment. 'And to think I've had aeroponics on my ass about the fucking *plants* this morning!' He laughed bitterly, looking around for support. 'The plants!'

'We should condense our living space,' suggested Hobbes.

'What d'you mean?' asked Ella.

'Shut off the quarters, the common areas, even medical, and set up a dorm somewhere in the offices, maybe centred here. Kill the power in the rest of the place and suck the air out. We'd use a fraction of the energy that way, buy ourselves a little time. We can re-compress the air and save it.'

Halman was nodding thoughtfully. 'Yeah,' he said slowly. 'And as for aero – they can spin on it.'

Alphe laughed again, with slightly more feeling this time. 'Yeah, that's what I told them,' he agreed.

'Amy,' said Halman, 'We'll do it – condense our space, I mean. Get the word round. I want everyone to pack a single bag of personal items. A *single bag* only, okay? Two hours, and I want the whole staff within these two corridors.'

'Sure, Boss,' said Amy, her eyes lighting up. She turned and practically ran out, looking like a bloodhound that had caught a scent.

'Alphe, you guys get everything you'll need out of maintenance and the warehouse. We'll re-power the hangar when we need it, but maintenance will stay off.'

'Of course,' said Alphe, as if this should have gone without saying. 'They'll have most of what we need in the hangar anyway.'

'Good,' said Halman. 'Now what's the story with the gennies? Last thing I saw was you and Fionne wading around knee-deep in the floor down there.'

'Ha!' barked Alphe. 'No joy, the last time I was there. Fionne's next door with Rocko, on a well-earned break, and Win Ling is on the power relay. But the actual turbines were damaged too, and to be honest we probably aren't going to be able to even get one of them running without the servicing kit from the shuttle.' He cast his gaze about, defiant, as if someone might try to blame him personally for this disastrous situation. 'Sorry,' he added warily.

Lina found herself to be unsurprised by this. She didn't think there was any bad news that *could* surprise her any more.

'Right,' Halman said. 'And the air system? I think everyone has noticed that there's something wrong with it by now.'

Alphe rubbed his chin with the back of one hand. He looked like he needed a shave. 'Well, the last gases we took did show some traces of refinery contaminants. Nothing to worry about yet, and of course the refinery's down now. But it might still get serious before long. And of course, when the battery goes, the air goes. Currently, it's on about eighty percent. It's also possible that something else is burning out in the system. We simply haven't had a chance to investigate further. We're sinking damn fast if I'm honest.' Everybody nodded sympathetically. None of them envied Alphe his job right now, however hard their own tasks might be. 'And if we're pulling back to a few corridors, my guys'll have to wear suits to even *look* at the scrubbers. Right now, we can still breathe, so we have higher priorities. Now *there's* something I never imagined I'd say. Higher priorities than the air scrubbers.' He shook his head in wonder.

'Yeah,' agreed Halman. 'Power is everything. The cold'll kill us first at this rate.' Lina was suddenly aware that it *was* cold in here. She shivered, joggling the table and causing the torch to fall over. Halman replaced it without comment. 'I wondered if we could put out some solar panels,' he continued. 'Don't we keep spares for the laser-relay satellites?'

'There are some panels stacked in storage,' agreed Liu. 'I can drag them out for you before we kill the power. Maybe we can–'

Alphe was shaking his head. 'No, no, no,' he said, overriding Liu. 'It sounds great in theory, granted. But how are we going to fit them? The loader is the only thing that can even carry those solar panels, and in case you all forgot, we don't have the loader any more. We'd have to place them by hand, in suits. I don't honestly think it's possible. And if we could, it would probably take us so long to set them up that we'd run out of battery before we even got them going.'

'Mmm,' grunted Halman. 'When what we should be doing is getting that damn shuttle back.'

Alphe stretched out one hand to Halman, palm up, as if trying to physically hand over the decision. 'Your call, but that's my take on it, yeah. If we had the extra staff I asked for ten months ago. . .' He trailed off pointedly.

'I put it to Farsight Platini,' said Halman, with irritation prickling in his voice. He was used to being harassed for more staff and more resources, and his default position had become defensive and somewhat pessimistic over the years. 'Talk to them about it.'

'Yeah, good idea,' said Alphe, sounding irritated himself. 'Oh wait – we can't.'

'I refuse to play this game, Alphe,' said Halman, a little haughtily. 'Just cut that shit out and put your helpful hat back on, please.'

Lina saw Alphe clench his teeth, drawing deep breaths between them. He looked like he might be counting to ten in his head. 'Sure,' he said at last. 'Sorry, Boss.'

'Don't sweat it,' said Halman, more diplomatically now. 'Throw one of your guys the solar panel bone to chew on if there's time.

230

But first, I want you to get those Kays modified and checked over. I want them as clean as we can get them.'

'Sure,' said Alphe. 'No problem.'

'Next on the agenda,' said Halman, stroking his balding pate. 'Any news as to why this has happened? Motive, etcetera?'

'Well, Hobbes has something for you there,' answered Ella. 'Hot off the press. Hobbes?'

'Yes indeed,' said Hobbes. 'We took some blood tests from Eli when he came into medical. They showed positive for fader.' He made a *there-you-go* gesture with his hands, palms spread.

Halman's brow furrowed deeply. '*Fader?*' he parroted. 'Where the fuck did he get fader from?'

'From Platini, of course,' replied Hobbes. 'Via shuttle.'

'So those fucking dockyard drones have been crating up psychoactive drugs at Platini?' asked Halman incredulously. 'And sending them here to fuck up my happy little family? Those bastards!'

'Must have been, I guess,' agreed Ella. 'My team do random checks on the incoming crates, but to be honest it's a token gesture. So much crap comes off those shuttles – heavy plant equipment, sealed electronics, radioactive material – that we actually *can't* check, that it wouldn't be hard to slip something through. I suspect it's been going on for ages.'

'Maybe someone's synthesizing it on board,' suggested Liu. His smile had become small and tight. It was well known that Liu was vehemently anti-drugs – he didn't even drink. Lina wondered if he knew about his ground crew's moonshine.

'I can't believe I didn't know,' said Lina quietly. Fader? Eli? *Really?* This was a man she'd worked with every day for years. How could she not have known? She supposed there had been a few things she hadn't known about him. She thumped the table, feeling a thrumming, numbing anger rise inside her. She couldn't tell if that anger was centred on Eli or on herself. 'Damn it!' she cried.

'Lina, chill,' said Halman harshly, as if she could just be ordered to do so. 'This ain't your fault, or mine, or Ella's, or anyone's. It's

231

just one of those things, and at least it makes a little more sense now that we know. That stuff has a bad rep for sending people batshit, and I guess that's just what happened here.'

'He claimed to be the *emissary*,' said Lina coldly. 'He said the *dragon* wanted Marco dead.'

Suddenly, she wanted out of here, wanted her son. She had gone to see him on the way to check in with Hobbes. She'd told him everything that had happened – she saw no point in trying to shield him any more, not after what had already occurred with Eli. He had accepted it quietly enough, but she'd thought she sensed a deep, dark depression inside the boy that had concerned her greatly. Her own blood-covered appearance hadn't helped matters, she supposed. She knew she should have waited until she'd cleaned herself up, but seeing Marco had been the overriding desire inside her at the time. He was currently waiting in Amy's office next door, still with Rocko, the hero of the day as far as Lina was concerned. Fionne had also joined them, probably shirking some vital maintenance duty in order to be with her young love. Lina didn't blame her at all.

'Yeah, he's authentically off his rocker, Li, we know that,' said Halman. 'I have to admit, I don't like all this dragon shit. Why a dragon? Why here? Why on *my* fucking station?' His shoulders slumped as he turned to Ella. 'Was there anything in his quarters?' he asked morosely.

'Er, I need to talk to you later about that,' she answered guardedly.

Halman looked a little puzzled, but he said, 'Okay, yeah.'

Lina wondered what Ella might have found that the rest of them couldn't hear. Normally, of course, she wouldn't have been privy to security information, but as she seemed to have been included in some temporary inner circle, she actually felt somewhat offended by Ella's cagey attitude. She looked at the other woman, but Ella seemed to be pointedly avoiding her gaze.

'Anyone not clear on what they need to do?' asked Halman.

'I guess I need to relocate the whole medical department,' answered Hobbes, sounding resigned but surprisingly upbeat about this idea.

'Good. That's right. Questions? No? Good. Now piss off, you lot,' Halman said, indicating the door with a sweep of one huge, apish arm. 'Not you, Officer Kown,' he added ominously. Obediently, they filed out, mumbling parting pleasantries more out of habit than real feeling, leaving a worried-looking Ella behind. Lina glanced at her as she left, but Ella still wouldn't look at her.

CHAPTER THIRTY-FOUR

'I thought I heard you talking to somebody last night,' said the man, without looking up from the shuttle's console.

Carver almost gagged on his water, struggling to hide it with a cough. He wasn't sure if he'd got away with it or not. 'Nah, man,' he said, wiping his chin. 'Maybe I was talking in my sleep.' Silence from the man, who still stared intently into the screen of the console, tapping its touch-sensitive surface with one index finger. 'I've been told I do that,' Carver added. 'Vivid dreams. You know.'

The man pinch-zoomed on a section of the screen, mirroring the display on the shuttle's main window. The shuffling debris of the belt vanished behind a magnified view of a tan-coloured planet, slightly blurred. 'I should think someone with your history may well have some disturbing dreams,' said the man critically, peering up into the main screen now. There was a shuddering bang as the shuttle's defensive mass drivers fired at some rock that had strayed too close. The sound reverberated through the walls and floor, fading away in diminishing waves.

You can fucking talk, thought Carver. He glanced towards the chair where the corpse had sat. The body itself was gone now, though blood had stained the floor and lockers around the chair in great spattered fans of dirty brown. Carver had noticed its absence when he'd gone to get the water from the locker, but the man hadn't mentioned what he might have done with it. Neither had Carver thought it wise to ask. He looked up at the screen. A fuzzy shadow moved across the image, presumably an out-of-focus asteroid.

'What's the planet?' asked Carver, trying to change the subject.

'Yuwan,' said the man distantly. 'Our local gas giant – the nearest planet to us. A Predecessor world. They found the ruins on

234

one of its moons, Safi-366.' He didn't sound hostile at all now, but thoughtful and introspective. 'They certainly seemed to like gas-giant moons,' he mused. He indicated the vastness of space with a sweep of one hand. 'Beyond that, outwards: Vagar, an icy little rock. Then Platini system, just under five light years away. In the other direction, towards Soros: Lillias; CET-11; Viking; Pallos; Hantii. They move around, of course, so they're not strictly lined up like that, but you get the idea. All dead worlds, never colonised or terraformed. The sort of places no species would want.' He looked round, his eyes distant and dreamy, twinkling with the reflected lights of the console, as if there were fireworks inside his head. Carver felt the sadness of the night before emanating from him still. He practically smelled of defeat. *No wonder your dragon is finished with you.*

'Why not?' asked Carver, trying to be polite. When was the bastard going to release him? *Was* the bastard going to release him? Neither man had mentioned the possibility yet this morning. Carver wondered if he had really heard the voice last night, or if it had just been a product of his own exhausted brain. It seemed unreal now, though he remembered feeling very different about it at the time. It had seemed real then, hadn't it? But he'd taken fader last night, and fader was notorious for inducing hallucinations. *Dream juice*, it had been called on the streets of Aitama. He wished he'd refused it now.

His current state of uncertainty wasn't helped by the fact that, regardless of whether he had heard the voice before, or just imagined it, it hadn't spoken to him this morning. Part of him was immensely relieved by this. Maybe he wasn't going insane after all. But another part of him wished it would speak again. That voice had seemed so sure, so calm, so soothing – balm to his racked and frightened mind. He remembered falling into a restful slumber, confident that the morning would bring release, relief and revenge. But now. . . now he was not so sure.

So he played the game, being polite and restrained with the crazy dragon-man, taking the crazy dragon-man's insults, listening to the crazy dragon-man's bullshit. He remembered the voice saying, *You, Prisoner Carver, are to be my new emissary*, and shuddered a little. Maybe, if it really was all real, Carver himself was the new crazy dragon-man, the latest edition. *Fuck it – whatever*, he thought. *I just want out of this. I'll play the crazy dragon-man for the rest of eternity if I can just be free again.* His gaze stole to the restraining device stuck to the vertical face of the console. *I hate you*, he thought at it, lest it might forget.

'Why *would* anyone want those places?' answered the man, turning to face Carver. His face was expressionless. 'They're dead.'

'I guess,' agreed Carver, unstrapping from the chair and pushing himself into something approximating a standing position. 'I need the toilet, man,' he said, which was true. He was almost bursting, in fact. He felt his face flush with embarrassment, a most annoying sensation.

'You're wearing a space suit,' said the man, a little frown creasing his weathered brow. 'Piss in that.'

'I don't want to,' said Carver, realising he sounded like a petulant child. 'I don't like it.'

The man nodded, sighing, politely exasperated. 'So,' he said, with what Carver took to be forced levity. 'Maybe we should let you go – you know, release you.'

Carver felt a grin trying to spread across his face, but he tried to restrain it, aware that it might be a sinister grin, a grin that might betray his secret intentions. 'Hey, that'd be great,' he said in his friendliest voice. 'I've worked hard cutting that rock. I mean, I know we ain't done yet, and I'll still help. It's not like I've got anywhere else to go, right?'

The man was studying him closely, that dead, vacant gaze seeming to wash over Carver like ice-water. 'No,' he agreed. 'I guess you don't.' He snaked his body out of his own chair and pushed across to the restraining device.

Carver felt his heart begin to hammer in his chest like an engine approaching the redline. He clenched every muscle in his body, trying to control it. 'Hey, look, thanks for this, man. It's pretty good of you to let me go.' His mind was spinning now, in dark and tightening circles, closing in on that grim, inevitable finality like a shark circling closer to its prey: *You're dead, you crazy fuck! Let me go, and you're dead meat. Go on! Do it!* His head was throbbing again, as if his brain had swollen tight against the inside of his skull.

'Well,' said the man, releasing the restraining device from the face of the console and raising it to look into its display, 'it's what the dragon wants.'

'That's great,' said Carver, floating closer to the man with nonchalant slowness. 'Good old dragon.' He wondered briefly if invoking its name would cause it to appear, to speak to him again – maybe to manifest in the flesh, vengeful and ravenous and angry – but he heard nothing. It occurred to him, also, that the crazy dragon-man hadn't been speaking to it, either, this morning. *No,* he reminded himself, *that's because it's pissed with him. He's failed it. And now he has to go. Out with the old, in with the new. . .*

The man was tapping at the screen of the restraining device now, his gloved fingers somewhat clumsy. He held it up for Carver to see the screen, his face a perfect poker-playing blank. A glowing legend on the screen read *NO PRISONERS*. 'Okay?' he asked. 'You're released.'

Carver, still floating closer, felt a euphoric thrill go through his body, almost a sexual pleasure. And the grin was breaking out on his face now – he couldn't help it any longer – like a predator breaking cover. 'That's great,' he repeated. And it was, wasn't it? First positive development since he'd been caught on Aitama, what seemed like a million years ago. 'Can I see it?' he asked, reaching out one hand for the restraining device. The shadows of the cockpit seemed to lean over him, enfolding and cocooning him. The man shrugged and passed it over. It was a grey metallic box, just small enough to hold in one hand. Heavy. Sharp-edged.

'Do it!' hissed the dragon, making him start and almost drop the device. 'Do it!'

'Yes,' he replied. 'I will.'

The crazy dragon-man tried to push himself away from Carver, but Carver grabbed his wrist and held on. The crazy dragon-man was strong and rugged-looking, but Carver was an absolute beast, almost half his weight again. '*What*?' asked the crazy dragon-man, his face twisted in confusion.

Carver just laughed – he couldn't help himself – and hefted the restraining device. Heavy. Sharp-edged. He felt the dragon smile – a vortex in the darkness, a cleft in reality. He swung the metal box, falling in. *Out with the old*, he thought, as blood flew in a thick scarlet gout. *In with the new*.

CHAPTER THIRTY-FIVE

Lina returned to the admin offices carrying two bundles in her arms like a human forklift – Marco's stuff and her own. People ran everywhere, carrying piles of clothing, dragging their children, jostling, shouting, dropping things as they went. Chaos had arrived, unbidden and unexpected, on Macao. The air tasted bad. It was cold. She walked through a Dantean scene of fear and disorder – scrolling images of rusty metal and clamouring refugees.

She wondered what Ella had stayed to talk to Halman about. Something she wasn't allowed to hear. Something to do with her? Marco?

Two men in space suits ran down the corridor carrying an immense length of water pipe between them, brushing people aside as they went. What the hell did they need that for? Maybe they were just moving it out of the way.

As she reached the corridor that connected the admin offices together, she saw Ella emerging from Halman's office. Ella noticed her at the other end of the passage and offered her a wan smile before walking off into the bustling crowd. Lina considered giving chase, trying to extract some information from her, but she didn't really have the strength for it. Instead, she returned to Amy's office – or what had once *been* Amy's office – which was to be the dorm where she would sleep until either the power was properly restored or they were all dead.

The dorm was rammed with people, sitting on mattresses with the defeated expressions of refugees everywhere. There was just enough space to step carefully between the makeshift beds, picking through the maze of sprawling bodies, bags and items of clothing. The chemical stink of the air was even further fouled by the smell of sweaty, nervous human bodies packed into close

239

proximity. There was a hubbub of fearful chatter in the air.

Si Davis was sitting on the bed of a young woman from aeroponics, over by the far wall, seemingly in an island of good-natured serenity just large enough for the two of them. They were laughing – actually laughing! – and leant together, reading something off a datasheet. Lina smiled a little to herself. She had to admire Si's opportunism. And his fast work. Lina couldn't remember the woman's name for sure – Michelle, she thought – but whoever she was, she was a pretty young thing. A passing twinge of emotion went through her – jealousy and nostalgia, mainly, entwined into an unpleasant, greasy sadness. She turned away from them, heartened and saddened in equal measure, and looked around for Marco. She couldn't see him.

She went to the bed that had been assigned to her – really just a thin mattress placed directly on the floor. She threw down her luggage and checked under her covers without much real hope. Then she checked under the heaped covers of Marco's bed, next to her own. He was, of course, not there.

'Where's Marco?' she asked the room as a whole. She could barely hear her own voice over the racket. She was not the only one calling somebody's name. 'Marco!' she yelled again, worriedly scanning around.

She spotted Ella's son Clay, sitting on his own bed with earphones in, staring into a handheld video game. She rushed over and dropped to a crouch in front of him. Apart from his hair, which was dark and crew-cut instead of blond and crew-cut, he looked like a perfect, smaller-scale, male version of his mother. He was also Marco's best friend and closest competitor at school.

'Clay!' Lina yelled into his young face.

Clay continued to stare into the screen for a moment, then he paused the game, took out one earphone and looked up at her. 'Hi, Lina,' he said.

'D'you know where Marco is?' she asked him.

Clay shook his head. 'He said he was going with Rocko,' he replied helpfully. 'But that was a while ago.'

'I only went to get our bags,' said Lina to herself. Niya Onh

240

went past, dragging a huge metal crate by one handle. Si Davis came to her aid, though possibly just in the hope of impressing his new friend. 'Have you seen Rocko?'

'No, sorry,' said Clay. 'Maybe Mum saw them?'

'Thanks, Clay,' said Lina absently, already rising and starting to look for Rocko.

She found him in the corridor outside, moving pieces of medical equipment into one of the offices for Hobbes.

'Where's Marco?' she asked without prelude.

Rocko's face took on an instant expression of concern that was so fearful and so genuine that Lina felt a chill run down her spine. 'Why?' he asked, wiping a sleeve across his sweaty forehead and leaning against the monitoring station that he'd been trying to manoeuvre through the narrow doorway. This blocked the doorway temporarily, trapping Hobbes on the other side and clearly incensing him. Hobbes shoved the heavy piece of equipment out of the way, making Rocko move aside, and dashed off down the corridor, muttering. 'Isn't he with Clay?' Rocko asked.

'He told Clay he'd gone to find *you*,' said Lina, tears beginning to swim in front of her vision. 'I only went to get our bags,' she said again, as if this exonerated her from blame.

'Hey, hey,' cooed Rocko, moving towards her and gripping her in a tight embrace. His skin felt smooth and warm against her. He patted her aching back with one hand.

'Where is he?' she sobbed, aware that she was suffering a totally unnecessary overreaction, but unable to stop herself nonetheless.

'He'll turn up,' said Rocko softly. Lina wept onto his chest, jostled by passers-by, lost in her own microcosm. 'He's just a little spooked out right now. He probably needed some space. I should have been watching him, but I thought he was with Clay.'

'Maybe he did need some space. . .' said Lina slowly, a new thought dawning on her. She lifted her head from Rocko's chest and looked up at him. *Rocko*, she thought. *Hero of the day*. 'You might be right,' she said, sniffing back the tears. She snorted back a runner of snot that had almost dropped onto his shirt. He didn't seem to mind.

'Sure I am,' he agreed encouragingly.

Lina released him gratefully and stood back. 'Thanks, Rock,' she said, slightly embarrassed. 'I, er, I have to go.'

'No problem,' he replied. 'You want a hand or something?'

But she was already away, moving through the busy corridor as rapidly as she could without actually injuring anybody, dodging trundling hardware and temporarily-deserted items of luggage. As she got further from Halman's office, the epicentre of the chaos, she began to pick up speed. Soon she was running through deserted corridors ignoring the twinges from her back, ignoring the headache that still raged inside her skull.

She ran through the rec area, dodging between the immense pillars, tripping once on a jacket that somebody had dropped, rising, throwing it away and continuing without pause. She passed the canteen, glimpsing the untidy jumble of chairs and tables, vaguely distressed to see them all vacant for the first time that she could remember. She headed through the plaza, past the shuttered-up *Miner's Retreat*, and then into the living quarters. She took the stairs up to the refinery level, emerging into the machine rooms, re-tracing the route that she had shown to Marco.

The machine rooms were an ominously silent robotic graveyard. Silvery gas tanks and complex-looking metalworking machinery loomed out of the darkness at her as she passed, levers and handles and outcropping corners seeming to reach for her.

She skirted around the outer wall of the great spoke, through the little side door, through the dark storage room, and into the spoke itself. She stood for a moment, staring up into that vast darkness, now almost as thick as pitch, where only a few feeble red LED-strips offered any illumination at all, stretching up into infinity like a runway into heaven.

She went to the lift, where her suspicions were confirmed. It wasn't there. She pressed the pad to call it, kicking her heels impatiently as she waited. The awe that she usually experienced in this place had turned into fear. The space was so vast, so dark, so. . . *industrial*. . . She stared around at the thick cables, feeling them

242

groaning under their unthinkably heavy burdens. Soon she began to hear the lift descending towards her. Then she saw it, and saw that the cage was empty.

She waited for the lift to slow to a complete stop then jumped into the cage and jimmied the latch shut behind her. She fumbled for the hanging control pad and hit the *UP* button. There was the traditional bang as the magnetic catch released and the lift began to rise into the blackness of the spoke.

The dense forest of cables towered around her, constricted by perspective, ending in a black pit above. The journey seemed to take a very long time.

She reached the top and virtually floated out of the cage. How long did they have left before the power went off and the air was sucked out? Halman had said two hours. Had it been closer to one or two by now? She cursed herself for not bringing suits. She should have thought. But somebody would stop them from draining the air, surely. Rocko had seen her go. Surely she had time enough.

She bounced and swam through the narrowing tunnels until she reached the ladder that led up to the hub itself. Exactly why there was a ladder here she had no idea, because it was easier to just jump up into the hub than to actually use it. This was what she did, and she shot into the steel drum of the hub itself with more speed than she had intended, flying right across to land awkwardly on the opposite wall.

'Mum!' cried Marco in alarm.

She looked up and there he was, floating dead centre in his jeans and T-shirt. She pushed off and headed towards him, crashing into him and banging her chin on the top of his head. They tumbled together onto the opposite wall, almost falling down the hatch to the floor below, locked in a death grip.

'Marco!' she exclaimed, letting him go. He scrambled to his feet, drifting away from the floor-slash-wall again, back towards the centre.

Lina pushed off again as well, and they floated together in that eye of stillness, equidistant between the curved walls. On either

243

side of them, perfect circles of space peered in: belt on one side, endless starscape on the other.

Lina extended one hand to gently touch his face. Marco flinched away from her, tears in his eyes.

'You ran away,' she said softly, not intending it as an accusation.

'I. . . I. . .' he stammered, tears streaming down his face now. 'I don't want you to go, Mum! Don't go out there!' He waved one arm angrily towards the belt. 'I don't want you to go out there!'

'Marco, I have to,' she said, knowing that this was true. 'Something bad is happening here, Son,' she said uncertainly. 'Something *wrong*. . . It's something that threatens us all. And I have to fight it. I have to try. So yes, I intend to go out there to the shuttle.'

He shook his head, angrily, refusing to even consider her words. 'No!' he cried. 'You *don't* have to! Don't go out there! *He's* out there!'

'Marco. . . We're all in serious danger here. That means *you*, my son, are in danger. If we leave the shuttle out there then we won't have the parts we need to fix the power and the air. And then,' she continued slowly, emphatically, 'we will die. I cannot allow you to die if there is a chance that I can prevent it. I made that promise before you were even born – it's an implicit one, a promise that all mothers make.' She snared his thin arm with one hand and drew him closer. 'I have to try and fight it. And it's going to be okay. I'm gonna fly that shuttle back in here tomorrow, and your old mum will be a hero.' She forced him to look at her, steering his face with one hand under his chin. 'And then, once Macao has everything it needs, I'm going to take that shuttle, we're going to get on it – you and I and anyone else who wants to come – and we are going to Platini Alpha. We'll sleep all the way and wake up in a new world. You were right. It's time we left this place. But first. . .' She stared into his quivering, tear-streaked face and felt herself beginning to cry again, too. She was turning into a veritable salt-water tap these days, it seemed. 'It's going to be okay,' she said again, drawing him to her chest and squeezing him

244

as tightly as her aching back would allow. But as she looked out at the belt, where it hung in the glasspex circle above his shoulder, she wasn't so sure. It stared implacably back at her like an eye, until she had to look away.

CHAPTER THIRTY-SIX

'Head through the corridor behind you,' said the dragon in its calm, insistent voice. 'Find the airlock.'

'Right,' agreed Carver. 'Right, that makes sense.' Everything the dragon said seemed to make perfect sense – it seemed a very sensible creature, all in all.

He swam through the doorway that led out of the shuttle's bridge and into the echoing bowels of the great ship, clawing his way along the handlines provided for that purpose. Drifting globules of blood surrounded him like evil fairies, sometimes spattering softly against his suit or face. He didn't look back at the bridge where the crazy dragon-man had died. *Crazy dragon-man mark one*, he reminded himself. He smirked contemptuously as he went. It was kind of funny, really, the whole thing. The old emissary was drifting in the belt now like the worthless jetsam that he was.

He passed through the thick doorway, designed also to act as an emergency bulkhead, trailing his gloves across the ancient metal as he went. Huge pieces of alien equipment loomed from alcoves on either side of the passage – gunmetal-coloured, statuesque machines whose purpose he would never understand. Thick, ribbed pipes and armoured conduits hung from the ceiling, wrapped around protruding brackets and corners like massive techno-snakes, threatening to entangle his clumsy body. The air tasted sharp and coppery, like the taste of a battery on the tongue. Steam hissed from a vent in the grilled floor, making him recoil, blinded, waving it away from his eyes. His body spun around, inverting, and he bumped his head on the floor before he could right himself.

'Careful, now,' said the dragon, a hint of wry amusement in its voice.

Carver swore, floundering his way back to the handline, where he paused for a second to compose himself. 'Yeah, yeah, that occurred to me already,' he muttered. He dragged himself along to the end of the passage, passing the boarding tube that led back into the great asteroid without even looking into it. *No more digging for now*, he thought to himself with some satisfaction. *Important business to attend to first.*

At the end of the passage was a junction. He knew that one side led to an airlock door into the cavernous cargo bay. The old, failed emissary had informed him that it was unpressurised in there and full of spares for the station. That, therefore, could not logically be the way to the docked ship in which the crazy dragon-man had returned to the shuttle. He took the other turning, leftwards.

The new corridor zigged and zagged with apparent randomness, its path presumably dictated by some fundamental constraints of the ship's design. He passed beneath some sort of shaft that led away into impenetrable darkness far above, offering a dizzying glimpse into the shuttle's soaring architecture. He stopped and peered up into it, squinting.

'Is that the way?' he asked.

'No,' said the dragon. 'Just carry on.'

'No,' agreed Carver. 'I'll carry on.' His brain felt pleasantly fuzzy, as if he were slightly drunk or very tired. It was a kind of reassuring fuzziness, though, as if it diminished Carver's own responsibility for his actions. He had already decided that he liked being the new emissary – the very notion seemed to fill him with a sense of importance, a new perspective on his own place in the universe. Finally, he had a purpose. Perhaps his whole life had merely served to prepare him for this moment.

At the end of the passage he came to a vast convex door, clearly another airlock, smaller than the one to the cargo bay.

'Is this it, do you think?' he asked the enveloping darkness around him.

'This is it,' replied the dragon calmly. 'Press the yellow pad there.'

247

Carver spotted the control that the dragon was referring to and reached out to press it. The pad required more pressure than he had been prepared to exert, and the force pushed his own body back away from the door. There was an undulating, whispering whoosh of sound and the door seemed to shiver in its mountings, then began to open. An irritating, beeping siren began to sound, setting Carver's teeth on edge. He floated closer again, wiping blood from his cheek with one sleeve. The old, failed emissary had clawed his face, probably with the zip of one of his gloves, and Carver's own blood was mixed there with the murdered man's. The wound still stung and burned fiercely. *Probably infected, knowing my luck*, thought Carver as he waited. *As long as the bastard didn't infect me with the disease of failure*.

The necklace of human fingers around the throat of his suit lent him great strength, though – it was a powerful item. Totemic. Surely it would protect him from the taint of failure. Some of those fingers had been pretty hard to bite off, but it had been worth it. It proved his dominance over the old emissary, his right to ascension. It was his crown, his sceptre. Yes – a powerful item.

'Fear not,' the dragon told him. 'You will not fail me – I will not allow it.'

Carver was unsure whether that was threatening or reassuring, and decided that it could possibly be both at once. Whatever the case, it was a little unnecessary. He had no intention of failing the dragon. *His* dragon. It had granted him freedom, he was certain of that. He supposed that he owed it his life.

Once the door had opened fully, Carver pushed off with his toes – he had learnt that gentle movements worked best in the micro-gee – and floated into the airlock. As soon as he was inside, the great door began to close behind him with a cyclical squeaking noise. He looked around the interior of the airlock, cold fingers of claustrophobia starting to work their way into his mind. There were no handlines here, so he clamped his magnetic boots to the floor while he waited. The airlock was cramped – only big enough for three or four people – and dimly-lit by a single LED-cluster in the ceiling. A rack of suits and matching helmets was bolted to one wall, and the suits hung limply like flayed skins.

'You're sure I don't need a helmet?' Carver asked the dragon, suddenly worried.

'No, it's fine. You see the sign on the wall there, above the exit?'

Carver looked up and saw the small screen to which the dragon clearly referred. It read, simply, *SAFE*.

'Okay, I'll trust you,' he said, still a little uncertain.

'You *must* trust me,' said the dragon. 'Do you think I let you go just to send you unprotected into a vacuum? Please.' It sounded a little irritated, and Carver thought it best to let the matter lie. Anyway, it had a point. 'The airlock cycle is just a precaution – it always goes through the motions, regardless of whether there's air on the other side or not.'

'I guess that makes sense,' Carver admitted, glancing around impatiently.

There was another whoosh of pumping gas and then the exit door, superficially identical to the one he had entered by, began to rise into the ceiling. Carver realised that he was holding his breath, and he let it out in a rush, gulping an experimental lungful of whatever atmosphere he was now immersed in. It was, as the dragon had promised, fine.

He moved through the airlock, passing through a series of reinforcing metal ribs, dragging himself along with ever-increasing dexterity. He looked around wonderingly, unsure of exactly what manner of ship he was emerging into. It was much more cramped than the shuttle behind him – darker, simpler, older-looking. He guessed it must be quite a lot smaller, too. There were deep gouges in the nearest wall where some heavy piece of equipment had been forced into or out of the airlock, and a fair scattering of rubbish and shiny curls of swarf drifted in the corners. It didn't look as if it had been cleaned in a hundred years. He could see the cockpit from here, and it looked small and simple after the relative technical complexity of the shuttle that had brought him to this awful solar system.

'Onwards, then,' he muttered to himself, feeling inexplicably nervous now, as if the ghost of the man he had murdered might materialise before him with a blood-curdling scream. It occurred to him how utterly alone he and the dragon really were out here. Anything could happen, completely unnoticed by the entire civilised universe. He imagined that he could feel the vessel pitching and rolling around him, even though he was fairly sure that without any gravitational reference point, that had to be an illusion.

'Remain calm,' said the dragon soothingly, instantly making him feel better, its words so similar to the rush of the fader he had taken the night before. 'Focus on the job at hand. You're doing just fine. Don't worry about a thing.'

'My dragon,' he whispered, craning his neck to peer down the passage ahead. Something began to hum deep in the mechanical heart of the ship – it sounded like an internal combustion engine revving up. Carver ignored it and floated towards the cockpit.

Inside the cockpit was a single pilot's seat with duct tape like scars on its cushions. The window was small and the ceiling low, hung with loops of cable cinched together with plastic ties. The console looked relatively simple – a multi-purpose main screen, a few ranks of switches, and a flight yoke which was shiny around the grip from long use. The window showed the scabbed and blistered skin of the huge asteroid. *Dragon-skin*, thought Carver distantly.

He drifted across to the console and began to rummage items out of the locker in its base: datasheets, one of them cracked right across its surface; food wrappers; an unidentifiable metal item about the size of a key; a bottle of beer; a pen with its point broken off. . . Not what he was looking for. Frowning, he cracked the top off the beer on a corner of the console, making it instantly fountain out of the bottle in a plume that snaked into the air, twisting and spraying droplets. Laughing, Carver intercepted the plume with his mouth, sucking it down with childish glee, chasing it back to the neck of the bottle, which he drained in one gulp.

He laughed aloud, and smashed the bottle against the main viewscreen in celebration, creating a scintillating firework of glittering shards that pattered off the walls and floor in a chaotic display. The beer had been good – very good – and he wondered how long it had been since he had last had one. Years? Was it years? If you counted the time he had spent in sus-an, it might be as long as seven years, he thought. He wanted another.

'Remember why you are here,' reminded the dragon, actually making him jump.

'Yeah, sorry,' Carver said guiltily. The dragon was right. It was always right. Hadn't Emissary Mark One said that? Or it always knew best – something like that. The crazy fuck had apparently been right about that, at least.

'Try the main console,' said the dragon.

'What? You think it'll be there?'

'Try it, I said,' ordered the dragon, a hint of impatience in its voice.

'Right, okay,' agreed Carver. He flicked the switch marked *Main Console Active*, which seemed like the likeliest candidate for the job.

'Hmm. . .' he mused, staring into the small screen, watching the indecipherable dance of white text as it self-tested, something beginning to whir inside it.

After a few seconds the console presented him with what was clearly a home-screen, with icons that looked as if they might conceivably represent various shipboard systems. He was pretty sure he recognised manoeuvring jets, and maybe docking clamps. One of the pictures looked like a book – a stylised blue cover and several splayed pages – and as a book was what he had originally sought, Carver tapped the icon with one gloved finger. Nothing happened.

'It's a conductive screen,' said the dragon. 'No pressure-sensitivity. Take your glove off.'

'A conductive screen,' Carver repeated, not entirely sure of what that meant. He thought that he might have known, once, but his intelligence seemed to have slipped a notch since the first time he had heard the dragon's voice. Anyway, it didn't matter – the dragon seemed more than capable of doing the thinking for him.

He fumbled to remove his glove, throwing it onto the pilot's chair. It bounced away and spun off into a corner, where it did a little low-gee dance before it came to rest. He hit the icon again, this time with his bare finger. The screen changed with an uncertain-looking flicker, and a simple legend appeared on it in rounded, idiot-friendly letters: *FARSIGHT FS-ISL107 IN-SYSTEM LOADER – PILOT TUTORIAL SIMULATOR.*

Carver felt a grin split his face. He thought it was probably a pretty nasty grin, maybe even a madman's grin, but he didn't care, didn't honestly give a burning shit in hell. He laughed aloud, throwing himself back into the chair and spinning it around.

The dragon, hiding just behind the gauzy film of reality like a thought that longed to be voiced, grinned too. Carver couldn't see it, but he *knew* it. 'Good,' it said. 'That's good.'

CHAPTER THIRTY-SEVEN

When Lina and Marco neared the dorms, Theo came rushing up to meet them, wearing his black combat armour.

'Come on!' he yelled, beckoning them to hurry up. 'We're waiting for you! Everyone's waiting. Halman's in a right state!'

Lina looked down at Marco, who grinned back up at her. That grin looked a little flaky round the edges, but she was glad to see it nonetheless. 'Uh-oh,' she said, breaking into a trot.

Marco didn't reply and they ran after Theo, who led them back towards Halman's office and the dormitories, stopping occasionally to hurry them along. They passed through the first corridor – which had been checked for air-tightness and would form a makeshift airlock – and into their own corridor, the one that connected all the dorms and Halman's office.

When they emerged into their little refugee camp, a sea of irate and fearful faces was staring back at them. It seemed that everyone was here, waiting, much as Theo had promised.

'Where the fuck have you been?' demanded Halman. He noticed Marco – a minor for whom he was technically at least partly responsible – and corrected this to, 'I mean where the hell have you been?' He stood a clear head above most of the crowd, a scowling monolith of a creature.

Lina was glad to see him, although she supposed she was in trouble. She couldn't help grinning at him as she forced her way through the throng towards him, dragging Marco by the hand. 'Hi, Dan,' she called out, embarrassed.

As she stopped in front of him, Halman seemed to melt. He smiled, too, and leant down to speak to Marco. 'You managed to get her back in time, then, kiddo. Just about. I'm glad someone sensible's keeping an eye on her.'

Marco grinned up at him. Halman looked big enough to eat the

253

boy whole. 'Yes, Sir,' he agreed. 'Somebody has to.'

Lina, amazed at his cheek (after all, *she* had gone after *him*), shoved him on one shoulder, making him stagger. 'Kids today!' she exclaimed with mock despair, throwing her hands up. 'Go and see Clay, Son,' she ordered. He ran off dutifully enough. She turned to Halman. 'Sorry, Boss,' she said more seriously. 'Thanks for waiting.' She was aware that a fair number of people were unabashedly listening in.

'Well you didn't leave me much bloody choice, did you,' Halman retorted, but he didn't sound too angry. He lifted his chin and addressed the crowd more generally: 'Somebody get Alphe! Tell him it's time to go!'

The word went round, rippling back down the darkened corridor. The crowd parted in such a cinematic way that it could have been choreographed and Alphe, in the station's standard-issue white space suit, appeared at the far end of the group. He moved down the gangway they had made for him, being slapped on the back as he passed. Lina was reminded of early footage of olden-day space pioneers leaving on the first terraforming missions – people who had been celebrities in their day. A few people shouted out encouraging slogans. Alphe's suit-light sliced from left to right as he turned this way and that, acknowledging various people.

He stopped before Lina, holding a large toolbox in one hand, and gave her an embarrassed smile. He turned to Halman and said, 'I guess I'm ready, then.'

'Good man,' Halman replied, arms folded across his chest. 'You sure you don't want someone with you?'

Alphe looked like he was genuinely considering this for a moment, then he said, 'No, thanks. It should be easy. I won't be long. I'm hoping to get some sleep myself soon.' A chant had gone up behind him now – *Alphe! Alphe! Alphe!* – and he rolled his eyes, set his face and made his way heavily to the door which would soon become the inner skin of an airlock. He turned once more, waved to the crowd, then cranked the handle to open the door. It seemed to take a long time, and he waited for it to be fully open

254

before stepping through. Just as slowly, the door inched down behind him. The chanting died away, leaving an awkward silence behind it. People milled around, some of them starting to dribble away back to the dorms. It was late. They were tired. And they were facing their first night as refugees within the walls of their own home.

'Is he killing the hangar as well?' Lina asked Halman.

'Yeah,' said Halman. 'He's killing the emergency power and drawing the air out of everywhere except here and the prison. Tomorrow morning, when you go with them to sort the Kays out, we'll re-power the hangar. You won't get air down there, though. It'll be suit-work, I'm afraid.'

Lina thought about this, biting her bottom lip. She had temporarily forgotten that tomorrow, if all went to plan, she was going to enter the shuttle through a hole in its hull. And if Eli objected, she supposed she would have to shoot him. She honestly wasn't sure how she felt about that. She only knew that she'd have to succeed. What she'd told Marco was the truth – she had to at least *try*.

'I'm sure it'll be fine,' she said.

But she must have failed to hit the right confident tone, because Halman leant down to her level and said, 'Lina, it *will* be fine. You should get some sleep. Alphe is gonna be a while, whatever he says. I want you fresh tomorrow. You'll go after breakfast – you, Alphe, Fionne and Liu. You'll sort the cutting discs out, full pre-flight, then you and Ella will go across. Okay?'

Lina couldn't determine if that was okay or not. She had never really liked to think about things too much in advance. She preferred just to do them when the time was right.

'I think I will go and get some sleep,' she said.

Halman nodded, his lips stretched into a smile, and he half-turned to go, then stopped himself. 'And by the way,' he added, 'there's gonna be someone posted at the airlock from now on and the other exit from this corridor is welded shut. But even so, keep an eye on that boy of yours, will you?'

'I will,' she said, a little defensively. And then she added, 'I only went to get our bags.'

Halman turned his smile up a notch without replying, then he strolled back towards his office, whistling. The sound was gratingly at odds with the bleakness of their situation. The corridor pulsed redly as the last stragglers wandered away. This was now their world.

CHAPTER THIRTY-EIGHT

They moved through the pitch dark corridors of the desolate station in a silent procession. Lina had, in fact, hardly managed to sleep at all. She'd also barely eaten anything for breakfast, managing half a slice of bread and a cup of coffee. Her stomach was rolling and sloshing queasily as she followed Alphe through the deserted passages of Macao, moving awkwardly in her space suit. Marco had hardly spoken to her this morning. She'd left Rocko to watch over him. *Hero of the day two days running*, she thought.

Their suit-lights made bright circles that skimmed across grey passageways and hulking machines. Doorways into utter darkness leant towards them from either side.

Prior to the extraction of the air, the heating had gone off. Moisture from the air had condensed onto walls and floors, then frozen there, making the architecture look as if it had been carved from dark and glittering crystal, and the footing treacherous.

They passed aeroponics, shining their lights onto rows of wilting plants that hung suspended like rotting piñatas. Stainless steel surfaces and shiny glassware broke the beams into shards and reflected them back, speckling the corridor they stood in. The frost was heavier in aero, where a nutrient-rich mist had circulated amongst the roots of the plants, and had now condensed like fallen snow onto every surface. They moved onwards, as if through a ghost ship, awed and frightened, hardly breathing.

When they reached the stairs that led down towards the rimwards hangar-level, they stopped, as if by silent consensus. Their suits blasted jets of expelled vapour into the sterile space. They stared into that well of shadows and exchanged nervous glances. Lina was honestly scared. This had been their home ground just a day ago. And to see it like this – an alien world of ice

257

and ruin – was just too much. She knew from the stunned, fearful faces behind their visors that the others felt it too. She heard only the sighing sound of her own powered respiration.

Fionne tried to say something, but her suit had an intermittent mic fault and her voice cut in and out rapidly, making her words utterly unintelligible. She shook her head, vexed, and tweaked the dials on the front of her chest unit while Alphe, Lina and Liu watched her mutely. She banged the unit with the flat of one hand, making a brief whine of feedback in everyone's ears. They winced, as one body.

'Sorry,' said Fionne. 'It's – *shhh* – bloody stupid – *shhh* – can't – *shhh* –' She actually stamped a foot in anger, clearly cursing behind her faceplate, and banged the chest unit again.

Liu turned to Alphe, splashing his light into Alphe's face, making him screw his eyes up and look away, briefly spotlit in spectral monochrome. 'Are we waiting for anything in particular?' he asked.

'No,' said Alphe. 'Just having a breather.'

Lina looked down into the stairwell, where black was layered on black in endless, impenetrable strata like seams of coal. 'Come on,' she said, and led the way.

They moved through the warehouse like ants through the depths of some vast machine, craning their necks to stare up into the soaring darkness. Icicles hung from metal beams like crystal tears, frozen in time.

They stopped before the hangar door and Alphe hefted the toolbox. He smiled thinly at the others and moved to an armoured junction-box between the hangar door and Charlie Stenning's office. He prised the cover off and began to closely inspect the electrical switching gear inside. He did something unseen with a small screwdriver while the others stood kicking their heels impatiently. Briefly, the whole of the warehouse flickered into brilliant, flood-lit visibility. The waiting group inhaled sharply. Then, the lights flickered off again and a small red warning sign lit up above the hangar door. The word *VACUUM* glowed there like a threat.

Alphe straightened and returned to the group, skidding on the ice. 'There,' he said simply. Lina saw that, in keeping with his usual theme, he had already managed to smear one glove with machine oil. 'Power.'

'Halman could've let us have air, too,' said Lina a little bitterly. 'This'd be easier without these damn suits.'

Alphe just laughed and said, 'Shall we, ladies and gentlemen?' He made a sweeping *after you* gesture with one arm, like a butler.

Fionne stepped forwards and entered an override code into the door's control panel. She stood back, taking a deep breath, then reached out and hit the pad. The door began to scrape laboriously open, crushed ice falling from its track in a fine powder. Inside, the hangar was lit in its customary sterile white – LED-white with a faint hint of blue in it – which served only to increase the feeling of cold.

'Will the heating come on?' asked Liu. 'I'm getting a chill, even in this suit.'

'Yeah, should do,' said Alphe. 'But it might take a while.'

He led the way into the hangar itself, his boots crunching unheard through the frost. 'Remind me which one is yours, Li,' he said. Lina pointed to K6-12. 'Good. Let's get to work then.'

Liu had already got one of his ground crew to pull out the larger cutting discs from the warehouse, and he retrieved these from where they had been left on the central desk and passed them to Fionne. Each was about half a metre across. 'They look a little worn,' he said apologetically. 'I hope they're okay – the heat can make them brittle over time. But these are the only two that Charlie could find.'

While Alphe and Fionne worked on her Kay, overseen by Liu, Lina took Ella to have a look at one of the other ships – K6-7, which she knew to be a relatively reliable vessel. She explained the differences between the Kays and the M-classes that Ella had flown in Platini system. Ella listened respectfully, even when Lina realised that she was patronising her a little.

'Sounds fine,' said Ella when she had finished.

'Yeah,' agreed Lina. 'I guess it'll have to be, won't it?' Suddenly, she felt the burden of her responsibility weighing down on her, physically crushing. She slumped back against the Kay and slid to the floor, her stomach clenching and knotting, her head still aching from her last meeting with Eli.

'You don't sound so sure,' said Ella quietly, kneeling down beside her.

Lina wondered if she had forgotten that, no matter how quietly she spoke, she was talking on the communal radio channel. 'Why are we here, Ella?'

'What d'you mean?' Ella asked, puzzled-looking. 'You mean *here*?'

'I mean why *you* and *me*? We both have kids back there. If we screw this up, they'll have to raise each other.'

Ella sucked her lip, giving this due consideration. Then she said, deadpan, 'They'll get bloody good at video games, then, won't they?'

Lina thought that was a pretty weak joke, but she appreciated the attempt. 'Yeah,' she said, even managing a little laugh. 'I guess they will. Come on – let's go and see how they're doing. They must be almost ready for this one.' She held out a hand so that Ella could help her up. Ella was just beginning to say something else when a red light began to pulse in the ceiling of the hangar. They stopped dead, lifting their faces as one to look at it.

'What on Earth is that?' asked Liu's voice over the radio.

'Come on!' cried Lina, terror sparking inside her. She leapt up and sprinted off back towards where the others stood around her ship, gawping up at that incongruous, unexpected red light.

Alphe turned to her, his mouth hanging agape. 'I think a ship is coming in,' he said. His eyes were wide and full of animal fear.

'A ship?' Fionne repeated.

'Eli,' said Ella coldly. 'It must be Eli.'

'What. . .' began Alphe, trailing off into nothing. The team stood rooted in place, dumbfounded.

And then the space door began to open in the floor, sheets of ice sloughing off it and tumbling away into space, forming a ramp that protruded like a tongue.

260

'The safeties are still off!' cried Liu. 'We can't stop it!' Lina looked across at him and saw, to her dismay, that even he had now stopped smiling.

'Weapons!' yelled Alphe, lunging for one of the tool-boxes.

'Weapons?' parroted Fionne. 'What for?' She tried to say something else but her suit's faulty comm shredded it into random noise.

'If that's Eli in that ship,' said Lina, reaching for a large wrench that lay beside K6-12 on the floor, 'we have to bring him in.' She didn't think she managed to sound any more excited by this prospect than she felt.

'Us?!' yelled Fionne, horrified. 'But I. . . I can't. . . I. . .'

'Look!' cried Alphe, straightening up with a hammer in his hand.

A ship was coming into sight, weaving carefully around the few errant asteroids that had come almost within mass-driver range of the station. It was a large and squarish vessel with manoeuvring jets jutting from its hide like porcupine quills and a small cockpit stuck onto the front like an afterthought: the in-system loader. It came about on a swooping arc, twisting about its lengthwise axis to approach the station with its wheels to the ramp. They could now make out the figure of a space-suited pilot behind the console.

'Oh shit. . .' breathed Liu – the first time Lina had ever heard him swear. He had found himself a handheld gas-torch, which looked virtually useless as a weapon. She thought he might be able to lightly toast Eli with it, but that was about all. *Eli*. She remembered what the crazy bastard had done to Sal, Nik, Jayce and Tamzin, and a lump began to swell inside her throat, making it hard to breathe.

The team shuffled nervously, their faces frightened behind their visors, bristling, trying to ready themselves. They stood poised, fearful, weapons outstretched. Even Fionne had found some sharp-looking implement to arm herself with, and it looked horribly unnatural in her hand.

The ship was rolling up the ramp onto the deck of the hangar now, gas jets erupting from its hull, landing lights winking red and green. Lina could feel the tension in the bodies of her companions – those minute muscular twitches as they fought the urge to turn tail and flee.

'We have to do this, guys,' said Alphe, sounding a little too uncertain himself to inspire much confidence. 'He has to be stopped here. It's okay – there's one of him and five of us.'

The loader was approaching, slowing, moving down the ranks of Kays towards them. They could see the pilot looking at them, now, and Lina had the sudden impression that it *wasn't* Eli after all. She had sat in the pilot's seat of the loader herself, and she was about the same height as Eli. There had been space above her head, she was sure of it. But this person looked as if they'd been *crammed* into the cockpit, and if so they must be absolutely *huge*.

Fionne was chanting, 'Come on come on come on come on. . .' in an endless mantra, her eyes stretched so wide open that they looked as if they might just pop from her head.

The ship turned sharply about its axis, sideways across the width of the hangar, blocking the flight deck and side-swiping Petra's Kay. The smaller vessel rolled silently onto its side, crunching into another of its fellows, shearing off tool arms and crumpling hulls. The loader ploughed on, wrecking a third ship as it finally came to rest with injured Kays littered around it like toys that it had tired of and discarded. The pilot was hidden from sight again.

The loader settled jerkily onto its suspension, lowering slightly, its jets sputtering to a stop. The hangar was deceptively still and silent. The last wisps of condensed gas trailed away, fading into nothing. The loader's landing lights filled the space with pulses of sick colour – putrescent green and bloody red.

At the top of the loader's short ladder, the hatch began to open.

CHAPTER THIRTY-NINE

Carver cycled the main hatch of the loader, as the dragon had told him to do, then rushed down into the vessel's small cargo hold with the cutter gripped in both hands. One of those hands wore an incongruous bright red glove from the ISL, a replacement for the one he had torn. It looked right, that red hand. *The red hand of vengeance*, he thought.

His head was thrumming and throbbing, beating like a drum, but he felt good. He felt *charged*. The power of the finger-necklace infused him and enfolded him. The dragon wound around his body like a shawl of dark feathers. Its voice was quieter here, further from its den, but he felt its presence nonetheless.

He emerged from the loader's cargo hold as quietly as he could, forgetting that they wouldn't hear his footsteps in the vacuum. He could hear their voices, though, over the radio. They were shrill and breathy, full of fear.

He ran along the body of the loader, crouched low and grinning ecstatically to himself. The cutter was heavy in his hands, solid and reassuring. As he crept past the loader's landing gear he saw his intended victims crowded round the ladder that led up to the ship's main hatch. They had fallen for his trick. Idiots. Let the hand of vengeance strike them down.

The cutter came alive, spluttering out globules of plasma which solidified into a continuous stream. He burst from the shadows at a run. Was that him laughing or the dragon?

Someone was slowly ascending the rungs of the ladder while the rest of the cowards hung back watching them. They looked like they were holding hammers and spanners, the hopeful fools.

Carver broke cover, accelerating to the fastest pace that he could manage in the suit, with the cutter poised above his head.

'Where is he?' asked a woman's voice over the radio.

And then, just as he was about to swing the cutter, which should have neatly cut through all three of the idiots standing on the deck like a sheathe of wheat, slicing them in half at their waists, one of them – a little Asian-looking fucker – turned round and screamed.

'LOOK OUT BEHIND!'

Clearly wired to the max, they turned as one, flinching away from him as the cutter went shimmering through the air. Its beam sliced neatly through one of the loader's radio antennae, then passed close enough to the belly of one of the men – some inbred who looked like a fucking farmer – to singe the material of his suit. Carver actually saw the white fabric blacken as the cutter swung in its wide arc, possessed of its own unstoppable momentum.

He brought it back round in another swipe, angling down in a diagonal line, stepping in. But his feet slipped on the deck, which seemed to be covered in ice, and he fell to one knee, the cutter sizzling through one of the loader's tyres, making the whole ship slump slightly as if threatening to simply fall on him.

Carver screamed in rage, scrabbling up, the cutter flailing in one hand, out of control. The dragon twined around him, faster and faster, hissing like a steam engine, utterly enraged.

'Kill them! Kill them!' it screamed distantly. 'Don't let them get away!'

But they were quick – quicker than he was, at least. The person on the ladder spun and leapt down onto the deck. Carver caught a brief glimpse of her face as she went. She looked like the sort who might enjoy some quality time alone with him: older than him, perhaps, but kind of handsome, with tangled blonde hair that hung across one side of her face. *I'll fucking get you!* he inwardly vowed. But she was already off – they all were – and running towards the large door that gaped at the end of the room like a portal into purest darkness. He felt the dreaded miasma of failure closing in around him like poison gas.

He regained his feet, slipping and sliding maddeningly, the cutter gouging deep lines into the deck, sending up gouts of steam that blinded him. He staggered after the fleeing cowards, waving

264

the steam away from his face, and lifted the cutter high again. One of the running figures threw a hammer back over their shoulder as they went, but Carver dodged it easily, gaining his stride, his legs pounding like great engines.

They burst out of the door and away into the station, but Carver was closing on them already. Their suits flashed whitely in his light – flapping spectres that he followed through the gloom, gaining on them, gaining on them. . . The cutter trembled keenly in his hands, spitting and gouting.

They seemed to be inside some massive warehouse where shelves like skyscrapers arced away into darkness above him. The fleeing cowards dodged around pallets of sheet metal, jumped over coils of hose, almost falling over each other as they went. He was almost close enough, now. . . almost. . .

And then his prey reached a T-junction and scattered – three left, two right. Carver skidded to a momentary halt, torn by indecision, his head bursting with pressure.

'The woman!' hissed the dragon. 'Go after the woman, you fool. She and I have business still to finish. Go! Right!'

Carver took off rightwards, bellowing his rage, the cutter taking little nips out of either wall as he ran. He saw the heel of a boot disappear around the next corner and he drove himself onwards, leaving long streamers of expelled vapour behind him like contrails.

He rounded the corner and saw one of the fleeing cowards sprawled on the floor, scrabbling to regain their feet. Was it the woman? *Let it be the woman!* he prayed to himself as he leapt forwards and kicked the figure's head like a football, making their helmet bounce against the floor. He dropped onto the figure's back, seizing the fabric of their suit in one huge hand, and pulled their head up off the floor to look into the face.

'You,' he snarled to the little Asian-looking fucker, 'are the wrong fucking one!' The rage bubbled up inside him, so hot that he thought it might emerge as fire from his mouth. The face behind the visor gibbered with fear. 'But you'll do,' he added, smiling with anticipation.

265

He knocked the little scaredy cat out by smashing his helmet on the floor a few more times, then dragged him back to the hangar and got busy. It was art, really – certainly his best work. And the dragon seemed to demand it. It hovered at the periphery of his mind, cajoling him, encouraging him, massaging that streak of darkness that pulsated in his brain like cancer. It had to be appeased. He should have caught them all, he knew.

But he didn't allow himself to get too carried away, because those other couple of fucks had escaped, hadn't they? Yes, and they would be back. Probably with some asshole friends, he suspected. Those sorts of people always had loads of asshole friends.

So he finished his work with the little scaredy cat and headed back out of the hangar again. He observed the small in-system ships as he passed, counting them. Fifteen in all, but one of them was in pieces, and those pieces were heaped with dust and metal shavings as if they hadn't been touched in months. Someone had taped a handwritten sign across the ship's partial hull, but the words on it were long-faded. And he had hit four more vessels on the way in, partly by accident and partly to appease his own childish desire for destruction. Three of these lay on their sides forlornly, clearly broken. The fourth one looked to have suffered only minor damage. Ten undamaged, then. And the loader, which he would take again.

Flying the loader had been easy, having run through a few hours of simulation. It mainly involved telling the computer where you wanted to go, and how fast, then employing whichever guidance routine was most appropriate. It hadn't been necessary to resort to manual controls at all, in fact.

He stood just outside the hangar doorway, staring into the cavernous vastness of the warehouse, marvelling at the massive machine-parts that nested in the racking, reflecting his light dully from their oily skins. He realised then, as he imagined one of those vast pieces of metal tumbling down and crushing him to death, that the station was making artificial gravity. It hadn't even occurred to him before. Of course, he'd known that the station would be a spinner, and even kind-of understood how that created the impression of gravity, but he hadn't realised how easily, how thoughtlessly, he'd slip back into the one-gee lifestyle. He honestly hadn't noticed until now, but now that he did, the sensation was an enjoyable one. He felt powerful, heavy, brutish, like a lump of malleable iron. But he still felt a little vulnerable beneath those infinite tiers of machinery. He cautiously moved along the gangway and took a left at the end.

One thing he had managed to extract from the little scaredy cat, besides some blood and teeth, was the route to the station's prison. He had no way of knowing, of course, if the man had been lying to him, but he suspected not.

The plasma cutter swung jauntily at his side, switched off, its ceramicarbide barrel pointing towards the floor. It had become like an old friend, now. Carver was considering giving it a name, but he'd never been good at names. *Fury*, maybe, for the job it had done on the little scaredy cat. Or *Dragonkey*, for the work it had yet to do, that most important job of freeing the dragon from its prison of ice and rock. He didn't really like either, though.

He climbed the stairs carefully, aware of the slipperiness of the steps — two floors, like he had been told. He passed a sign reading *MACHINE ROOMS* and moved down a narrow passage with glass-fronted workshops on either side. He turned into an even narrower, windowless corridor that continued straight until it faded into blackness.

Suddenly, something moved at the end of the passage — a flash of white — and Fury-slash-Dragonkey was in the firing position before Carver even knew what was happening. The fingers round his neck jiggled and jumped like the fingers of a gifted pianist. He stood, cutter poised, eyes squinted half shut, staring into the darkness, washing his light from side to side, seeing nothing but textured metal and rusty meshwork. Something had moved, though. *Attack of the asshole friends*, his mind warned him.

'Go and check,' said the dragon, but its voice was far away, like the voice of the sea on distant shores. 'It's nothing, but go and see for yourself.'

267

Cautiously, Carver worked his way down the corridor to the spot where he had seen the movement, trying to check both ways at once. His heart was large and slippery in his chest and his head was pulsing as if it was trying to breathe. It felt like it had swelled up tight inside his helmet. He was, for all his violent nature, something of a coward when it came down to it. Of course, he would never have admitted this, even to himself.

He reached the spot and shone his light around, immediately revealing the source of the motion: icicles had fallen from a hanging pipe and shattered on the floor here, leaving a crystalline spatter of fairy dust that Carver ground vengefully beneath his boot. He grinned to himself, shaking his head at his own foolishness. Had he really been frightened just then? There was nothing worse than him on this station, he was sure of that. *Well*, he thought, *maybe just the dragon. Maybe.*

Still grinning, he continued round the corner into a slightly wider area. Another doorway led away to the right, but Carver angled leftwards, beneath a sign reading *REFINERY*, creeping up the few steps and into a haunted house of leaning shadows and black metal. Immense crucibles and muscular crane-arms soared above him, cables and chains as thick as his waist drooping to the floor in places. He slunk past a control desk that overlooked some huge machine, a contraption that looked like a sewage treatment plant and stretched away into solid darkness. The place was utterly dead and still, veiled in frost and rock dust.

He picked his way through this industrial wasteland at a steady pace, trying not to linger, knowing that the asshole friends would be coming soon, looking for him, probably hoping to hinder his escape. Hopefully the sight of the little scaredy cat would slow them down a little, but he supposed it was also likely to make them angrier. And so he kept moving, not so quickly that he would miss something, get lost or even have an accident, but quickly enough.

His suit's limited HUD continued to show vacuum outside its own protective confines, and a temperature so low that Carver wondered if it was even right. The station was obviously damaged, even crippled, and he wondered if it was the doing of the old, failed emissary. He suspected it probably was, and he grudgingly acknowledged to himself that the crazy bastard had apparently been good for *something* after all.

Through the refinery, out into another corridor so alike the last one that he felt a brief but powerful sense of disorientation, as if reality had skipped a beat.

'Carry on,' said the dragon, its voice a faint but fervent whisper. 'Hurry.'

'Hurry,' repeated Carver, not even hearing himself. He moved onwards, passing a sign that read CLEARED PERSONNEL ONLY BEYOND THIS POINT.

He emerged into a small chamber that was divided in two down its length by a screen of icy armoured glasspex. He reached out, swiped away an arc of frost and peered through the screen. There was a desk in there and a trio of monitors hanging from the ceiling. Some kind of security checkpoint, he thought. On the wall below the monitors was a shiny steel cabinet of a type that Carver thought he recognised. It was a weapon locker.

He laughed out loud, hefting the cutter. He fired a brief burst of plasma at the sheet of glass, expecting to inscribe a neat doorway through which he could pass. The glass, however, shattered explosively at the first touch of plasma, exposing Carver to a brief gale of shards. He flinched instinctively, turning his head away, praying that none of the pieces had cut his suit. He waited, hardly daring to breathe, until he was sure that he was actually all right.

'Lucky,' said the dragon. 'Now hurry up!'

'Yeah,' agreed Carver. 'I guess that was stupid.'

The dragon said nothing, which Carver took to be a sign of agreement. He stepped into the small room that had been closed off behind the glasspex. He approached the weapon locker and tried its doors. It was, of course, locked. *No problem for me*, he thought to himself. *I have a universal key.*

He carefully positioned the muzzle of the cutter on the side of the cabinet, fired it up, and neatly sliced the entire front off it. The piece fell away, revealing what was inside: a gun. A smallish laser pistol, simple and cheap-looking, as were often used on ships or habitats where a projectile weapon might pierce the hull. Not powerful enough to fire through armour, but probably good enough to burn through a space suit – certainly not something you'd want to be hit on exposed flesh with. Carver lifted the weapon down, surprised at how light it was. It had a plastic security tag through the trigger-guard to indicate that it was unused. He ripped the tag out and threw it away, then stepped cautiously back though the frame that had held the armoured glasspex, and continued.

The door out of the security room had a warning hand-painted onto it in large red letters: *TEMPORARY AIRLOCK. SECURITY ONLY.*

'That's it,' hissed the dragon faintly. 'The prison.'

'Yes,' agreed Carver, stuffing the laser pistol into his belt and hefting the cutter in both hands. Despite the new addition of the laser, he still preferred the cutter. It was so much more *personal* than any gun. He squeezed the trigger and it came alive in his hands, fizzing and spitting, making the glass of his visor darken to protect his eyesight. 'This is it. The prison.' Reluctantly, he let the cutter fizzle out again. He might need to be stealthy at first.

He stepped forwards and hit the pad beside the door. As it cracked and juddered open there was a rush of gas from the darkness on the other side, a whitish stream that rolled and twisted, then rapidly dissipated. Carver waited until the door was high enough and then he stepped inside.

CHAPTER FORTY

'Calm the fuck down!' bellowed Halman, not very soothingly, rising from his chair. 'And tell me what's going on!'

Lina pressed herself into her own seat, unable to speak. She couldn't even remember entering the room. She still had the visor down on her helmet, despite the fact that the damn thing felt like it was suffocating her. Her breath wreathed her body like smoke, as if something was burning out inside her, an effect which didn't help her fragile sanity at all.

'Boss?' said a tentative voice from the doorway.

'Fuck off, Theo!' roared Halman. He cast his gaze across the terrified foursome who had been squeezed into the room with him. 'What happened? And where is Liu?'

Lina looked around herself, unable to believe the evidence of her own eyes. Ella, Alphe, Fionne. . . She looked again, trying to count them. Halman was right. Liu wasn't there.

'He. . . he. . .' she stammered. 'He was with me,' she managed to splutter. Her breathing was too fast, too shallow. She tried to slow it down. 'He was with me,' she said again, more steadily.

'The bastard must have got him!' exclaimed Ella, who was standing directly in front of Halman's desk and as such was subjected to the full close-up glower.

'*What*?' Halman demanded. '*Who* got him?'

'A giant,' said Fionne in a whisper, slowly raising her head as if surfacing from a dream. She, at least, had managed to open her visor. 'With a necklace of human fingers.'

'What the hell are you talking about?' Halman asked, with more control this time. 'What *happened*?'

Alphe's jaw was visibly trembling as he spoke: 'We. . . well, we. . . we were working on Lina's Kay, I mean we're almost done, but. . . then. . .' He faltered, clenching his eyes shut. 'Shit!' he cried in

271

frustration, clearly unable to continue.

'He had Eli's fingers round his neck,' said Fionne quietly, looking up. Her pretty face – the face of a girl from a skincare advert more than that of a deep-space engineer – was glazed and stunned, her eyes unfocused. She looked around Halman's office as if seeking something sane and real to latch onto.

'*Who did*?' growled Halman. '*Who*?'

'A ship came in,' continued Alphe flatly. 'Cycled the hangar remotely. I guess the safety systems are still off-line after Eli's escape. Anyway, we thought it was him. But it wasn't. It was. . . I don't know who it was. . .'

'A giant,' said Fionne wonderingly. 'A giant with Eli's fingers. Covered in blood.' She stared blankly into Halman's face. Lina pressed herself further and further back into her chair, trying to distance herself from this reality. Her mind was railing inside her, a desperate prisoner in her skull.

'What happened?'

'We thought we'd be able to bring him in,' Alphe went on. 'But it wasn't Eli.'

'Carver. . .' breathed Halman, turning away to stare out of the window. 'Ronnie Carver. Six foot eight, ugly bastard, last seen on a supply shuttle bound for here.'

'He cycled the main airlock on the loader, but he tricked us. He came out of the cargo hold, and he. . . he. . .'

'We ran,' said Fionne in a disbelieving voice.

Alphe nodded. 'Yeah,' he agreed, still speaking to Halman's back. 'We ran. He had a plasma cutter. So much for fucking heroics!' He looked to Fionne and then Lina, his eyes pleading. 'He must have caught Liu.' His voice cracked, and the rest of his words were slushy with sudden tears: 'He must have caught Liu, he must have. . .' He put his head in his hands, shielding his face while great silent sobs racked his body.

'He's dead,' Fionne said. She looked too shocked to cry, her gaze unfocused and unblinking. Lina had seen people on the news, emerging from the embattled mines of Platini Alpha with that same expression – soldiers who'd seen their buddies die from exposure to chemical weapons or plasma traps. She knew that some of them never lost that look, never really recovered. She wondered if that same look was on her own face. 'He must be dead!' Fionne cried, her voice rising to a wavering treble.

'You ran?' asked Halman, turning back to them. 'But you lost Liu?'

'Yeah,' agreed Fionne bitterly. 'We ran. Like cowards.'

'No,' Halman insisted. 'You did the right thing. I'm going to organise a sweep of the station, but I want you guys to stay here. Don't move a muscle.'

'I'm coming,' said Ella in a low, flat voice that brooked no argument.

Halman paused, biting his lip. 'Okay,' he said.

Lina heard a voice say, 'Me, too,' and then she realised that it was *her* voice. Had she really just volunteered to go back out there?

Halman turned his stare on her. His dark eyes seemed to bore into her, as if probing for weakness. 'Okay,' he said again. 'Come on.' And he swept across the office and out of the door. Ella and Lina scrambled to follow him.

Halman stalked out into the corridor, the two women dragging along behind him. He went quickly from dorm to dorm shouting names: 'Theo; Si; Murkhoff; Rocko; Petra. . .' Panic spread in his wake, voices raised in question, fearful scrambling. 'Meet me by the airlock! The rest of you stay put!' he yelled as he went back out into the corridor. Those he had called came slowly, apprehensively out of their rooms, asking questions that he ignored. He turned instead to Ella. 'Ella – get me laser pistols for everyone here.'

'Sure,' she said, nodding once.

'Do you have enough?'

'I think so, yeah,' she said, and then she ran off, calling for someone to help her.

Halman scanned around for Theo, physically picking him out of the crowd by one hand. 'Theo – suits for everyone. We have to go out there. Hurry now.' Theo simply nodded and ran off.

'Lina,' said Halman, rounding on her.

She fell back a step. 'Yes?'

Murkhoff appeared at Halman's elbow and tugged on his sleeve. He looked thinner than ever – emaciated, really, and the bandage across his ruined eye looked dirty and unsanitary, even though Hobbes had changed it twice a day.

'I'm not coming,' said Murkhoff quietly. His voice was a dry rasp.

'*What*?' demanded Halman, as if he might not have heard correctly.

'I don't know what's going on,' said Murkhoff in that same disinterested tone. 'But I don't want any part in it. I'm *not coming*.'

Halman stared at him for a moment, and his mouth fell slowly open. 'Fuck it, Murkhoff,' he said. 'Whatever.' He sounded offended, but personally Lina couldn't blame Murkhoff for his reluctance. He had suffered enough at the hands of Macao's psychos already.

Murkhoff stalked off without another word, back towards his dorm. Lina and Halman watched him go in silence.

'You can't blame him,' said Lina once he was out of sight. She felt a little better now that her visor was open. The air here tasted bad, but she felt better all the same. A little.

Halman shook his head dismissively. 'Lina,' he said, attempting to pick up again from where he'd been interrupted, 'are you sure you're up for this? You don't have to come, you know. Hell, if that ass can opt out, then so can you. In fact, I'd rather you did.'

'Dan. . .' she sighed. 'I have to go. I–'

Something struck her in the side and she looked down, shocked, to see Marco. He hit her again with the palm of his hand. His face was clenched and tear-streaked.

'You can't go!' he shrieked, lashing out again and again. Lina struggled to grab his wrists but he was too fast, too wriggly. 'You can't go! Don't go out there again! Something else has gone wrong, hasn't it? *Hasn't it*?!'

'Honey. . .' she began weakly, tapering away to nothing. What was there to say? She had said it already. Nothing had changed. 'I *have* to. . .' she finished lamely. She finally managed to snag his arms and hold onto them. She knelt to look into his face. 'Somebody came in on the ISL, Marco. Somebody dangerous. We have to catch them.'

'Well that's fucking *fine*, then!' he screamed, worming free.

'Don't you swear at me!' she retorted automatically, totally stunned.

'Lina!' said Halman, grabbing her by the shoulder and raising her up so that he could speak directly into her ear. 'Lose the kid, or you're not coming,' he said in a low growl. Then he turned and strode away, shouting for Ella.

'Marco. . .' Lina began. But she didn't have anything else to follow it up with. 'My son. . .' she managed to add.

Marco shook his head, tears streaming down his face, mouth working soundlessly. He turned, almost colliding with Petra Kalistov, and ran away down the corridor. Lina stood in indecision, poised to pursue him, but Si's huge hand landed on her shoulder, stopping her.

'Lina,' said Si. 'You okay?'

She looked up into his broad, lantern-jawed face. That question again. 'Yeah,' she said, without any real idea if this was true or not. 'I guess.'

'Good,' he said. The hand squeezed briefly, then moved away.

'Gather round!' called Halman.

The little group closed in around him in a nervous huddle. Theo reappeared pushing a rack of space suits, then joined the back of the circle. Many of them eyed the suits suspiciously before turning back to Halman.

Lina squeezed in next to Si, whose large and solid presence was a reassuring bastion of solidity.

Halman looked at his tiny army, into the eyes of each in turn. 'People, we have a problem. . .' he began.

CHAPTER FORTY-ONE

'Close the outer door,' said the dragon. 'This is an airlock, remember.'

'Oh yeah,' agreed Carver, slightly mollified. He went back and shut the outer door, then returned to the one that would, all being well, allow access to the prison.

'Are you ready?' asked the dragon hungrily. 'Be prepared to fight. They may not be pleased to see you.'

Carver could feel the dragon's excitement like a cloud that surrounded him, prickling his skin. It reminded him of the tension in the air before a storm, which had been a common, almost daily occurrence back on the electrically-volatile world of Aitama. 'I'm ready,' he breathed. He hit the pad to open the inner door.

The door slid slowly into the ceiling, spilling dusky reddish light into the corridor like blood, revealing a world of sanguine shadow and glass panels beyond. Moving nonchalantly, so as not to panic anybody who was watching him, Carver stepped into Macao Prison, the cutter held as out of sight as possible behind his back, checking from side to side for company. Somebody was crying softly down one of the glass-walled corridors. Another voice answered the crying – a woman's voice. As quietly as he could, Carver crept down the passage towards it.

The first cell he passed contained a man lying naked in the middle of the floor, face down and unmoving. Carver didn't linger to check if the man was alive or not – now was not the time. The second cell he passed contained a scrawny, balding little rat of a man who was sitting cross-legged on his crude prison bed, the back of his head against the wall and his eyes shut. That was good.

Carver crept on past, occasionally checking back up the passage behind him, closing in on the voice. He turned his suit-light on, but he kept it pointed down at the floor for now. Its little circle of brilliance skimmed along the pitted metal like an eye staring up at him from hell.

The next cell contained a smooth-looking, oldish man, who stood stock-still in the centre of his tiny cell, regarding Carver with reptilian eyes that glittered in the red light. Only those eyes moved, following him, as Carver stalked past. The man was smiling a neat little smile, but it wasn't a smile that radiated any warmth at all – it looked like the smile of a crocodile that would be perfectly content to snap your leg off and eat it. Carver stared back at him, shaking his head, one gloved finger raised to his lips. The man made no acknowledgement, but he didn't make any noise either, and that was the main thing.

Suddenly, the voice at the end of the passage stopped, and Carver heard an intake of breath. 'Theo?' called the voice, its owner the merest suggestion of a shape in the shadows. He dared not spot her with his light yet. The sobbing stopped as the crying person paused to listen, too. 'Is that you? Man, you made me jump.' Carver saw movement up ahead and the voice took on new tones of suspicion. 'That *is* you, isn't it?'

He saw the figure congeal out of the darkness – a woman in a space suit, but no helmet, coming towards him squinting. She was a large, strong-looking woman of the type that Carver naturally associated with penal workers, but she didn't look too bright.

He splashed his light into her eyes, dazzling her, and making her fall back a step as he quickly covered the remaining ground between them, his huge boots ringing on the metal floor, the dragon leering over his shoulder ravenously, its breath a musky, charnel house stench that filtered even into his suit and filled his head with the taste of dead meat and ancient dust.

'Yeah,' he said, firing up the cutter, 'it's me all right.'

'Oh good,' said the woman, shielding her eyes, her words almost entirely lost in the rising bellow of the plasma cutter. The noise quickly swelled to fill the space with deafening volume, the sound echoing back hugely from the metal walls, layer on layer, loud enough to blot out all thought. 'Hey – what the hell is–' she shouted.

She got no further with the question, and her voice was all but inaudible anyway. Carver brought the cutter up in a smooth, controlled arc, not aiming for a killing blow just yet. It took the woman's gloved hand off at the wrist just as she tried to pull it back. The hand went sailing gaily into the air behind her and was lost in the darkness of the passage. Carver could feel the eyes of the prisoners on him, awed and terrified in equal measure, staring out of their cages like the trapped, desperate animals they were.

The woman held the stump of her hand up in front of her face and looked dumbly at it for a moment. The cutter had cauterised it so neatly that there wasn't as much as a drop of blood. Carver drew the weapon back and paused. The woman looked from her missing hand and back to him, her mouth hanging open and a thin trail of spittle depending from her lower lip.

'Wait!' she cried in a tone of dawning horror. 'You're not–'

'Not Theo, no,' Carver shouted, his grin stretching so wide that he thought the edges of his mouth might meet up at the back of his head. His brain felt like it was going to burst and rupture his skull like a fragmentation grenade.

He plunged the lance of blinding plasma into the woman's chest, sending out a great gout of steam, then whipped the weapon upwards, virtually tearing her torso in half. He kicked out, sending her convulsing remains flying into the darkness, and roared with bestial triumph, shaking the cutter above his head like a caveman's club. He felt exultant, wired, truly alive. This was what it meant to be free! The dragon twined around him, empowering and protecting him, phasing in and out at the edge of reality, a ghost of a dream of murder. Although it was distant, weakened in its cage of rock, for a moment Carver felt it there in the passage with him, relishing his triumph.

An eruption of noise came from the cells around him – cheers and cat-calls, whoops and crying, shouted reports that went rapidly down the line of cells as he turned in place with the cutter held aloft, revelling in the admiration of the dragon, his dragon, *his* dragon. Presently, he fell still, killed the cutter and stood breathing deeply, trying to regain his composure. He looked up and saw that he had gouged a thick, jagged line down the ceiling of the passage like a scar. Water dripped slowly from the cut like seeping blood in the red light, pattering softly onto his right boot. The suit felt like it was suffocating him, but he didn't want to take the helmet off. All being well, he wouldn't be here too long.

He went back to the cell he had passed where the man with the reptilian eyes still stood in the same place as when Carver had first seen him, smiling benignly. Carver shone his light into the cell, letting its beam play across the sparse furnishings and rusty walls. The man's bed was neatly-made and the few personal items in the cell looked to have been carefully arranged. The metal toilet in the corner had been polished to a mirror shine. He saw that the notepads and pens on the table had been positioned at perfect right angles to the room.

'Are there any more?' Carver asked, looking into the man's face.

'No,' said the man, his voice as prim and polite as his smile. He didn't even narrow his eyes when the beam of Carver's light fell across his face. 'No more. And may I say – well done.' He nodded once, agreeably, towards Carver.

'What's your name, Prisoner?' Carver asked him.

'Welby,' said the man. 'I've been expecting you.'

That was a little odd, thought Carver, but never mind. The guy was probably just crazy, but that was okay, wasn't it? If you bobbed for apples in the sewers, you came up with turds, right? He let the comment pass.

'Welby, I'm here to set you people free, just like the dragon did for me. We have much work to do.'

'The dragon?' asked Welby politely.

'Yes, yes,' said Carver hurriedly. 'The dragon in the asteroid sent me, I'm it's emissary, and I'm here to set you free. But first–'

'I knew it,' said Welby, his smile widening, showing perfect white teeth. 'The Old Ones sent you. An emissary. Of course.'

'Welby, I'm gonna let you people out, but I need to know that you aren't gonna fuck me around, okay? Is there anybody here who's gonna fuck me around?'

279

'I knew you would come,' said Welby smugly. 'I told the faithful as much. The time for vengeance is at hand.'

Carver felt himself smile too. He was already starting to like Welby. 'Yeah,' he agreed. 'I guess it is.'

CHAPTER FORTY-TWO

'Quiet!' commanded Halman, holding up one finger. He looked ungainly in his space suit, huge and awkward.

Lina held him in her light, breathing in heavy, ragged chunks. 'What?' she whispered, head cocked. Whatever he had heard must have come through the comm-channel, because they were moving through a vacuum and there was nothing else to hear.

'I thought I heard voices on the radio,' he said at length, shaking his head. 'Several of them. Faint, but. . .'

'Ella's team?' suggested Lina uncertainly. 'Or Si's?'

'I guess,' he replied. 'Almost *too* faint for them, I thought. Anyway, it's gone now.' They stood silently for a moment, oppressed by the darkness of the passage. Open, deserted doorways lined the walls around them and the metal panels of the corridor were crusted with ice. Lina, Halman, Waine and Theo stood for a moment, exchanging warning looks, their suit-lights turning the world around them to black and white, like some terrible dream sequence. The passage shuddered suddenly, dislodging powdered ice from the ceiling. It fell around them like snow.

Lina wiped her visor with one sleeve, clearing it. 'Mass driver,' she whispered, unsure of why she was whispering.

Halman nodded, towering over her. 'Do you hear me, Ella?' he asked into his mic. 'Si?'

Their replies were clearly audible, if muddied somewhat by the radio.

'Did you hear anyone else on this channel?' Halman asked.

Ella's voice said, quite understandably through the static, 'No, Boss.'

'Nope,' said Si.

'Are you at the prison yet, Ella?' asked Halman.

'Not yet. Something wrong?'

'No,' said Halman. 'Don't worry about it. But keep your ears open. I could have sworn somebody else was on this channel for a moment there.'

'Okay, sure, I'll. . .' replied Ella, the tail-end of her answer tattered by interference.

'Will do,' said Si, slightly more clearly.

Halman visibly steeled himself. 'Let's continue,' he said to Lina and the others, his jaw set determinedly.

Onwards through that surreal cavern of white ice, grey metal and thick black shadow. Lina felt the blood rushing in her ears, swarming through her veins, throbbing within her hammering heart. Where had the invader – Ronnie Carver – gone? Was he around the next corner? Within one of the rooms that led off this corridor, maybe lying in wait for them, cradling the plasma cutter? Even worse, maybe he had doubled back, got behind the teams somehow as they fanned out, made his way back to the offices where Marco waited for her to return. She didn't think that last was likely – and he'd have quite a fight on his hands if he tried to breach the dorms – but her mind kept suggesting it as a possibility all the same. She was glad that someone was on guard inside the makeshift airlock. *Marco*, she swore to herself, *I am coming back from this.* But it didn't sound that convincing, even to her. Death had proven itself to be easily obtainable of late. It seemed to be everywhere she went.

They rounded a corner where somebody had deserted a huge pile of rubberised pipework, presumably in the scramble to vacate the main body of the station. They stepped over its snakelike coils carefully, concerned that they might slip and damage their suits. Such an accident could easily prove fatal in this environment. A tiny rip in the fabric, or a knock to the famously unreliable control units could result in a rapid, unpleasant demise. Lina stepped cautiously through the pile, her boots feeling uncomfortably heavy on her feet, her calf muscles aching from walking in them. The laser pistol felt flimsy and inadequate in her hand. She had never even held a gun before. She'd never even struck anybody in anger before this nightmare, let alone shot them.

They continued to the end of the corridor, following those jinks and jags that the designers of Macao had felt necessary to incorporate into its construction, checking into the deserted living quarters that they passed. Each of these showed them a little sneak preview of somebody else's life: a half-eaten apple left on a table, now frozen solid; two pairs of slippers arranged beside a door – his and hers; an unmade bed; a framed photograph of Aitama's yellowed plains, its glass crusted with frost; a thousand relics of a time, not so long ago, when this frozen, empty space had been their home. A little twinge of sadness went through her, but it was only the merest spark beside the fear and trepidation that dominated her thoughts.

The notion of actually taking a Kay and returning to that dark and hulking rock where Eli had secreted their shuttle filled her with a chilling dread that increased in magnitude with every step she took towards the hangar. She wondered if she had been insane to volunteer. She couldn't imagine how she'd ever arrived at that decision. She felt as if the intrinsic, inherent bond that joined mother to son like an unseen umbilical, was stretching, weakening, fading, as she picked her way deeper into the bowels of the station's corpse.

They had long-since lost radio contact with Amy Stone, who had been left in charge back at the dorms. The construction of Macao virtually denied the use of internal radio altogether, and it hadn't taken long for Amy to become inaudible as they ventured out, barring the occasional freak burst of signal here and there, which offered barely coherent snatches of speech and fizzing static that hurt the ears. Marco might as well have been on another planet. Lina felt a wetness developing in her eyes, and she blinked it away, unable to put a hand to her helmeted face, trying to clear her mind of all but the job at hand. *Focus*, she told herself. *Focus, and come back from this. You cannot afford the luxury of screwing up and getting killed. Nor the luxury of crying like a little girl.*

'Lina, you want to go back?' asked Theo, appearing at her elbow as they neared the steps down to the hangar level. He was smiling a small, concerned smile.

'No,' she said, a little offended. She affected looking into one of the rooms they passed in order to avoid his scrutiny.

'It's going to be okay, Lina,' Theo said. Waine shouldered his way past them and stood at the top of the steps, peering down into the darkness below.

'Sure,' said Lina, blinking her eyes to clear them and treating Theo to what she hoped was an encouraging smile. Judging from his expression, it missed the mark somewhat. 'I'm just a bit jumpy.'

'Come on,' called Halman softly, beckoning them onwards.

They descended the steps carefully, mindful of the slipperiness of the surface, gripping the hand-rail as they went, half expecting Ronnie Carver to peel away from the shadows and fall on them at any moment. Had he really killed Eli, as suggested by the fingers around his neck? Oddly, Lina didn't seem to feel anything at all about that possibility. She supposed that she had already mourned Eli – the Eli whom she had known for so long – once it had become clear that the old Eli was gone, replaced by some drug-addicted psychopath. And now, if that new Eli really was dead, then what concern was it of hers? He hadn't been *her* Eli any more by that point – he had been some sort of monster. *It'll eat you up, Lina!* her mind sang. It had eaten *him* up in the end, she supposed, thinking of the shadow in the belt.

And what *was* that shadow? She thought she had almost *seen* it in the belt when she had been in pursuit of the ISL. But had she? She had seen it first in a dream, after Sal's death. Maybe she had just imagined it in the belt. She suspected that it was simply an embodiment of her own fear. But a nagging, doubting little corner of her mind kept wanting to tell her that it was something real, tangible, maybe even evil. Who knew for sure? She hadn't mentioned the shadow to Halman or the others, maybe for fear that acknowledging it would cement its reality, somehow give it substance. Whatever it was, she had agreed to go out there again. She shook her head, wondering at her own recklessness.

At the bottom of the steps, the passage continued straight for some fifteen metres, flanked by storage cupboards and tiny utility rooms, before angling to the left into the main part of the warehouse. They moved along in a fearful huddle, treading carefully. The airless space was eerily silent, a collage of grey and black. A water leak in the ceiling had formed stalactites of ice that stretched down to the floor like giant fangs, and the group unconsciously stepped around them as if afraid of being bitten. Lina's boots slipped in the puddle of ice and she went painfully to one knee, cursing under her breath. Theo helped her to her feet again, lifting her by the arm as if she were of no weight at all. His compact body was obviously stronger than it looked. She thanked him and they continued.

Every nook and cranny of the warehouse was a hiding place from which the dreaded Carver might spring. Every outcropping piece of machinery, every tarpaulin-covered pallet, every massive spool of cable, was a skulking human form. Lina's breathing seemed to fill the entire world. She held the pistol in front of her like a ward. Frost glittered everywhere like fairy dust, making the place into a sinister wonderland. There was only silence from the comm. Ella and Si were too far away to talk to now. Lina wondered if they were all okay, and who, if anyone, would find the escaped prisoner first. She hoped, for all her most altruistic desires, that it would not be her own group.

The hangar door was standing open, dangerously inviting. The lights were on inside, showing rows of gunmetal ship's hulls and reflective cockpit glass. They crept inside, explorers in their own lost world.

The in-system loader loomed in the centre of the hangar like a vast beetle that had landed there, surrounded by its cowed harem of battered Kays, almost blocking the flight deck completely. The space door hung open at the far end like an unravelled tongue. It was disturbing to see it left like that, just hanging open, almost inviting the void to spill into the station, living shadows and all, to drown the remaining survivors like flood water.

'My ship,' said Lina, pointing towards K6-12 with her gun. It sat over on the right-hand side of the hangar, in the shadow of the loader, with just enough of an angle to be able to move it without moving the loader first. She was sentimentally glad that the incoming vessel had not damaged it. 'I could just take it now and go out there. If Carver's here, maybe there's nobody alive on the shuttle at all.' She looked at Halman, who froze in place, his face scrunched in thought. 'I could just go, Dan.'

'No,' he said. 'No, we take care of this first. Eli could still be out there, or the pilot. We deal with this first, then you and Ella go together as planned.' Lina started to object but he stopped her with a single shake of his head. 'Don't fucking argue with me now, Lina,' he said with soft menace. 'Not now.'

Lina huffed, annoyed, and turned away. She let her light play across the ships, caress their battered hulls. 'Fine,' she said.

'Lina and Waine, wait here and guard the door,' commanded Halman softly. 'Keep your wits about you. Anything happens, shout – I won't be far. Actually, if you see Carver, shoot first and then shout.' He beckoned Theo with his laser pistol. 'Theo – with me. We'll sweep down to the other end, check the control room, then come back.'

He waved Theo over to the other side of the hangar, and they moved off down the rows of Kays with their weapons cocked at the ready. Lina tried to take some comfort in the fact that Halman had once been a low-ranking officer in the Farsight army at Platini Alpha, but she couldn't do it. He was still a large man, but he looked too old now, too hunched, too drawn, and although she knew the shadow of a fighter still dwelt within him somewhere, it was at best well-hidden.

Halman could be seen in silhouette, gun outstretched, skirting the central control desk and Ilse's broken and upturned Kay while Theo moved away down the far side of the hangar. Halman approached the dead-lifter, which was parked in the middle of the flight deck, overshadowed by the loader that had pulled up on the far side, almost touching it. Suddenly, his suit-light flashed as he turned to look back towards Lina and Waine.

'Oh shit,' said Halman's voice over the radio. 'Oh shit. Oh no.'

'What?' demanded Lina. 'What is it?'

'The bastard. . .' muttered Halman. He had stopped before the dead-lifter and was seemingly frozen in place staring at it. It looked like something was on the lifter's forks, something torn and tattered that Lina couldn't distinguish from her distant vantage point.

'Come on!' she called to Waine, already setting off at a run. Theo was also heading towards Halman, calling out to him, unanswered.

Before she actually reached him, Lina saw what Halman had found. Halman himself hadn't seen it until he'd been right upon it, but with the benefit of his light, which was now firmly planted on the object in question, Lina could make it out quite clearly. She stopped, skidding to a halt, transfixed by what she saw hanging from the lifter's forks. She willed her feet to continue moving, but they seemed to be stuck to the floor. Maybe she had inadvertently activated the magnets on her boots.

Whatever else Ronnie Carver might be, he was certainly creative. He seemed to have made a sculpture in human remains. The body hanging from the lifter's forks had been not just butchered but almost entirely *reworked*, cut right open and somehow *peeled*, reshaped into something inhuman and monstrous. Ribs had been splayed open like wings, limbs had been broken and re-jointed, hands twisted into talons, flaps of meat carved crudely but enthusiastically into new forms. Scraps of space suit hung here and there like streamers. Pieces of skin and intestine, cauterised by the plasma cutter, lay strewn around the floor like bits of rubbish.

Lina knew instantly what it was: a dragon. A dragon made from a sacrificed human body, strung up with wire that had clearly come from the large spool on the floor by the central desk. A message, an omen, a harbinger of disaster cast in human flesh and blood.

'Dragon!' she gasped, her mind reeling in horror, flailing, grasping for something to latch onto before sanity slipped and fell away, possibly to be lost forever. *It'll eat you up!* She was falling, falling into darkness that loomed beneath her like the mouth of a waiting monster. *I'm going to take my son to Platini Alpha, and*

287

one day all this will seem like a bad dream, something that never really happened at all. . . And although she didn't really believe it herself any more, that was enough – *just* enough – to hang onto. She stood reeling, hands to the sides of her helmet, her muscles suddenly as limp as rags, holding her up out of mere habit.

'Oh shit,' sighed Theo, approaching the lifter with his hand out as if to touch that hideous creation of murdered meat.

'Don't!' cried Lina without thinking, as if the thing might suddenly come to life and eat Theo whole like a wolf in a children's fairy story. She reached out one unsteady hand, meaning somehow to stop him, but it was all right – Theo stayed his hand and simply stood staring in awestruck revulsion.

Waine walked slowly past her, gliding silently as if on rails, to stand shoulder to shoulder with Halman. But Lina saw his eyes as he passed, and they looked dull and glazed in his wrinkled face.

'That fucking bastard,' snarled Halman, moving closer to Liu's destroyed corpse. He turned around, his face full of horror and slowly-growing anger. 'Poor fucking Liu,' he said.

Lina regained control of her muscles, and she forced her feet to carry her forwards. Her throat was hitching and constricting, making her breathing heavy and hard. The thought of going out there again, into the belt, now seemed utterly unthinkable. For all her earlier determination, all her speeches to her son, she simply didn't think she could do it now.

In her earpiece, she heard Waine begin to cry. This seemed significant to her – another bad omen.

'This changes nothing,' said Halman, still staring at the abomination that hung from the dead-lifter's forks. 'We'll secure this area, lock the space door with my personal code, then move back towards the plaza and meet up with the other teams. Then, if we haven't seen Carver, we'll spread out again from there.'

Waine began to say something, his voice still unsteady, but his words were drowned by a sudden burst of noise from the radio. It sounded like massed human voices, screaming, shouting. . .

For a second Lina couldn't work out what was happening. She scrunched her eyes shut, as if by doing so she could lessen the

288

volume in her ears, and a question began to form on her lips. She looked at Waine, and was alarmed to see the expression on his face.

Waine's eyes fell wide open and he said something to Lina which was inaudible against the background noise. He pointed to the hangar door behind her. Halman stared in shock. As Lina turned to look, it dawned on her what that noise was.

A veritable mob of people were storming into the hangar, the massive figure of Ronnie Carver at their fore, taller than Halman and at least as heavy as Si Davis.

As she watched, the plasma cutter came alive in Carver's hands, making her visor darken protectively. She clutched the pistol, completely forgotten, in one fist and stared dumbly as the mob rushed towards them.

Theo was quicker to react. He ran to meet the giant, levelling the pistol at him. He fired once and the beam briefly danced around the feet of the onrushing Carver. Theo steadied himself to fire again. Nothing happened. He held the gun up, looking at it in confusion. Lina saw a red warning light glowing on its body. And then Carver was on him.

Carver brought the cutter down in a mighty overhand swipe. Theo made to block the strike with his dead pistol, but the beam of the cutter went right through the gun, sending its end twirling away into the shadows like a propeller. Then the beam went through *Theo*, as if he was no more substantial than a cloud of smoke, dividing him roughly about the waist in a great rush of vapour. The two halves fell away, gas rupturing from his suit. Carver's mob of followers spread out into the hangar, whooping and jeering, leaping into cover.

Lina stood stupefied and watched as Theo died. Who the hell were all these people? Where had he found all these *people*?

Halman was running already, under cover of the Kays, firing his laser pistol on the fly, without pause to aim. The roaring of the attackers still filled the comm, making communication impossible. Lina looked to Waine, totally lost, knowing that her life – all of their lives – hung in the balance.

Somebody in the attacking group was firing a laser, too, as they ran along the furthest row of Kays. The shots went wild, most of them zipping away into the cable-festooned darkness of the ceiling. One bounced off the mirrored cockpit glass of K6-4 and hit the dead-lifter, where it left a small and understated burn in its paintwork. It was clear, however, even to Lina's stunned mind, that the shooter was aiming for her and Waine.

'Quick!' she yelled, unaware that her voice was inaudible beneath the continuous war-cry of the attacking group. She darted across the open deck, feeling horribly exposed, and under the nose of the nearest ship, her boot skidding on the ice, almost slipping out from under her. She hit the deck and looked back over her shoulder.

Waine was behind her, but he was not so fast. He took a hit from the laser pistol, high on one shoulder, and his suit shredded itself like a burst balloon. He collapsed, writhing and clutching at his throat, grabbing instinctively for Lina's leg as she scrambled further into cover. She peeked out and saw him thrashing on the floor, twisting and arching like a fish out of water. Shots from the laser stroked the deck in front of her, probing, making her duck back again, powerless to help the man who now lay dying only feet away.

The roaring was subsiding now, and Lina heard Halman's voice over the radio. 'The prisoners!' he shouted. 'The prisoners!' Other voices came from the radio, too – desperate, aggressive exclamations and screams of rage.

Halman was right, of course – it made perfect sense. Carver had freed the prisoners and brought them here to escape on the ISL. Not just one homicidal maniac any more, but sixteen of them. How could things get any worse?

Lina scampered round to the other side of her Kay and peeked out again. The prisoners were fanning out into the hangar, running in clumsy half-crouches, keeping to the shadows. Two of them dashed into the shade of the dead-lifter where she had been only moments before, peeping out at her with ugly, feral faces. They would flush her from her hiding place at any second, as soon as they had summoned up the courage to make the next dash.

'Halman!' she yelled, poised in indecision, feeling like an animal caught in a hunter's sights.

'Lina, follow me!' he yelled back. 'We have to get to the door!' She couldn't see him any more, but she knew he was right. They had to get away. There was no hope they could win this fight.

Without allowing herself to stop, think, and then possibly die in that moment of consideration, Lina launched herself out from behind the ship and onto the open floor of the flight deck. She caught another glimpse of Halman, pinned down behind a Kay to her right, exchanging fire with the laser-armed prisoner. She ran towards him, knowing that a beam of light could end her life at any second, leave her gasping and suffocating like Waine, or maybe just blinded and convulsing in agony on the floor. She thought about what might happen if Carver captured her, about what had happened to Liu. *Dragon!* she thought madly. *It'll eat you up!*

She landed beside Halman with a jarring crash, laser beams playing on the deck behind her. He popped up from cover, but was forced to duck back again without even getting a shot off.

'Shit!' he cried.

Lina, staying low on her belly, edged round the landing gear of the ship and took a quick glance towards the door. The shooter was out of sight, hiding, and she couldn't tell where he was. But Carver was running from cover to cover, closing in on them. She caught a glimpse of the face behind the visor, and it looked pink and stupid and horribly eager. And he was close. Her mind began to gibber in fear.

Halman popped up again, letting off another shot. An answering beam flashed silently past his helmet, missing him by perhaps a hand's breadth. It seemed the enemy had got his eye in now. Halman ducked down again, cursing.

'Come on!' cried Lina, desperately seizing the initiative. She knew that if they stayed put, they would die for sure. Sadly, the odds didn't look much better if they broke cover. But what other option was there?

She threw herself round the back of the Kay, squeezing between the ship and the hangar wall, safely out of the enemy's line of sight, but also virtually blind to what was going on. Halman was right behind her. They ran, crouched, ducking under outcropping winches and brackets and ventilation units.

And then they came face-to-face with Carver.

They skidded, Halman falling over Lina, and the giant towered above them, the cutter held high for the killing blow. She saw the fingers jumping on their string around his neck and the face behind the visor, streaked with blood. Still crouched low, she tried to shy away into the wall itself, raising one hand in a pointless attempt to protect her head, knowing that she was about to die. Oddly, she felt only a drifting, timeless sense of calm now that it came down to it. Everything slowed down. Her heartbeat sounded loud in her ears, like a war drum. The world flattened and spread like oil on water. This was the end.

But Halman rolled away, his training taking over, crashing into the wall, firing the pistol as he went. Either he had been something of a crack shot in his day, or he was lucky now. Whatever the case, the beam of the laser hit Carver right in the visor of his helmet. He staggered back, dropping the cutter, which sliced a neat segment from the radar dome of the nearest Kay before going out. He reeled away, into the open, almost hit by a shot from his comrade's laser, hands to his helmet. He screamed into the comm – a sound of maniacal rage and frustration more than pain, groping blindly for the person who had shot him.

'Go!' screamed Halman, scrambling to his feet.

Lina ran, her feet skidding on the icy floor in excruciating slow-motion. It was like a dream she'd used to have quite regularly back in the days when her marriage had been failing but she hadn't had the sense to overtly acknowledge it – a dream in which she'd always found herself running from some faceless aggressor, but running without moving, as if caught in treacle, frozen in a single, hellish slice of time.

Her flight from the cover of the ship to the door of the hangar seemed to take minutes, though in fact it must have been closer to two or three seconds. Laser lights played around them, deceptively harmless-looking, miraculously touching neither of them. Suited enemies moved towards them from every angle, but too slowly.

They were out, away into the warehouse and running as fast as their suits would allow. One slip now, one tiny pause, one stumble, would mean death. Lina felt her heart beating in her head, compressive waves that made her vision fade and swim. The exhausted breath from her suit stretched out behind her in a long silky plume.

Halman seemed to keep pace with her effortlessly, and he ran beside her although she knew he could have just stormed away, leaving her easily behind. The warehouse was utterly dark after the relative brightness of the hangar, and their suit-lights bobbed and weaved crazily as they ran, slashing and slicing through the darkness. They didn't pause to look behind them, and there was only silence from the radio. They ran beneath the crushing shadows, over the frosted metal, through the airless void of their hostile home, leaving more friends dead behind them.

CHAPTER FORTY-THREE

When they reached the next floor, Halman slowed Lina with a hand outstretched in front of her. At first, she didn't think she *could* slow down, but gradually she managed to control her aching, pumping legs. They decelerated to a walk, checking behind them. There was no sign of any pursuit and nothing from the comm.

'I think we're clear,' Halman said between heaving breaths. They were passing those empty living quarters again, and the area was even more desolate to Lina's mind than the industrial coldness of the hangar had been. People should have been living here, and instead there was only this lifeless metal warren, frozen in the moment of desertion.

'I think you're right,' she said, trying not to look through the doorways that they passed, keeping her light fixed on the wall at the end of the passage, where it took a turn to the left.

'You heard anyone recently?' asked Halman. He was still holding his laser pistol, cocked at an angle against his shoulder.

'No,' said Lina. 'You?'

'Not for a while, I don't think, but to be honest I've had other things on my mind. I should have locked the hangar door. I wasn't thinking.'

'Carver could just cut through it. If we'd paused we'd have been killed. Like Theo. And Waine.' Two more. She couldn't even remember how many that made now. And what had caused it all? How had her world degenerated into *this*? She couldn't work it out. Something about dragons and psychoactive drugs and shuttles and prisoners. It was all a blur inside her mind.

'Yeah,' said Halman darkly. 'I guess.' He adjusted one of the dials on his suit's chest unit. 'Ella!' he yelled into the comm, with such sudden volume that Lina physically jumped.

'Damn it, Halman!' she yelped, feeling her heart shudder inside her as adrenalin surged through her body. She only narrowly avoided peeing in her suit, a humiliation which, although private, she certainly didn't need.

'Sorry,' he said more quietly. They reached the end of the passage and Halman peered round suspiciously, gun outstretched, before leading Lina round. 'Ella!' he yelled again. 'Si! Somebody fucking copy me!'

Lina wondered how she would react if *Carver* copied, or maybe one of his escaped mental-case friends. She thought she might scream if that happened, but luckily it didn't.

The next time Halman called Ella, she answered.

'I'm here, Boss,' said Ella's voice. But it had lost its usual strong and confident tone. Ella sounded frightened and possibly out of breath.

'Ella,' said Halman with a sigh of relief. 'Bad news.'

'I know,' she answered. Ella sounded as if she might be running. 'We're on our way towards the plaza. Carver's freed the damn prisoners! And he murdered Rachelle. Where are you?'

'We're back on two now,' Halman replied, coming to a halt. He turned in place, casting his light around. 'In the refinery quarters corridor. Don't go near the hangar, though, Ella. Carver's circus of freaks just fucking rushed us there. They killed Theo and shot Waine – one of the bastards had a laser.'

Ella replied with a single word that, although shredded by interference, Lina understood to be *fuck*. 'Is Lina with you?' asked Ella, and Lina was touched to hear the note of concern in her friend's voice.

'I'm here,' she said, but the words came out in a croak. She licked her lips and tried again: 'I'm here, Ella. I'm okay.'

'Good. That's good. Hi, Lina.' The relief was clear in Ella's voice.

'Hi,' echoed Lina, feeling a little foolish. It seemed there were more important things to be said. 'Have you seen Si's team?' she asked.

'Look where you're going!' cried Ella, which seemed a pretty strange answer until Lina realised that she was talking to someone at her end. 'No,' said Ella in a more conversational tone. 'But we last heard them only a minute ago. We could back-track and get a message to them, probably.'

'Do it, please,' said Halman, leaning his back against the wall of the passage and stuffing the pistol into a tool-loop on his suit. 'I want them to head back to base and get me Alphe and Fionne. I know they're fucking traumatised, but right now they can join the club. I want them, and your team, and Si's team to meet us here soon-as. And tell them to bring every spare air cartridge they can find for these suits. I assume the prisoners have escaped back into the belt. But if they're still in the hangar I want us to return in force. If they've left the station, then we'll go ahead as planned, with the slight change that we'll now take as many Kays as we can fly. Then we'll cut our way into that shuttle and take it back.'

'Sure,' said Ella's voice. She sounded pleased. Ella liked to have a plan. Even a plan that was, in Lina's opinion, now one hell of a long shot. In fact, it was probably suicide.

'I know the odds are sounding worse and worse,' said Halman, as if reading her mind. 'But what choice do we have?'

'And Ella?' asked Lina. 'Will you give a message to Marco for me?'

'Of course. What is it?'

Lina's mind suddenly went blank. What could she possibly say to him that would make everything all right? How could any words even begin to do that? There had been more deaths. She was about to put herself right into the midst of a very grave danger. Hope was trickling away like sand through the waist of an hourglass. The assault on the shuttle now sounded like a death sentence. What could she possibly tell him?

'Just tell him I'm okay,' she said lamely.

'Will do, then,' said Ella. 'We're turning back. As soon as we can get a message to Si's lot, we'll come and meet you there. Stay put. Oh, and Boss. . .'

'What?' asked Halman cautiously.

'I want a pay rise when all this is over.'

'Dream on, Officer,' countered Halman tiredly. And then he began to laugh. The sound was eerie in the deserted corridor, and a little too close to the edge of insanity. But after a moment, Lina found herself joining him. They leant against the wall, shoulder to shoulder, as the radio went quiet, and waited.

CHAPTER FORTY-FOUR

Blinded! He was fucking blinded!

Carver lurched, sightless, feeling for the bastard who had shot him, but he couldn't get his bearings. His eyes stung and burned, streaming with tears that he couldn't even reach to wipe away.

'Kill them!' hissed the dragon. Its voice, although still faint, buzzed with raw, desperate energy. 'Kill them! Before they get away!'

But he couldn't – he couldn't even tell where they were. His head was beating like a heart, the blood rushing inside it with audible force. He had dropped the cutter, but that seemed like the least of his concerns. He knew that he was in the open, vulnerable. The asshole friend with the laser might shoot him at any moment.

'No, you idiot – they've escaped!' scolded the dragon. 'It's too late.'

'Fuck!' cried Carver, shaking his head in an attempt to clear his sight, as if he could shed the blindness like a dog shaking off water. He felt a hand on his shoulder, and he twisted away violently, lashing out. His fist connected with something soft and he heard a startled intake of breath over the radio. He didn't care if the target was friend or foe.

He tried to force his eyes to open – they burned like hell, as if somebody had rubbed salt into them – but he could already see a little better. The world was still a vague, shifting haze of light and dark patches, but he thought he might not be permanently blinded after all. Staggering, hands outstretched, he reached a wall, where he turned around and sat, holding his head in his hands, wishing he'd brought the strip of fader caps with him. Not, he supposed, that he'd have been able to take them with his suit on.

'I'm sorry,' he muttered, not caring if the escaping cowards heard him or not. 'I'm sorry.'

'Don't concern yourself too much,' said the dragon a little more calmly. 'We can still do what we need to do. Find somebody to fly the loader first. I don't think you can do it right now, and you need to get away before they return. Welby can be trusted – ask him to find another pilot for you.'

'Yeah, Welby thinks you're his god. Maybe you are,' Carver said. The dragon didn't answer, but he knew that it was right, that Welby would do as he said. How much control Welby had over the other ex-prisoners remained to be seen, however. 'Welby!' he called. 'Come here!'

He felt the clanging of approaching footsteps through the deck, and when he looked up he could make out the shadow-shape of the little man standing over him. 'Carver,' said Welby's voice in his earpiece. 'What shall I do?'

'Find out if one of the others can fly the loader – the big ship in the middle. It's big enough to take us all out of here.'

'Certainly. Would it be impudent of me to ask where we intend to go?'

Carver felt his jaw clench as he answered. 'It might be, Welby, it might be.'

'Some of these men will follow me to the grave. They are my congregation – the faithful – and they have been awaiting this salvation. I believe that the Old Ones have sent you. This one you call *the dragon*. I am eager to find out more, I confess. My people will obey you without question. But others among them – those who are lost, who will not listen – will want to know what we intend to do.'

'What others?' demanded Carver rudely, blinking his eyes.

'This might work well for us,' said the dragon slyly. The eager, hungry note was back in its voice now. 'These unbelievers.'

'Did you hear that, Welby?' asked Carver with sudden suspicion. He had to know. Before going any further, before bringing this little cultist and his friends right into the court of his precious dragon, he had to be sure.

'Hear what?' asked Welby neutrally.

'I thought there was someone else on the radio, I guess,' said

Carver with immeasurable relief. Of course, Welby could be lying. But he thought not. 'Just ask about the loader, will you? I need you to help me until I can see properly. And we're going back to the asteroid. Where it lives.'

'Fine.' The dark patch that represented Welby faded away, and then Welby began talking to the other ex-prisoners. Somebody asserted that they had flown an identical ISL at Platini Dockyard and the matter was quickly settled. Doubtless they'd be better at it than Carver was. That was good and soon he'd be back where he belonged, in the dragon's lair. And this time he'd have an army with him. He was wondering what the dragon had meant when it had said that the presence of the unbelievers might work well for them.

Interesting. . . he thought. *It'll be interesting to find out.* He couldn't wait for his vision to come right again. His eyes still stung like nothing he'd ever known and the burning was almost more intense than before. But those patches of light and dark were already beginning to crystallise at the edges. The others were talking excitedly. It sounded like the new pilot was starting the ship up. Carver felt a hand on his shoulder again. He turned to see the now-slightly-clearer shape of Welby standing over him again.

'Come on,' said Welby. 'We're good to go.' He helped Carver to his feet. Good old Welby. Carver was lucky to have found him. He just hoped Welby could maintain order until he himself could see properly again. Surely the dragon wouldn't let things fall apart now. Its own freedom was near at hand. It needed him. He needed the prisoners. Maybe when his eyes were truly better he'd kill one or two of them, just to make the point.

'That's right,' said the dragon, reading his mind.

Maybe that was what the unbelievers were for. . . Carver grinned to himself, despite his stinging eyes and ringing head.

'Get my plasma cutter,' he said. 'I dropped it, but I'm not sure where.'

'It's okay,' said Welby, helping Carver along with a hand under his arm. 'I already retrieved it.'

'Good,' said Carver significantly. 'I'll be needing that.'

CHAPTER FORTY-FIVE

They soon received word from Ella that she was on her way, having sent Si back to base to retrieve the two techs and as many air cartridges as they could find. Lina checked her own air reserve. It showed just over sixty-percent. Halman's, he being somewhat larger, was down to just over half.

'Dan?' said Lina, turning to him. They were sitting next to each other on the floor of the corridor, facing the darkened doorways of the refinery team's living quarters, their suit-lights making two bright circles on the opposite wall like eyes.

'Yeah?'

'I've been thinking. . .' she began slowly. 'About this dragon thing. . .'

'Yeah,' said Halman unenthusiastically. 'So what's up with that?'

'I've been wondering if it's a real thing.' She scanned his face, trying to gauge his reaction. Perhaps he'd think she'd finally gone nuts. Perhaps she had. 'You know – if maybe there is really something out there.' She indicated the vastness of space with a vague sweep of one arm. 'In the belt.'

'What do you mean?' he asked.

'Well. . .' She shuffled her backside closer to the wall, trying to make herself comfortable. Halman was holding the pistol in his hand again, toying with it. 'When it was just Eli, I thought he'd simply gone crazy. That the whole dragon thing was something out of his drug-riddled head. But now this Carver. . . you know, that fucking monstrosity he made in the hangar.'

'Mmm. . .' grunted Halman. 'A dragon, yeah.' He was silent for a moment, then he turned to Lina. His primitive face was lined in thought. 'Maybe he passed the delusion on to Carver in some way. Carver sounds like a pretty messed-up individual – the sort of freak who might believe any old shit. Maybe he's on the same drugs. I can just imagine the two of them sitting in that damned asteroid, smashed out of their tiny brains, talking about dragons and emissaries.' He paused, then added, 'Bastards!' in a vicious snarl, so heartfelt that Lina almost laughed.

'Yeah, I thought that. Everyone knows that fader causes mass hallucinations. Or maybe just Eli suggesting it was enough to make Carver believe in this dragon, too.'

'You don't sound sure, though,' said Halman, looking at her with his brows raised in question.

Lina sighed, rubbing at her knee. She couldn't remember hurting it, but it ached deep inside the bone nonetheless. 'I'm *not* sure,' she said, looking away uncertainly. She could make out the spindly silhouette of a dining chair through one of the doorways opposite. It had been upset in the evacuation and now lay with its legs in the air like a dead thing, shiny with ice. 'I know it sounds pretty tenuous, but I've been feeling as if there is something out there. Something. . .' She searched for the right word at some length, then settled for, '. . . else.'

'Something else?' repeated Halman. 'A dragon?' He laughed, but it sounded a rather bitter laugh. 'As in *here there be dragons*?'

Lina was struck by a sudden pang of sadness, so sour that it burned inside her like acid. She remembered Sal joking about that, out in the belt, what seemed like a million years ago. *Here there be dragons, right? That's what they used to write on the uncharted parts of the map in times of old.* It seemed like ancient history, but Lina remembered the words exactly. Sal. Sal Newman. The woman who had almost stolen her husband, long after he'd been worth keeping. The woman who had earned Lina's trust and friendship over the years since, and who had then died in a cloud of shredded guts. She remembered that tooth hitting the glasspex canopy of her Kay and shivered.

'Yeah,' she agreed. 'Something like that.'

'I don't know,' replied Halman in a slow and measured voice. 'I don't know. There could be any number of things out there that we aren't aware of. But I *do* know that if this dragon is a real thing

– be it some Predecessor relic, or an evil spirit from another dimension, or some fucking military experiment gone wrong – then it has our shuttle. Without those parts and those supplies, we die. So we're gonna go out there, and if it *is* real. . . well. . .' He made a noise that was probably supposed to be a laugh. '. . . Then I guess we'll find out.'

'Maybe we can kill it,' said Lina. 'If it is real.'

Halman shrugged. A reply formed on his lips, but was forestalled by a voice from the radio – Ella's voice.

'You still there, guys?'

Halman sat up straighter, looking around himself. 'Yeah, still here.'

'Si's team have headed back. We're on our way to you. Everything all right there?'

'Yeah, fine here,' answered Halman. 'You know Tryka? We're right outside his place.'

'Okay,' said Ella. 'Ten minutes max.'

'Fine. We ain't going anywhere.'

'Out,' concluded Ella simply.

'Maybe it's a bit of both. . .' said Lina, mainly to herself.

'What is?' asked Halman, turning a bemused expression on her.

'The dragon,' she explained. 'Maybe it's both real *and* a product of the fader.'

'What d'you mean?'

'Maybe it is something real, something left by the Predecessors. And fader acts as a sort of tuning device, that allows the user to listen on its frequency. Nobody ever noticed before because this thing exists only here, in the belt. Or this is the only one people have ever found. Maybe the Predecessors left fader for us to find, for just this purpose. Everyone knows the urban myth about it coming from one of their worlds. You and I can't hear this dragon's voice, or see it, because we haven't taken the necessary drug.' Halman's puzzled expression exaggerated into a caricature. 'Unless you want to confess something to Doctor McLough, that is?'

303

'Me?' he asked, his eyes widening. 'I never so much as smoked a joint, Lina. I'm still a military man at heart, I guess.'

'Well, maybe something really is out there in the belt, maybe physically inside that rock. I've had a bad feeling in the belt recently. Even looking at it. I know that's hardly submissible evidence, but still. . .' She realised just how painfully stupid and unlikely this all sounded, but she *needed* to say it. 'And Carver has also been taking fader, hence that horrendous sculpture he made for us. Maybe Eli started him on the drug, or maybe he already had an addiction. I don't know – I haven't seen his record.'

'Hmm,' grunted Halman, who had seen his record but couldn't remember if Carver had a drug addiction or not, truth be told. 'Maybe. But I have to say, Lina, I don't like where all this is going.'

Lina realised that he had essentially shut the question out of his mind. He didn't really have the right sort of brain for such abstract considerations, she knew. She didn't think he cared, really. He was concerned with the practical problems of getting the shuttle back and repairing the station before it was too late. *Fair enough*, she thought. *That does seem like a reasonable prioritisation.*

They waited in silence for a while, each lost in their own thoughts. Suddenly, something glimmered in Lina's mind – something she had shelved for later consideration. She brought the thought forwards and examined it. She had to ask. She took a deep breath and said, 'What was it that Ella didn't want to tell you in front of me?'

Halman gave her a sideways look. She could see that he was debating whether he should tell her or not. And that was enough to confirm that she was right. It was something about *her*. Halman sighed, the expelled air boiling around him, cloaking him.

'Shit, Lina,' he said. 'I didn't want to tell you this. But I almost *did* anyway. . .'

'Dan,' she said, turning what she hoped was an imploring expression on him, 'we might not have long to live. I don't know if you've done the maths but I have. We still have to get that shuttle. And now there are sixteen nut-cases out there, assuming they are

304

going back to the shuttle. Maybe eighteen if Eli and the pilot are still alive, although I honestly doubt that very much. Carver trashed four of the Kays when he came in. That means we can, at most, get ten people out there. Those aren't great odds in my mind. I'd never accuse you of genius, Dan,' she continued, offering him a smile, 'but I reckon you've done that sum yourself by now. If we're gonna die, I think you might as well tell me. I know it's something that concerns me, so. . .' She spread her hands and let this filter through to him for a moment.

After what seemed like a long pause Halman said, 'Ella went to Eli's quarters after he was supposedly confined in medical. Before he killed Jayce and Tamzin.' Halman was staring intently at the corridor floor now. His voice was flat and robotic. 'She found a lock of hair in Eli's bedside drawer.'

'*What*?' asked Lina, genuinely puzzled. 'Is that what she told you?'

'It was your hair,' said Halman. And then he forced himself to look at her. His eyes looked hollow and incredibly sad. 'She was sure that it was yours.'

'*What*?' asked Lina again, utterly failing to decipher the intention behind these words. 'He had my *hair*? Is that it? Is that your big secret? Well I can die happy now. Thanks, Dan!'

'Lina!' Halman almost shouted. 'Think about it. Not his ex-wife's hair, not a lock of hair from some cherished grandchild. *Yours*.'

The words began to sink into her brain like heavy rocks sinking into mud. 'Holy shit. . .' she breathed, finally wringing the meaning from what he had said. 'You don't mean he was in *love* with me, do you?' Suddenly, she felt almost overpoweringly sick. She clenched her jaw, trying not to actually puke inside her suit. That would *not* be a good development in this little adventure.

'That is one interpretation of the facts,' said Halman guardedly. 'Maybe that's why he started the fader in the first place. He had to work with you every day, saw you all the time. He knew you wouldn't have been interested in him, knew you were all about your son. He. . .'

305

'Stop, Dan! Please just stop!' she cried. She struggled against the now almost-ubiquitous tears. This was too much. She couldn't think about it. This was too much. If true, then this was all her fault. She was the root from which this great tree of misery had grown. 'No!' she wailed. '*No. . .*'

'Lina. . .' Halman started. She waved him to silence, and they sat that way for some time. Lina tried to let her mind go blank, but her mind seemed to have other ideas. It kept re-writing events as she remembered them, this time inserting little tags all the way through: *that was my fault. . . and that was my fault, too. . . that was because of me. . . and that one. . .*

And then she was mercifully jerked from this dark reverie by Ella's voice. Ella sounded clearer this time: 'We're just around the corner now.'

After another minute or so, Ella appeared, moving cautiously at the head of her little group. Lina was encouraged to see that Ella was still on high-alert and she walked with her laser pistol held at the ready.

'You going to actually shoot me this time?' asked Lina as Ella came towards them. She already felt better. Ella generally made her feel better. That was one of Ella's redeeming qualities as far as Lina was concerned. She'd have to put the Eli-having-her-hair matter on the back-burner for now. Hopefully, she could leave it there for ever, although she suspected not.

'Maybe,' said Ella, lowering the gun all the same. 'If you give me any shit.'

'Well,' said Halman, getting to his feet a little laboriously. 'Let's hope it doesn't come to that. Good to see you guys.' And he went to Ella and, amazingly, crushed her in a clumsy embrace. He turned to Hobbes, who took a cautious step back and held out his hand for Halman to shake. Petra he simply slapped on the back. Her handsome, angular face was arranged in a tolerant smile, but she didn't look particularly receptive to hugging.

'They won't be far behind, all being well,' said Hobbes. Clearly he meant Si's team. Hobbes had found himself the neatest and cleanest space suit that Lina had ever seen. The face behind the visor was as immaculately shaved as ever. She wondered how he did it. She had caught sight of her own reflection in one of the windows they had passed earlier, and she had been alarmed to see the deep shadows of exhaustion beneath the surface of her features. She felt dirty, dishevelled and ill-used.

'Good,' said Halman. 'I hope Alphe and Fionne will be all right to finish the work on the Kays.'

'Have the escaped prisoners left the station?' asked Petra, her face intent. She had not just one, but two laser pistols in the belt of her suit. Lina looked to Hobbes and saw that he, however, carried only a small medical kit.

'Well I fucking hope so,' answered Halman. 'The plan now, my fine friends, is to take as many ships as we have out to that asteroid, where we will take the shuttle back as originally intended. All that has changed is that there are now more of *them*, and that we will have to take more of *us*. This is gonna be our last roll of the dice. We'll take the best pilots and the best fighters we can. And we will succeed. Because we must.'

'Right,' said Petra curtly. 'I'm coming.'

'Well, I see no other choice, either,' said Ella. She sounded almost alarmingly upbeat about it. 'We do have more lasers than them. That bastard stole one weapon from the back-door security desk, but luckily he never found the main locker in the prison armoury.'

'Yeah, one of those shit-bags shot Waine with it,' said Halman.

Ella took a deep breath and held it for a moment. She let it out in a long sigh, grim-faced. 'I was sorry to hear about Waine and Theo,' she said. 'We all were. There's been too much of this, now. Too much. I want to force it to an end.'

'Well the good news is,' offered Hobbes, 'that the station's now so damn cold outside our dorms that the lack of power to the freezer isn't really an issue any more. We can set up a makeshift morgue just about anywhere we choose.'

Halman turned on the much smaller man, his face incredulous. 'Well fuck me, Hobbes,' he cried, 'if you don't know how exactly to cheer a man up!'

307

'What?' asked Hobbes, unaware of having said anything wrong.

Halman shook his head wonderingly and walked away down the passage, hands clasped behind his back. But he didn't go far. He turned and came back, setting up a repetitive cycle of pacing that Lina found rather tense. She tried not to watch him, and instead chatted with Ella and Hobbes.

Hobbes was poor conversation at best, so Lina and Ella soon fell into an essentially private discussion about Platini Alpha and, more specifically, Lina's intention to take Marco there. Neither of them mentioned the fact that simply surviving the next twenty-four hours had become something of an uncertainty. Petra sat alone on the floor at the far end of the corridor, scrunched into a ball with her elbows over her knees. Her two pistols lay in front of her like a yin-yang.

After a while, they heard Si's voice from the radio. He was close, just checking in to confirm that they hadn't gone anywhere since he'd last spoken to Ella.

'I wish,' said Halman. 'I'm getting fucking sick of waiting here.'

A few minutes later, Si's massive figure appeared at the end of the corridor, spotlit in Hobbes's suit-light, virtually filling the passage from side to side. Lina could see that he was grinning widely, his squarish, lantern-jawed face showing no sign of the worry that she herself felt. Rocko, Niya Onh, Ilse Reno, Alphe and Fionne were with him. They tramped down the passage towards the others, moving slowly in their heavy suits.

The group assembled there in the deserted living area, milling about and exchanging greetings. It occurred to Lina what an odd little family they made — a much reduced family now, she supposed. She wondered how many of them would return from their next mission. The odds had not been kind to them so far.

They made their way back to the hangar, moving in formation as directed by Halman. He sent scouts down every side-corridor, into every doorway, to check for lurking enemies. The station was a frozen relic of the home they knew so well, and they passed through it in dreamy silence for the most part. Lina felt as if their lives hung in a delicate equilibrium, a state that could be upset at any moment by a laser beam, or an escaped murderer rushing from a shadowy alcove, or maybe a booby trap left by Carver's gang. They processed through the warehouse to stand in a nervous group before the open hangar door. Relatively bright light still spilled from it into the warehouse, staining the floor like whitewash.

Lina peered round the edge of the door into the hangar, scanning the shadows for human shapes. She saw nobody living, but Theo's body lay in two twisted halves not far inside, the stump of his pistol next to him. She couldn't see Waine's remains – he had fallen behind her Kay, and was out of sight from her vantage point. The loader was gone, but the space door still yawned open at the far end of the flight deck.

'Let's go,' said Halman. 'Carefully, now. Ella, Si – I want you to go round the back and check the control room. Rocko, Lina – down the far side. I'll go down the right with Petra. Everyone else stay put and eyes open.'

The hangar proved to be empty except for the corpses of their friends. The toppled Kays lay around the deck forlornly. Lina was almost personally offended by this, and she realised with a glint of dark amusement that she considered the ships – all of them – to be hers.

Si found a pair of dirty and ancient-looking tarpaulins and he threw one over Liu's desecrated remains and another over Theo and Waine, whose corpses he dragged together to lay beside each other in death. He said nothing while he did this. As he finished and turned to walk away, Lina caught a glimpse of his face. It was utterly blank but for two patches of angry red high on his cheeks.

They closed the space door – it looked too easy for someone too stray to close, slip on the ice and fall into space. They parked a Kay right on the lip of the ramp, anchoring onto the deck itself, to obstruct any further unwanted attempts to land. Halman stationed Petra and Si at the hangar door to guard against any attack from that direction, even though they were all agreed that Carver's mob had surely left Macao.

Alphe and Fionne, quiet and shell-shocked, returned to work on the Kays, trying not to look at the tarpaulin-covered humps that represented the butchered bodies of their friends. The others formed a rough perimeter around the two techs, facing outwards with their guns drawn. It seemed to Lina like a classic case of too little, too late.

After a while, Ella distributed spare air cartridges to those who needed them. The suits were clever enough to allow hot-swapping of these, as long as it was done relatively quickly. It was still a dangerous procedure, though, as any delay with the installation of the new cartridge could leave the recipient airless and in serious trouble. Luckily, all the replacements went well enough, and Lina chided herself for being a little surprised at that. She was getting too accustomed to disaster. She wished that she had gone back to the dorm with Si's team. It might have been her last chance to speak to Marco. But it was too late now, so she supposed she would simply have to survive the coming assault.

Alphe and Fionne progressed in silence, sharing the telepathic link common to long-time work partners everywhere. They finished the installation of the enlarged cutting discs and then checked all of the Kays for obvious defects. It had been agreed that they wouldn't fly any of the ships that had been bumped by the ISL. Several of them looked superficially all right, but Alphe and Fionne admitted that they needed Liu to confirm that. Without him, they said, it might take them some hours to be sure. They had done what they could.

The others came and stood beside Alphe, regarding the modified Kays in critical silence. Eventually, Halman turned to Alphe and asked, 'Are you happy with them?'

Alphe sucked his lips thoughtfully. 'Yeah,' he said at last. 'Happy as I can be.'

'Good,' said Halman, laying a hand on the younger man's shoulder. 'Listen up, you lot!' he began, turning to address the group as a whole. Lina felt numb and detached, as if this was all happening inside a holo and she was merely watching from her sofa. 'We have ten operational Kays. The following will go to the

310

shuttle: Myself, Lina, Ella, Hobbes, Si, Rocko, Petra, Ilse, Niya and Alphe. Fionne, as the only non-pilot here, you are excused, and hereby ordered to return to the dorm. Report to Amy Stone and tell her what's happening. She is, of course, in charge 'til I return.'

'Okay,' said Fionne in a quiet little voice. Lina wondered how she felt about Rocko going without her. Not too good, she suspected.

'Lina will cut into the shuttle's hold. Ilse will fly the other modified ship, in case something goes wrong with Lina's. We will enter the shuttle as quickly as we can, flying across in suits. Anyone who wants to play fuckaround with us, we shoot them. You all up for that?' He cast around for agreement, his expression deadpan. Nobody answered verbally, but their faces were set and hawkish. 'Good. Once inside, we head for the bridge, where we will release the clamp on the boarding tube that joins the shuttle to that damned rock, and. . . away we go.'

'Piece of piss,' said Si, with some small trace of his habitual ebullience.

'Let's hope so,' said Halman.

'Well,' said Ella decisively. 'No time like the present, eh?'

'Fionne,' said Halman. 'Go home, okay?' She nodded sadly, then ran to Rocko. She embraced him, their suits briefly making one amorphous whole. 'I love you,' she whispered, the words clear in everyone's earpieces. They pointedly looked away, trying not to listen. 'Yeah,' said Rocko. 'I love you, too.' Then she released him, turned around and simply walked away.

They went to their respective ships, climbed the steps, and strapped themselves in. Ella took the one they had parked across the ramp, and she moved it out of the way with apparent ease, even skill. Lina watched in her HUD as a field of identifier-tags came to life. The enlarged cutting disc looked obvious and somehow wrong.

As she let the cockpit pressurise so that she could remove her helmet for a while, she considered the trial that lay ahead of her. Out there in the belt, a strange and bloodthirsty enemy awaited them. Eli was almost certainly dead, but still a reckoning was at hand. She realised that she was no longer afraid, though. A conclusion was approaching, most likely a bloody one, maybe a personally fatal one. But nonetheless, she welcomed it.

'Come on,' she whispered, looking to the left, where Halman was bringing his Kay round with the halting uncertainty of someone who hadn't flown for years. Ice dusted down from its landing gear and shivering hull. Was it significant that he was in Eli's old ship? She wasn't sure, but she no longer cared about the omens. She just wanted it to end, one way or the other. 'Come on,' she whispered again. 'Let's go.'

The Kays converged on the runway behind her, manoeuvring around their injured fellows. She waited for their icons to align, then hit the pad to open the space door. The ramp dropped away, angling out of sight. Lina caught glimpses of dark rock and endless night as she dialled up the gas, aware of the slipperiness of the deck. As the vessel accelerated off the end of the ramp, she risked a backward glance at the station. It was rising away behind her already, dark and vast and silent, like a gravestone in space. It disgorged the following Kays in a regular arc.

'I'm coming back,' she whispered, wondering who she was speaking to. Her hand was sweating on the yoke, making it slippery. She angled it down, heading towards the belt.

CHAPTER FORTY-SIX

By the time they made it to the shuttle, Carver's eyes were stinging worse than ever. His sight, however, had almost returned to normal. Seriously, he hadn't doubted that it would – would the dragon allow its emissary to stay blind? Hardly likely. Although he sat in the back looking down at his own knees, squinting and blinking in pain, he could tell that the prisoner was flying the loader with a fair degree of skill. The other prisoners sat around him in silence and he could feel their tension and excitement all around him. Everything was going to plan.

'Is that it?' Welby suddenly asked. Carver looked up and saw that he was pointing at the small screen affixed to the ceiling of the personnel compartment in which they sat together on steel benches, strapped in.

The shuttle, adhered to its rock like a leech, was coming into view on the screen, looming up between the tumbling debris of the belt. Carver's heart lifted. *Home*, he thought. *I'm coming home.*

'That's it, Welby,' he said. 'Where the dragon lives.'

'Amazing. . .' sighed Welby, his gaze fixed firmly on the screen.

Cratered steel and jagged stone scrolled beneath them as the prisoner guided the loader in to dock with the shuttle, giving expert little kicks with the manoeuvring jets, flying without computer aid.

Welby turned to Carver and said, 'See? He's a decent man, Fuller. One of my people.'

Some of the other prisoners shuffled nervously in their seats. *Unbelievers*, thought Carver, looking sidelong at them through his burning, watering eyes.

They congregated in the loader's hold and Carver explained his plan for the prisoners to assist him with the digging. Thus, by their combined strength, they would finally extract the dragon from its rock. They would need more mining equipment, and they mounted a space-suited expedition into the shuttle's icy, airless hold to search for it. Welby, it transpired, had actually been a ship-fitter at Platini Dockyard in his former life, and he suggested that it might be possible to tweak the air scrubbers and flood the hold, but Carver didn't see the point. This revelation from Welby did seem to confirm the man's usefulness, though. But they had other fish to fry. Much bigger, hungrier fish. The dragon hadn't spoken to him for a while, but Carver took this to be a sign of approval if anything. He felt certain it would tell him if he strayed from the path in any way.

Deep in the forest of racking and huge magnetic crates, they found the perfect twin of Carver's plasma cutter. He wondered briefly about the wisdom of putting such a thing into the hands of one of these men, who might eventually seek to betray him, even turn it against him, but he decided it was a risk he would have to take. Surely the dragon would warn him if he was in any danger of betrayal. It would know.

They also found many smaller, less impressive tools, including a simple pneumatic drill and matching compressor. Welby showed Carver a crate filled with dull grey metal cylinders, which he identified as shaped explosive charges. Carver didn't think he'd dare to use them on the rock face, but he took them anyway. Shaped explosive charges? It would have been ludicrous not to. The name itself had a certain power to it, a sound he liked when rolled off the tongue. *Shaped explosive charges.* He liked that a lot.

They also found a fair cache of weapons in a solid-looking banded trunk that sat on its own at the foot of one tall shelving unit, deep in the shuttle's hold. Helpfully, it was labelled *SECURITY – STANDARD WEAPON SET 04*. Carver opened it with his own, original plasma cutter, feeling an expression of childish delight spreading across his face. It was, as promised, full of the tools of murder. The most dangerous items therein were more of the cheap-looking laser pistols, but there was also a decent selection of other kit. Carver brushed aside his previous concerns about equipping the freed prisoners with weaponry, and armed the lot of them. He let Welby distribute the limited number of pistols, assuming that Welby would choose the people he himself trusted most, and hence the people least likely to cause any trouble.

They returned to the machine rooms of the shuttle, which led to the bridge and the boarding tube into the asteroid. Carver gave what he considered a rather rousing speech about the task at hand, the reason for their freedom. Most of the prisoners gaped in awe, as convinced as Welby was that Carver's dragon was indeed one of their venerated Old Ones, and that he himself was a prophet sent to gather disciples to its cause. Maybe they were right – he really didn't care. His only interest was in using these people for his own ends, which meant for the dragon's own ends. It wanted to be freed, so who better than a gang of prisoners to do the job? There was a certain poetic justice to it.

There were a few ex-convicts, however – a tall black man named Marcus, a heavy-set and tattooed simpleton named Josh, an ill-looking little scarecrow of a man named Ballic or Ballich or some shit – whose faces bore sullen looks of suspicion when he spoke to them. Carver marked these faces in his memory, his fingers itching on the handle of the cutter, which he hadn't put down for hours now.

'*Unbelievers*,' the dragon whispered. 'Beware.' And it told him of its plan for them.

In an uncharacteristic bout of generosity Carver distributed rations from the hold, then watched over his flock as they ate with apparent gusto, stuffing the food into their mouths like animals at trough and washing the starchy powders down with canteens of water. *I am Carver*, he thought, *emissary of the dragon and leader of men*. He knew it was a last meal for some of them. That was okay. This was a time of finality – he could taste it in the air. Things were coming to a head, the future racing away towards a conclusion that he could, as yet, not see. He felt no fear, only a slowly-culminating sense of elation.

He didn't let them rest for long. He led them out into the ice-slimed cavern of the asteroid's interior. The debris had completely filled the space without anybody there to keep it under control, and they set to work clearing it, manhandling pieces back through the tube and stowing them in a large, empty hold just off the shuttle's machine rooms. Even in the micro-gee this was a fairly laborious task. Already the debris half-filled the new dumping ground, and there was much more to follow. They'd find another place to store it when it came to that. Maybe they could eject it out of the airlock.

Then Carver showed them where to dig and detailed a group to remove the waste as they went. He asked Welby to choose another whom he trusted to be left temporarily in charge at the dig site. Welby picked out a large, greasy-looking man with a heavily-scarred face, and Carver gave him the second plasma cutter. He looked more than strong enough to manipulate the tool and his expression suggested that he took Welby's trust in him seriously.

Then Carver picked out those people who had looked at him so scornfully during his earlier speech and led them away into the shuttle. Welby accompanied him, staying behind the unbelievers with one of the laser pistols in his belt. The unbelievers, though, were armed only with stun-batons. Carver wondered if they had noticed anything amiss in this fact yet, or if they would do before it was too late.

'It is already too late,' said the dragon. Carver smiled as he led the group towards the shuttle's machine rooms.

'Yes,' he agreed. 'I guess it is.'

'Is what?' asked Marcus suspiciously, his voice an incredibly deep and sonorous bass. He was following behind Carver with some difficulty, pulling himself along the handline with irritating slowness.

'Nothing,' said Carver, turning his face away to hide his grin. The pulsing of his head had become so fierce that even his ears were ringing now. He'd have another hit of fader when this task was through. 'Nothing you need concern yourselves with,' he elaborated. He stopped before the doorway that connected the shuttle to the parasitic ISL and turned to face the others. 'Welby,' he said. 'Shoot them.'

Welby proved his worth again. He didn't pause for consideration; he didn't ask Carver to repeat himself; he didn't go *What?* or even *Right!* He just shot them – one, two, three – each in the chest. Two of the men convulsed and died quickly, gurgling their last like little babies. But Marcus writhed, spinning away and clutching at the burn in his suit. He pushed back towards Welby, attempting to swing his baton, teeth clenched in an animal snarl.

Welby, unfazed, shot him again, this time in the face. The laser burned cleanly through the front of Marcus's skull. His eyes glazed instantly, as if net curtains had fallen behind them, then rolled up into his head. The baton drifted away from his hand and Carver caught it smoothly, laughing softly to himself. It couldn't have been choreographed better if he'd tried.

'Good,' said the dragon.

'Yeah,' agreed Carver. 'Easy.'

'I'm hungry. . .' crooned the dragon. 'So hungry. . .'

'How will you eat?' asked Carver. Welby looked up into his face indulgently. 'Should I take them to the rock face?' Maybe the dragon would want the prisoners ground up and poured into a fissure in the stone.

'Until I am free,' explained the dragon wistfully, 'I must live my life through you.'

'I don't understand,' said Carver, but he thought perhaps he did.

'You, Emissary, must be my eyes, my ears, my claws. . . my *teeth*. . .'

'Of course,' breathed Carver, staring at those three drifting corpses. He was suddenly and ravenously hungry.

CHAPTER FORTY-SEVEN

They flew through the belt in loose formation. Lina steered mainly by Halman's and Alphe's Kays, which stayed ahead of her and to either side. Her ship's safety systems were running, but her trust in the safety of anything that came from Macao had long since dwindled. She half expected, at any moment, to be smashed to smithereens by an errant belt object, but even this was not enough to really frighten her. The conclusion was coming. Let it come. All she felt was a distant sense of relief.

Halman had ordered a change of radio channel, concerned that the prisoners might hear them on the default frequency. Nobody felt conversational anyway. They flew in silence.

As the belt thickened, a virtual infinity of potential ambush-points and hiding places flourished about them. The loader might spring out at them, even try to ram one of the Kays, but still Lina was unable to feel afraid. She wondered if Carver's gang had seen them coming yet. Hadn't she herself once joked to Eli about Macao's prisoners escaping and establishing a pirate base out here? Another joke that had proven to be prophetic. Perhaps, in some impossible way, they'd seen it coming.

When Eli's rock came into sight, she regarded it with disappointment. It was just a rock — large, but not so unlike a million other rocks out here. Except that this one had the ugly grey shuttle attached to it like a leech and the loader attached in turn to that. The whole thing looked lifeless, unthreatening, kind of sad. But the enemy was there, and in greater numbers now. She wondered what they hoped to achieve on that isolated boulder beyond starvation and an eventual, lonely death. She wondered if the dragon was real, if it was in there, sitting at the centre of its monstrous web, pulling the strings and watching its puppets dance to its bloody, savage tune. If it was real, would it somehow try to

318

stop them? *Could* it somehow try to stop them?

Although the belt was eerie enough, the shadow that Lina had sensed there before was not in evidence now. She supposed it probably never had been and she regretted mentioning it to Halman. If, as she suspected, it had merely been an externalisation of her own fears, those fears seemed much diminished now. Perhaps the continual fright and horror of recent days had dehumanised her, burned away all of her capacity for real emotion. Even her love for her son seemed a distant concept, something she knew was genuine and solid, but that she couldn't tangibly feel at that moment. Now she was just glad that an end was coming. That was enough.

Soros glinted through chinks in the asteroid field, pale and watery and distant, fading in and out of sight like a thief flitting between patches of shadow. She thought wonderingly about how far away Platini system was, and tried to gauge the possibilities of ever crossing that vast, desolate emptiness with her son, fleeing this merciless outpost at the end of the universe, desperately seeking something better.

She wanted the shuttle that Eli had stolen. Not just for Macao, not just for the desperately-needed supplies and parts that it held, but for her own selfish reasons too. The shuttle was her and Marco's only ticket out of here, unless they were somehow to survive the wait for the next one. She had to have it. She would risk her life on this one throw of the dice. And she would earn the right to take the vessel to Platini. Damn it, she'd *demand* the right if she survived this. And she'd take anyone else who wanted to go with her. To hell with Macao Station. It had been the grave of too many of her friends.

Their Kays converged on the unwelcoming mass of rock and machinery, the tiny threads of their gas trails wavering through the belt like spider silk. The shuttle was unlit, deserted, the loader just as dark and silent. The asteroid loomed large against a backdrop of endless grey and black, its facing side in shadow. It looked like a hole in space, a vortex into which a person might fall upwards and away into the archives of the universe and disappear forever.

319

Slowly, they approached.

They spread around the asteroid in a wide fan, encircling it and checking for danger. Finding nothing, they edged closer, tightening the net.

Si stopped his ship at the wide end of the rock and shone his headlight onto it. 'It's just an asteroid,' he said, echoing Lina's own disappointment. She wondered what they had expected to see.

She looked to her side, and there was K6-3, tagged with Ella's name, hanging in space, appearing to regard the asteroid with the cyclopean eye of its cockpit glass. Ella's ship rotated slightly to face Lina's, and beckoned with one of its tool arms. Lina thought she caught the meaning of the gesture: *Let's get on with it*. She waved an arm in return and brought her Kay around in a careful arc, moving down the length of the asteroid back towards the shuttle. The asteroid's scaled surface slid along below her, gaudy with bright instawall patches.

She stopped halfway along the shuttle's hold – the vast, curved belly that formed the greater part of its bulk – and unfolded her tool arms. The new cutting disc looked fragile and unwieldy. She flexed the arms, checking the diagnostics one last time.

'I'm ready,' she said.

'Go to it,' answered Halman. His Kay coasted across her field of vision, left to right, just above her.

She approached the shuttle warily, as if it might bite, and applied a magnetic anchor. She also spun up a screw anchor, pressed it gently to the skin of the shuttle and let it wind itself in tightly. She applied a little burst of reverse thrust, testing the strength of her grip on the larger vessel. Her Kay didn't budge at all.

'Right. . .' she said under her breath.

She fired up the cutting disc and touched it to the shuttle's hull. The vibration reverberated through the body of her Kay, making her teeth chatter together. Glittering jets of dust arced away from the cut, dissipating into space. The disc sank into the metal. She worked it carefully down in a vertical line, then withdrew it, turned it ninety degrees, and cut a horizontal. When she had inscribed a neat door-shape, she drew the cutter back. She looked to her right and saw Ilse Reno's ship hovering next to her.

'Nice work,' said Ilse.

Was that the first compliment Ilse had ever given her? Lina thought perhaps it was. 'Thanks,' she said.

Lina put out a claw and pushed against the vertical rectangle she had cut. Silently, it gave way and popped neatly out of the hole. The door-shaped chunk floated away into the ship and was lost from sight in darkness. The lights were off in there.

'Ladies and gentlemen,' said Lina with mock grandiosity. 'Please step inside.'

'Is everyone ready?' Halman asked.

The ships drifted, equidistant, their computers keeping them safely separated. The hull of the shuttle soared away above them like a cliff face. There was a general chorus of affirmation. Lina heard real fear in many of their voices. Niya Onh sounded as if she might be crying.

Lina released the clamps that held her Kay to the shuttle and burned briefly away from it, then stopped and floated stationary just behind Ilse. 'I'll go first,' she suggested, deciding that recklessness might be the better part of valour.

She closed her visor and called up her suit's HUD. She scanned the figures that floated before her eyes. All within ideal parameters. Plenty of air. She killed the main console of her ship without bothering to shut it down properly, then braced herself in the seat. The soft darkness of space rolled away into the distance, monotonous and eternal. A brief stab of longing – for bright sunlight, solid ground underfoot, trees and seas and houses, things she hadn't seen since childhood – struck her somewhere deep inside. She was going out there, into *that*, with nothing more than the space suit she wore now. It didn't look like a place where any human being belonged. And worse than that, she had to go into the shuttle. *Into the dragon's lair*, she thought darkly. *It'll eat you up!* But would it? *Could* it?

She reached up and turned the twin cockpit release handles.

The canopy popped open a hand's breadth with a vomited expulsion of air. She reached out her hand, pushing it all the way up, then paused in wonder, trailing her fingers through the vacuum. Curious that this medium, anathema to human life, was itself completely invisible – just nothing. A vast, fatal nothing. This was the stuff of which the universe was made. It was a wonder life existed anywhere.

She undid her harness and pushed away from her seat, a little too hard, flying between the rim of the cockpit and the open canopy, sending herself floating away towards another Kay. She saw Rocko ejecting from this other vessel, clumsily pinwheeling into space.

The air of her suit smelled sickly and somehow burnt, not unlike the noisome air of Macao itself. She didn't think she'd ever felt so alone and vulnerable, floating in space with only a few layers of fabric between her and oblivion.

Lina had never had occasion to use the in-built manoeuvring jet of a space suit before. She'd always flown pressurised vessels. In truth, she'd only ever worn a suit twice before this whole mess had started. She hoped it would be instinctive to use, because Alphe hadn't allowed them to waste any fuel in practice. She pointed the sleeve-mounted jet away from the shuttle and fired a brief burst, sending herself drifting smoothly towards the doorway that she had cut. She hit the hull of the shuttle shoulder-first, hard enough to send a jarring shock through her body. Alphe had warned her that the jet only had about thirty seconds total burn time available, but so far she'd used less than one, so she thought that would be plenty.

She imagined the psychotic Carver waiting for her in there, all bloodthirsty grins and human-finger-necklaces. She could almost see him crouching in the metal-smelling darkness of the ancient ship, grinning. Waiting. Madness was patient, after all. That was one thing that Eli's deception of his friends had taught her: madness was patient.

She clawed her way along the blistered surface of the shuttle. In some places the metal was so deeply pitted by impact marks that she could have put her whole hand into the dents. She gripped the edge of the rough doorway she had cut and looked back over her shoulder. Her companions were drifting towards her in a tentative-looking swarm.

It occurred to Lina that if there was indeed a greeting party waiting for them then Carver's people could just sit there and blast them one by one as they came through. It'd be little more than a turkey-shoot. It was possible that someone would be able to get a radio message off, but the radios in the suits were pretty weak, and the shuttle's hull was pretty thick, so probably not.

With this thought in her mind, Lina dragged herself round the lip of the doorway and fell into the blackness of the shuttle's hold. She tumbled, suit-light flashing over and over, showing blurring snatches of metal railings and spidery walkways. She let out the smallest burst that she could from the suit's arm-jet, hoping to right herself. She spun away, end over end, and hit one of the railings back-first. She cried out in pain but gripped onto it, finally managing to still herself.

When she cast her light back onto the doorway in the hull, she saw the unmistakable shape of Si Davis squeezing through, dragging himself down the metal wall with clawed hands. He looked up when her light fell on him and grinned his broad grin. 'Hey, Lina. I saw you spinning out then. Thought you were an expert pilot.' He gained one of the walkways above Lina and grabbed onto the railing, bracing his feet against the floor.

'I'm still a better pilot than you,' she retorted. But it was an automatic reply and the exchange seemed a pretty weak imitation of their usual banter. Si let it drop.

Other suited figures were clambering into the shuttle now, one by one, like great white crabs, scampering in slow motion down the walls to mass on the walkways around Lina and Si. Halman stopped beside her, holding onto the rail with one hand while his legs trailed in empty space above what would, in a one-gee environment, have constituted a very dangerous drop. Lina leant over and shone her light into the depths. She couldn't even see the floor down there. Above her, heavy crane arms were folded tight against their ceiling gimbals.

'Hello, Dan,' she said.

'Hey, Lina,' he said. The face behind his visor was shiny with sweat, swarthy and old-looking.

Alphe dragged himself along the rail towards them, also trying to run along the walkway with his feet and mainly just managing to look ridiculous.

'I know the way to the bridge,' said Alphe without preamble. 'And I have the printed schematic with me, just in case.'

'Good,' said Halman. He turned and looked around at his little army. 'Are we all ready to move?' Nobody said otherwise. 'Then let's go. And take it easy, now. Although you don't have any weight to speak of, you do still have mass in this environment. That means you have momentum, and that means you can get hurt if you go crashing around the place like fuckwits. Alphe – lead on. To the bridge. And for fuck's sake, keep your eyes peeled and your guns handy. My earlier speech about asking anyone we meet to surrender no longer applies. Now we're outnumbered and we can't afford such luxuries. Now we shoot first, ask questions later.'

They swam through a silent treetop village of steel mesh and flaking paint. They passed occasional small rooms – little more than sheet-metal huts – dotted here and there amongst the walkways. At one point they found their way barred by a thick forest of chains that stretched away into the great pit of shadows below them and snaked alarmingly when Lina tried to squeeze through.

'Let's find another way,' she said, backing off. Her companions floated behind her, holding onto the railings.

'How about we jump to the next walkway?' suggested Ilse. Her eye glowed demonically red in her face and her straggly grey hair, not tied back, had fallen across her forehead beneath her visor. She looked small and mean and dangerous.

'Yeah, no problem,' said Si.

'Don't use your jets,' said Halman. 'Not unless you have to.' He was leaning over the edge, casting his light onto the next walkway. It looked a very long way off and quite far below them. Lina knew

324

that she was just constrained by her usual one-gee way of thinking, but she remembered Halman's words about momentum. 'Go slowly and accurately. If anyone ends up spinning out of control it might take them ages to get back to the group.'

'I don't think I can do it,' said Hobbes.

Halman turned a glowering look on him. 'Well, Doctor,' he said, 'at least if you crash and die, we won't have to take you back to the morgue to freeze you.'

'That,' said Hobbes a little haughtily, 'is *not* funny.'

They clambered over the railing and hung from the outside of the walkway, suspended above that bottomless well. Lina looked to her left, where Ella was poised with her hands behind her on the bar and her feet braced against the walkway, ready to push off.

'Let's fly!' cried Ella, and she sprung away from the ledge. Lina watched her go, her heart pulsing high in her throat. Ella's white-suited body went sailing through space, spotted in half a dozen lights, her legs pulled up beneath her and her arms out to either side like wings.

'She's going too fast!' yelled Niya, her voice cracking with panic.

'Shit!' cried Rocko.

But Ella soared gently over the nearest handrail of the lower walkway, grabbing onto the furthest rail with one hand and managing to arrest herself. Lina heard her grunt of exertion over the comm. Ella floundered, legs flailing, then managed to pull herself over and down onto the walkway's floor. She righted herself, hovering just above the steel mesh, and waved.

'Come on!' she called. 'What're you all waiting for?'

Rocko laughed nervously. 'I knew she'd make it,' he said.

Someone else laughed — Lina wasn't sure who — and then Si pushed off, more slowly than Ella had done. Then Rocko, Alphe, Halman, Hobbes. . .

Lina took a deep breath and jumped. Remembering her recent time in the hub with Marco, she pushed off gently and drifted, slower than anybody else, across the yawning chasm of the shuttle's main hold. She hit the nearside railing of the new walkway squarely, cushioning herself easily with her hands, using them as buffers. Petra landed next to her, whooping with exhilaration. Several of them laughed, but it was a sound filled with tension and dangerously close to the edge of sanity. They dragged themselves onto the walkway and continued their journey.

The various walkways began to angle downwards and together. Soon they could see the main door to the hold – a large airlock door, wide enough to admit a dead-lifter easily. The floor ramped more sharply downwards and, although they could have simply drifted through space, they followed it, conditioned to obey the laws of up and down.

Suddenly, Halman's vice-like hand gripped Lina's shoulder from behind. She turned and looked up into his face. He pulled her to a stop and the rest of the group halted behind them. He pointed, down and to their left.

Lina followed the direction of his pointing finger and her chest seized tight. She saw it: a flash of white, down at floor level, moving between the cargo racks, a light briefly flashing ahead of it, then gone again.

'Somebody in a space suit?' she whispered, before remembering that there was no need to keep her voice down. Either the enemy was on their channel and would hear her, or not.

'Yeah,' said Halman. 'I think so.'

Everyone was craning to see, leaning over the railing. Several people were pointing pistols. Lina stared, seeing only strapped-down piles of crates and boxes down there, magnetised together in tall, improbable-looking columns. That flash again – white – someone in a space suit, for sure.

Somebody fired – a silent stitch of green in the darkness. The person below them turned with panicky speed and their light glinted briefly in Lina's eyes. And then a laser beam passed above her shoulder, harmlessly into the depths of the hold.

'Shoot!' cried Halman.

The figure below was swimming quickly just above the floor,

firing on the fly, missing them all again. Several people from Lina's team responded, although Lina herself stood uselessly holding her pistol at her waist, pointing down at her own feet. The figure flew from one stack of crates to another, crashed into something and went cartwheeling out into the open. Several shots from the walkway hit the unfortunate enemy at once. One shot put out their suit-light, another caught them high on the chest and a third hit them squarely in the head. The figure's suit burst, leaving the victim twisting and thrashing in the vacuum, their laser discharging hopelessly into empty space.

'I got him!' cried Rocko fiercely.

Lina had to look away – she couldn't stand to watch that struggling, asphyxiating death. It reminded her too much of Waine. She felt no joy at this small revenge, no sorrow for the murdered man, only a faded kind of revulsion at the spectacle.

'Another one!' somebody screamed – Petra? Ilse? – and panic gripped the group as they spun around, trying to look in all directions. Si lost his grip on the rail and drifted slowly out into open space, suspended magically above the drop.

'Up there!' yelled the voice again, and Lina knew this time that it was Ilse Reno. 'Look!'

Lina turned and saw Ilse pointing up towards another walkway that was almost invisible in the darkness above them. A flash of white – someone dragging themselves along the rail up there, legs kicking behind them.

This time Lina managed to aim her own weapon. She fired, but her laser beam flashed away into the shadows of the ceiling. Other people were firing, too, their shots making a brief but dazzling cat's-cradle of light. The figure dived down a set of steps, rolling over in their haste, and Lina fired again. She missed again, too, although she was closer this time. She suspected that the cheap laser was pretty inaccurate and that the fault wasn't all hers.

The figure gained the next walkway down, slightly closer to them, and it paused to return fire. The laser winked green. Halman reeled back, hitting the rail behind him and bouncing off to crash into Hobbes, with whom he entangled. They both fell, spinning away together along the walkway. Another shot from above barely missed Si where he floated, exposed, on his back. He returned fire, his broad face locked in a savage rictus.

Lina tried to fix the figure in her suit-light, but it was moving again, pushing off to fly along the walkway. She saw Ilse and Rocko sighting along their weapons. One of them missed by an even longer margin than Lina herself had. But one of them hit the figure. Lina didn't see where the shot had landed exactly, but she saw a flurry of white shreds as the enemy's suit exploded. The figure shot up into the darkness, convulsing, scraps of suit fabric shimmering in the team's torch beams, then rolled away into the cavernous depths of the cargo bay. The dying man faded from the range of their suit-lights, swallowed by the darkness. Gone.

They waited in silence, stabbing the barrels of their pistols in all directions, full of adrenalin, expecting more company. Gradually, they began to relax, lowering their guns. Hobbes extended a hand to Si, pulling him back to the walkway.

'You okay, Hobbes?' Halman asked.

'Yeah,' said Hobbes. 'But you hit me pretty hard there. You?'

'Fine,' said Halman. 'Sorry about that.'

'Do you think that's it?' asked Petra.

'For now,' said Rocko ominously.

'Let's go on,' said Halman. 'But expect more. Weapons ready.'

'Poor bastards,' said Hobbes. Nobody ventured so far as to agree with him.

As they continued down the incline of the walkway, nearing the airlock door that led to the pressurised part of the shuttle, Lina accidentally glanced down towards the dead man near the floor. His body floated, still rolling gently in the micro-gee, arms and legs spread, suit hanging in shreds. *One less to fight later*, she thought. She supposed that was a good thing. At least her team had all survived. That *had* to be a good thing, right? *We're winning*, she told herself. *So far, we're winning*.

'Is it far?' asked Petra, swimming past Lina with surprising agility. She held her pistol at arm's length, pointing to her side, as if trying to distance herself from it.

'Not that far,' said Alphe meaninglessly.

They descended to the floor level, following the handlines that stretched between steel poles bolted into the floor. Those towers of crates leant over them. They passed a dead-lifter, secured against low-gee inside a cradle in the wall.

'It's quiet,' said Ella in a whisper, scanning around herself. '*Too* quiet.' She laughed nervously. 'That's a bit clichéd, isn't it?' she asked, a little quiver in her voice.

Lina looked around. The dead man in the shredded suit was behind them now, gently pirouetting in a perpetual dance of death. Halman pushed to the front of the group and hit the pad beside the airlock.

Rocko and Ella hung back, acting as rearguard. Lina cast her light up into that night sky of soaring cranes and vaulted metal, seeing only a collage of black layers, watching for the incongruous flash of white that would mean more danger.

The airlock door opened silently and they followed Halman inside. The airlock looked old and well-used, its walls heavily scarred by collisions. Lina noticed a dangling bundle of plastic relays held together with insulating tape, which did little to reassure her.

Halman pushed through to the far end and cycled the airlock. The door by which they had entered dropped suddenly into place, trapping them. There came the building rush of pressurising air and then the opposite door slid open.

They emerged into a wide corridor lit by LED lights. Pistons moved beneath the grated floor like ligaments stretching and contracting. The airlock closed behind them with finality. They raised their visors and pulled themselves along the handline in a rag-tag procession.

'Shhh!' hissed Ella suddenly.

Lina turned to see Ella behind her, frozen in place with her head cocked to the side and one index finger raised for quiet.

'What?' Lina whispered.

'I thought I heard something,' said Ella.

'I can't hear anything,' said Halman. 'You think it was trouble?'

Ella shook her head. 'I don't think so. Sounded like some sort of machine noise. I want to scout ahead for a minute before we rush in *en masse*.'

Halman floated past her, towards the opposite wall. He dragged himself along it, clawing with his gloves, trying to see round the corner at the end of the corridor. 'I'll come with you,' he said. 'Si – you too. Everyone else sit tight and make sure nothing comes out of that airlock behind us.'

Halman swam off down the corridor, followed by Ella and then Si, who ricocheted clumsily from floor to ceiling as he went, cursing quietly.

Lina placed the palm of one hand against the wall, trying to temper the feeling of instability that she was suffering from. Through the padded skin of her glove she could feel a distant, low thrumming in the shuttle's structure, as if something was vibrating in the bowels of the ship, some kernel of life-force trembling inside it. She felt a frown crease her face. Ella had thought she'd heard machine noise. What were Carver's escaped psychos doing in there?

Of course, the answer that presented itself to her miner's mind was: *Digging. Mining*. But mining for what? Metals? Surely not. What, then?

'They're digging for *it*,' she breathed, making Alphe glance up at her, his honest face open in enquiry.

'Eh?'

'Nothing,' she answered, unwilling to explain herself. She had already tried that with Halman and she was pretty sure that he thought she was crazy. She shut the thought from her mind and looked away. 'It's nothing,' she repeated. How would spouting mystic bullshit about buried dragons actually help at this stage? It wouldn't change the fact that, whatever happened, they had to get this shuttle back to the station.

'Nothing?' he pushed, alerted by the tone of her voice. 'Sure?'

Petra dragged herself over, Hobbes close behind her. Niya floated just before the corner of the passage, watching Si's back as he disappeared off into the ship's innards.

Lina glanced around, aware that she had drawn a crowd. 'It's just that Ella thought she heard machine noise. If you put your hand on the wall, you can feel a vibration through it.' The others did as she suggested. 'You see? I wonder if they're mining for something.'

'I just want to get to the bridge, release the clamp and get the hell out of here,' said Petra. She looked around herself. Peeling walls loomed at unnatural angles, a world devoid of true directional reference points. They had oriented themselves with the floor as best they could, but the impression of order felt tenuous at best. Petra shivered, hugging herself. 'It's creepy.'

'Don't worry,' said Hobbes in a flat tone that was a long way from his reassuring doctor-voice. Lina wished that he had agreed to carry a gun, but she supposed it probably breached the Hippocratic Oath or something.

'They're coming back,' said Niya quietly. Her voice was almost too cutesy to belong to a real person – she always sounded like a cartoon character to Lina, an effect enhanced by her tiny figure and angelic face. They dragged and swam their way towards the corner. Si returned first, followed by Ella and then Halman.

'Well?' asked Lina. 'What's the plan?'

'We think we know the way to the bridge,' said Si. 'The shuttle's interior seems to have been changed a little from the schematic that Alphe has.'

'Changed?' asked Petra. 'How so?'

'It's old,' Halman said. 'The architecture of these things often gets altered a little over the years. But we know which way to go. We think.'

'Any sign of life?' Lina asked. Hobbes floated at her elbow, struggling to stay still despite having hold of a handline. He steadied himself on Lina's shoulder with the other hand, almost making her lose control herself.

'Nobody we could see,' answered Ella. She absently scratched the side of her nose with the muzzle of her pistol. 'That noise is louder down there though. But we can't tell if it's coming from the shuttle's machine rooms or the asteroid. No more of *those* bastards,' she said, indicating the hold behind them, where they had left two men floating dead in the vacuum, 'so that's the main thing.'

'Come on,' ordered Halman, beckoning them to follow him. 'Let's move out. Eyes and ears open, folks. Petra and Rocko take rearguard. I don't want anyone popping out of some unseen hatch or some shit and getting the drop on us.'

Halman led them round the corner and into a longer, narrower passage. The tension was high, like a current that flowed through all of them. The noise grew steadily louder as they progressed, becoming a continuous murmur that none of them could deny. They turned right at the end of the long corridor, passing beneath a wide grate in the ceiling from which steam hissed in roiling bunches, ivory-white in their lights, blinding them. They dragged themselves through, fearful of being attacked in their temporarily vulnerable state.

They continued. Right, then left. Down, then right. Past looming doors through which strange machinery and angular ducting could be glimpsed. They let Alphe push to the front of the group and lead the way, reading from his schematic, which, although wrong, was still the best guide they had. The metal walls pressed in on them, tightening like jaws. Macao seemed to be another world, an impossibly distant base, hardly a sanctuary itself. They passed no windows – except for the bridge, the shuttle had none. They crawled and swam through a grey, self-contained world of growing, growling machine noise and rough metal walls marred by amateurish welds. *Marco*, Lina thought. *Platini.*

CHAPTER FORTY-EIGHT

Marco sat on Clay's bedroll staring out of the window at the soulless enormity of the belt. He, like his mother, had begun to hate it. He wondered if that vast blackness would eat her, render her dead, erase her from his life and from the universe itself. So many had died – adults all, those invulnerable giants who ruled his world with such confidence, but who had now become the victims of fate themselves, subjects in a new kingdom of horror.

The fear inside him had become so steady, so ubiquitous, that he hardly felt it any more. That was another thing he had in common with his mother, although he didn't know this. It did, in fact, never occur to him that she *could* be afraid herself. Mothers weren't afraid. End of.

Clay had given up trying to talk to Marco some while ago and was now immersed in his handheld games console, his stubbled head bent closely over the device. The game was *Corp Wars* – a good one – but Marco had lost all interest in it. He'd been winning effortlessly – he had played it a lot more than Clay – but the lack of challenge wasn't the issue. Attempts to engage himself in the game had quickly begun to feel artificial, like lying to himself. All that mattered was what was happening out *there*. Murderers and thieves – people who seemed to want them all dead – roamed out there amongst the tumbling stones.

Macao was a dying body, a failing flywheel that spun in darkness, hope diminishing with every turn. Nobody had admitted it to him, not openly, but he knew this to be true. It wasn't that he had no faith in his mother. He practically revered her. She was the only one who had never left his side. At least, never before. He no longer even cared to know his father. With time and distance had come, inevitably, detachment. His mother, however, had always cared, always protected him. But despite his faith in her, he was

333

angry with her for taking such a risk. He also had faith in disaster, a faith acquired across the bloody days he had endured of late. Disaster was a voracious, living thing, and he felt that it had stolen into Macao from the belt outside and taken up residence. He could not have expressed this feeling in as many words, of course, but it was no less tangible for that. Disaster had moved upon them under cover of the endless night, stealthy and scheming and fatal.

For a while, his teacher had attempted to lead a class, there amongst the squalor of the dorm. She had bumbled along, fudging her words, confusing the subject. *Triangles*, he remembered. Something about triangles. As if triangles mattered right now. It wasn't as if the key to finding the relative lengths of their sides was the same key that would restore the power, return the shuttle, bring his mother back alive. And his teacher had seemed to agree, because she had faltered, stopped, then put her hands to her face. She had been weeping silently behind those hands when she dismissed the class. Her only accomplishment had been to scare her charges. Triangles remained a mystery to them. Nobody cared.

And so he sat. And waited. And wondered why Clay didn't seem as concerned as he was. Ella was out there, too. Did Clay not care? Or was this just his way of coping? Whatever the case, after a while, Marco began to resent it. He would have left Clay alone and returned to his own bed, but this one had a better view of the window.

Personal possessions still lay everywhere, scattered across the dorm like fallen soldiers, but now there were almost no clothes amongst them. It was getting cold – really cold – and people had put all their clothing to use. And the air didn't just taste bad, now – it actually seemed to sting the nose and throat. Marco wondered if it might be connected with his growing headache. Looking around him, he saw an alarming number of people rubbing their foreheads or massaging their temples.

Time, he knew, was running out. And almost everyone who mattered to the operation of the station had gone out there into the belt. He wondered if that was wise. Previously, he would have trusted the adults implicitly, especially Halman. He knew his mother trusted Halman, and that was as good a recommendation as Marco could have wished for. But now. . . now he was no longer sure.

They had taken their collective eye off the ball and Eli had let madness grow inside him like rot, unseen and unsuspected. Amy Stone was now in charge at base, but barely. Marco had seen two fist-fights already since Halman and Ella had left. People talked in tight, secretive groups, in hushed and desperate tones, shooting suspicious glances at those around them. The extended family of Macao had become a gaggle of disparate, sullen little groups.

One of the refinery guys began to play the guitar – something slow and sad and beautiful – but his attempt lasted only a minute or so before he was harangued to stop. They were in no mood for entertainment. Others watched the windows, too, waiting for salvation to emerge from that endless abyss. Maybe it still would. Maybe. The darkness shifted and swelled out there, chaos and pattern intermixed, shards of black and grey scattered like broken glass across the floor of the universe.

CHAPTER FORTY-NINE

'Down there,' said Alphe a little uncertainly, indicating the short flight of steps at the end of the passage. 'The bridge.' Above the steps down was a metal ladder leading up through a hatch in the ceiling.

'What's upwards?' asked Halman. The noise of machinery was louder here and he had to shout to be heard, which seemed somewhat at odds with the intended theme of stealth. His dark eyes were darting like flies in a jar.

'The passage to the machine rooms,' Alphe shouted back, 'and the boarding tube.'

'Is the noise coming from the machine rooms?' asked Niya.

Alphe shrugged. 'Maybe,' he replied. 'But I suspect not. The machine rooms are for stuff like scrubbers, filtration and hydration systems, auxiliary drive systems. . . None of it's really that loud.'

'It's coming from the asteroid,' Lina shouted. 'The sound's echoing back down the boarding and rescue tube.' She looked around at the faces of her companions. 'They're mining,' she added darkly.

'For what?' asked Hobbes, hovering at Lina's shoulder, holding fast to a handline on the ceiling.

'Come on!' ordered Halman from the front of the group before anyone could reply. He waved them onwards, but as he moved off he shot a meaningful look back at Lina. He knew, she thought. He might not be in danger of winning any chess tournaments, but she thought he knew. Ilse shoved her on the shoulder from behind, setting her moving.

They squeezed into the shuttle's bridge one by one, guns probing the multicoloured cavern of overhanging control panels and angular metal surfaces. Two chairs – pilot and co-pilot – were bolted to the floor before the console, conspicuously empty. The

sliding covers that would rise and seal around them to make sus-
an casks were retracted into the floor like drawn-back lips. Rocks
tumbled outside, tagged on the main screen with distance and
direction indicators. The ship's computer was silently working
away, alone, the ever-watchful idiot-guardian.

Lina floated past Halman, feeling claustrophobic in her space
suit. Bunches of cable hung from the ceiling like tendons, linking
one mute hunk of equipment with another. Red and yellow
telltales marbled the shadows. She braked herself against the main
screen, momentarily face-to-face with the asteroid belt outside,
then turned to survey the room. The others squeezed in behind
her, fanning out. The grinding, hammering noise was very loud in
here, the rattling growl of a machine-monster in a frenzy.

There was another seat at the opposite side to the viewscreen, turned away towards a complex-looking navigational
panel. Blood had spattered in great sprays around it, darkening the
lights of the panel, crusted and brown where it had pooled. Lina
wondered if it was Eli's. She decided that she didn't really care,
and was vaguely surprised at the coldness within herself. A large
spanner lay on the navigational console's dashboard: the murder
weapon.

'Lina!' called Halman. She turned to see him regarding her
impatiently, holding onto the pilot's chair. 'Don't worry about that
now.'

'Sure,' she said. Someone had died here. So what? A lot of
people had died. He was right – they had to focus on the task at
hand. 'Let's release that clamp and then get the hell out of here,'
she said.

'How do you do it?' asked Halman, forcing his body into the
pilot's chair.

'You see the row of injector switches?' she asked him, floating
closer.

He peered at the panel closely. 'These?' he asked.

'Below those, in the middle – the switch with the cowling over
it.' Lina's companions floated, silent and spectral around her.

'Oh yeah,' Halman said absently, flicking the cowling up to

expose the actual control beneath it. 'Here goes. . .'

He flicked the switch. There was a muted bang, surprisingly understated. Halman uttered a partially-formed curse as his legs and feet were suddenly swallowed by an explosion of yellow foam. It swelled out from beneath his seat with a whispering, hissing noise, trapping and enveloping him. He half-turned, his eyes full of horror as the foam bloomed around him. His face contorted in agony as the power of the expanding instawall simply tore his arms from his body and sucked them in. Lina stared helplessly as Halman's mouth filled with foam, choking off his cry before it could even be voiced. People were yelling, clawing to escape, and still the foam was growing. It completely covered Halman's face and he was swallowed, thrashing weakly, then was suddenly and simply gone.

Lina seized one of the bunches of cable on the ceiling and pulled as hard as she could towards the doorway of the bridge. Someone was screaming, 'It's a fucking booby-trap!' but she couldn't tell who. They shot from the bridge in a single, struggling mass. Lina's leg caught on one of Si's arms and they entangled, struggling against each other. She turned, with Si's hand grabbing for purchase on her suit, and saw that Niya had not been fast enough.

The still-growing foam snared Niya by the foot as she made for the doorway, stopping her dead. She extended a desperate, questing hand towards Lina. Lina tried to scrabble free, somehow get to Niya, reach the hand, the hand, maybe she could save her if she could just reach that *hand*. . . But no – she was too clumsy, devoid of purchase on any surface, almost suffocated by the struggling Si. Niya's eyes opened wide, her face a caricature of terror, and then the instawall's terminator overtook her and she was enveloped.

Lina pushed Si off her with a titanic effort that sent fresh agony crackling down her spine and launched herself away from the bridge. But when she turned to look behind her the instawall had stopped expanding. Its colour was darkening rapidly as it set hard, cocooning her crewmates like flies in amber. The bridge was sealed off. And her friends were gone. A yawning, dizzying blackness swirled inside her like vertigo. The rusted metal of the passageway swayed and swung around her. She put a hand to her head, her vision darkening. *Don't pass out, don't pass out*, she chanted in her mind. She bit her lip, drawing blood, and the pain served to sharpen her senses, bringing her back from the brink of that dark abyss. Somebody was crying, an inhuman sound of shock and misery. Ella? Surely not Ella.

Si landed beside her, shoulder-first, breathing hard. 'Halman,' he said. 'Oh shit, Halman. What the fuck was that?' He looked into Lina's face, his wide mouth hanging open. 'What was that?'

Lina heard her own voice say, 'Instawall,' but it sounded very distant, disembodied. She pressed her nose to the floor of the passage and shut her eyes, feeling the jagged little edges of rust flakes against her skin. 'Oh shit,' she muttered. 'What now?' She didn't expect an answer. Surely there was none. Death had played an unbeatable hand. Full house.

She felt somebody land gently beside her and looked up to see Petra towering over her. Petra's dark hair had escaped her helmet to float around her face like an anti-halo. Hobbes appeared, too, extending a hand to help her up. She took it and heaved herself upright, utterly numb. The clattering of nearby machinery had ceased, but nobody noticed.

Rocko was dragging himself along the ceiling towards her like a great human spider, laser pistol still clasped in one hand. When he was almost above her, he pushed off, twisting gracefully in mid-air, and landed beside her. His dark skin was shiny with sweat. 'Well, fuck,' he said simply.

'Where's Alphe?' demanded Ella sharply, casting around herself. 'Oh shit!' she screamed. 'Where's Alphe?'

They looked around themselves stupidly, calling his name, but it was clear that he was gone. As he wasn't in the passage that left only one place. He hadn't made it out of the shuttle's bridge.

'Oh no,' said Ella, more quietly now. Those two little words bore a vast weight of resignation.

Lina forced herself to stand, wincing at the new pain in her

339

back. She supposed it would hurt much worse if she ever made it out of this micro-gee environment and it had to bear her weight again. She looked around at the faces of her companions, but they were all downcast, staring at the floor. Nobody spoke for a while as they gave silent homage to their fallen comrades. Three more. Three more. It had happened in the blink of an eye. One by one, the members of Lina's little family were being taken, snuffed out, scrubbed from her world. She wondered if she would ever see her son again. She wished that she'd stayed behind. That way, at least they could have died together. She felt tears begin to seep from her eyes, which was odd, because she felt only a washed-out, empty shadow of resignation. This was it. This was the conclusion she had sought. *Be careful what you wish for*, she told herself.

'What the fuck do we do now?' asked Rocko after a while. 'Just what the fuck do we do *now*?' He looked around at the faces of his comrades. Petra was slowly shaking her head. Hobbes was silently weeping, his tears dispersing into the air like liquid crystal.

'Seal off the asteroid,' said Ella decisively. 'Assuming Carver's gang are all inside it. Then burn the jets from the engine rooms.'

At first, lost in her own bottomless reverie, Lina didn't hear her. Gradually, the words filtered into her mind. And made sense. 'She's right!' said Lina, knowing that she should have thought of it herself. 'She's right. Trap the bastards and burn the jets manually. But we'd have to cut through the boarding tube. I don't think it's safe to fly with the rock joined on. The altered C-of-G would make it impossible to steer without computer. Don't get me wrong, it won't be easy anyway. But I think it can be done.'

'They all have to be in the rock, though,' said Ella. 'Or we just arrive home with a shuttle full of maniacs. But if we can cut them free, we can just leave the fuckers here to freeze.'

A slow smile spread across Rocko's face like the shadow of a storm cloud. 'Yeah. . .' he said. 'Let's do it. Let's kill those fucking murderers.' He seemed totally unaware of the hypocritical nature of this statement.

'Which way?' asked Lina. Shaken heads all round. Alphe had had the schematic. 'I guess it must be up,' she suggested. She wished she could remember for sure.

They crawled and bounced and swam their way back to the ladder that led up into the ceiling outside the bridge. The ugly instawall flower hadn't extended far enough to block the ladder, but it had come close. Lina was pretty sure the stuff had become inert now, but they all avoided touching it as they cautiously stepped onto the ladder one by one.

They reached the top without incident and found themselves in another corridor – lower, darker, more jumbled with machinery. Great pipes stretched away into darkness, visible inside the meshwork walls. Blueish LEDs shone from the ceiling like cold stars. Missing wall-panels showed battered junction-boxes and badly-soldered wiring.

'Come on!' called Lina, moving off down the passage. The others followed behind her, frightened but infused with fresh purpose.

Rocko sped past her, snagging a cable to stop himself. 'You know how to fire the jets manually?' he asked. 'Cos I don't think I do. I mean, I could do it on a Kay, but this thing must have loads of them.'

'I think so,' she replied. In truth, she had no idea – not specifically – but she was confident that she could work it out. She thought about Carver's gang finding themselves suddenly trapped within their new prison of rock, desperate with fear and disbelief, and that renewed her energy and determination. She wondered how they could be certain that all the prisoners were actually stuck inside the rock and not wandering free somewhere in the shuttle. For all they knew, the enemy might be in the engine rooms waiting for them. She gripped her gun tightly and dragged herself onwards.

They emerged into a wide space filled with battered industrial equipment: air scrubbers; water purifiers; a row of sus-an casks intended for passengers; racks of hand-tools; magnetic-bed trolleys; other things that Lina couldn't even identify. The ceiling soared above them, three times the height of the corridor's, criss-crossed with suspended walkways and hung with winches and brackets.

'The machine rooms,' said Rocko. 'It's not far from here.'

Petra slid silently past Lina, her gun cocked at her shoulder. Ella followed behind her, checking between computer cabinets that towered on either side like standing stones. Lina trailed along, falling further behind until she brought up the rear with Si, who drifted beside her silently, a strong and reassuring presence on her mental radar.

There was a sudden bang – a little exclamation of noise, nothing really – and Petra flew backwards, crashing into Ella and sending her somersaulting into a pile of canvas drive belts where she landed on her back. Petra's flight continued, past Hobbes, who just managed to dodge out of the way in time. She smashed into an empty shelving unit to Lina's left, thrashing and jerking. Lina recoiled, gasping for breath that suddenly wouldn't come. Blood was spraying from Petra's head in a thick, beautiful fountain of escaping life essence. A rock pin – a twenty-centimetre steel spike – had been fired into her skull, right in the centre of her forehead, where it protruded like a unicorn's horn. Petra arched her back, throwing her limbs out, rolling up the shelving unit and onto the ceiling, globules of blood spreading around her in a ruby-red constellation.

'Ambush!' Ella screamed, diving for cover behind a cabinet.

Si raised his pistol, firing as it came up into position, almost hitting Hobbes in his urgency. He kicked off, flying backwards towards cover, shooting as he went. Lina was firing too, aiming into the mass of white-clad, swarming shapes that was flooding into the room from the far door. At the forefront of the oncoming group was a massive giant of a man, wielding what was unmistakeably a plasma cutter. Carver.

Lina hooked one foot around a lever that jutted from some nearby machine, pulling herself down into its protective shade as she loosed shot after shot at the giant who ran towards her, dodging and ducking low, his magnetic boots clanking and banging on the deck as they released and reattached with each step. None of her shots hit him, though. One of them actually bounced off the shiny barrel of the plasma cutter itself and hit the shoulder of another prisoner. Although the beam had diffused as it rebounded, it still had energy enough to do its job. The prisoner lost control and hit the ceiling, slapping and clawing at his shoulder. Someone shot him again and he jerked once, then fell still. A pistol drifted out of his hand and floated gently away.

Lina hit the deck behind the machine, a large square thing with a plastic hood and a startling array of switches. The breath went out of her in a painful rush. Laser beams zig-zagged across the floor beside her, making her pull her knees up close to her chest. There was a loud, concussive *bong!* sound as something – probably another rock pin – hit the other side of the machine like a sledge hammer.

Si appeared beside her, firing as he came, ducking into cover, yelling something that Lina couldn't hear. Shouting voices; the deafening noise of the plasma cutter; bouncing lights whose touch meant death, stitching the darkness with brilliant lethality.

She caught a glimpse of Ilse Reno, a petite figure with a red-glowing eye, clawing her way behind a large fuel tank. Lasers danced across the tank and it erupted into sudden flame, splashing Ilse with gobbets of blazing liquid as she scrabbled around it, immolating her instantly. She screamed, the pitch so high that Lina could barely hear it, and turned over, writhing as she tried to put herself out. She dragged herself around the shattered, flaming tank, as if it might still offer safety. Then, blazing and dying, she collapsed with just one burning foot protruding.

The sprinklers in the ceiling gushed to sudden life, spouting water that rebounded from every surface, clumping into crystal balls that drifted like bubbles through the air and burst afresh where they landed. The flaming fuel tank guttered but did not extinguish.

Hobbes was pinned down on the other side of the main aisle, behind a crate that was barely as big as his body, one hand over his head and the other trying to hold him still. Lina peeped out of cover and saw Rocko bouncing from behind a computer terminal, clutching his shoulder, trying to back-track towards her and Si. A prisoner flew out of the shadows to his left, and she tried to cry out, to warn him of the flanking attack, but she could not. Her voice simply died inside her throat.

Rocko spun with amazing speed and shot the man twice in the face, hitting him a third time as he fell. But Carver was almost upon him. He had the plasma cutter raised above his head, slicing into the ceiling, sending out gobbets of white-hot metal.

Lina fired at him again, but either he was somehow charmed or she was just a terrible shot, because she missed him by several metres. Ella darted out from between two tall shelves, moving like a striking shark, coming from Carver's blind-side and hitting him bodily, knocking him back. But his magnetic boots retained contact with the floor and he immediately rebounded, swinging the cutter at her head, Rocko forgotten.

Rocko came instantly to Ella's aid, kicking out, knocking Carver's aim off and bringing his gun to bear on the giant. Another prisoner – a hugely fat man with a heavily-scarred face – came from behind Carver and struck Rocko on the side of his neck with what looked like a metal bar, sending him flying backwards into a rack of equipment. Ella stepped in close to Carver, kicking out at his groin. Although she connected, sending herself shooting backwards, it only seemed to anger him, and his back-swing grazed across the belly of her suit, coming within inches of her flesh.

Lina, unable to even get a clear shot at Carver, fired instead at the huge man who was floating in the air above Rocko's prone and struggling form, hefting the metal bar in his gloved hands. Amazingly, she hit him right between his shoulder blades. The man released the bar and drifted up towards the ceiling, hands going to the burn and pawing at it in disbelief. Rocko recovered and shot him again.

Carver kicked out, doubling Ella over and launching her like a missile through the air. Instantly, he charged after her, running through a blizzard of water, the cutter flaming and blazing in his hands. Lina saw the picture of insane, murderous rage on his pinkish idiot's face as he slashed through a power-press with the tool, sending up thick blasts of mineral steam.

344

Ella landed just behind Lina, crashing into a tool-rack, stunned. The pistol came out of her hand and flew away into the shadows behind them. Lina noticed a sneaky-looking, rat-faced little man with a pointed chin trying to creep up on her left, and she sent him scurrying for cover with a shot from her pistol. A red light illuminated on the weapon's side. It had overheated.

Hobbes launched himself out from behind his box, hands still covering his neck and head, into the more substantial cover of a large waste compacter. He dragged himself over it to the other side, but Lina saw a laser beam hit him in the sole of one foot as he disappeared.

Carver was almost upon her now, but he was utterly intent on Ella, who still lay stunned and motionless. Lina popped up, aiming the laser at him. Of course, it didn't fire. *Oh shit*, she thought as he turned his murderous face on her. *I forgot about that.* She saw Eli's fingers strung around his neck and wondered fleetingly if her own would join them soon. Maybe he'd make a bracelet from them instead. Why not? He could start a whole fucking accessory line. In a few seconds she'd be dead, so it hardly mattered to her.

'Aaaaarrgghhh!' screamed Carver, flexing his huge arms at her. She could see the cords of muscle standing out above the neckline of his suit, the beads of sweat on his skin. And there was nothing in his eyes. Nothing.

Suddenly, Rocko popped up next to Carver and shot him in the side. Carver didn't fold over in pain and he certainly didn't die, although the hit was clearly a clean one. He did, however, spin to face Rocko, bringing the cutter around in a flickering backhand swipe. Rocko fired a burst of thrust from his suit's arm-jet, flying back out of range. The cutter passed through some indiscernible snarl of machinery without slowing at all, sending electrical components and shorn wires flying. Smoke from the blazing fuel tank spread and drifted around the combatants. Lina smelled the repulsive savoury odour of burning meat.

'Lina!' Si screamed next to her. She turned to face him, feeling dreamy and slow. 'Get out there and cut the tube! Go! Take Ella with you! We'll push them back. There aren't that many of them –

we can do it! In thirty minutes, we're gonna fire the jets. It's our only chance. Now move!'

And then he rose up next to her – fearless, towering – and pushed up towards the ceiling. He passed right over Carver's head, bounced back down to the floor and landed behind him. Carver spun, trying to bisect Si with the cutter, but Si checked his elbow, stopping the swing. For a split-second, Lina saw the two giants locked together, each straining to overpower the other, and then, with an immense effort of will, she leapt from cover.

She threw herself towards Ella, feeling something buzz angrily past her cheek, millimetres away from her skin – probably another rock pin. A laser beam, scintillating green, stroked the metal next to her, probing for flesh. She landed beside Ella, dropping her own gun and seizing her friend by the shoulders. She managed, somehow, to drag Ella round to the other side of the tool-rack. Her handhold on the rack slipped and she almost sent them both drifting into the open air, where they would have been easy prey. But she made it by sheer effort of will. The rack didn't offer much cover, though. As if to prove this point, a laser beam passed right through one of the gaps in it, hitting the floor between Ella's splayed legs and making a neat little burn there.

Lina slapped Ella round the face. 'Ella!' she screamed, spluttering out water. Rocko was shouting behind her. Hobbes too. He sounded like he was in pain. 'Ella! Come on!' There was a loud crash. She saw a tower of crates come apart and float away from each other, off to her right.

Ella jerked, her eyes flickering, and stiffened in Lina's arms.

'Wh. . .' she managed to croak.

'Ella! Come on!' Lina repeated, shaking her friend by the scruff of her suit. Ella flopped uselessly, scratching Lina's face with the zip of one glove. 'You have to help me! Move, damn you!'

'Lina. . .' said Ella, fixing her with a glassy eye.

Another projectile hit something nearby, making a sound like a struck gong. Someone was moving along the racks to their left, closing in through the smoke and water vapour. The sound of Carver's plasma cutter filled the world.

346

'Move!' Lina screamed into Ella's face, and this time Ella moved.

They launched themselves back towards the door they had come in by, Lina grabbing for whatever handholds she could reach. Ella became less and less of a burden as she fully returned to her senses. They dragged themselves along handlines, clawed their way along pitted walls and metal-tiled floors. Lasers probed the space behind them. Rocko was shouting, but Lina couldn't hear the actual words. Neither did it matter any more. They had a plan. One last plan. For it to work, though, they had first to get away. Even as long shots went, she thought this was a pretty unlikely one. Would the others be able to actually beat the prisoners back to the asteroid? Maybe, if Si could defeat Carver. . . then maybe. Thirty minutes. That tube had to be severed. Their last chance.

Lina fled, rat's teeth of panic nibbling at the edges of her mind. She tried to concentrate only on the task at hand – where the handlines were, which way to go, how much time they had. When she finally dared to look behind her there was nobody in pursuit. She had left her friends, and she felt a twinge of guilt that she thought might become an unbearable sense of remorse if she survived this and they did not. But this was how it had to be. Whatever had befallen her comrades, they had clearly slowed their attackers down enough to allow Lina's escape. As for pushing the enemy back to the asteroid. . . who knew? *Thirty minutes thirty minutes*, her mind chanted. How many left?

She imagined Marco, waiting in the freezing dorm, maybe looking out at the belt, wondering whether she would return. Clay would be waiting with him. Maybe that was why Si had suggested she take Ella with her. How exactly she had ended up subordinate to Si in this matter, she didn't know.

They flew down the ladder to the bridge level, not even bothering to touch the rungs. The vile instawall bloom protruded from the bridge like a massive fungus.

Lina was achingly aware that neither of them was armed any more. The noise of Carver's cutter had become inaudible, but still they didn't slow. Perhaps he had simply switched it off to mask his

347

pursuit. Perhaps her friends were dead. Or perhaps Carver was himself dead, his posse forced back to the asteroid. Who knew? From the radio, silence punctuated by bursts of static and the occasional indecipherable yell.

She wondered if they might somehow trigger another trap, but what could they really do except attempt to touch nothing and hope that it wouldn't happen? They hurried onwards, back towards the cargo hold, deep in the haunted bowels of the vessel.

'What do you have in mind?' Ella asked after a while. She was dragging herself along the line on one of the walls, giving a hard yank and then letting it run through her hand until she slowed, whereupon she would repeat the process. Lina was using a rather less elegant frantic scrabbling technique. 'What are we going to do? You have a plan, right? Surely we aren't just running away.'

'I want to get back to the Kays,' she answered, forcing the words out through the gaps in her laboured breathing.

'What for?'

'I'm going to cut through the boarding tube. If I can.'

Ella coasted along silently beside her for a moment. 'Won't that cause the dreaded blow-out?' she asked after a while. 'Maybe we *should* let it blow out?' She turned to look at Lina, her expression cautious, clearly aware that she was suggesting the condemnation of anybody left aboard, including their friends.

'The tube will seal itself at both ends,' Lina replied. 'It senses vacuum, in case you try to board a damaged ship and the ship suffers a hull breach or whatever. They used them in the Corp Wars for battlefield recovery.'

'Then why the hell didn't we just cut it to begin with?' Ella demanded.

'We were going to release it from the bridge, remember? When there *was* a usable bridge. Also, I guess Halman wanted to know the shuttle was clear of hostiles first. Si said he'd try to push them back to the asteroid. He gave us thirty minutes before they try a manual burn, if they can. But when we cut into the tube, any prisoners left aboard the shuttle will be stuck there with Si.'

'Poor them,' said Ella. It took Lina a moment to realise that this

348

was supposed to be a joke.

They were almost at the airlock of the cargo hold now. Just a few more corners to go. They passed a large room where huge tanks stood on thick metal legs, interconnected by a complex weave of pipework. Lina didn't know if the tanks contained water, fuel, or what. She thought about Ilse Reno, burning. The smell of roasting meat. She wondered how it felt to be burned alive. Or to drown in instawall. Or to be shot in the head with a rock pin. Maybe they were all better than freezing slowly to death in an unpowered space station.

'Shit, Lina, this sounds like a long-shot to me,' said Ella as they rounded the corner into the last corridor, seeing the airlock door at the far end ahead of them.

'I suppose it is,' Lina admitted.

'I don't understand why *I'm* here,' said Ella. 'What use can I be?'

'Si told me to take you,' said Lina. 'So I did. He probably wanted you to act as my bodyguard.'

'Bodyguard?' asked Ella, frowning deeply. 'I don't even seem to have a gun. I was out of it for a while, there. I think that bastard knocked me out cold. So that was the dreaded Carver, eh?'

'Yeah,' said Lina. 'That was him.'

They stopped before the airlock door. 'Check my suit over,' said Ella. 'Then I'll check yours.'

Lina did as instructed. Ella's suit was clearly scuffed and marked in places, scorched across the belly, but none of the grazes looked like they had gone all the way through.

'Looks okay, Ella,' said Lina. 'Is there anything on the HUD?'

Ella closed the visor of her helmet and checked, her eyes reading left to right, left to right. 'No,' she said. 'But you know what the computers are like in these things. Cheap plastic-printed crap.'

'Check me,' said Lina, holding her arms out to facilitate the process. Ella floated round her, examining her closely.

'Looks fine. Let's go.'

'Yeah,' agreed Lina, closing her own visor. Glowing text

349

overlayed her vision. 'Let's.'

Lina hit the cycle control and they swam inside. The door silently sealed itself behind them. They waited while the rumble of expelled air died away to nothing, leaving *VACUUM* warnings glowing in small text before their eyes. They headed out, back into that disturbing cavern of congealed shadow and soaring walkways. Lina's light flashed over the still-spinning body of the man whom Rocko had shot. She looked up, where another corpse floated somewhere in the vaulted darkness, invisible.

They launched themselves through open space as quickly as they dared, using their arm jets, terrified of hitting some unseen balustrade or railing and injuring themselves or damaging their suits. But they landed intact on the wall near to Lina's makeshift doorway, braking themselves with careful dabs of reverse thrust. Lina dragged herself along the wall and curled her fingers round the lip of the doorway.

She looked round at Ella. Her friend looked frightened and possibly in pain. 'Here goes then,' said Lina with forced levity.

She pulled herself out of the shuttle and emerged into the belt. Rock and ice and dark oblivion. She floated towards her ship, the nearest one to the doorway. It looked somehow small and sad, like a lost child, drifting in that vastness. At least it hadn't been smashed by a belt object while its computer had been off. Ella emerged behind her and drifted past, tumbling and cursing. She fired her jet – the tiniest burst – and managed to regain control. She looked clumsy and ridiculous, floating there in her cheap space suit.

They looked at each other uncertainly for a moment. Then Lina nodded and fired her sleeve jet. She flew towards her Kay, her course and speed almost perfect. She reached out to grab hold of one of its tool arms. Then she worked her way through the gaping crocodile-mouth of the cockpit lid and into her seat. Checking back over her shoulder, she saw that Ella had overshot her own ship and was coming back towards it, arms outstretched to catch hold.

She closed the cockpit and fired up the console. It rebuked her for her failure to shut down correctly last time, and she cancelled its requests to run self-diagnostics. She let the cockpit flood from the onboard air tanks. The ship felt snug and comforting around her, like a second skin. She wondered how the others were doing back on the shuttle, if they were still alive. Maybe they had been captured, tortured, sculpted like Liu. *You left them*, said the voice inside her. *Yes*, she answered it. *I know.*

She let the gas run straight into the jets without bothering to warm them up, then brought the ship about. The shuttle looked dead, deserted from here. Surely it could conceal no danger, contain no life. It was simply a sprawling slab of metal, utterly inert.

Ella's ship was coming around, too. Several of its tool arms began to move randomly as she hit an incorrect control, then the vessel's main headlight flickered on, off, then on again. The tool arms stilled and the ship turned towards Lina's.

'Ella, stay here and listen for the radio. Your ship will relay anything it hears to mine,' suggested Lina.

'Sure,' replied Ella. Her Kay fired retros and was quickly left behind. 'Maybe I can even be some use, eh?'

The lumpen hull of the shuttle paid out beneath her as Lina dialled up the gas, heading towards the point where the shuttle's belly was nestled against the asteroid, leaving a gap just large enough to fly through. She pushed the yoke gently forwards, bringing the nose down to point into that crevasse, dark shiny stone forming one wall and impact-scarred metal the other. Her headlight sliced through the darkness, making the asteroid sparkle as if its jagged skin concealed a wealth of tiny stars, condensed into solid matter.

Soon she was deep in the trench and could see the curved outer skin of the boarding tube where it joined the two walls together. She was bringing the cutting arms online as she went, flexing them, testing their responsiveness. The gas torch flared pitifully in that canyon of darkness. The cutting disc spun silently at the end of its arm.

She approached the tube and anchored onto it with the Kay's magnetic clamp. A little jolt went through the ship as the clamp banged into place. She applied the gas torch to the ribbed skin of the boarding tube. Metal began to melt at once, forming little globules that drifted away into space. A brief burst of air rushed from the cut, brightening the torch's jet. But then it stopped. The tube had sealed itself. That was good. She began to work the torch around the wide cylinder, but it was slow, painfully slow. *Thirty minutes*, she thought again. *How many left?* Rock and steel stood around her like frozen waves of impossible mass and density, looming, threatening, filling the universe.

Suddenly, there came a deafening blast of noise from the radio. Lina jumped, jerking the small stick that controlled the gas torch, making it come away from the metal. The noise was gone again. It had sounded almost random, like white noise, but Lina didn't think it had been. There had been something in there, below the hissing and crackling of the muddied radio signal. She thought it had been screaming.

'Ella! What was that?'

'Somebody's trying to contact us!' cried Ella. 'Hurry, Lina!'

'I'm trying, I'm trying!' Lina called back, re-applying the torch. She was aware of what that noise had meant. They weren't all dead inside, not yet. But they were in trouble. Was it already too late to save them? Would she, at best, manage merely to cut loose a tin can full of insane murderers and slaughtered personnel? How would they ever get Carver's gang out of there if Si had failed to push them back? Maybe Fionne really would have to create some sort of poison gas. Lina just couldn't imagine her being prepared to do that.

She realised that she had cut as far as she could without moving the ship itself, so she withdrew the gas torch and detached the clamp. She backed carefully away to survey the boarding tube better.

Another burst from the radio. This time the screaming was clearer, and there was another voice, too. Somebody must have worked their way close to the shuttle's hull, and was trying to talk to them. Friend or foe? She couldn't guess.

'Lina!' said Ella in a small, high voice. 'You hear that?'

'Yeah,' said Lina distractedly, gently turning her ship to present the gas torch to a new section. Maybe she should try the rotary cutter – it might be faster after all.

'I couldn't make out the words!' Ella shouted.

'I know,' Lina replied. 'Just stay there and listen.'

She slowly drew the gas torch along the boarding tube's armoured skin, inscribing a neat incision through which a milky glow emanated, as if it was bleeding light. Again she hit the limit of the tool arm's reach and released the magnetic clamp. She drew a hand across her forehead and it came away slicked with sweat. Her heart was practically buzzing, its rhythm had become so fast.

'Come on,' she whispered to herself, backing away for a better view. She saw that the asteroid was blocking the way to where she needed to go next. A great, jagged protrusion of rock jutted above her, preventing her from continuing the cut from here. She would have to fly out of the canyon then return from the other side. More time. 'Shit!' she cursed, damning herself for her inability to go any faster.

She backed the ship up until she reached a point that was wide enough to turn in, then brought it about and dialled up the gas. She emerged from beneath the belly of the shuttle, seeing Ella's vessel hanging in front of her. The other Kays were clustered roughly in the distance. Some of them still had their headlights showing, as if their pilots had just popped out for a minute. In reality, she knew that most, if not all of them, would never sit in those ships again.

'Lina?' asked Ella's voice. 'You done?'

'No, I just have to hit it from the other side,' Lina answered, already turning to fly across the top of the shuttle.

'Well, when you–' But Ella's voice was cut off by a gasp. Lina's nerves jangled like wind chimes. 'Lina! Look!' cried Ella, her voice shrill with excitement.

Lina spun her Kay around, expecting the worst, honestly terrified. The shuttle's huge manoeuvring jets were sputtering to life. Serpent-tongues of incandescent gas licked the vacuum, stuttering then steadying. The shuttle wallowed, shivered, and

353

began to move.

'Lina, they've done it!' cried Ella. 'They've done it, Rocko's done it!'

'No. . .' Lina shook her head, trying to deny that it was happening. 'No, Ella, this could be bad. . .'

'Bad?' asked Ella. Lina could hear the joy drain from her voice. 'Why?'

'Because I'm not done! I'm not done!'

'But what's—'

'Get away!' Lina yelled, realising what was about to happen. 'GO!'

She slammed the gas all the way to the stop and her Kay took off with enough gees to pin her uncomfortably into her seat. Her vision began to cloud, grey monochrome bleeding in from the edges. She struggled to remain conscious, feeling her suit clench around her legs, driving the blood to her brain.

The shuttle and its massive asteroid moved slowly at first. The great symbiotic construct of rock and metal ploughed into the field of abandoned Kays, narrowly missing Lina and Ella as they accelerated out of the way. The Kays piled up against the hull of the shuttle, then were spilled off into the void, scattering like nine-pins, spinning away into the night, broken tool-arms shattering off them. Lina brought her ship to a stop, Ella drifting nearby. As one, they turned to look.

'It's fine, Lina!' said Ella. 'Look – the course is good.'

And sure enough, Rocko had somehow got the bearing right. The shuttle was heading in the direction of Macao. But it looked far from fine.

The half-cut boarding tube, instead of forming a rigid link between the two objects, was now something more akin to a hinge. As the awkward conjoined mass began to pick up speed, the nose of the shuttle came down to meet the asteroid. There was a silent collision that dented the shielded hull of the ship and sent chunks of rock shattering off in all directions. The shuttle rebounded, twisting on the severing link of the boarding tube, and this time its back end hit the rock. The manoeuvring jets exploded,

354

scattering debris and illuminating the glistening asteroid in a flash that lasted just the briefest instant.

Lina watched in silent horror as the shuttle was blown clear of the rock. The asteroid flew on, its course almost unaltered by the loss of its man-made parasite. A host of smaller rocks, its swarm of progeny, flew with it now. Lina maxed the gas again, giving chase. Shadows twined through the belt around her – imagined, real, both or neither of those things – ink and oil swirling on the canvas of the night.

The shuttle hit a smaller asteroid and rebounded, crashing into Eli's rock for a last time as the pair flew towards the station. This time the whole asteroid shattered, breaking in half in a hideous slow-motion dance of destruction – chaos from order, entropy in action. The shuttle flew off on a tangent, up and port-wards. Half of the asteroid deflected to the other side, hitting one jagged iceberg, then another, disintegrating as it went, spreading boulders and gravel in all directions.

The remains of the other half flew onwards, ever onwards, towards the station. It smashed a smaller rock out of its way, setting off a chain of collisions that almost killed Lina. The ship's computer swerved the Kay around one spinning rock and then another, as she struggled to keep the large chunk in her sight. Her mind was reciting the names of the dead as she went: *Sal, Nik, Jayce, Tamzin, Eli, Liu, Rachelle, Waine, Theo, Halman, Alphe, Niya.* . .

The shuttle was slowing down, ploughing through asteroids that shattered into dust against its deuterium shield. It would miss the station. But the rock might not. . .

Macao came into sight, rising through the haze of asteroids like a sailing ship appearing through sea-mist. Marco was in there.

'No,' Lina breathed. 'No. . .' She flew on, tailing the spinning chunk of stone as the shuttle slowed to a halt, gently rotating, with the ISL still clinging to its back.

Although Macao was dying, its kinetic defence systems were still working. The station fired once from the mass drivers on its hub, once more from its rim. The half-asteroid burst apart. Some small chunks continued on, colliding again and again, being whittled down to dust and finally petering safely out. Lina brought her Kay to a halt before the towering edifice of the station, that great dirty wheel. Macao remained untouched, inviolate, turning. Eli's rock had become a cloud of sand and gravel.

The shuttle, however, was mostly intact. Lina floated in her Kay, dumbstruck, fearing the worst. They had the shuttle. But people had died. More family gone. She could not imagine that Rocko, Hobbes and Si could be alive in there. Surely not. The jets had exploded. She realised that she had been conditioned to accept disaster, but she was unable to envisage any other outcome. The silken blackness of space pressed in on her – the raw material of loneliness, the base colour of defeat.

'Oh no. . .' she sighed. 'No, no, no. . .'

'Lina. . .' began Ella. But she had nothing else to say.

Suddenly, the radio blared with static, a hissing jumble of electromagnetic interference. But within that jumble there were words:

'Lina! Ella! Are. . . there? We. . . the shuttle! Repeat: we have the shuttle!'

CHAPTER FIFTY

Si clambered up into the ISL and pushed Lina bodily aside, shoving her into the middle seat, shoulder to shoulder with Hobbes.

'I'll fly,' he said, grinning at her. 'I'm a better pilot than you.'

Lina laughed and shoved him back, which barely affected him at all. 'Screw you, Davis!' she retorted.

'Never,' said Si, reaching down to flick the manual injector safeties. 'Not in your wildest dreams.'

'Believe me, Si, that would be a nightmare,' she replied, wriggling her backside into the thin cushion of the bench in an effort to get comfortable.

Si just laughed and turned around in his seat to look behind him into the crew compartment. The benches were filled with volunteers from Macao – as many as would fit in the ISL. 'You ready, shift B?' he called over his shoulder. There was a general noise of affirmation. 'Then let's fly!'

He flooded the jets, bringing the loader rumbling round in a wide arc, skirting the stricken dead-lifter. The hangar was conspicuously devoid of functioning Kays apart from the two that Lina and Ella had managed to bring in, which sat nestled beside each other like frightened pack animals. Those damaged by the ISL had been shunted into a far corner, where they would remain isolated until someone could inspect them.

The klaxon sounded and the ramp began to drop. The belt appeared before them, but this time the shuttle could be seen out there, off to the right, surrounded by a cloud of debris from its smashed manoeuvring jets. It was upside-down relative to Macao, slightly dented at the front, but essentially intact.

'Wheee!' cried Si childishly as the loader accelerated off the end of the ramp and curled away into space. He pinned the yoke, flying unnecessarily fast, clearly enjoying himself.

The shuttle grew quickly to almost fill the screen. Lina could hear the crew chattering behind her. It wasn't a happy chatter, as such. But it was a cautiously excited one. There was much work to be done – shifts had toiled around the clock, the ISL ferrying a continuous stream of volunteers out to the damaged ship – but there was hope. Real hope. Fionne was leading a team of the more technically-able members of the crew in the re-fitting of the air scrubbers. They still had to fix the power, but there were only so many people who were actually of use in such endeavours. Time was very much against them still. But there was hope. And that was a good starting point.

'So, I guess we're looking for the gennie parts today?' asked Hobbes.

'Yeah,' said Si, tugging at the collar of his space suit. 'And we'll take as much food as we can. But generator parts first.'

'I can't imagine when Fionne will manage to actually fit them,' said Hobbes, a little darkly.

'I know,' said Si, bringing the loader swooping along the upturned belly of the great shuttle. 'Busy, busy. We could use another nine or ten of her.'

'How long do think it'll be until we can. . .' began Hobbes, trailing off, not wanting to say it.

'Fly the shuttle?' asked Lina, turning to look into his face. Hobbes nodded. She thought she saw a little glimmer in his eye. 'Why? You coming with us now?'

'Yes,' he said. 'I thought I might, actually.'

'It'll be a long ride, you know?' said Si, peering into the screen, slowing the loader as it rolled over to fly along the top-side of the shuttle. 'It looks like we'll have to re-attach the loader and use its engines for propulsion. Might take ten years instead of five, sleeping shifts in sus-an.'

'I don't think many people will want to stay behind, Simon,' said Hobbes, glancing back over his shoulder. The team back there were laughing now, and the sound was good to hear. It was kind-of infectious, actually. Lina felt herself beginning to grin too. 'By the time we've made Macao safe in the short-term and checked the shuttle for flight-worthiness, I think we might have a full complement.'

Si laughed. 'I hope so, Doctor.'

'Me too,' said Lina. Faces scrolled before her mind's eye – the faces of the dead. She still could hardly believe that Si had killed Carver, survived himself, and he and Rocko had actually pushed the prisoners back into the now-destroyed asteroid. So many comrades had died. It would be a disservice to them to stay here. And she thought Hobbes was right: once the immediate danger was dealt with, everyone would come with them to Platini. 'To hell with Macao,' she said. 'I'm glad you're coming, Hobbes.' Hobbes smiled back at her and pushed his little glasses further up the bridge of his nose. Lina shoved Si on his powerful shoulder again, making him glance over at her. 'But I'll fly the shuttle until it goes auto, Si,' she said. 'I am, after all, a better pilot than you.'

Si laughed – a deep, rumbling bass. 'Screw you, McLough,' he said.

'Never,' replied Lina, craning to see the shuttle's docking point, which was coming into view beneath them now. 'Not in your wildest dreams.'

CHAPTER FIFTY-ONE

Murkhoff adjusted the grimy bandage that covered his ruined eye. There was nothing he could do to make it comfortable. He thought it was becoming infected. He hadn't dared look for a day now. Nobody seemed to care. They were all too busy with their precious shuttle.

His skull burned and ached inside, a vortex of perpetual agony which poured from his eye into the back of his head like sunlight focused through a lens. He was grinding his teeth. He'd found that he couldn't stop it any more – the pain in his jaw almost served to distract from the pain in his head. But not quite. In fact, even the fader had ceased to really touch it. And, joy of joys, he didn't have much left. There would be more on the shuttle. But the pilot had been his contact, and without the pilot he'd never find it. And they'd hardly allow him to search for it anyway, would they?

He glanced around at the dorm, pulling his fleece jacket tighter around his shoulders. *Look at them*, he thought sullenly. *Scurrying about like their asses were on fire, trying to save themselves. Nobody gives a shit about me, though, do they? Well, I've some news for you, people: I don't give a shit about you, either.*

It was true. Nobody cared. He had been forgotten. Maybe he should have gone with Halman's shuttle mission after all. Perhaps he could have found the bastard prisoner who'd stabbed him with the pen, maybe throttled the fucker before he died himself. What revenge was he ever going to get now?

He knew he'd have to go with the others to Platini. He supposed they'd fix his eye if he ever made it there. But the possibility seemed so distant, so hypothetical, that it offered little hope.

'Bastards,' he muttered through his clenched teeth. He wasn't sure exactly who he meant. All of them, he supposed.

Outside the window, the belt hung suspended in silence. Yuwan, on a slightly lopsided orbit, had faded below the rotational plane and hence from sight, taking its Predecessor moon with it. Vagar was in ascendance instead – a bright, tiny pinprick of light. Darkness lay in wait out there, squeezed into every rocky crevice, spread as far as the eye could see, barely restrained by Soros' distant glimmer. Eli's rock had been smashed to dust, and that dust had clumped, forming a cloud that hung before the station like a veil. They'd been so busy with their shuttle that he didn't think anyone else had noticed it.

Fionne was attempting to fix the scrubbers, he knew. But she was hamstrung by a team of bumbling amateurs and they were having problems. It wouldn't work. He knew that, too. They'd see. They'd fucking see. The air was now so thin that he was short of breath even standing still. His head swam and ached and pulsed. His teeth squeaked as they ground together.

It was fascinating, really. Even with only one good eye, he could see the *patterns* out there. It wasn't truly random, was it? There was order within the chaos. He moved closer, placing the palm of one hand on the window. The belt was thrumming gently: alive. He could feel it through his skin. Order. Chaos. Darkness, frozen in a wave of pent-up energy. A force in its own right.

That dust cloud. . . It was moving. Something was moving inside it – little eddies, little currents. . . order within the chaos. *Patterns.*

And then it spoke to him.

'My emissary. You have come to me. . . Listen. . .'

'Yes. . .' he breathed, pressing his face to the cold glasspex. 'I'm listening.'

Also by this author:

XENOFORM

City Six is a dark and brutal place, mired in crime and corruption. Gangs rule the streets of the Undercity and every private police force is for sale. The rich live in secure enclaves, oblivious to the suffering and violence that plague the city's poor. Sinister and powerful corporations trade stolen bodymods, fearless of the law, and human life itself is just another saleable commodity.

In this harsh environment an unprecedented threat is emerging. Whistler and her team of professional abductors start to see a new parasitic organ in the bodies of their victims. Debian, a young cyber-criminal turned commercial hacker, finds a terrifying computer virus in the databanks of an AI-research company.

An unknown enemy is attacking the city, altering the populace into nightmarish creatures and decimating computer systems. It seems unstoppable.

Can these unlikely heroes find a way to fight it? Or will City Six fall prey to an environmental and technological catastrophe on an unimaginable scale?

Xenoform: A near-future nightmare for the networked generation!